Slayter and the Dragon
LEGACY OF SHADOWS

Slayter and the Dragon
Legacy of Shadows

TODD FAHNESTOCK

F4 PUBLISHING

SLAYTER AND THE DRAGON
Copyright © 2024 by Todd Fahnestock

Trade Paperback Edition

All rights reserved. No part of this publication may be reproduced, distributed or transmitted in any form or by any means, including photocopying, recording, or other electronic or mechanical methods, without the prior written permission of the publisher, except in the case of brief quotations embodied in critical reviews and certain other noncommercial uses permitted by copyright law.

This is a work of fiction. Names, characters, places, and incidents are a product of the author's imagination. Locales and public names are sometimes used for atmospheric purposes. Any resemblance to actual people, living or dead, or to businesses, companies, events, institutions, or locales is completely coincidental.

Cover Art by:
Rashed AlAkroka

Cover Design by:
Rashed AlAkroka, Sean Olsen, Melissa Gay & Quincy J. Allen

Map Design by:
Sean Stallings

Ordering Information:

Quantity sales. Special discounts are available on quantity purchases by corporations, associations, and others. For details, contact us via our website.

Slayter and the Dragon / Todd Fahnestock — 1st ed.

ISBN: 978-1-952699-54-2

Dedication

To my fantastic beta readers. I hoped you would love this one, and you did. Thank you for everything.

What is Eldros Legacy?

The Eldros Legacy is a multi-author, shared-world, mega-epic fantasy project managed by four Founders who share the vision of a new, expansive, epic fantasy world. In the coming years the Founders committed themselves to creating multiple storylines where they and many others will explore and write about a world once ruled by tyrannical giants.

The Founders are working on four different primary storylines on four different continents. Over the coming years, those four storylines will merge into a single meta story where fates of all races on Eldros will be decided.

In addition, a growing list of guest authors, short story writers, and other contributors will delve into virtually every corner of each continent. It's a grand design, and the Founders have high hopes that readers will delight in exploring every nook and cranny of the Eldros Legacy.

So, please join us and explore the world of Eldros and the epic tales that will be told by great story tellers, for Here There Be Giants!

We encourage you to follow us at www.eldroslegacy.com to keep up with everything going on. If you sign up there, you'll get our newsletter and announcements of new book releases. You can also follow up on FaceBook at:

facebook.com/groups/eldroslegacy.

Sincerely,

Todd, Marie, Mark, and Quincy
(The Founders)

MAPS

Prologue

Tovos dreamed.

He didn't sleep, of course. Sleeping was a Human weakness. There were a hundred ways to rejuvenate the body, and Human sleep was by far the most inefficient.

Some of the Eldroi had actually fallen to emulating it, actually sleeping. Some slept for centuries. The Eldroi, modeling their behavior after scuttling mortals. Disgusting. It was akin to the ridiculous Drakanoi and their dragon forms. The Eldroi, emulating lower life forms.

So no, Tovos did not sleep.

But he dreamed of murder, carnage, and a revenge against the mortals so complete the mountains would run red with blood. Tovos had been taught at the foot of the most powerful Noksonoi since Noktos, the father of all Noksonoi. The fearsome Harkandos had not only been Noktos's heir apparent, he'd also been Tovos's mentor. Everything Tovos knew about the world, he'd learned from Harkandos.

And then Nhevalos The Betrayer had killed him.

Harkandos had been everything to Tovos, had been everything a Noksonoi should be. If the ridiculous Drakanoi had wanted to emulate something, they should have emulated Harkandos. Every Eldroi should have, on every continent.

Instead, the Noksonoi had allowed Nhevalos The Betrayer to undermine them, line them up on a cliff, and push them over.

So Tovos dreamed of revenge on The Betrayer's little cockroach protégés. Tovos hadn't seen them in time. They had scuttled through the tall grass and he'd recognized them only when it was too late. He cursed himself for that. He had thought Rhenn was Nhevalos's pawn, the only one who mattered....

But Khyven had been Nhevalos's ringer all along.

Now that Tovos had seen Khyven in action, it was clear. No Human should have been able to do what he did, to circumvent Tovos's defenses, to hurt Tovos that badly. The others had helped him, of course, but it was Khyven who had mysteriously avoided Tovos's strikes. His ability to evade them had been precognitive.

The Human was using Lore Magic.

Somehow Nhevalos had imbued Khyven with a special kind of Lore Magic, had leveraged the mortal's latent Eldroi blood, elevating him.

Tovos clenched his fists. It was all so obvious now. Only now, when he must wait.

He glanced down at the thick, golden manacle around his ankle. The Dragon Chain not only stopped him from leaving this place but also from using any of the streams of magic.

Tovos had actually helped create this artifact. All the Noksonoi had. Dragon Chains had been designed to trap other Eldroi, specifically the Drakanoi. They'd been made long ago before Humans were a threat, when the only wars that waged across Eldros were the Elder Wars between other Eldroi: Noksonoi, Pyranoi, Daemanoi, and of course Drakanoi.

Now, thanks to Khyven and his friends—especially their Human mage—here Tovos sat, trapped by a tool he'd made to thwart his enemies.

He had only one possibility left, a thin one: his connection to the Dark. He had been sending his will into the noktum day after day and night after night, trying to call one of his servants to him.

But because of the nearby Lux—whose sole purpose was to shatter the power of the noktum—Tovos knew the message, if it was leaving the cave at all, would be barely a whisper. Someone had to be listening for it. Someone had to want to hear it.

After so many days, he feared no one would, though he kept trying. At some point, one of his minions might feel the ripples and be drawn to this place. All Tovos required was the single touch of a hand, a foot, anything at all. The release of the Dragon Chain was so simple, a necessary weakness as a counterpoint to the powerful spell.

But a creature had to come to this place first.

The dragon Jai'ketakos had remained here for two thousand years, bound by the Dragon Chain. He'd only been freed when Tovos had sent Zaith the Nox and that damned Luminent Lorelle to this place. Tovos had thought it would be a master stroke: unleash the powerful dragon, create an ally in the upcoming war. Jai'ketakos should have been grateful. Instead, he had slaughtered Tovos's minions and vanished. If Jai'ketakos had just seen that the Eldroi, no matter which continent they came from, had to band together to stop these arrogant Humans, he would have ...

Tovos raised his head. His thoughts fluttered away.

Was that a footstep?

He reached into his tenuous connection to the Dark and tried to feel who was coming. His ears had caught a sound, but the Dark revealed nothing. It was almost as though ...

As though whoever was coming was shielding himself from the Dark.

Tovos rose from his sitting position at the edge of the mound of gold. He looked down the irregular hall of the cavern, which bent to the left a hundred yards distant.

"Ventat?" he called, wondering if his most competent mortal

servant had returned from Daemanon to look for him. Or perhaps it was Olgirios the Gargoyle, Tovos's castle steward.

A tendril of smoke wafted around the bend, and a giant, clawed talon came into view.

Tovos's hope flickered and faltered as Jai'ketakos rounded the corner. The Drakanoi's huge talons touched the rocky floor so lightly for such a huge creature. His enormous horned head bent low to keep from striking the cavern's ceiling.

"Well hello Tovos," Jai'ketakos said.

Tovos had worked to master deceit these past centuries. He'd done it to counter Nhevalos's cunning. He'd done it even though Harkandos had always hated deceivers. The glorious Harkandos had demanded that the Noksonoi be exactly who they were, no dissembling. They should indulge in their abilities. They should show who they were in every single moment, and Tovos had originally modeled himself after that philosophy.

But Nhevalos had defeated Harkandos. Tovos's ill-fated mentor had also preached adaptation, rising to whatever challenges presented themselves. So Tovos had schooled himself to think in cunning, sidewinding ways. It had been difficult, but in this moment, he was grateful for the training. He strove use everything he'd learned as he responded to the Drakanoi.

"Brother," Tovos said in a genuine voice. "It is good to see you."

Jai'ketakos smiled. "It is."

"I sent creatures to free you," Tovos said. "Clearly, they succeeded."

"Ah." Jai'ketakos raised one scaly brow. "Then it is as I suspected. You sent the Nox and his luminous companion."

"I felt you had been imprisoned too long, a cruel a fate for one so worthy. Whatever crimes you had committed, surely your penance had been paid." Tovos paused, dropping his voice. "And more than that, Jai'ketakos, the world has come to a precipice. Noksonon needs you."

"Noksonon? Or *you*?" the dragon asked.

Tovos's concern became icy certainty. The dragon was

toying with him. He had not come here with the purpose of freeing Tovos, which meant Tovos must convince him.

"I was not the one who imprisoned you," Tovos said.

"No." The dragon's mouth split in a toothy smile. "But I wonder how long you have known about my plight. A few hundred years? A few thousand?"

"I sent Zaith and Lorelle here because I knew they would free you."

"Yet you could have come here at any time since the war. You just left me, like all the others."

"Do you want to see these mortal fleas continue to build their little kingdoms and pretend the world belongs to them?" Tovos angled the topic away. "Noksonon is ours by right! And the time to strike is now. The cusp is upon us. Do not let your focus scatter to old grudges that have nothing to do with me."

"Old grudges ... Mortal fleas ..." Jai'ketakos cocked his head as though thinking it over. "You know, Tovos, I like these fleas. They cavort. They lament. They burn so nicely. Have you ever sampled sizzling Nox, Tovos? Your minions are tasty."

Tovos yanked at the Dragon Chain in frustration. "Don't toy with me, Jai'ketakos. You know of what I speak. Would you let the opportunity pass us by?"

"Us?"

"Your casual actions serve the wrong side!"

"Side? On which side do you calculate I stand?"

"Would you like the mortal races to continue strutting across this world?"

"Oh, I especially like it when they strut."

"They aspire to the grace that once only belonged to the Eldroi."

"The Eldroi ... The Eldroi ..." Jai'ketakos mused.

"I agree that we have all had our differences in the past. The Noksonoi, the Drakanoi, the Pyranoi, the Daemanoi. But we must put that aside. We must put the fleas in their place or we will continue to hold only a fraction of our rightful grandeur. The world belongs to *us*."

"That is a pretty speech." The dragon smiled. "And you include me in this grouping of Eldroi?"

"You are Eldroi! All of us are—"

"During my stay shackled to that manacle you now wear, I had time to think upon many things. I came to a beautiful revelation."

"Jai'ketakos—"

"Human, Luminent, Nox, Delver, Wergoi, Noksonoi, Drakanoi ..." the dragon continued, stepping on Tovos's words, "Mortals or Giants. Gods or animals. They all have only one thing in common."

"And what is that?"

"They all burn...."

Tovos raised his chin. Even when the armies of the Humans and Luminents overran the bulwarks of Harkandos Keep seventeen hundred years ago, Tovos had never felt so helpless. Without magic, without minions of any kind to free him or fend off the dragon, Tovos was utterly vulnerable. Exposed.

The dragon's smile widened, as though he could feel Tovos' thoughts.

"Quell your fear, Lord Tovos. I'm not going to kill you. I'm going to give you a choice."

"A choice?"

"Of course. It is not up to me to choose your destiny. A sentient being should chart his own course."

"What choice?"

"You will determine my next action. You stand at a crossroads, and one fork in the path is this: I will decline your gracious offer to join your war, and I will leave this place right now. I will leave you as you are, bound by the Dragon Chain. But I will come back every month. And each month, I will give you another chance to recruit me to your war."

The Drakanoi watched Tovos, eyes glimmering as if he was enjoying this. Tovos waited.

"The other fork is this: I will free you, and you may do as you wish. You may go wherever your body will carry you and whatever you wish. If it is still your desire to pursue this war against the fleas of the world, then I say, 'Huzzah, and more power to you.'" The dragon became solemn. His smile receded. "But if I do this, you will never see me again as long as you live. You will never again have the chance to recruit me to your cause."

The dragon stared intently at Tovos, clearly seeking to read him, but Tovos kept his face unreadable.

Tovos had the dragon now, but he kept the satisfied look from his face. The ridiculous Drakanoi always were so puffed up, thinking themselves such high thinkers when they were, in fact, idiots.

The Drakanoi thought, just as Tovos intended him to think, that Tovos's greatest wish was to unite the Eldroi in the war. But Tovos didn't need Jai'ketakos to join the war, not really. What Tovos needed was freedom. Once he had his magic back, once he was back in his castle, he would bring the dragon to heel.

"You would be a fool to stay out of this war," Tovos warned, playing out his part. It wouldn't do to give even a glimpse of his desperation to the dragon.

Jai'ketakos blinked lazily, like the statement was boring. He let out a small breath, and the gaps between his teeth glowed with an orange fire. "If such is your choice, then a month hence, we may discuss that. You may ply me with your pretty speeches once more, and I will listen. But I am done listening today. Make your choice."

"You make me sad, Jai'ketakos," Tovos said. "I thought you would be smarter than this. I will not hold you to your decision. Because you do me this service, I will not turn from you when you change your mind and come to your senses."

"Then you have made your choice?"

"I choose for you to free me."

The dragon's smile stretched to that impossible width again, and behind those tall teeth, orange fire turned yellow, then white.

"Oh ..." the dragon said softly as though Tovos had made him the happiest creature on Eldros. "A good choice, Lord

Tovos. The best of choices."

Jai'ketakos drew a deep breath, rising up to the limit of the cavern. The enormous trunk of his body grew as he took all the air he could into his lungs.

"Jai'ketakos!" Tovos shouted "What are—"

The dragon fire hit Tovos in the chest, so fast he didn't have time to move, to think.

He screamed as the fire seared him, blew through him. He turned his face away and threw up his arms. His clothes burned away. His skin melted. Muscles and bones charred. His hair flashed off and his right eyeball exploded in his head. But still the fire went on and on and on. Every nerve in his body screamed, and Tovos screamed with them.

After an eternity of unbelievable pain, he realized he was still alive. He lay on his back on the molten golden soup of what had once been the coins of the dragon's treasure mountain.

Tovos moaned weakly through a lipless mouth. Ragged blades of agony raked through his dying body. He felt the dragon draw closer, felt his presence like terror incarnate. A massive claw fell on Tovos's gamey chest. Tovos howled like an animal.

"I free you," the dragon whispered in Tovos's good ear. The Dragon Chain opened, separating from his bubbling flesh and falling to the cavern floor.

Tovos tried to scream the dragon's name, but only a howl emerged.

"I free you forever," Jai'ketakos said.

A single claw, like a curved sword, punched down through Tovos's chest and tore through his heart. Tovos sucked in a half-breath, mouth open ...

And died.

♦ ♦ ♦

The tortured, melted body went limp, and Jai'ketakos pulled his bloody claw from the corpse. He smiled down at the dead Noksonoi lord.

"You may now go wherever your body will carry you. Pursue your war. Recruit your soldiers. Retake your power. Take all the power you can carry. Do whatever you may, as I promised." The dragon chuckled until the laughter finally petered out.

He watched the smoking, charred corpse for a long, satisfying moment, then he took a breath and turned toward the entrance.

"Now, my lord," he spoke to Tovos as though he was still there. Jai'ketakos had long ago become accustomed to talking as though there was someone around to hear. "There is a curiosity regarding this Dragon Chain, something that is tickling my mind. Someone had to put it on you, dear Tovos, and I do not know who it could be. I sense from your anger that it must be one of those fascinating mortals you mentioned. After all this time, Nox or Human or Shadowvar shouldn't even know what a Dragon Chain is, let alone how to use one. Some mortal out there was clever enough to use it against you. That is clever, especially for a mortal. And I do so enjoy a bit of cleverness." He glanced over his shoulder at the smoking corpse. "So I will seek your killer, Lord Tovos. For you. For the honor of the Eldroi." He chuckled again. "I will find your imprisoner, Lord Tovos. I will find him and see if he burns as nicely as the one he imprisoned...."

Chapter One
SLAYTER

Slayter planned to save the world, but he wasn't sure exactly how to do it. Yet.

His mind was alive with Giants when he entered his laboratory, but the familiar surroundings lent an immediate sense of ease, a respite from thorny thoughts. That was, after all, the main purpose of having a laboratory at all.

All five mage candles flickered with light, standing nicely upright in their candle holders. Two large ones perched on walls and each pillar around his worktable also held a candle in iron holders. The candles did not provide enough light to work by, of course. Bright lanterns hanging from the vaulted ceiling overhead did that. The candles were ritualistic, and a key component to bringing calm. Five was the mage's number. There were five streams of magic: Love Magic, Lore Magic, Land Magic, Life Magic, and of course, the stream of magic Slayter used: Line Magic.

Five was the power number of Eldros. The destined number. There were five continents, after all. Five major tribes of Giants before the Giant War. If one looked one could find the number five everywhere, in fact.

Not everyone—not even every mage—focused their energy on the power of five. Halenza, Slayter's mentor, certainly had not.

The mage's number was *not* three, but Halenza had only installed three lanterns to provide light and three worktables.

But then Halenza, as talented a mage as she had been, had been focused on acquiring social power and influence, which was a poor objective for a mage, in Slayter's opinion. As a result, she had been only a shadow of the mage she might have been. She could have tried to peel back the mysteries of the world. Instead, she had served as Vamreth's catspaw. She had seen the world as a pyramid with herself close to the top.

But the pentagon was the mage's shape, the true shape of the intent of the world. Points that met at angles, that linked from one to the other. There was more to the workings and the harmony of all things than one top point. That was something worthy for a mage to understand.

This laboratory had flaws, but searching for a "perfect" location could waste time, and he had much to do. He'd had much to do since he was ten years old. So he had made a mental adjustment instead and put up five mage candles to remind him that he served the accumulation of knowledge and the understanding of magic, and all had been well since. All situations were multi-faceted jewels. Turning the gem to a different facet often worked wonders. After all, life rarely came in an orderly fashion.

Speaking of which, he turned to look over at Shalure. She was here already, of course. That seemed to be her purpose at the moment. She sat in the corner. Ever since the discovery of her magical talent, she had become a regular installation in his lab. She had become ...

Well, he supposed she'd become his apprentice, if one wanted to look at it that way.

The conscientious girl had taken to coming here before he

arrived to prepare the laboratory, light the lanterns, light the candles, and organize whatever he'd left strewn on the worktables the night before into perfectly straight lines. She'd even ensured that all the candles stood straight up and down.

Such things were like warm blankets wrapped over cold hands to Slayter. They calmed his heart and made him ready to work. She was gloriously attentive to him.

"*Good morning Shalure,*" Slayter gestured as he closed the door behind himself.

The water clock against the far wall read five o'clock precisely. Even Slayter considered anything before five o'clock brutally early, but Shalure made a point to be here with enough time to do her morning tasks.

Slayter used to come in at six in the morning, but the sun rose at seven o'clock in early spring in Usara, and he'd pushed his schedule earlier because he wanted to make sure that if Rhenn—who slept during the day now when she slept at all—had a solid two hours of his best and most intellectually productive time before the sun chased her away.

"*Good morning Slayter,*" Shalure signed back.

"*I trust you slept well.*"

"*I did.*"

A lie. Both ways, really.

Slayter forced himself to use typical social protocols to make his friends more comfortable. Sometimes it even worked. Social protocols were a fountain of ridiculousness that rarely yielded useful information. He had asked after her sleep because that was what was expected. And polite, they said. It was also, of course, entirely unnecessary. He already knew how Shalure had slept at a glance. The persistent dark circles beneath her eyes told the real tale.

So they lied to each other. She through telling him the opposite of the truth. He through acting like it would add to his knowledge. And somehow this made people more comfortable.

"*Thank you for your ministrations.*" He indicated the lab.

"*It's the least I can do,*" she said.

Which was, he knew, her way of saying she wasn't doing the *most* she could do. That she wanted to do *more*. That he'd been remiss in teaching her the things that she actually wanted to—

The laboratory door banged open and Rhenn strode through. She marched across the room and threw her sword on his clean and tidy worktable. It clattered on the polished stone surface and slid to a stop at the far edge, knocking a quill and parchment to the floor. Rhenn had become far more serious since her adventure in Daemanon, but she was still as impetuous as ever. And rough on her equipment. Slayter was glad he'd made adjustments to the pommel ruby on that sword since he'd first given it to her. The initial iteration of that sword would have exploded if she'd thrown it on the table like that.

"Take it out," she demanded.

Slayter glanced at the water clock. It was five minutes past five. Five and five. Two fives.

"You're angry," Slayter said, turning his attention back to her. He wasn't always correct about his friends' moods. People often surprised him about what they got angry about, so it was always best to confirm.

A flush rose in her cheeks and her lips curled in a snarl.

All right. Definitely angry. He'd called that correctly. He glanced at the sword, then back at her.

"You want me to take out the gem?" he guessed as she opened her mouth to expel whatever vituperations lay behind her teeth. He turned his focus to the sword. The enchanted ruby spun lazily in place, held aloft by magics that bound it in place.

"The damned thing is tainted and I want it out," she said. "This sword was E'maz's last gift to me. I told you in the beginning I didn't want it altered. You said it would make the …" She shook her head. "It doesn't matter. I've tried it. I want it out. I want it back the way it was."

"Is it not working?" he asked.

"No, it's not working!" Rhenn clearly tried to master her anger, her fists clenched at her sides. "The gem is evil!"

"It's not the same gem N'ssag used—"

"I want the sword the way it was!"

Slayter narrowed his eyes. A new thought occurred to him. She was angry. She attached this anger to the sword. However, this might not be about the sword at all. This could be about something else entirely, and she was *blaming* the sword.

Last week, after he had adjusted the sword's magics, she had sheathed the blade with satisfaction, with an air of possession. Last week, the gem had not bothered her.

"What happened?" he asked.

"Nothing happened," she said too quickly, like she'd been prepared for the question. "I hate the gem. You took my sword and you didn't ask me and you created this abomination and …" She twitched, noticing Shalure for the first time. Rhenn blinked, seemed to gather herself, then said in a calm voice, "My apologies, Shalure. I didn't see you there."

It's all right. I don't mean to intrude. I'll go. Shalure signed to her. She stood up, but Rhenn waved a pacifying hand for her to sit back down. Shalure froze.

"It's influencing my mind," Rhenn turned back to Slayter. "That's what it's doing."

Slayter narrowed his eyes. Well, that was just impossible.

"It is … influencing you?" He repeated. There were many things Slayter didn't understand. The world was full of delicious mysteries. But Slayter knew his craft of Line Magic as well as anyone. The spells he had put into the gemstone—and thereby bound to the sword—were Life Magic spells. They had only to do with the transfer of the life force from a creature, or multiple creatures, into the sword, and then into Rhenn. It was not Love Magic. It had nothing to do with mental control. Not even a little bit.

But Slayter had long ago discovered that people didn't like being told they were wrong, even when they *were*. Especially when they were. And it went double for Rhenn.

"Tell me more about that," Slayter said, giving himself a moment to think about what the real problem might be. "What exactly is it—"

"It wants me to go into the noktum, Slayter. The sword is driving me into the noktum."

"Driving you into the noktum?"

A thrill ran through his body. This was a new mystery almost certainly having to do with Rhenn's miraculous transformation. Something magical. Rhenn's new state—a powerful bit of Life Magic interwoven with darkness and crafted by a master Life Mage from Daemanon—was interacting with the magical darkness of the noktum. That was just ... delicious. There was something important to know here, and he *had* to learn it.

"Well that's ... amazing," he breathed.

Rhenn's eyes narrowed. "It's not amazing, Slayter. It's horrible. Fix it."

He blinked at her vehemence, then realized she'd misunderstood him. "I mean, yes, I would fix the sword, of course. Except there isn't really anything to fix. Well, I mean ... What I mean to say is that it's not the sword. It's you."

Rhenn lifted her chin.

"It's ... I mean it has to have something to do with your transformation. Daemanon bloodsuckers are creatures of the dark. Their hunger for blood is built into them using darkness as part of the process. They are literally bound to the dark. And Vohn and Lorelle just discovered a sentience within the noktum. And now you're telling me that this sentience is speaking directly to you, like it did with Vohn. Like it did with Lorelle. It sees you as one of its creatures, even though you weren't made here." He waved his hands excitedly in the air. "I can't believe I didn't think of this before. This could be a revelation of epic ..."

He trailed off as he noticed that behind Rhenn, Shalure was jumping up and down frantically, waving her hands. Once she had his attention, she signed hastily.

Isn't helping! Rhenn doesn't want to ...

Shalure was so agitated that the last word was garbled. It was either "ear split" or "hear that."

Shalure signed again.

Look at her!

Slayter glanced at Rhenn. The queen's face had lost all color, and tears stood in her eyes.

"A creature of the noktum?" she asked in a husky voice. "Is that what I am? A monster that runs around sucking blood?"

That wasn't what he had been saying at all. "No. Well, I mean yes, but ... What I meant to say is this is a perfect opportunity to—"

"To experiment with my life?" she interrupted, chin still high. "An opportunity to hone your skills?"

Slayter opened his mouth, but he suddenly saw the conversation from the other side, from Rhenn's perspective. She was taking his words as an offense, as Shalure had frantically gestured, not as the opportunity to learn that they were. He desperately searched for the words to correct the situation, to show her that this could be seen as an advantage.

He didn't find them.

"Er ..." He glanced at Shalure again, but she seemed frozen, eyes wide as though she couldn't come up with anything either.

Rhenn's tears spilled over and ran down her cheeks, but her face was stony. "Get the damned gemstone off the sword." She threw the command over her shoulder as she stalked out of the room.

Slayter blinked. He paused there for a moment until even the queen's footsteps on the stairs outside had faded. He walked to the door and slowly closed it, then glanced at Shalure. He stared at her, but he wasn't really seeing her. He thought about how he might have played that differently. People simply didn't see things sometimes. This new change in Rhenn could connect the large to the small. It certainly could.

The real problem wasn't Rhenn's dislike of the stone. The real problem was that the Giants were coming for them. It was more important than Rhenn's emotions about E'maz. It was more important, really, than everything. If the Giants returned and had their way, *nothing* would matter ever again.

Knowing more about the noktum—the master spell cast over all of Noksonon long ago—could be the difference between saving every person on the continent or dying at the hands of the Giants.

Are you going to remove the gem? Shalure signed.

Slayter came out of his reverie, signed back to her. *It's not the stone. If the sentience in the noktum is talking to the queen, understanding why is the key.*

He looked at a little patch of amorphous darkness hovering above a small circular wooden stand, encased in glass and held there by a series of spells.

She said it was the stone in the sword, Shalure persisted.

She is mistaken.

He walked toward the little patch of noktum he had captured and brought here after Vohn told them there was an active sentience in the Dark. Lorelle called it the "Dark" with a capital D.

Slayter had discovered many interesting things about the Dark once he'd begun to study it. Prevailing wisdom was that there were many noktums scattered all over the entire continent of Noksonon—the "prevailing wisdom" was wrong. There weren't hundreds of noktums. There was one. Still. The master spell the Giants had cast over the continent seventeen hundred years ago remained intact. There were simply very thin spots and very thick spots. Some of the connections were so thin that they couldn't be perceived by the naked eye, but they were all connected.

To the layman, this made no difference whatsoever. But for Slayter's purposes, it had enormous repercussions—or opportunities—if facing Giants in a war.

Shalure remained silent and unobtrusive, as was her way, as Slayter got to work. She either watched over his shoulder as he worked with the bit of noktum, which he didn't mind, or she read in the corner as the hours moved past.

Slayter's objective was to tease out this sentience Vohn had described and Lorelle had experienced to see if it would talk to him. Over the course of the next five hours, he made seven disks with different spells to see if it would manifest.

He failed seven times.

Unlike other people, Slayter was unperturbed by failure. He loved the learning process above all things, and each failure offered learning. Of course, in a combat situation it was apparently different. Khyven had quite pointedly told him that trial and error when lives were at stake was not the optimum—

The lab door banged open. Khyven himself stepped through as though Slayter's thoughts had summoned him.

"You!" He pointed at Slayter as though it was a surprise to find him here, in his own laboratory.

Slayter was impressed by how Khyven could step into a room and fill it. There could be a thousand books and dozens of powerful experiments all around him, but it would seem like Khyven was the only thing of importance. It was like he had sucked all the light into himself and the only thing you could look at was him.

Slayter glanced at the water clock. It was ten after ten. Five and five and five and five. And added to the fives on the clock when Rhenn had visited at five minutes after the fifth hour of the day, well that was ... Well, there were three different ways to calculate the fives.

"Did you give her a sleeping potion?" Khyven demanded, walking toward Slayter like he was going to chop him in half. That was another of Khyven's gifts. When he was angry, everyone around him felt it. It was as though he wore a magical cloak of rage that touched everyone around him.

Slayter wasn't afraid, though. He had analyzed each of his friends and knew their primary motivators. He would have bet everything in his laboratory that Khyven would never, ever raise a hand to him. Ever since the War of the Usurper, Khyven would rather die than let any of his friends come to harm.

"Did you?" Khyven towered over Slayter, chest heaving as though he'd leapt down the steps to the laboratory.

"Lorelle?"

"Yes Lorelle! Who else would I be talking about?"

"There are any number of—"

"Slayter!"

"No, I didn't."

"You didn't," Khyven repeated flatly.

"It's not a potion."

Khyven sighed. "But you gave her something."

"A sleeping spell."

"Slayter ..."

"I took the idea from the Leaves of Charnen Wynne. She was also a Line Mage—quite insane—but every now and then she hit upon something ingenious. You see, the trick is to carve all but one line of the spell onto a water-resistant clay disk, which as you know keeps the spell quiescent. Then you cover half of the disk in Wynne's phosphorus-sugar mixture. When it dries, you finish the line, completing the spell, but while half is obscured by Wynne's mixture. So the spell remains inert. But ..." Slayter made a releasing gesture with his fingers. "Drop it into a cup of water. Plop, fizz, and the phosphorous-sugar mixture breaks down into solution. The design on the disk is revealed, and the spell takes effect."

Slayter grinned at Khyven. He did not smile back.

"A sleeping potion," Khyven growled.

Slayter felt a keen disappointment. "No, it's not a potion, it's—"

"You activate a spell in water and she drinks it."

"Yes."

"That's a potion."

"Well ... All right, I see your confusion. Here is the explanation: the magical properties aren't in the liquid. I mean, not at first. It's in the disk—"

"I. Don't. Care."

Slayter blinked. "I thought you wanted to talk about the properties of the spell."

"No. That's what *you* wanted to talk about. I'm telling you to stop talking about it, and I'm telling you to stop drugging my lover!"

Slayter sighed. "It's not a drug, it's a—"

"Stop doing it!"

"Is it not working?"

"Oh, it works."

Slayter wrinkled his brow. "But if the spell is working—"

"She's asleep, Slayter. All night. From the moment she puts her head to the pillow to—"

"Sunrise. Yes. That was how the spell works—"

"Slayter!"

Slayter narrowed his eyes. Khyven's anger wasn't about the workings of the spell. Nor its efficiency. It was about something ... else.

"You don't want her to sleep," Slayter said.

"I can't rouse her even if I wanted to."

"Why would you want to?"

"Slayter, just stop giving her—"

"What is this?" Lorelle's voice interrupted.

Both Slayter and Khyven turned.

Lorelle stood the doorway, arms folded over her chest. The bottom of her noktum cloak settled with a flamboyant final ripple, as though it was bowing. Slayter had noticed the cloak did that same little flourish every time it finished a teleport. Magically, that had to mean something. Such a repetition indicated the inner workings of the cloak. It was quite intriguing.

He glanced at the water clock. Seventeen minutes after ten. Well, so much for the fives. That was disappointing.

Khyven opened his mouth to respond, but he seemed not to have considered what he would say once he got that far.

"You're following me?" he asked.

"You're interrogating Slayter about me?" she asked.

"I'm not interrogating him. I'm just ..." Khyven trailed off.

"Go on. Finish that sentence. What are you doing, exactly?"

Khyven looked at Slayter angrily, as though this was his fault.

"This isn't ..." Khyven fumbled. "Maybe we discuss this elsewhere."

"Oh, I quite agree. We *should* have discussed this elsewhere. But that horse has left the stables. Do go on. Finish your sentence."

Slayter decided to help Khyven out. "He wanted to know—"

Khyven cut him off with a vicious swipe of his huge hand and a glare that could have melted rock. "Lorelle, I think we just take this back to our room and—"

"Let me see if I can piece it together," she interrupted. "I made a decision. You didn't like the decision, so rather than telling me, you come to Slayter in an attempt to undermine the decision?"

Again, Khyven opened his mouth to speak and simply held it open. Finally, he blurted. "You've been dead to the world. Every night for five nights!"

She gave him a flinty stare. "And?"

Slayter had a suddenly, illuminating revelation.

"This is about sex!" he exclaimed.

"Slayter," Khyven growled, and his glare was so full of violence that Slayter suddenly wondered if Khyven would actually strike him.

Lorelle narrowed her eyes. "I have a reason for Slayter's spell. An important reason. You didn't think to ask me?"

"And you didn't think to tell me about this important reason?" Khyven retorted, anger sneaking into his tone as though he'd found a path to the high ground.

"So if I don't immediately inform you of something having to do with my own life, you're going to go behind my back and try to undo that thing? That ..." She turned, and her cloak swirled around her. "... is good to know."

"Lorelle!" Khyven leapt toward the doorway.

The black cloak seemed to melt with the shadows, obscuring her, then shrank into nothingness and she was gone.

Khyven landed where she had been a split second ago, just a fraction too late. "Damn it!"

He whirled, shot Slayter a white-hot glare, then vanished up the stairwell.

Slayter stood there for a good long moment, fingertips lightly touching the polished surface of the worktable. He knew that Shalure would be listening, watching. He'd tried to make a habit of revealing his discoveries as he thought them, so he spoke aloud.

"You know. I've done some calculations, and I've determined that if sex were removed from the Human race, couples would relate in a much smoother fashion." He turned to Shalure. "Don't you think—?"

She was crying.

She sat in her corner on her stool, and her body shuddered quietly. She held one hand to her mouth, and her red and teary eyes stared at the doorway where Khyven had been.

Slayter looked at the doorway, back at Shalure, back at the doorway, then back at Shalure.

He took a wild shot in the dark.

"You are upset."

She flicked something with her fingers—so garbled he had no idea what it was—and lurched from her stool. It wobbled back and forth and clattered to the stone floor as she fled through the doorway. Her soft-slippered feet tapped lightly on the steps as she ran up them.

He glanced around his laboratory, at the piece of noktum, at Rhenn's sword, at the half a dozen other projects that needed his attention. Usually, this would fill his mind with excitement like food filled the mouth with flavor.

But today the only taste was ash and paste.

"Well this won't do," he said aloud, this time to no one. But someone answered him.

"Difficult morning?"

Slayter turned again to find Vohn in the doorway. He wore a black jacket over a dark gray shirt tucked into black pants. As always, it was understated clothing that blended with the shadows, but his face and hair *actually* vanished against the dark behind him. He could have been an empty suit of clothes standing upright. Only his bright white horns indicated he had a head at all. He stepped into the light of the lanterns and his features reappeared.

The magic of the Shadowvar. Slayter found it fascinating every time. Vohn had other magic too, a kind that even most Shadowvar didn't possess. He was what the layman would call a banshee, a creature who could discorporate and join the noktum as a howling wind.

Of course, there were a half-dozen reasons why he should absolutely *not* do that, especially right now. It seemed the Dark hungered for all of Slayter's friends in one way or another. The great Giant Nhevalos—known as The Betrayer—had branded Khyven as a Greatblood and planned to use him for some mysterious purpose. The noktum race of the Nox had tried to recruit Lorelle to their ranks. But then a dragon had destroyed them. The Dark wanted Vohn so badly that Slayter had had to pry him from its grip. And now the Dark seemed to have turned its attention to Queen Rhenn.

Vohn crossed the laboratory and took Slayter's hand.

"I have work to do," Slayter protested.

"You do." Vohn led him to the doorway.

"But we are going for a walk?" Slayter offered.

"We are."

Walks actually had an amazing effect on Slayter, clearing his mind, helping him to think better, faster. Over the past weeks since Slayter had brought Vohn back, the Shadowvar had been showing up at random times and encouraging Slayter to take a walk. Interestingly, it always seemed to be at a time when Slayter most needed one.

"How do you know?" Slayter asked.

"It doesn't take a genius to know when a friend is in need."

"What does it take?"

Vohn just smiled. They started up the stairs.

Chapter Three

SLAYTER

Slayter chased the memories.

He had not been with his parents when they passed; he'd been in Vamreth's court. And Slayter hadn't really cared they had passed. He'd never shed a tear, never felt one way or the other about it. It had never seemed particularly important until this moment. His parents had never understood him, and he'd never felt a particular loyalty to them. Their actions had been predictable and pedestrian, and not dedicated to serving any particular higher cause, like Rhenn's actions had. When Slayter had left Wheskone Keep before his tenth birthday, he'd had no doubt his parents—either quietly or outwardly—had celebrated his departure. Slayter certainly had.

He hadn't been close to his siblings, either. Only his older sister Yvelle had ever tried to see the world through Slayter's eyes. She'd failed, but she had tried, and he'd always remembered it. His two older brothers had tortured him and his two younger brothers had been following closely in their footsteps at their father's behest. The most interesting behavior

Slayter had ever received from his parents or siblings had been a mystified, barely-veiled fear. Slayter had been able to do things other children couldn't. He'd been a nuisance, and even a political liability at times.

At age seven Slayter had seen through the lies of Baron Sendrin, a visiting noble who'd wheedled himself into a hundred acres of Father's land. Slayter had called out his plan in front of everyone at a well-attended feast. What Slayter didn't know was that Father had actually manipulated the baron into wanting to take those swampy holdings and was fully aware of what was happening.

Slayter had stirred a pot his father had wanted still.

After that disaster, Father had banished him to the duke's treasury during the next feast to keep him out of sight. By the time dinner was done, Slayter had proposed a new and more efficient method of keeping track of the duchy's balance sheet. The treasurer never spoke to Slayter after that and insisted he never be allowed back in the treasury again.

Slayter had fomented a similar situation after being banished to the armory instead. After watching the smith work for a day, Slayter suggested a different way to heat and bend metal. They'd banished him to the kitchens after that, where he had freely given his ideas about cooking. After that, the stables. After that ...

Well, soon he'd been banished from just about everywhere in the duchy but the library. He hadn't been able to help himself. Whatever the mystery, he had to pierce it. And once he did, he'd felt compelled to tell those around him, who rarely understood. He had clear vision. They did not.

And they hated him for it.

So when he was nine years old, his parents had shipped him off to the capital of Usara to apprentice to a hedge wizard who sold fake charms and colored potions to bumpkins. The man had no idea what real magic was, and it hadn't taken Slayter more than a few days to realize it. Of course he couldn't stop himself from pointing it out, and the man took to beating him every time he did.

Slayter reckoned the hedge wizard would have killed him soon enough, but Vamreth—then just an ambitious baron—had a court mage named Halenza Gaurlyn. She had stumbled across the charlatan's shop one day and noticed Slayter's talent. She'd immediately seen past his bruised face to his quick-thinking, agile mind, and she'd plucked him from the shop. The hedge wizard had been delighted to transfer Slayter's apprenticeship for a few silver pieces.

That had been the defining moment of Slayter's life. It had been the fork in the road that had taken him here, rather than to an early death.

Up to that point, Slayter had been a thirsty boy trying to dig a well with his bare hands. He'd known there was water down there—he could sense it!—but he'd only ever come up with handfuls of dry dirt.

Halenza gave him a river.

She unlocked his abilities. The water flowed, and he drank and drank and drank. The world, so gray and confining before, was suddenly alive with endless colors of possibility. Slayter suddenly knew exactly what he was and what he must do with his life.

In his first three months under Halenza, he outstripped her other apprentices. Within a year, he was doing spells for her—even spells for Vamreth—which she claimed as her own.

Halenza had actually been a talented mage. Unlike the rest of her apprentices, she could cast strong spells, had precise hands, and a creative style. But by the time Slayter was ten, he had outstripped her in every way.

And she knew it.

She kept him hidden from Vamreth as long as she could, claiming his talent as her own.

Slayter didn't care about that one whit. He saw her petty connivances as a weakness. It was the reason she had never fulfilled her potential as a mage. She cared too much about Vamreth's favor, and about the court's perception of her.

Slayter hadn't cared how anyone perceived him, and he ignored it all. Her lies. Her power jockeying. The important thing was that Halenza was teaching him magic. If she wanted to take credit for his work, fine. If she wanted to use him to further her own ends, fine. She could tell the world that he was a three-eyed huska beast with the intelligence of a bug as long as she kept offering him knowledge. Only after he had drunk her river dry would he even care about the next step.

Until the night of the coup.

Halenza had awoken him sometime around midnight, and there were torches in his room. After ten years, that was what Slayter remembered about the beginning of that pivotal night. The torches. The lights burning in the dark like the eyes of angry animals ...

"Wake up," Halenza had said. Curling black smoke from the oil-soaked torches had filled the room . It stung his eyes and he squinted at the light. Slayter couldn't help thinking about how those tall tongues of flame could light the low rafters on fire, how a person should really use lanterns inside, instead of torches.

"Leave the boy. What are you thinking?" the brutish, bearded man with the oiled chainmail shirt had said. The mace at his side was a chunk of thick, heavy steel.

"He comes with me," Halenza had said.

"This is red work. For men and not boys."

"We will need more than muscle and steel this night," she had retorted.

They had left the baron's manor and moved quietly through the night. It seemed with every street they passed, their horde grew.

They had slipped into the palace past a bribed guard, and then the massacre had begun. Vamreth and his soldiers had slaughtered everyone. That night had defined the word "horror" for Slayter.

He'd done what Halenza asked of him, little spells here and there through the screaming and the blood. For the first time in his life, Slayter's mind seemed unable to think, so he just did what he was told.

After the palace was secured, after all the enemies had been killed or run off, Slayter spent a year continuing his apprenticeship to Halenza much like he had that horrible night. She told him to do something, and he did it. He worked his spells by rote, but his voracious appetite had vanished.

He thought and thought. He reviewed the slaughter, putting the memories and every player's motivations into place in his mind, ordering everything and trying to draw satisfying conclusions that put him into that picture. He couldn't. Instead, when he finished, he came to one unavoidable conclusion.

Halenza had no moral code and, through his connection to her as her apprentice, neither did Slayter.

Vamreth was a greedy, petty, power-hungry man, and Halenza had chosen to serve him. She allowed her power to be used by this man and by extension Slayter's power.

Slayter realized that he was like them both. He was selfish like Vamreth, focused only on absorbing more knowledge. He was weak like Halenza, allowing his power to be used without bringing his intellect to bear on why.

The realization left him feeling ill. Slayter was a victim of fate, yes. He'd had few choices when Halenza had plucked him from a sure death, yes.

But he did have choices now. And that changed everything.

It took him that first year to organize these thoughts, but his final realization was that just learning magic wasn't enough. There had to be a higher purpose to life. There had to be a ... rightness. Otherwise he was no better than her. Or Vamreth.

At first, Slayter didn't even know—or care—what it meant to have rightness. Before that moment, rightness had simply meant learning magic. His entire life had been filled up by trying to quench that unquenchable thirst.

Now, with magic as his ally, he had a new thirst. To solve an impossible puzzle. He was trapped in a nest of vipers. How could he possibly free himself? He would need a plan and a masterful one at that, or he would never escape. They knew his value. Slayter was a piece of treasure in their minds. Halenza and Vamreth would never let him go.

It took five more years after Slayter's initial revelation for him to find the window to act. Soon after his sixteenth birthday, Wheskone Keep burned to the ground, killing almost all of Slayter's family.

Interestingly, the deaths of his parents had become the key to his escape.

The fire hadn't been an attack like Vamreth's bloody coup, just a stupid accident. A torch fell during a feast, lit a wall hanging on fire. The straw on the floor went up. Then the tables.

Earlier during the feast, Slayter's drunk brother had brought in the four stallions he'd trained to do tricks. He'd wanted to show them off. The stallions had panicked at the fire, kicked a table. The table wedged into the alcove of the main doorway. Fleeing the fire, the mob rushed the now-obstructed door, wedging it more firmly into place and creating the perfect barrier. The crush of a hundred people seeking to save themselves had, instead, doomed them all.

After the fire, they'd found an enormous cluster of people burned alive right there, trying to get past the throng of bodies, clearly never realizing that if they had just worked together for a critical moment, they could have extricated the table and made it outside.

Slayter knew that he should be upset. His youngest brother and Yvelle were all who had survived, but the first thing he saw was the opportunity to extricate himself from the nest of vipers. This was his way out.

Not even Halenza and Vamreth could deny him a trip back to his ancestral home after losing nearly his whole family.

By then, he had become so valuable that Vamreth hadn't wanted Slayter to be free of the palace even for a day, but neither Vamreth nor Halenza had any idea Slayter had been plotting his escape. Why would they? He had been sure to perfectly mimic the behavior he'd exhibited before the coup. In their eyes,

Slayter was enamored with learning magic under Halenza's wing. In their eyes, that was his only desire.

So Vamreth had graciously allowed Slayter to go to his northland home and set things in order. And in a further show of "affection," he had sent along a retinue of eleven Knights of the Steel and one Knight of the Sun—one of Vamreth's elites named Sir Ehvron. This was, of course, to "protect" Slayter from any banditry by the newly arisen Queen-in-Exile, who had started harrying royal coaches over the last year.

Vamreth had orchestrated a plan to ensure that Slayter went, took care of the funeral, and most importantly, returned quickly.

But Slayter saw Vamreth's intentions immediately. Lies and deception worked only in two ways: The first was to manipulate a lesser intellect, to craft a complexity that took them by surprise because they could not anticipate it. Or alternatively to play on a person's emotions. Make them feel like they owed you, make them fear you, make them trust you like you were their best friend.

But there wasn't a conclusion that Vamreth or Halenza had ever come to that Slayter hadn't seen long before it dawned on them. Besides, they were often distracted by their emotions and their urges, choosing diversions over truth. Slayter could barely understand *why* people let their emotions drive them, let alone to be trapped by such behavior.

He went along with their transparent lies, laying down the lines of his plan one at a time. By the time Vamreth ordered his "protection" detail, Slayter had already solved that problem—and many other potential problems—days before.

Slayter and his detail rode out into the forest, headed north. The first night they camped, he snapped a sleep spell over the entire group. His guards slumbered while he went deeper into the woods, found the Queen-in-Exile. He'd known where she was hiding for more than a year now.

Rhennaria Laochodon was suspicious of him at first. But he had anticipated her reaction, and he dealt with it by concentrating on each of his words and saying exactly what he knew would put her at ease. He also exhibited a good amount of his power to illustrate that, if he had wanted to betray them to Vamreth, he could have already done so.

In her moment of doubt, where she actually seemed to be considering taking him at face value, he made his proposal. He wanted to become her spy. He wanted to help her overthrow Vamreth.

Rhennaria had put her hands on her hips, glanced at her friend the Luminent, and smiled a crooked smile.

"A spy, is it? What do you know about being a spy?" Rhenn asked.

"Spies build loyalty with a person of power. Then they betray that loyalty by giving information or opportunities to that person's enemies. Often, there is the donning of a specific persona involved to perpetuate the deception. There must also be instances where the spy will—"

Rhennaria narrowed her eyes, and her smile grew. "So you know the definition."

"Several definitions, actually. Some of them have different nuances, but—"

"Have you ever been a spy?"

"No."

"And what would you envision doing for me?"

"Would you like me to kill Vamreth? I was assuming you'd like me to do something like ..." Slayter trailed off, noting two clearly different reactions from Rhennaria and her friend Lorelle. Lorelle recoiled and raised her chin. Rhennaria's eyes, however, glowed.

"Much as I would like that," she said in a husky voice. "It wouldn't work."

"I kill him. Then you come take his place."

"If only it were that easy." There was true remorse in her voice, and she shook her head. "No. Me and mine would be dead in a week. We need to flush him out of the palace and destroy him in front of the entire kingdom. I need to come at him with an army."

"Do you have an army?"

She glanced at Lorelle, then back at Slayter. "Not yet. But soon enough. That's not really the question, though."

"What is the question?"

"Can you do what you claim you can? Can you hide in Vamreth's court and be there when I need you the most?"

"I have been doing it for six years. Ever since he overthrew your parents."

That surprised her, and again she glanced at the impassive Luminent, who shrugged.

"Very well, Sir Mage. Let's try it. We'll do this for a few months, and if I'm convinced you're real and that you can actually manage it, then we will make our plans."

She extended her hand. He shook it, and the elusive sense of rightness he'd wanted so badly was suddenly there. His chest filled with a warmth he'd not felt since he'd first started learning magic. Yes, he was meant to learn and know magic. But this was what he was meant to *do* with it.

He gave her a stack of clay disks, a little metal scratcher, and a bracelet with a blue gemstone on it.

"Complete this line on one of these when you wish to talk to me. Complete it, and snap it. I will know you want to talk. Then I will contact you through the bracelet."

That was how he left them. That was how it began.

He had returned to the camp and Vamreth's guards, removed the sleep spell, continued to the north, finished the charade, and returned to the palace.

A week later, he killed Halenza.

She had been experimenting with making magically poisoned weapons for Vamreth, weapons that never had to have reapplications and that would never poison their wielder. Vamreth loved having edges that allowed him to lord his power over others. The spells were fairly complex, trying to effect something like that, but not beyond Halenza's skills. And with the proper precautions, which she took, the spell preparation was quite safe. The odds of an accident that would fatally poison her were a thousand to one.

But Vamreth didn't know that.

So when he found her sprawled in her laboratory, dead, he'd called for Slayter to explain what had happened. He did so.

And, of course, he lied.

He'd included all the details that sounded plausible. He let Vamreth fill in the gaps with what he wanted to see. Because what Slayter had seen years ago—what Halenza had blinded herself to seeing—was that Vamreth actually wanted Slayter as his royal mage, not Halenza. And now Vamreth had exactly what he wanted.

Manipulation, it turned out, was primarily achieved through overwhelming someone's intellect with complexity, and then telling them the story they wanted to hear.

Vamreth made him royal mage on the spot.

From that moment forward, the only person who could have unraveled the lines of Slayter's deception was Halenza. And she was dead. The rest of Halenza's apprentices fell in line. To them, he gave orders. To Vamreth, he fed lies and truths in appropriate measures until Khyven the Unkillable burst into the palace with his Helm of Darkness and a horde of noktum creatures at his heels.

Slayter lost a leg that day, but every bit of him felt right. And that was what was most important.

That was the most important thing of all ...

Until now.

Slayter felt that thirst again. This time it wasn't for magic. And it wasn't for a sense of rightness. The world had changed. His life had changed. Now he had a family, and that family was in danger.

This time the puzzle was grander, possibly beyond even his capacity, but that only made him want to solve it all the more—

The shadow of a cloud passed over the moon.

Moon?

Slayter emerged from his reverie to find that he had come much farther, and taken much longer, than he realized. His stump hurt, jammed tight within his prosthetic. The shaping of the thing, some well-placed padding, and a modest spell lessening contusions had made it so Slayter barely felt it anymore, just as long as he did only a modest amount of walking.

Clearly, he'd exceeded that.

Not only had the sun set some time ago, but he had meandered to the eastern edge of the city. The city wall's dead end loomed above the warehouses that lined the street. He heard the wharf somewhere to his right: the calls of sailors as they made fast the final lines, loaded supplies, or invited friends to nearby drinking establishments.

He took in all of this as well as a sudden certainty that something was not right. He brought his mind back from its wandering and focused on the here and now. He looked and listened for anything out of the ordinary.

The morning's rainstorm had wetted the cobblestone street, but rainstorms were common in late spring. The street was empty, but that wasn't unusual either for this time of night. The warehouses would have shut down for the day. The noises from the wharf were normal. Working men and women off to spend their daily earnings.

What was out of place?

That shadow passed over the moon again, and a chill went up Slayter's spine. That was no cloud. Clouds moved slower. That thing, whatever it was, had flicked past, cutting out the whole moon for an instant. Something fast. Something flying. Something huge.

He scanned the sky, but he couldn't see the thing. He didn't have the same physical abilities as his friends. Khyven's awareness of danger was almost preternatural. He'd have been aware of whatever this thing was minutes ago, most likely. And Lorelle, with her new connection to the Dark, would have seen it in detail against the black sky.

But as belated as Slayter might have been to notice it, it took him only a second to calculate the number of creatures that flew at night, that flew that fast, and that could blot out the entire moon with their bodies. There was a night albatross from the Cliffs of Qhor. Weighing close to two hundred pounds and with a thirty-foot wingspan, the night albatross might replicate such a thing, but only if fairly close to the viewer. And it was highly unlikely to replicate such an effect twice in thirty seconds. Likewise for a noktum Gylarn, which was about twice the size.

The only other thing that could blot out the entire moon moving that fast would be a whale thrown from a monolithic catapult. Since there was no catapult of sufficient size in Usara and since it would be impossible for even a horde of people to lift a whale and set it in this imaginary catapult, Slayter came to the only logical conclusion.

That had been a dragon.

Chapter Four
SLAYTER

layter searched the sky. He didn't have Lorelle's eyes, but he put all of his attention into catching that elusive silhouette again.

According to common belief, dragons were myths, beasts that were once real perhaps, but no longer. Even those who believed in dragons knew they had been lost to the mists of time a thousand years ago.

Of course, the same had been said of Giants for a thousand years.

Until the adventure into the Great Noktum with Khyven and Vohn, Slayter had accepted that dragons had once been real, but that they'd died out long ago.

Then he'd seen the great dragon Jai'ketakos incinerate a party of Nox hunters. Shortly after, he'd seen the devastation of the entire Nox city, all in a matter of minutes. The sheer power of the creature ignited the imagination.

Dragons were very real, and at least one of them was loose in Noksonon. Slayter remembered thinking at the time that if that dragon could leave the Dark, nothing on Noksonon would be safe.

Now he belatedly thought: why would a dragon be *unable* to leave the noktum?

Slayter's gaze flicked about the night sky and he found the giant creature, was barely able to track it until it blotted the moon again. The dragon seemed like it was idly sweeping back and forth over the city, studying it. Slayter saw its shadow flash across the ground and followed.

He broke into a limping run as the shadow flowed over the rooftops, climbed abruptly up the city wall and vanished.

The pain of his stump hampered Slayter, and the prosthetic felt like a waterlogged stump tied to his knee. When he ran he always felt like a crab trying to scamper on mismatched legs, but now it just hurt.

He pulled the top spell disk from the cylinder at his waist. It just so happened that the top disk was, and always would be, a spell against dragon fire. After Slayter luckily pulled this same spell from his cylinder when he'd saved Khyven and Vohn from the dragon in the noktum—that had been sheer happenstance—he'd determined that as an homage to luck, he would forever keep that same spell on top.

He stopped in the center of the street a hundred yards from the wall, the spell between his fingers. He reminded himself to go slowly as he reached into his robes to withdraw his scratcher. He had nearly fumbled the scratcher in the Great Noktum and had almost died for it.

He poised it over the clay coin.

Of course, protection against dragon fire would do him no good against a dragon's bite, but the odds that the dragon would bite him—or even notice him—were minimal. Dragons didn't need to pay attention to individuals. The dragon hadn't incinerated a single person in Nox Arvak; it had incinerated the whole city. Slayter was irrelevant.

The black form against the dark night, barely a speck in the distance, turned. It grew larger and larger, and Slayter held his breath. It was going to pass right over him. Last time, he had been so concerned with saving his friends he'd barely gotten a glimpse of the thing. This time, he planned to see every detail.

He checked his assumption. No. It wasn't going to fly over. It was slowing. It was going to—

The dragon's wings flared, wider than the street and both rows of warehouses on either side. Its sleek body reared upright, black scales glistening in the moonlight as long, powerful legs extended down to touch the street fifty feet in front of him.

He forced himself not to flinch, waited for the enormous talons—each as tall as a man and curved like giant wagon wheels—to crunch into the cobblestones, cracking them and digging a furrow.

They didn't.

Instead, the mighty wings beat fast, barely missing the warehouses beneath them. The powerful wind shoved Slayter back a step and forced him to shield his eyes, and the great talons clicked down as daintily as a duchess' pointed shoe.

The wings beat a few more times, tucking in and narrowly missing the warehouses. The front of its body landed as though the enormous beast was as light as a feather. Its wings folded neatly against its back as the dragon settled its bulk.

Slayter catalogued every inch of the creature. Something of that size simply didn't just alight like a sparrow. There was Land Magic at work in combination with those mighty wings and muscles. Slayter was dazzled at the nuanced usage.

The histories indicated that elder dragons were all Giants who had transformed into this preferred form. Giants could work all five paths of magic at the same time, a feat no Human could ever hope to achieve. That was what was happening. The dragon was using Land Magic, and perhaps other magic as well.

Slayter's gaze remained glued to the thing's appearance. He would have thought the creature's face would look like that of an alligator or some other reptile, but it didn't. Its snout came to a beak-like point beneath two huge nostrils. He wanted to see it open its mouth. Were there teeth in there? Or was it actually a beak?

Thick, black horns poked out from its neck, and two larger horns sloped backward from its head just above its ears.

Its jet-black pentagonal scales created fascinating patterns. Large scales covered its head behind its eyes then became smaller as the shape of the head demanded. The cleft between its brows was smoothed flat just behind its eyes, then rose into an impressive ridge that then turned into a wicked, backward-pointing horn, making three at the crown of its head.

Smaller, barely discernible pentagonal scales surrounded its bulbous eyes. Every scale glistened as though wet, but Slayter doubted there was a single drop of water on the creature.

Two circles of ominous orange light lit up the hollows of the dragon's nostrils, and the creature's eyes sparkled with intelligence.

"You are ... magnificent." Slayter spoke his thoughts aloud.

The corners on either side of the scaly mouth turned up. "Hmmm ..." it said, and Slayter's breath caught again.

The voice of a dragon! How many Humans in the last two millennia had heard the voice of a dragon? That would be zero. None.

"You ..." The dragon rumbled. "You are *that* mage."

Slayter's thoughts froze. The dragon had recognized him. Recognized *him*!

"You know me?"

"You, a Human fighter, and a Shadowvar banshee. You stood at the edge of the forest outside of Nox Arvak. You were about to start a fight with a batch of Nox. I incinerated all of you. And yet, here you are. Unincinerated."

"You *saw* me?" Slayter had barely been able to make out the shape of the dragon, it had been so far away at that moment, flying so fast.

The dragon chuckled, a deep, crackling sound that promised fire. "A dragon can see for miles. I can see beyond, and I can see through. A dragon can see an ant crawling a kingdom away. A dragon can see into the hearts of Humans."

Slayter's breathing came fast.

"So yes. I see you, mage. Your thirst for knowledge. You are not the first such to die for such a need. And I could slake your thirst, oh ... Yes I could."

"Please do."

"That spell in your hand ..." The dragon glanced to Slayter's disk. "Is a derivation of Fyrdevon's Sigil. You've changed it. Clever, for a Human. But did you know there are three different languages for Line Magic? And did you know there are a dozen other spells like that one, and far more effective for your purposes, which I assume is to protect you from me."

"Three languages?"

"How many rune sets do you use for your work?"

"One," he whispered. "There's only ... I thought there was only one."

"There are three."

"Senji's Boots..."

"Did you know you have no need for that crude disk you hold? You could wield magic without being tied to this limitation of clay and water. Would you like that?"

"That would be ..." But Slayter couldn't find the word to accurately describe his excitement. To learn how to wield Line Magic like a Giant ... It would be an unfathomably valuable weapon in the coming war.

Sparks floated up from the dragon's nostrils. "What do they call you?"

"I am Slayter. The, uh, the mage."

"Slayter the Mage ... Not 'Her Majesty's Royal Mage' or the 'Head of the Arcane Conclave of Usara?'" The dragon smiled, its scaly lips turning up on the sides of its head. "Or perhaps you've been called 'Dragon Master' for your feat in the Great Noktum?"

"Only two of those things, actually," Slayter said. "Not the, uh, not the last one."

"Yet they are not poised on your lips. A Human uninterested in titles ..." The dragon cocked his head. "That is interesting,

Slayter the Mage."

"Might I have the honor of *your* name?" he asked. He needed to know if Lorelle had been right. If Zaith had been right. There were, after all, so many dragons in the myths that had trickled down over the last two millennia. It was too much to hope that this was, in fact, the legendary Jai'ketakos.

The dragon's scaly lips pulled back further and now Slayter could see that, yes, it did have teeth. Many rows of teeth. Enormous teeth.

Slayter didn't have a spell to protect him from the teeth. He did, however, have one that could record his last thoughts. Oh, the knowledge he had gained in just twenty seconds!

"Like you, I have titles, but why clutter a fine meeting with an abundance of inanities? For what is a title, after all, save a posturing for strangers. I am done with posturing. My name is Jai'ketakos."

He *was* Jai'ketakos! Jai'ketakos the Fire of the Dark. Jai'ketakos the Wall of Worlds. Jai'ketakos the Protector who stood at the gate between continents. There were three ancient texts that made reference to this great black dragon who guarded the Thuros at the center of the world.

"Well this is … worth dying for," Slayter murmured.

The dragon chuckled again. "Well said. We are in a strange confluence of belief and reality. You are prepared to die, and I was certain you already were. I am rarely surprised, yet you have done it. I have a novel idea, Slayter the Mage. Will you entertain it?"

"Of course."

"I submit we be honest with each other."

"Yes."

"I will tell you a truth, then you tell me a truth."

Slayter blinked, and his heart raced faster. There were barbs in this. This creature was not his friend, but he couldn't resist. "Very well."

"I came to kill you." The dragon's smile returned.

"Of course you did," Slayter said.

"Of course?"

"Why else would you be here?" Slayter said. "You burned a Nox city, and I can think of eleven reasons why you would burn Usara. I can think of no reasons why you would spare it."

"Eleven? Not a dozen?"

"Only eleven. You said truth."

The dragon chuckled. "Indeed. Most Humans are not interested in the whole truth."

"I often moderate the exactitude of my thoughts for my friends. It makes them feel at ease."

"Moderate your exactitude...."

"I can do the same for you, if you like."

"Do you take me for a Human?"

"I can't even imagine that."

"You're attempting to be polite."

"No."

"Indeed ..." the dragon mused to himself, gazed past Slayter for a moment, then back to him. "I didn't come north just to kill you. I came looking for a sign of my old adversary from long ago. I saw this grandiose Human city pretending at the greatness of the Noksonoi, and ... Well, I became distracted. I intended to bathe it in fire."

"Yes."

"Then I recognized you. And I saw a crossroads."

"A crossroads," Slayter said. The way the dragon said the word, the way he injected it with emotion, meant something. It was as though the dragon was saying it from the depths of his soul.

"Oh yes ..." The dragon grinned, showing those tall rows of teeth. Twin flames licked up from its nostrils.

"You've decided not to burn the city," Slayter said.

"When I meet someone of consequence, there is a crossroads. My path forward is no longer mine to decide. It is theirs. I am but the keeper of the crossroads; those I meet are the keepers of the decision. Do you understand this?"

"You aren't going to kill me."

The dragon showed even more of its teeth.

"Exactly, Slayter the Mage. Instead, I'm going to give you a choice …"

Chapter Five
SLAYTER

"A choice?" Slayter asked.

The dragon shifted left and right, hunkering down even lower. He extended his forelegs in front of himself, claws scraping against the cobblestones, then rested his head between them. His gaze never left Slayter.

They were currently alone in this darkened street, but that wouldn't last. Even if no one saw the dragon land, another citizen would soon happen across this street. It was rather miraculous they hadn't already. The wharf and the late-night taverns were no more than six blocks away. Slayter calculated some wayward sailor or drunk would stumble across this incomparable moment in the next five minutes.

He also knew that most people would react to the dragon's presence with panic. Another slight few would react with foolhardy violence. Like Khyven.

If either of those things happened, two things would follow.

First, Slayter would die, as would whoever had the misfortune to stumble across them.

Second, Slayter would lose this unparalleled opportunity to learn, a regret he would carry with him for the rest of his short life.

"Most never realize every second of their life stands on a knife's edge," the dragon mused, still pinning Slayter with that enormous, glittering stare. "And if they do, they fail to grasp the excruciating beauty of that transience, that each choice in each moment is a crossroads of exquisite importance. They let their choices flutter away like butterflies. I have come to make sure that doesn't happen."

Slayter studied the dragon's eyes intently, and he did not respond.

"But I think you do understand the weight of your choices, Slayter the Mage. Yes, I think you do."

Slayter waited.

"Your thirst for knowledge is so thick I can taste it," the dragon said softly. "Shall we?"

"My crossroads?"

"Oh yes."

Slayter nodded.

"This is your choice: I will slake your thirst. I will tell you the answers to every question you can think to ask. This will go on and on as long as you can stand it, as long as you can keep your eyes open. I will tell you about dragons. I will tell you about the Noksonoi. I will tell you secrets you cannot even fathom. Then I shall circle your city and leave forever."

"And my other choice?"

The dragon narrowed his eyes, searching for something on Slayter's face. "No reaction? I expected to see saliva drip from your chin. Are you truly considering all I could do for you?"

"I have considered it."

"So quickly?"

Slayter shrugged. "It is but half the choice."

"You are eager to meet your fate."

"I'm eager to see the road ahead."

"Oh, I will be sad for you to die, Slayter the Mage."

"We are of one mind in that regard."

The dragon chuckled. "The other half of your choice is this: I will tell you nothing. Nothing at all. You shall receive no information from me now or ever. Not if we should meet at a future crossroads. Not if I was on the brink of death and giving knowledge to you was all that would save me." He opened his mouth slightly, then snapped it shut. "Then I shall leap over this wall and fly east, never to return."

Slayter nodded. "I see."

"Which will it be, Slayter the Mage?" The dragon's eyes glittered.

Thoughts fluttered in Slayter's head like caged bats. "The choice. It's important to you."

The dragon raised a scaly eyebrow. "Crossroads are all that matter. And at every crossroads, there is a choice. Make yours."

"Spare your knowledge."

The dragon blinked, raised his chin slightly. "Spare my ... You do not wish to know all that I know?"

"I choose the second path."

The dragon's eyes narrowed. "You will never have this chance again."

"I know."

"Why would you turn me away?"

"If I choose to learn what you know, you will burn the city. If I don't, you won't."

The dragon narrowed his eyes. "I said no such thing."

"You said, 'I shall circle the city and leave forever.' But you made no promise to leave without violence. Circling the city was what you did at Nox Arvak. You could burn all of Usara in that time. And I believe you want to."

"Do you?"

"Are we still talking truth?"

The dragon smiled coldly. Each sharp tooth was nearly as tall as Slayter, and he was keenly aware that he had no magic to stop those teeth. For the longest time, the dragon said nothing.

"Well played," he said, but the playful tone had vanished.

Slayter watched him.

"Since we are being honest," the dragon said. "Tell me how you came to your decision."

"If you give your victim their heart's desire, you give yourself permission to take yours. That is the nature of your crossroads."

The dragon let out a long, slow breath. Blistering hot wind swirled around Slayter's ankles. He winced, but didn't move. "That is dangerous knowledge, Slayter the Mage."

Slayter said nothing.

The dragon rose to his full height, towering over him. "This is the second time I have underestimated you. There won't be a third."

An explosion of fire erupted from his mouth, engulfing Slayter.

Chapter Six
SLAYTER

Slayter snapped the disk the moment the dragon drew breath. Orange light flared. The spell took effect, but the dragon was fast. Perhaps Khyven might have snapped that disk quick enough, but Slayter felt unbearable heat for one white-hot instant as flames surrounded him, angry and churning.

The cooling effect of the spell followed just in time, and he didn't die.

The flames curled up, leaving the cobblestones glowing hot and melted. Only the stone Slayter stood upon was unaffected. The warehouses to his left and right became bonfires. Screams and shouts rose behind him and to his right. The wharf.

The dragon stayed true to his word. His barely visible silhouette cut the dark sky above the roaring flames as he climbed toward the moon, up and away from Usara.

Slayter shook his head. The edges of his hair were singed, as was the hem of his robe and his sleeves. He stood in the middle of the fiery maelstrom a long minute, his spell slowy fading.

But the unbelievable heat remained from the fires all around.

The spell had easily handled the dragon fire in the Great Noktum, but this time it had run out. Jai'ketakos had seen the rune upon the disk. He'd known exactly what the spell could do, and he'd poured enough dragon fire on him to overwhelm the spell.

Slayter hissed and crouched as the heat increased, turning away, but there was no way to turn. With the bonfires of the warehouses, the heat-warped air, and the melted street, he completely lost his bearings. Every direction was a fiery death. And even if he knew which way to run, he had no idea if running over those melted stones would kill him quicker. All he knew was that he couldn't stay here—

A cowled and cloaked man barreled into him, swept him right off his feet like he was a piece of paper. The man wrapped his arms around Slayter and cradled him against his chest like a baby.

"Got him!" Khyven shouted. Slayter squinted through gummy eyelids to see Khyven's bared teeth beneath the smoking cowl. But the air cooled almost immediately. Clearly, Khyven knew which way to go.

In seconds, Slayter could breathe again.

They left the flames behind, but the big man didn't stop until they were at least two blocks away. He set Slayter on his feet, patted out a few small fires on his robes and swatted at his hair.

"That was ... magnificent!" Slayter said, turning and blinking his gummy eyes at the inferno against the eastern wall of Usara.

"Magnificent?" Khyven was angry. "What the hell happened?"

"Jai'ketakos. The dragon from the noktum."

"Here in Usara?"

Slayter nodded.

An armored shape leapt from the rooftop behind Khyven, a silhouette as black as night against the orange fire. It landed on the cobblestones without breaking its legs.

Slayter recognized the queen once she stood upright, and

again he marveled at the extent of her new superhuman abilities. The last time he'd seen her running about, she hadn't been jumping from rooftops.

"You faced a dragon alone?" Queen Rhenn's eyes flickered with an inner light, like a flame's reflection on polished silver. It was the only thing visible in her black silhouette until she stepped into the light of the fires.

Vohn entered from the alley to Slayter's left. Behind him came Lorelle and Shalure. That surprised Slayter, and for a moment he realized that if they'd brought Shalure she had been either close at hand, or they'd *thought* to bring her.

"I knew it had to be you," Vohn said. "I knew it."

"We saw the explosion," Lorelle said. "Vohn immediately thought you had something to do with it."

"Fire erupting up to the stars?" Vohn said. "Who else would it be? Besides, he always ends up around the docks."

"I do?" Slayter asked.

"Let's get this fire out," Rhenn said, wincing at the blaze even at this distance.

"You stay away from it," Lorelle said.

"I'm fine."

"Yes, and you'll stay fine if you stay away from it."

Rhenn growled.

"We'll handle it," Khyven said.

They split up, intent on quashing the fire. Slayter's face and hands felt like he'd held them too close to a campfire for hours. Everything was tender, but he ignored the pain and worked his magic. Between two disks in his cylinder as well as an impromptu spell scratched into the dirt at the edge of the conflagration, he dampened the flames, keeping them from spreading.

Rhenn rallied the shocked sailors and dock workers, and within minutes she had a working water line with half a hundred buckets pulling water from the sea and bringing it to the burning warehouses.

Within an hour, they had the fire out. In the end, four

warehouses had burned. Two of them to the ground. After, Rhenn climbed atop a half wall and gave an inspirational speech. The people cheered her.

She stepped down and turned to Lorelle. "Take us back to the palace."

They walked into a dark alley and Lorelle's cloak swirled around them all. Slayter's gut wrenched. The alley vanished as though it was all spinning in black water, and he got sucked down the drain.

With a gasp, he suddenly stood in the queen's dark meeting room. The magical lanterns Slayter had fashioned—the ones that didn't hurt her—hung in the four corners.

After he'd barely managed to stop the urge to vomit, he looked longingly at his usual chair toward the room's window on the left side of the table, limped to it, and fell into it with a sigh.

"That feels better."

Vohn took up his usual spot next to Slayter. Khyven plopped into the chair on the other side and put his half-melted boots up on the table. He didn't seem to be any worse for wear. Slayter rolled his eyes. He had been right in the middle of those flames, same as Slayter. Why wasn't he singed?

Lorelle sat next to Khyven, descending elegantly into the chair as though she weighed nothing. Shalure kept her gaze down and stood awkwardly to the side. She nodded to Slayter, then headed for the door.

"Stay," Lorelle said, looking at Shalure with a strange expression that Slayter couldn't decipher.

"Stay for the meeting?" Khyven asked.

Lorelle turned a flat glance upon him, and it was clear even to Slayter that the argument they'd begun in his laboratory wasn't finished. "You have something to say?"

Khyven opened his mouth, glanced at Vohn, who did a bad job of pretending to study the tapestry at that moment. Khyven gave him a withering stare.

"No. I have nothing to say," he said softly.

"Please sit," Lorelle said to Shalure.

Rhenn nodded as though giving the royal approval, then turned her gaze back to Slayter. "The fire is out. No one died. Now if you would please, tell us what happened?"

"Ah, well," Slayter said. "A dragon paid a visit to Usara. He came to find his enemy and burn the city."

"A dragon."

"The dragon."

"*The* dragon? The one from the noktum?"

"Jai'ketakos." Lorelle pulled a couple of vials from her pouch, mixed them, and passed them to Slayter. "The dragon I set free."

Slayter relayed the story of his most recent encounter, from the moment he spotted the dragon in the sky to the point at which Jai'ketakos tried to kill him.

"And I would be dead now. His blast was calculated to kill me, despite my spell. Except, well, he had not expected you to act so quickly. Lorelle's cloak, I imagine, got Khyven there. And Khyven's speed and ..."

A new thought occurred to Slayter. What if none of this was an accident? Jai'ketakos had said he wouldn't underestimate Slayter again. And he hadn't. Underestimated Slayter. But he had underestimated Slayter's friends' response speed and their individual abilities.

Or more likely than underestimated them, he simply didn't know about them.

That could be vitally important to the puzzle.

Slayter thought of the slippery, half-hidden way Nhevalos had dealt with Khyven and Rhenn. He also thought of the minimal notes about The Betrayer in the histories. Nhevalos moved through others, always half-hidden, only revealing his full game when the last move was about to be made.

Nhevalos had told Rhenn he was fighting for Humans, that a war of Giants was coming. More and more, it was beginning to seem like The Betrayer hadn't been lying. What if he was putting together a team? What if Khyven meeting Rhenn ... What if the bonding of Lorelle and Khyven ... What if even the addition of

Slayter and Vohn and even Shalure ... What if none of this was an accident? What if Nhevalos was orchestrating all of it ...

And keeping it hidden from the Giants like, say, Jai'ketakos.

Lore Magic was not Slayter's strong suit, but he knew enough to know that everything he'd just considered could be manipulated by Lore Magic. This is exactly what a master of that stream could do: bring together seemingly unrelated elements to effect a great change.

More thoughts came, one after the other.

What if Rhenn's inner circle weren't the only team? Senji's Footsteps! Nhevalos could—and probably was—doing this on every continent.

Of course that was true. Slayter could see it now, written large. That was the entire purpose of Khyven's recent abduction to Daemanon, to meet his brother, to reveal his parentage.

A thrill of excitement ran through Slayter. This was what he needed. This was the next piece.

It was but a small piece, and one that perhaps Nhevalos was trying to reveal on purpose. But it was a piece, and if Slayter could wrap his mind around the entirety of the puzzle, then he might be able to pull his friends free of its clutches.

"*Slayter!*" Rhenn shouted.

He snapped from his reverie to find everyone staring at him expectantly. Apparently Rhenn had been calling his name for some time.

"You stopped talking in the middle of a sentence," Rhenn said.

"Yes, well ... I think none of this is an accident."

"The dragon?"

"Yes."

"You said he came here to burn the city."

"No. Well, I mean yes. But that was secondary. He came here to search for his enemy—which I calculate refers to Nhevalos—but he saw the opportunity to do what he loves. Or rather he meant to, except he came upon a crossroads."

"Slayter ..." Rhenn showed her fangs in frustration.

"You've left us behind again, my friend," Vohn said softly.
"The crossroads tripped him up," Slayter explained.
"You mentioned he gave you a choice," Rhenn said.
"He has to give choices."
"He *has* to?"
"Yes. I think Jai'ketakos is a bundle of rage. I think all he wants to do is destroy. But for some reason, he has limited himself to a strange kind of code in the dispensing of this rage. It is his only governing thought. If not for this code, this need to see and dispense crossroads, he would simply be laying waste to the countryside."
"Why? Why would he limit himself?"
"That is the question."
"So what is the answer?"
"Well ... Why does anything happen?"
Vohn frowned. "That's not an answer."
"Why does Khyven get frustrated that Lorelle is asleep at night? Why does Shalure burst into tears when she watches Khyven and Lorelle together? Why does Rhenn fight against the thing that could make her life easier?"
Everyone in the room tightened up, eyes flashing with anger.
"Because we've all been marked by our past. We cannot help ourselves. I don't know nearly as much about Giants as I would like to, but Jai'ketakos seems to me to be acting very much like a Human in this regard. He was the guardian of that Thuros for two thousand years, and we have evidence to suggest it wasn't voluntary."
"The Dragon Chain," Lorelle murmured.
"He was a captive. There are plenty of histories suggesting that captivity drives people insane if they're held long enough. Imagine being imprisoned for two thousand years."
They all blinked, thinking about this.
"I'm only speculating, but what if Jai'ketakos made the decision to be locked in that place. Or what if he made a single decision that led to being locked in that place. And then he had two thousand years to think upon that one decision. That one

crossroads. What if his mind snapped somewhere in there, and the only thing he wants to do is destroy. And the only thing lodged in the center of any kind of control of himself is this notion of crossroads. To spread his pain upon everyone else. To force them to make the bad decision he made."

Everyone was silent.

"That's ... that's a lot of supposition," Vohn said.

"He's right. You can't possibly know that," Rhenn agreed.

"I don't know that," Slayter said. "But I came to the conclusion yesterday that we can't win this war."

"Which war?"

"The war that is coming. The war Nhevalos mentioned to you. We can't win it using only what we know. I've calculated we can barely win it even if we make wild guesses, bet everything upon them, and win. That is the only option we have open to us until we know more. If we don't fight our way out of our own prison, a prison we can't see, we're going to get swept into this war exactly as Nhevalos wants us to."

"That's not happening," Rhenn said through her teeth.

"Oh, but it's already happening," Slayter said. "I'm pretty sure he has us exactly where he wants us to be."

"I escaped him," Rhenn said.

Slayter paused, and he gave himself credit for doing so. A year ago, he wouldn't have. Rhenn's tragedy was wrapped up intimately with Nhevalos. The loss of her old self. The loss of E'maz, who she had clearly been in love with. And it all happened because of Nhevalos. In her mind, she had given up everything to escape him, and she didn't want to hear what Slayter was about to say.

But it was the truth, so he had to.

"I don't think you did," Slayter said. "I don't think any of us did. I believe it's likely that what happened to you—every bit of it—was exactly what Nhevalos wanted to happen."

"No. He wanted me to bear a child with A'vendyr."

"That's what he told you."

"Yes, that's what he told me! And that's what he had set up!"

"Except this is a being who has manipulated Humans and Giants and every other race since the beginning of recorded time. I've only known you for ten years, Rhenn, and I can see that you would have rebelled against that situation instantly. Nhevalos has probably known you since you were born. Do you think he wouldn't have been able to predict that if he abducted you, put you in a foreign land with foreign pressures and then demanded that you form a union not of your making ... that you'd actually go along with it?"

Rhenn said nothing, but her face had gone white.

"You don't know that," Lorelle said, echoing Rhenn's earlier words.

"No, I don't. But it seems extremely likely based on what I do know."

"You're saying me running to N'ssag ... You're saying me and E'maz ... You're saying Nhevalos orchestrated all of that?"

"No, you did," Slayter said. "But I think Nhevalos knew what you would do with the correct pressures applied to you."

"That's not possible."

Vohn put a hand on Slayter's wrist, urging him to stop talking, but Slayter was done. There was nothing more to say. This was information Rhenn didn't want to hear, but they all needed to stop fearing the truth and start embracing it. If they didn't, they could never prevail.

"So we're just puppets on a string?" Khyven growled. "I won't believe that."

"You most of all," Slayter turned to Khyven.

"No."

"Zaith called you the Greatblood. Nhevalos confirmed it. You have Giant's blood in your veins, part of it put there by me, but part of it was yours from birth. You've been shaped since childhood. The Old Man you talk about. Nhevaz. The Night Ring. Even your introduction to Rhenn and her rebellion. None of that is beyond the abilities of a Giant who wields Lore Magic. Perhaps all of us have been."

That got a round of looks from everyone.

"All of us?" Rhenn asked the question that was on each of their faces.

"We cannot afford to believe otherwise," Slayter said. "We are in a battle not just for this kingdom, but perhaps the entire world. And until Rhenn got snatched from her own palace, we had no idea we were even in a fight."

Rhenn's gaze hardened as she saw what he was saying. She should. She more than any of them knew what Nhevalos was like.

"We are pawns," Slayter said. "At least, we have been. Pawns have no idea why they are being moved, and we are beginning to. So perhaps we are something else now. I plan to see the entire board. I would rather us know what is coming our way, rather than simply wait for Nhevalos to move us."

"You're saying we take the battle directly to Nhevalos."

"And be prepared for the others."

"Others?"

"We are pawns. Or rooks. Or knights." He gestured to Lorelle and to Khyven. "Some of us queens."

"You're leaving me behind again, Slayter," Rhenn warned. "What others?"

"The other side."

"Slayter—"

"Of the board," Lorelle said softly. "He's talking about Nhevalos's game board."

"We might be Nhevalos's power pieces," Slayter said. "Certainly Khyven is, and probably Rhenn. Nhevalos plays us, but who is he playing us against? As much as you might hate him, Rhenn, he may be more on our side than whomever he is playing against. We need to know who that is."

"The Giants?" Khyven offered.

"Of course. But which Giants? And more importantly at this moment: who are their power pieces?"

Chapter Seven
N'ssag

N'ssag surveyed his new kingdom. Nox Arvak's burnt husks of buildings spread out before him. The resilient purple trees had already begun to sprout from the ground where they'd been charred into stumps. The glowing ferns had long since returned to full flourish. It was still impressive to N'ssag that these plants could grow at all in complete darkness, but of course that was the way the Giants had developed them. They were not normal plants, but it still astounded him how resilient they'd been to the dragon's destruction. The Nox had not been so resilient. Those that had been burned had stayed dead.

Until, of course, N'ssag had arrived.

Behind him sprawled the Nox palace, which had mostly been destroyed, but the southwest wing was still intact. Ventat Obrey had said that was the part of the palace where visiting Nox dignitaries would sleep, and that it was fitting for N'ssag to make his home there.

So he had.

N'ssag had thought he was going to die in that cursed nuraghi when Queen Rhenn's henchmen had arrived. One moment he was about to rule the V'endann Barony, and the next he was being shoved out a window by that stupid Giant he'd brought back to life.

That was how Ventat had found him, bleeding and staggering through the wet forest. Ventat had brought him here, told him what was expected of him, and had given him a home. N'ssag had nursed his wounds. The cuts had been deep, had severed muscles. N'ssag would always walk with a limp now, and he'd never again be able to raise his left arm completely over his head. Ventat had given him some healing salves. He had magic, but not a healing kind of magic. Ventat was a Land Mage. And while Life Magic was N'ssag's hallmark, he did not know how to heal the living. Only how to raise the dead.

N'ssag now stood upon what had most likely been a dancing floor. It was mostly unmelted, and he envisioned what this place must have been like before the attack. A half-wall to his left cordoned off a ten-foot-by-twenty-foot space where, perhaps, musicians had gathered to play.

N'ssag had brought back to life nearly all of the city's previous inhabitants in the last few months, and he was well acquainted with how the lithe, strong Nox were formed. He imagined what they must have looked like dancing, throwing themselves about with supernatural grace.

That first month, N'ssag had been so grateful. He'd been given a new home, time to recover, and more material than he'd ever had to work with in his life. The conditions for making primes were optimum in the Great Noktum. With the amulet Ventat had given him as well as all the materials he needed for his laboratory, N'ssag had brought back nearly every single corpse in this burned city.

He'd created an army.

Even now, they were ravaging the countryside, sucking the blood of the plentiful creatures within the noktum, and every single Nox was loyal to him. N'ssag had fixed that little problem.

He had no intention of ever facing the near-death problem he'd faced with his queen. His system was far more sophisticated now.

Life, materials for work, and all the time in the world to realize his dreams. N'ssag should have remained happy.

But once he'd finally achieved all he'd ever wanted, his mind had wandered to what might have been if he had succeeded in Daemanon. He went over the battle again and again. He had been so close!

It preyed upon his mind.

Another man might have blamed Rhenn for the catastrophe, but it wasn't her fault. Love was difficult even at the best of times. Love was a give and take. His queen had made mistakes, true. She'd leaned on her fear and her rebelliousness too much. But N'ssag had made mistakes as well. He hadn't properly conditioned her. He hadn't perfected his process when he'd made her, and they'd both paid for it. Rhenn had made a run back to her old life, which she could never have again of course. And N'ssag had had to recover from a gut wound that nearly killed him.

He and his queen were wiser now, though. The next time they met, their love would flourish. He would make sure of that.

So no, it wasn't Rhenn who drew his wrath.

Some might have assumed it was her henchmen who should be blamed, but no. Oh, they had been troublesome, but they weren't the real source of N'ssag's dismantling. Henchmen did what henchmen were trained to do. The big warrior named Khyven was an idiot with a sword. Slay slay slay. He was a sharp tool made for a single task, just like N'ssag's primes. A man like Khyven was no real threat. N'ssag would simply make sure the next time they met, he overwhelmed the muscled moron with his primes. After the warrior was dead, N'ssag would simply let that arrogant swordsman rot away like so much offal. He would not give the man the honor of coming back as one of his high primes.

The other henchman was the Nox girl Lorelle. She was

much the same as the warrior. Perhaps she was more subtle in her approach and her powers, but she was a follower, clearly born to do what others told her to do. He doubted she had any more intelligence than the idiot swordsman. She, too, would be taken in hand. Ventat had told N'ssag all about that noktum cloak and how to neutralize it. At his next meeting with the lovely Lorelle, he would overwhelm her with his primes, strip her of that noktum cloak, then strip her of her life.

She would simply be another lithe and ready body to infuse with N'ssag's brand of life, as well as an undying loyalty to him. She was ... a delicious resource, and he salivated at the idea of laying her down on a slab and turning her into one of his own. He could picture it all.

So no. Neither of those followers of his queen were to blame. Rhenn's little clutch of friends would have gone down under the overwhelming wave of his primes. N'ssag had walked through the steps of that battle over and over, and each time he saw it ending the right way. In his favor. It should have gone that way. It *would* have gone that way, save for one thing.

That damned Line Mage. Slayter.

N'ssag closed his eyes and relived the horrible moment when his plan had fallen apart. He felt it again like a crushing hammer blow to his heart. It wasn't the stupid warrior with all his slashing about, trying to cut through an army that was clearly too much for him. It wasn't the Nox with all of her teleporting about, trying uselessly to topple a wave here and there when his army was the entire ocean.

No, it was when N'ssag had spotted the mage standing in the doorway. Slayter had held something so simple. A mirror, but somehow he had directed a blinding beam of sunlight down that hallway, and that single mirror, that single, simple tool became a sword of light that cut through N'ssag's most powerful creations. It tore them apart like N'ssag's power was nothing.

He clenched his fists around the golden, stringless harp in his hands. He'd met a dozen like Slayter Wheskone. The privileged. The arrogant.

The high-level priests of Nissra, many of whom were mages, were like that. Every mage he'd ever met had scoffed at N'ssag's talent. And Line Mages were the worst.

The academics of the towers of Saritu'e'Mere had organized magical talent into categories: Jot Mages, Talent Mages, Adepts, Masters, and Archmages. The more versatile a power, the greater it was lauded. A narrow definition indeed.

They classified "great mages" as those who could apply their magic to multiple endeavors. For Life Mages it was growing trees. Calling upon animals, sometimes even seeing through their eyes. Healing the sick and injured. Imbuing artifacts with life charms.

For Land Mages, it was being able to call upon all four of the elements: throwing fire, moving earth, bringing rain, pushing the wind. Using all together, rather than just one or two, was defined as a higher-level power.

For Love Magic, being able to elicit fear as well as love or anger or inspiration.

He was sure it was the same for Lore Magic. N'ssag simply didn't know enough about Lore Magic to know what its different flavors were, but he was certain those mages were judged similarly.

And Line Mages ... Well, they were the worst. Line Magic was, by definition, the stream of magic that could combine all four other streams. Line Mages were borrowers. They didn't have their own legitimate stream, so they stole from the other four. And then they looked down their noses at everyone else.

The academics of Saritu'e'Mere had classified N'ssag as a Talent Magic. Not the lowest of the low, but almost. Which, of course, made him barely worth noticing. He had been thrown into this lesser category because of their short-sightedness, and they treated him like trash. His power was not versatile. He could only do one thing: siphon life-force from the living and put it into the dead. Or sometimes the right artifact. He'd never drawn animals close. He had never healed anyone. He couldn't even heal himself.

And so the mages of the high towers and of Nissra's priesthood had looked down on him. They'd thought his brand of Life Magic was disgusting at best. Useless at worst.

Because they currently lived in a world that prized magical versatility above all else.

And N'ssag had been on the verge of proving them wrong until Slayter Wheskone had undone everything with his little mirror trick ...

Clearly, Slayter was the real threat. He didn't just use his magic. He used his intelligence, as N'ssag had always done. Slayter had seen through N'ssag's power, seen it from head to toe, and then he'd dropped the floor away.

So when they met his queen's henchmen again, he would teach them where they really belonged. He would bury the warrior. He'd claim the Nox woman and her sleek body. And the mage ...

He would claim no position of esteem amidst N'ssag's primes. He would not be afforded a quick death. N'ssag would torture Slayter until the Line Mage screamed his name. Until he begged for mercy. Until he admitted N'ssag's magical supremacy with every quivering nerve of his dying body.

N'ssag realized he'd clenched his fists around the horns of the harp. He was breathing hard like he'd hiked a mile.

He was nearing the resurrection of the entirety of the Nox city. He was so close. And when he had his army ready, he was heading north—

"N'ssag," Ventat's deep voice cut through his daydream.

N'ssag spun, and a fiery little pain lanced down his spine. He hated moving too fast. Now he was going to have the burning fire in that muscle for days. Wincing, he rubbed his neck and looked balefully at his partner. Why did he always have to go sneaking around like that?

"What are you doing?" Ventat glanced at the empty dance floor, then at the direction N'ssag had been staring.

"Plotting the first stages of my war."

Ventat narrowed his eyes. "Your war?"

"I have a number of scores to settle in Usara."

Ventat shook his head slowly, and his face took on that sour expression N'ssag had seen so many times in the academics in Saritu'e'Mere, or in the faces of the high priests of Nissra. Ventat clearly didn't think N'ssag understood what was really important. But like the academics and the high priests, Ventat would realize only too well—and too late—that N'ssag knew everything that was important.

"Tovos's war isn't about settling your scores," Ventat said.

N'ssag wanted to sneer, wanted to tell him that very soon his opinion wouldn't mean a thing, but Ventat Obrey was a Master Land Mage. He could shoot fire from his fingertips. He could open up crevasses in the earth.

He could kill N'ssag, and there was nothing N'ssag could do about it. Yet.

In this moment, right here, N'ssag was at a deadly disadvantage. N'ssag's power built slowly, and Ventat could make the very air strangle him, right now.

And so N'ssag had to remain silent and simply nod. He had spent a lifetime bowing and scraping to the arrogant. He could do it for a few more days.

But one day... One day soon... N'ssag's high primes would surround him, all loyal to him alone, and he would show Ventat what real power was.

"Of course, Ventat. Of course. My apologies. I misspoke."

Ventat looked down on N'ssag for a long moment as though he was searching for imperfections in the fabric of his robe. Finally, he must have found what he was looking for because he nodded once.

"Bring your harp," he commanded. "We have business."

N'ssag gripped the harp in his hands. Of course he would bring it. He rarely let it leave his side. "Where are we going?"

"For a ride."

"A ride?" N'ssag's eyebrows went up. "On a horse?"

"A Talyn. Come with me."

N'ssag swallowed but stayed where he was. His hands

gripped the harp nervously. Talyns were big, fierce land birds that the Nox had used to ride long distances. That didn't sound good at all. N'ssag didn't get along with animals. The only use they'd ever been was as a source of life-force. Every animal N'ssag had ever met seemed to sense that all he wanted to do was kill them, and they reacted accordingly. "I don't ... I don't ride things."

"You are today."

"Isn't there something I can do to help you from here—"

Ventat whirled at the top of the steps and pointed a finger at N'ssag's face. The air suddenly became so thin that N'ssag gasped. His beloved harp tumbled from his fingers and struck the stones with a ringing sound. He was torn. One hand grappled with his throat, the other reached for the precious harp.

"Listen, necromancer," Ventat growled. "You will do whatever I ask of you. If I say you're riding a Talyn, you're riding a Talyn. Never forget who saved you from certain death, who brought you here, who gave you a second chance. You serve Lord Tovos, and none other. Say it."

N'ssag fell to his knees, nodding vigorously. Black spots appeared in his vision. He abandoned his reach for the harp and he clawed at his throat with both hands.

"Say it," Ventat repeated.

"Tovos!" he gasped. "I serve Tovos! Please ..." He waved a hand in the air that he hoped Ventat would see as a request for mercy.

"Follow me." Ventat turned on his heel, his black cloak whipping about him with dramatic flair. Suddenly N'ssag could breathe. He sucked in a whistling breath.

"Of course," N'ssag gasped. He took three deep breaths, but he knew Ventat would not wait long without a second attack. Hastily, he collected his harp and shuffled after. He caught up with Ventat and trailed just behind him. "Where ... Where are we going?"

"Shut your mouth and follow me."

Chapter Eight
N'ssag

entat did not understand N'ssag's greatness. He was just like the academics of Saritu'e'Mere. They had not understood either.

Ventat treated N'ssag like an underling, a lackey who should use his poor talents to benefit his betters. But he could not see the greater picture. No one could see the greater picture.

The academics of Saritu'e'Mere, and now Ventat, saw N'ssag as a minor mage, a one-trick novelty. They also saw him as a coward because he disliked direct conflict. And of course they saw him as a weakling because his delicate body couldn't withstand pain.

So Ventat, and the academics of Saritu'e'Mere, fell to ordering N'ssag about, making him do ridiculous things like ride a vicious, dangerous beast to some unknown place.

The ride was torture. Every jolt of the Talyn's odd gait brought another lance of pain from N'ssag's poorly healed wounds. It seemed that no matter which way N'ssag moved, it sliced him.

It felt like daggers were being shoved into his butt and thighs as his and Ventat's horrible mount topped the rise. The near-blinding spears of light that pushed into the eternal darkness overhead should have awed N'ssag, but the pain was nearly overwhelming. He simply didn't have any resources to appreciate the awesome magic before him.

"This ..." he gasped. "Is as far as I go."

"N'ssag—"

"No. I can go no further."

"Stop whining, you wretched bag of Sleeth dung," Ventat said. "We are here."

With a gasp of relief, N'ssag winced as he brought his leg up, intending to slide off the Talyn and collapse on the ground to seek a position for his legs and back that didn't hurt so bad.

Ventat grabbed him and shoved him back into the saddle. N'ssag cried out as the daggers jabbed him hard.

"You will stay there until I tell you to get down."

"It's killing me!"

"I'll kill you, you insufferable coward. I brought you here to help my lord, and by all that is holy you will fulfill that one task or I will end you myself."

Over the interminable hours on these horrible beasts, Ventat's temper had become shorter and shorter. N'ssag finally had a chance to see what the Land Mage really thought of him. Ventat was no brother. No partner. He wasn't even a friend. He saw himself as N'ssag's master. He was just like the priests of Nissra. To Ventat, N'ssag was merely a tool to give greater glory to his master Tovos, and thereby greater glory to Ventat himself.

He couldn't see N'ssag's greatness any more than the priests could.

"Come on," Ventat growled and led his Talyn into the bowl of the valley. N'ssag hissed as the beast started moving again.

"What is ..." He grit his teeth at a particularly bad bounce. "What is down here anyway? Lord Tovos lives here? I thought the castle—"

"Shut your mouth."

N'ssag could have explained that praise and support was a far better motivator for him, but talking to Ventat was like talking to a wall. Just like the priests.

He bit his lip and bore his pain as the stupid beast clambered down the slope. Ventat didn't pause again. A half dozen times during this journey, N'ssag had tried to get the Talyn to obey his commands, but the thing was somehow slaved to Ventat. It wouldn't turn around and head back to Nox Arvak, wouldn't even pause if N'ssag screamed. All it did was follow Ventat's Talyn.

So when they approached the forbidding cave mouth—N'ssag would swear it looked like the mouth of some enormous beast—his stupid Talyn didn't change course even when he beat on its neck and yanked its reins.

"Be quiet unless you want to die on sharp teeth as tall as you are," Ventat snarled.

N'ssag went completely silent, eyes wide. "Teeth? What is it? What's in here?"

"This is a dragon's lair. And if the thing is awake because of your whining, I'll feed you to it face first."

"A *dragon*?" N'ssag dropped his voice to a whisper. "The dragon that burned Nox Arvak?"

"Yes."

"Then why would you bring us here!"

"Because I think my master might be in here. After months of searching, I found this." He held up an enormous finger with a ruby ring on it. The thing had to be as thick around as N'ssag's wrist and nearly as long as his forearm. Its blackened skin was peeled away from red muscle and white bone.

"Nissra's Hell, Ventat! What is that?" N'ssag still recoiled.

"I pray it is not my lord's finger. But it is certainly his ring."

"Where did you get it?"

"A Sleeth."

"Sleeth?" It was one of the flying, devilish otter things. N'ssag had seen them from a distance, and they frightened him. There were no flying, carnivorous otters in Daemanon.

Thankfully, the damned things didn't enter Nox Arvak because some spell or other that protected the place. It was yet another reason N'ssag would rather be there than here. "It just dropped it off?"

"Shut up."

They wended their way deeper into the cavern, stalactites pointing down from the ceiling like spears, stalagmites reaching up to them like eager teeth. Corridors branched off here and there, and N'ssag imagined any number of hungry predators within, ready to pounce.

"Why do you think he's here?" N'ssag whimpered.

"Shut *up*."

They rounded the final bend in the huge hallway and N'ssag *did* shut up. A mountain of gold, jewels, and valuables of every kind sloped up to a point near the ceiling, almost touching it. N'ssag's mouth dropped open. This was the den of just about every dragon story he'd ever heard. A vast treasure of incalculable wealth.

"What ... is this?" N'ssag murmured, agog.

"Master!" Ventat leapt from his Talyn and sprinted to the base of the pile. N'ssag followed with his gaze to what looked like a charred corpse laying in a melted and solidified pool of gold.

Ventat skidded to his knees next to the corpse, gripping its hand. He peeled up the charred forearm and, sure enough, the right hand was missing its middle finger, the charred piece that Ventat carried.

Wincing, N'ssag lifted his throbbing leg over the Talyn and dismounted. He landed on rubbery knees and almost fell. He pulled hard on the saddle to maintain his balance, and it was a miracle he stayed upright.

The Talyn curved its neck around and snapped at him. The rapacious beast would have bitten off his entire hand if N'ssag hadn't let go with a squeak. He fell onto his butt.

And screamed.

His injuries forked through him and he twisted desperately

to take the direct pressure off them. The Talyn squawked and looked down on him hungrily, but it didn't move to attack again.

"Get over here, necromancer," Ventat growled.

N'ssag crawled gingerly toward the pile of gold.

"Faster, necromancer, or I swear I'll leave your body here."

With a squeak, N'ssag levered himself painfully to his feet, staggered a few more steps forward. With each step, he hated Slayter Wheskone a little more.

Finally he made it to Ventat's side. N'ssag looked the corpse up and down. Not much of the original body remained. Strips of muscle and skin clung to exposed bones. The thing's toe bones poked out like spears of white asparagus. Its left hand had clenched in a fist, protecting the meat of its palm while the bones of its fingers were open to the air. Its ribs wrapped around its blackened heart like a dead mother cradling a baby, all except for a grisly hole that had been punched straight through.

The wound wasn't made from any weapon N'ssag could think of. He'd seen many wounds working with his bodies. This was no sword, no axe or arrow. It was huge. It was as though someone had shoved a sharpened fence post through the Giant's chest. But there was no such weapon nearby.

The Giant had also been horribly burned. The right half of its face was blackened muscle and bone, but the left half was almost completely intact, eye open and staring at the ceiling, long black hair flowing off its scalp. That was almost impossible to believe. The fire that had hit this Giant had been hot enough to melt gold. How had half the Giant's face been spared?

N'ssag was still lost in a reverie when he heard Ventat's voice.

"I said now, necromancer."

N'ssag shook his head, realizing Ventat had been talking for a while. "I'm sorry, what?"

"Revive him."

"Mmmm," N'ssag said, and for the first time since they'd begun this journey, he didn't feel scared. This was Ventat's weakness, this destroyed Giant to whom he had attached his allegiance.

"Bring him back to life," Ventat demanded.

"Of course ..." N'ssag said. "I will need my harp. And I will need that beastly Talyn's life."

Ventat let go of his beloved Tovos's burnt hand and stood up. He went to the Talyn and led it up to the edge of the treasure pile. With a whisper, Ventat raised his hand, palm up, and thin stalagmites rose around the beast, hemming it in and creating a roof over it. In seconds, the beast had been hemmed in by a stone cage.

N'ssag tamped down his jealousy of Ventat's extreme power, the versatility of what he could do. It didn't matter. One day, Ventat would wish he had never doubted N'ssag. He would see N'ssag's greatness. One day, they would all see ...

N'ssag felt his magic gathering. Oh yes ...

What he had learned in his last week in Daemanon ... What his queen had taught him ...

... was that the worst failures birthed the most powerful successes.

But those days of failure were over. It was time for N'ssag to stand up on the pedestal of history.

"Stab this into the beast," N'ssag murmured, withdrawing from his robes the long, thin spike with its glowing, life-holding ruby.

He passed it over to Ventat, who reluctantly took it, looking at it like it was a snake.

"I am not your assistant, necromancer—"

"Do you want him back?"

Ventat's lip curled. He turned and thrust the spike through the bars and into the chest of the Talyn. The movement took the creature by surprise, and it shrieked as Ventat buried the point unerringly into its heart.

N'ssag was surprised by the brutality and accuracy of the strike. The man was a mage, but he'd just lunged like an expert swordsman as well.

The rod's magic flared to life, pulling the purest essence of the creature's blood and life into itself. N'ssag felt the power across the scant distance. The Talyn sagged against the bars, and Ventat reached out to remove the rod.

"No," N'ssag whispered. "Patience. Patience, my ignorant friend ..."

Ventat bared his teeth, but he didn't say anything. Oh, the weak were so predictable. No doubt Ventat was plotting his revenge against N'ssag for such a slight. But N'ssag could throw any diminutives he cared to throw at this moment. Ventat would do nothing while the resurrection of his precious lord hung in the balance.

The other Talyn squawked and backed up, skittish, as his fellow slid to the ground inside the cage.

"Ahhh ..." N'ssag exhaled as the last of the caged Talyn's life-force went into the rod. "Now, my dear Ventat," he said. "Remove the rod and give it to me."

Ventat's face flushed a deep purple, but he yanked out the rod and handed it, dripping, to N'ssag.

N'ssag didn't care about the blood; he just took it and inserted it into the curve of the harp, creating a single "string" with the golden rod, straight up the middle. He'd found this glorious artifact deep within the Hepreth Nuraghi and married it with his lifekeeper, a perfect union. On the verge of an incredible victory, the forces of fate had delivered to him the one tool that would ensure it all.

He'd found it beneath an altar of one of the dead Giants in the room where he'd brought his beautiful queen to life. At first, he hadn't known what it was, but it drew him to itself. He had felt its vital importance.

As he had pulled the life-force from one of his primes to animate a Giant corpse, the stringless harp had vibrated so strongly he could hear its song in his head.

And then it was clear to him, almost as though the song had spoken the harp's secrets. It was a magical amplifier. Whatever N'ssag could do, the harp could increase tenfold, twentyfold, a hundredfold! It could give as much as N'ssag's own frail body could stand to channel.

When he had brought that first Giant back to life, stripping the goblin of its own stolen life-force and funneling it into the huge body, the harp had hummed with song. That old Giant body should have been decrepit and barely able to move with the small amount of life pushed into it. Once upon a time, with N'ssag's normal methods, it would have been. But with the harp, the Giant—and shortly after its fellows as well—had not only risen and begun walking, but he'd been able to wield magic!

"Oh, he will be magnificent, my ignorant friend." N'ssag climbed atop Lord Tovos's burnt corpse and saw Ventat twitch with anger. But the powerful Land Mage only watched. Ventat was playing his own game, and he needed N'ssag to bring his lord back. Just as N'ssag had been helpless to take a breath under the power of Ventat's magic, so too was Ventat helpless to help his lord without the power of N'ssag's magic.

N'ssag drew a deep breath, raised the harp overhead. The single point of the ruby rod poked below the bottom curve of the artifact, three inches of sharp gold dripping with Talyn blood. The harp hummed. The life-force, the rod, was attuned to the harp now. N'ssag yanked the rod out, wielding it like a dagger. He aimed for the charred flesh to the right of the hole in Tovos's chest.

And thrust downward. The strike was good; it sank satisfyingly into the crispy flesh, buried to the ruby.

The ruby blazed with light. The magic took hold.

Tovos's body rocked. N'ssag sat down hard, straddling the burnt waist and entrails, but his fist remained clamped around the gem of the rod, willing all of the Talyn's life-force into the body, willing it to multiply, to fill up every piece of flesh and bone that remained to this lord of Giants.

The harp sang, quivering in his hand like an excited hunting dog. Tovos's body shook harder, and it sat up, dislodging N'ssag.

He yanked the harp and rod out and rolled awkwardly to the side, sliding down to the ground on a small cascade of golden coins. But he'd felt the life-force go into the Giant. He'd felt all of it go. There was nothing left.

He sagged under the weight of the following exhaustion. These days, with the harp's assistance, filling up something like a single Nox barely drained him. He could do twenty a day without hurting himself. But this ... this was N'ssag's masterpiece. He had given everything to it.

The Giant sucked in a breath and roared through a ravaged throat. His one good eye opened, looking wildly about.

"My lord," Ventat knelt before him. N'ssag scuttled back a healthy distance. The awakening was a tricky time, even with all of N'ssag's new precautions. His queen had taught him that.

Tovos's one eye tracked over, spotted Ventat. "Ventat Obrey," he gurgled through a ravaged throat.

"Yes, my lord. I found you. I found you at last."

Tovos looked over at N'ssag. N'ssag smiled and bowed.

"You ..." Tovos gurgled, looking back at Ventat. "Brought me back from death."

"Yes, my lord. Death cannot stop you from enacting your will, and from exacting justice upon whoever did this to you."

"True ... True ..." He gestured with a blackened arm at N'ssag. "And this is ... N'ssag?"

Ventat blinked. He hadn't expected that, hadn't expected his lord to recognize N'ssag.

"Y-Yes, my lord. You know him?"

"Of course," Tovos rasped.

Ventat glanced at N'ssag, who smiled.

"He is your new master," Tovos said.

Ventat hesitated, stunned momentarily by his own confusion. But though Ventat was ignorant of what was really important, he was no idiot. It took him only a moment to realize the truth. Tovos was now loyal to N'ssag.

"You bastard!" Ventat spun, raising his hand and pointing at N'ssag. Jagged chunks of rock peeled up from the ground and flew at him—

N'ssag flinched, but a foot-thick, solid stone wall rose up to block the projectiles. They shattered on its surface.

Ventat's eyes went wide and he spun back to his lord. The Giant's fist was clenched, a nimbus of blue glowing around it and the sudden earthen wall.

"My lord, he has cast a spell upon you. Do not heed him!"

N'ssag walked around the edge of the wall that had protected him, slipping and sliding on the coins awkwardly, but he couldn't hide his triumphant smile. He glanced at Ventat smugly, then at Tovos.

"Kill him," N'ssag ordered.

"N'ssag!" Ventat raged, but Tovos opened his fist. The earthen wall crumbled into a pile of broken rocks. Tovos clenched his fist again, and the air whooshed away from Ventat.

Ventat opened his mouth to murmur, to curse, to shout, to scream.

Nothing came out.

He collapsed to the ground, thrashing, uselessly grappling at his throat as his face turned lavender, then purple, then dark purple. N'ssag daintily made his way down the gold to stand close, though not too close, to Ventat. The man's eyes bulged from his sockets and his chest spasmed.

And then Ventat died, mouth open, tongue lolling out.

N'ssag knelt next to the man now, cocked his head and studied his grisly purple mask of death.

"You understand it now, don't you?" N'ssag whispered to him. "You see my greatness ..."

Chapter Nine
ELEGATHE

Elegathe rose from the bed and took the sheet with her. It was partially tucked under Prince Tarventin, but he snuffled, shifted off it, and rolled over, pulling the thicker covers with him. A sleeping consent to his lover.

As though this good man had consented to what was going to happen in his life, to what she had brought upon him.

She closed her eyes, clutched the sheet to her breast, twisting the fabric in her fist.

She lifted her eyeglasses from the nightstand with two fingers, twisting them back and forth. She moved silently to the expansive balcony, a semicircle of white marble with a wide guardrail held up by smooth, shaped pillars as thick as her thigh. A warm breeze flowed over her skin. Imprevar was a cold country in the winter, every bit as cold as Usara. Spring was violent, with slashing rainstorms and hailstorms for a solid month.

But that fierce spring gave way to an early and long summer that was the most pleasant in all of the Human lands. The other kingdoms began their summers almost two months after Imprevar. For the people of Triada, the summer days were almost upon them: days of wine and harvests, parties and lovemaking, bright dresses and music, and a contemplation of how they were the most beautiful and cultured kingdom in all of Noksonon.

That was what they were expecting, what they had known for half a hundred years, but that was not what was coming. That beautiful, deceptive sunrise was a lie.

A storm was on its way, and it would consume every person on Noksonon. She lifted her eyeglasses with one hand and put them on.

Elegathe could barely remember last year when she had traveled through the Thuros with Darjhen, met the High Masters from the other continents. She could remember being angry with him for making her feel like a little girl again, making her feel like she knew so little of the world after she'd been the High Master of the Readers of Noksonon.

He'd been right, but she'd changed since that day. She knew everything now, it seemed. She knew more than she wanted to. She wished she could be that little girl again. Innocent. Hopeful. Honest. She tried hard not to hate herself, but some of Darjhen's last words came to her ...

Sometimes I think that I am an evil man.

She hadn't fully understood him at the time. She did now.

For the last several months, Elegathe had become everything she'd ever wanted. A woman at the center of the web. A Reader who knew the fate of the lands, who stood so far above the layman workers, the mothers with babies at their hips, the peacock nobles in their self-indulgent opulence, even the rulers of the lands, who thought they saw so clearly. She had attained this, had become that person.

She was the tip of the sword, moving events toward a future that would save the mortals of the world: the Humans, Luminents, Shadowvar, Taur-Els, Delvers, Brightlings, Nox, Vertigyans, and so many others within the noktum that she had not met.

It had been so much easier to be a Reader when she had been tucked securely in the Reader House, looking at everything from a distance, looking at the people who inhabited the world as pieces that must be moved on a board.

But for the last several months, Elegathe had mixed with the world. No longer standing at a distance, she had become the instrument of fate she'd always wanted to be, and not a mere watcher. Darjhen had opened this world to her, and she had matched him stride for stride. She had pushed Nhevalos's chosen in the kingdom of Usara. She had orchestrated preparations in the kingdom of Triada, becoming trusted, becoming a woman who was instrumental to their greed. She had secured influence among the Sandrunners' nomad kingdom, becoming a wise woman, a foreign prophet. And in the kingdom of Imprevar ...

She gazed over at Tarventin, the handsome Prince of Imprevar. His muscular form lay sprawled beneath the covers. His golden wavy hair spread across the silken pillow.

She had secured Imprevar's loyalty as well. Or rather, she had secured the loyalty of its future king.

She closed her eyes again, and her fist tightened on the sheet so hard her fingers ached. If she looked at him too long, she began to see that soft hair matted with blood. If she looked out over the city too long, she could see it smoking and broken, bodies in the streets, draped in an eternal night....

She had seduced the prince at about the same time she had convinced the King of Triada to make her a Merchant Diplomat. It had all been planned, just as she had wormed her way into the Council of Wisewomen for the Sandrunners. To the Sandrunners, she was now a bringer of water and knowledge. To the King of Triada, she was now the doorway to greater trade with the Shadowvar and Demaijos. To the Prince of Imprevar, she was the woman who held his heart, who enflamed his desires, who had become his confidante.

A woman he now said he wanted to make his intended.

Tarventin believed these things about her because she

wanted him to. He'd never had a chance to make his own decisions. She had stacked the odds in her favor so he never knew what was actually happening.

This was the power of true knowledge.

She had it. He did not. She knew everything about him. She knew what to say to him, what he longed to hear, what he needed to feel. She played her part perfectly because she had been trained. He was a harp beneath her hand, and the song was exactly what she wanted it to be.

Soon, Tarventin's father would be dead. Tarventin would ascend to the throne, and in the flustered confusion of those unexpected days, he would reach out to Elegathe for help. When he did, she would steady him. In his rush of gratitude and passion for her, he would make her his bride despite the fact that she was not of the royal line in this kingdom or any other. Then she would provide him with the exact information to make him successful. She would whisper into the ear of the King of Imprevar, and he would heed her.

She would whisper into the ear of the King of Triada, and he would believe her.

She would whisper into the ear of the Burzagi, and he would follow her.

And because they listened to her, when the Dark came for them all, the Human kingdoms would survive....

Of course, there were many futures where she had not come to Imprevar. The old king continued his rule. Tarventin continued as a blissful and adventurous prince. And they would all die when the darkness came.

But because of Elegathe, the king would be dead in two weeks instead. She had orchestrated that coming event. She had made that choice. There would be far less blood, far less death because of her choices, but on mornings like this, she could not see herself as anything but a murderer. If not for the events she had set in motion, the king would still be alive in two weeks. That was the truth—

"Darjhen is dead," a voice echoed her morbid thoughts,

rising from the shadows behind her. Once, such a thing would have startled her, but not anymore. She'd been expecting him. Nhevalos had come at last. She hadn't seen him in a possible future, not like she'd seen the fate of the Imprevaran kings. Nhevalos was almost impossible to predict with the *kairoi*, but she didn't always need the *kairoi* to predict the future. Nhevalos was predictable in a different way.

She held herself perfectly still except that she opened her eyes, looked again at the deceptively peaceful city, at the beautiful fields beyond lying in the cool, predawn shadows. Beyond that, she looked at the lightening horizon, a crust of yellow along a fragile line of mountains. A crust of hope along a fragile line of the future.

"Yes, I know," she finally said.

"You know," the Giant replied, and she imagined she heard a hint of approval in his voice.

"Did you think I'd let him leave me again without knowing everything about where he was going? About how he was doing?"

The Giant was silent for a time. "You read the *kairoi*."

She didn't answer him, for two reasons really. First, she wanted to serve him some of his own medicine for a change. Nhevalos never answered a question he saw as having an obvious answer. Of course she'd read the *kairoi*. She was a Reader. This arrogant, emotionless killer could suffer what it was like to be kept in the dark. There was nothing she could hide from him for long, of course, but he could drift for one satisfying moment.

Second, she had cheated. Yes, she'd read the *kairoi*, but it wasn't the *kairoi* that had told her Darjhen died.

Before she and Darjhen had begun their individual journeys into the lands of Noksonon, they'd spent several weeks together preparing, coordinating. During that time, when Darjhen was asleep, she had placed a ring gently on his toe. She had left it there for the requisite three hours and then removed it. It was a spell she'd commissioned from a powerful Line Mage. Its function was to imbue him with a benign spell that would report his location and the status of his life-force to the whomever wore the ring.

She'd worn it on the index finger of her left hand since that night. The spell had told her the location of her mentor—she could point to where he was within thirty miles if looking at a map—and the direction he was in if she didn't have a map. And she could feel any strong emotions he had. If he was happy, she felt slightly happier herself. If he was sad, she found herself pulled down as well. If he was excited, she gained a spring in her step.

It had still been on the index finger of her left hand yesterday when she'd felt him die. Her heart had wrenched as though someone had grabbed it and twisted. She'd been in the palace courtyard waiting for Tarventin when she gasped at the pain. It was as though she'd been spun about by some terrible wind and couldn't find her bearings, but her gaze had been drawn to the south. He'd died somewhere to the south. Somewhere near the Great Noktum.

The echo of his death lingered within her, but after an hour the ring went inert. It became just a normal ring. She hadn't realized how much she'd grown accustomed to it. A reassuring bit of Darjhen had been with her always. Then it was gone, and she'd never felt more alone, at least not since Darjhen had rescued her from the streets and made her a Reader. He'd changed her life. He'd *given* her a life.

And now he was gone. And it was just one more event in the inevitable march toward Nhevalos's outcome.

She turned away from the rising sun and looked at the Giant. He stood in the shadows at the foot of the bed. His black hair was pulled back into a ponytail, and a single earring glittered in his right ear. He wore a black long-sleeved shirt and a scarred leather vest, open in the front. Black breeches. Black boots. His intense gaze was still hard for her to meet, and she hated that. Elegathe didn't look away from the gazes of men, not unless she was manipulating them to a purpose and a coquettish glance was part of the act.

Nhevalos was also much taller than when she'd first met him. At first, she thought maybe it was the dramatic entrance, the direness of his news that made him seem larger. But when she took two steps closer to assess him, that thought evaporated.

He was definitely taller. He had been six and a half feet the last time she'd seen him. He was well over seven feet tall now. He was growing. Was he reverting to his normal state as the war approached?

She glanced back at Tarventin. He still slept, blissfully unaware that there was a Giant in his room. Nhevalos wouldn't hurt Tarventin, of course. Tarventin was part of his plan, and if there was one way the Giant was predictable, it was that nothing was more important than the plan. Nothing. Tarventin was who Nhevalos wanted on the throne, which surely made him one of safest Humans on the continent.

His father, on the other hand, was just as surely doomed....

"Tarventin will not wake." Nhevalos followed her gaze.

"You wouldn't be much of a Giant if you couldn't make one prince stay asleep, I suppose."

"I am sorry about Darjhen."

"I doubt that. I don't think you've been sorry about a single one of the deaths reaped for your plans," she said. Darjhen would have told her that she shouldn't provoke Nhevalos, but Darjhen was dead, so who gave a damn anymore?

"He did more than anyone to ensure the future of your people," Nhevalos said.

"And he died exactly as you wanted, I'm certain." She wondered when it would be her turn. At what point would her sacrifice serve his vision more than her service? A year from now? A week? Tonight?

"We were orchestrating three futures. Any of them would have sufficed, but five others appeared at the last moment. In every one of those five, Darjhen died."

She turned her gaze up, held his for a long, excruciating moment. "You misread the *kairoi*?"

"Other Eldroi have now taken an interest in the game. This was expected, though sooner than I would have liked. Our fight will become increasingly similar to a common battle among mortals. There are those who can change the future as fast as we can."

"You're saying Darjhen encountered a Giant."

"Tovos."

"Tovos killed him."

"It could have been worse."

"Please tell me how it could have been worse."

"Had Tovos known what Darjhen was, he'd have tortured him, leveraged him for information. But he misjudged, and Darjhen died in the battle. Torture would have been worse."

The thought of Darjhen tortured to death hit her hard. She couldn't help but imagine Darjhen's agony, Tovos "taking his body apart." She swallowed and fought the tears. She wasn't going to cry in front of Nhevalos. "Am I to finish Darjhen's job?"

"No."

"You don't want me doing ... whatever he was doing? It was more important than what I am doing."

"No. The north is where the fate of Humans will be decided. We will lose a few cities to the south. You are where you should be."

"A few cities? They are already attacking?"

"There have been preliminaries."

"Which is where Darjhen died."

"Yes."

"Which city?"

Nhevalos didn't answer. He just stared at her, and she was forced to look away again. "I also came to say that Darjhen was right about you. You were everything he promised and more. You have done better than Darjhen himself could have done."

She swallowed as she felt a swift chill up her spine. "Is that why Darjhen is dead instead of me? Because I'm more useful? Is that what you're saying?"

Nhevalos glanced at Tarventin and back at Elegathe, his face was expressionless. "I'm saying it would have been a mistake to breed you instead of this."

She tried to keep the shock off her face. Breed her? *Breed* her!

Then it hit her. That was the source of the tension during their first meeting, when she hadn't known who Nhevalos was, when Darjhen had told her to keep her mouth shut. He'd been afraid. Nhevalos had been breeding Greatbloods for centuries, and Darjhen had been afraid Nhevalos would simply take Elegathe and vanish, use Love Magic on her, breed her with some noble, and that would have been her fate instead of this. To be a brood mare for the next Khyven the Unkillable.

She should have put that together before now. That was short-sighted. She was a mage, which meant she'd always had some quotient of Giant's blood in her veins. Of course she'd have been a possible candidate. Darjhen had saved her once again.

She suppressed a shudder and tried to act like the very thought didn't turn her stomach....

Then she glanced again at Tarventin. The cold moved from her spine around her body and sat like a lead ball in her stomach. Tarventin was of royal blood. Most of the Greatbloods were bred from royalty.

Her feelings for Tarventin... Had Nhevalos used Love Magic on her?

Her hand went to her belly—

Nhevalos shook his head. "Tarventin's blood is not pure enough. That is not why you are here, Elegathe."

She swallowed.

"As I said, you are more valuable as a Reader. There is no more need, indeed there is no more time, to make Greatbloods. We have what we have. The war has begun."

"The war has begun..." she echoed.

"You will see me more often now. You may finish your... liaison if you wish." He indicated Tarventin. "But you must leave soon."

She glared at him, but he didn't flinch, just looked back at her.

"The next moves are coming," he said.

"Khyven and Rhenn. Slayter and Lorelle."

"And others, yes."

"You were wrong about her," she said. "About Lorelle."

"That remains to be seen."

"You thought she had to die."

"Mmmm."

"She has done as much as any of them to drive your plans. Why do you hate her?"

"Hate her?" Nhevalos shook his head. "Hate is a luxury reserved for Humans. I do not hate any Humans. Lorelle threatens to pull Khyven's attention from where it should be. That is all."

Elegathe closed her eyes, shut out the view of this incomprehensible, demanding being who had, of course, come here to demand more. Last year when she'd stood in the room with him and Darjhen seemed like ten years ago. She'd seen Nhevalos as some upstart ordering around her mentor. Back then, she would have told him to go to hell.

She wanted to attack him, stab him with a dagger. If her life belonged to her, if she didn't know what she knew, she would have done that. She would have tried, at least, and probably died before she could draw a single drop of blood …

But in these last few terrible months she had traveled the continent. She had gone places that would have turned her mind inside out if she hadn't had the training of the Readers, if she hadn't been prepared by Darjhen.

She'd seen the inside of the Great Noktum. She'd viewed the blinding, unfathomable Lux up close. She'd been to Nokte Shaddark and Demaijos, from the Vellyn Isle to the cliffs of Mallorn, from the ordered pastures of the Taur El to Lumyn, the haughty capital of the Luminents. In each place, she had seen where Nhevalos had planted his seeds, the other Greatbloods.

Each had been guided by the Giant to be another Khyven the Unkillable, each bred to have a high concentration of Giant's blood, each with some sense of precognition. Triada had one. Laria had two. There was a Shadowvar in Nokte Shaddark as well. Three Taur-Els. Two Demaijos. One Human in Nokte Vallark. One on Vellyn Isle.

There had been one in the Sandrunner's ruling clan as well. A Champion of the Sun Ring called Txomin. But he and Khyven had clashed during Khyven's rise, and Txomin was no more.

There had also been a Greatblood in Imprevar, but he had died in a childhood accident years ago. Imprevar had no champion, no Greatblood to lead them into the Dark. It put them at a horrible disadvantage, but they'd just have to do it the hard way. And Elegathe would help them. She'd help them or she would die trying.

So no, she couldn't just stab Nhevalos in the throat. He was a bastard, but he was the only bastard who could see this through, the only one of the Eldroi who was on their side. He'd spent centuries setting up the thin possibility that Humans could defend themselves.

When he asked, she had to say yes. There was no other answer, because there was nothing else.

"Elegathe," Nhevalos prompted. "Are you ready?"

She let out a breath and opened her eyes. "Of course I am."

"Good. It will be more difficult without Darjhen, but you will have other help. The places you've visited before, they will need assistance to face what is coming." He pulled something from the shadows. It flowed out like a river of black silk, and he laid it across his arm.

She glanced at it and knew instantly what it was.

"Darjhen's noktum cloak," she said.

Nhevalos did not acknowledge the obvious, so he said nothing.

She crossed the distance. One hand was still bound up in the sheet, so she let it go. Modesty was laughable in front of Nhevalos. She wasn't a person to him, just a pawn on a board.

What did one care if the pawn covered itself or not?

The sheet fell to the floor and she took the cloak with both hands.

"I'm going on a journey," she said.

"Soon."

Her heart hurt. She never thought she was going to stay in Imprevar forever, but she didn't think she was going to fall in love with Tarventin, either. She felt torn in two. One Elegathe wanted to stay and make this charade real. To love a man and be loved in return, to face the future together without lies. The other Elegathe knew that love—that the common relationships between people—could not happen again for anyone if Nhevalos didn't win this war. He needed all the pieces he'd put in place. Khyven was one of those pieces. Darjhen had been one. And so was she.

"Everywhere I've been before?" she asked.

"And places Darjhen went. It is time to reveal yourself, to tell the leaders who you really are."

"Some will try to kill me if they know I'm a Reader."

"Then you will handle them."

She hesitated, then nodded.

"You will go to Castle Noktos first."

Her eyes widened. Castle Noktos was a nuraghi inside the Usaran noktum, near the crown city of Usara. It was the Usaran noktum that had burst with the creatures that overthrew King Vamreth and cleared the throne for Rhennaria Laochodon. The Readers had studied a great deal about Castle Noktos. It was perhaps one of the most dangerous places in the noktum. Elegathe knew what lived there. More Kyolars and Sleeths, Gylarns and Cakistros than anywhere else. But more than that. There was a steward in that castle, a monster that devoured anyone who dared to cross his borders.

"What of the keeper, Rauvelos?"

"Wear this." Nhevalos extended his fist, an Amulet of Noksonon dangling from a chain.

"I have one," she said.

"And this one is marked by me."

She took it. "Rauvelos will recognize it?"

"Tell him you want access to the Vault."

"What is in there?"

"A thousand years of preparation. Take the treasures you find. Distribute them to those you visit."

"You're not going to tell me what's in there?"

"Rauvelos will explain."

"Explain what?"

Nhevalos said nothing. He never told more than he needed to, as though the release of too much information could disrupt the *kairoi* he had seen.

"When do I need to leave?" she asked.

"Now."

"I'm not leaving right now."

Nhevalos said nothing. She thought maybe his eyes narrowed just the slightest bit, but she couldn't tell.

"I'll leave tomorrow," she amended, though she didn't want to leave tomorrow either. She had hoped for at least another week here, a month even. She couldn't simply slip out immediately like a paid harlot. "If I vanish, the work I've done here is worth nothing. Is that what you want?"

Nhevalos stayed silent for a moment, then spoke in a low, serious voice. "Beware your steps, Reader. Darjhen stumbled, and it took his life. There are pitfalls everywhere around us. Ensure that your steps are guided by our goal, not by distractions."

He moved deeper into the shadows, and it was her turn to say nothing.

"Beware your steps ..." he said, then he was gone.

She gave one glance over her shoulder at the impending sunrise, then climbed onto the bed and caressed Tarventin's cheek. He awoke with a sleepy smile.

"Elly," he murmured.

She kissed him passionately, slithered on top of him.

His arms awakened and wrapped around her. "Elly?"

"The sun is coming," she murmured into his neck.

"The sun?"

"I want it to see us," she breathed. "I want the sun to see that this ... That this is true."

"True?"

"Shhh ..."

"Is something wrong?"

She kissed his mouth to make him stop talking. He kissed her back and allowed her to sweep him away. He allowed her this because he didn't know any better. None of them knew any better. And none of them would until the sun had been blotted out and the streets ran red with blood.

The Dark was coming, and it would swallow them whole.

She ignored Nhevalos's demands and shut away the vision that he had orchestrated everything, including her desire to rebel in this very moment. She took the morning with the sun's new rays upon their naked bodies, told herself that she was just a woman. She loved the man she had chosen.

And she pretended that the world wasn't about to end.

Chapter Ten
SLAYTER

Slayter limped from the queen's meeting room still thinking of how to get ahead of someone who could see the future. He started down the steps in a daze, letting his hand follow the rail as he made the slow journey. Step, clomp, step, clomp, step, clomp. He descended the four flights to the main floor, and then the two flights down from that.

While the nature of Line Magic was to dabble in all of the streams, it wasn't particularly effective at Lore Magic. He had dabbled, but Lore Magic required a mage to go deep, to develop an intimate facility with the threads of fate called the *kairoi*.

The nature of Line Magic was to span a wide range of magical facility, but dive only so deep. For example, a Line Mage could never fight a Land Mage toe-to-toe in a battle of fireballs. The Land Mage would always win within those parameters. A Line Mage's true strength was to be able to come up with a solution from any angle necessary. If the Land Mage attacked with fireballs, the best way for a Line Mage to defeat him would be by using a spell of Love Magic, temporarily making the Land

Mage terrified of fire. The reason Slayter loved Line Magic—and why he was good at it—was because it required a high problem-solving ability to use it properly. There weren't any legendary Line Mages who had been idiots.

The same could not be said of Land Mages.

But Lore Magic required a depth of commitment and practice that never seemed to weave well with Line Magic, at least it hadn't for Slayter. He calculated he would never be able to manipulate the *kairoi* effectively enough to manipulate the future over even a year, let alone ten or twenty. And the best Lore Mages, certainly the Giants, did exactly that.

Slayter looked up and realized he was at his laboratory door. It was only at that moment he realized that the quiet Shalure had followed him.

"Shalure," he said, blinking. "Apologies. I didn't see you."

That's all right, she signed.

"Why are you ..." He shook his head to clear it. "I don't think I require your help this afternoon."

Yes, you do.

"Do I?"

You're hurt. Let me help you.

Slayter looked at his reddened arms, and he suddenly felt the parched heat in his cheeks. His nose had started excreting pus along the bridge. Maybe he'd been more badly burned than he'd thought.

"Lorelle gave me a balm. I'll ... I have a spell I can use, as well."

Let me help you, Slayter.

He opened his mouth to protest, but realized it was silly. He was still getting accustomed to having others help him.

"You may not be able to heal me," he said. "We haven't done much training to get you to—"

And whose fault is that? She interrupted him with a gesture even as she deftly undid the protection spells on the door as he had shown her. She pushed the door open then gestured that he should enter.

She followed, closed the door, then went across the laboratory to the comfortable chair where she usually sat to watch him. She looked at it meaningfully, and he followed her and sat down.

Just relax, she said.

"It's going to take life-force from you, Shalure," he said. He was too tired to make hand signs to her, and his burned fingers hurt too much, so he just talked.

Of course it is.

"You need to moderate your output. What you did with Vohn wasn't ideal. You helped him, but you fell unconscious. As a Life Mage, you need to be careful of that. If you get used to knocking yourself unconscious every time you perform a healing, it's going to kill you. It won't be long before you overdraw, and that 'falling unconscious' will be falling into a coma from which you will never awake. Then you starve and you die—"

I understand. She smiled tolerantly at his dire description. *I will only heal you as much as I feel I can.*

"Well ... All right."

She knelt in front of the chair and took his hands in hers. He really didn't think she'd be able to do much, but it was good for her to practice. His inclination was to use the spell he'd created for just such a burn, but she was right about one thing. He'd been neglecting her education, and this was a perfect opportunity to practice.

Shalure closed her eyes. To his surprise, he actually felt something, a tingling in his hand, a ... reaching out of Shalure's magic.

A rush of warmth flowed into Slayter's face and his hands. For a painful moment, it felt like pins and needles, and he hissed. Then the flesh became less sensitive. The reddish hue of his hands softened to pink.

He looked down at Shalure.

"Well done," he murmured.

She didn't answer him. Mostly, he thought, because both her

hands were occupied by holding his, but perhaps there was something else. Shalure's brow was furrowed like she had smelled something she didn't like.

"What is it?"

She didn't answer him for another moment, and the tingling receded then vanished altogether. Shalure took a deep breath and blinked open her eyes. Rocking back on her heels, she contemplated him, but she didn't look at his face. Instead, her gaze lingered on the center of his chest, like she was trying to see through him.

"What is it?"

She paused for a moment longer, then her fingers flicked several gestures. *Your robes. Can you remove your robes to the waist?*

"What? Why?"

Maybe nothing, but ... I don't know.

It was an odd request. If anyone else had asked Slayter to remove his robes, he would have had at least a dozen questions for them before complying. But Shalure was a fledgling mage following something she'd sensed, something she could barely grasp. He knew that feeling well. Even if her intuition revealed nothing at all, it was important to let her explore these feelings. He believed the best mages followed their intuition.

"Very well."

He stood up, unfastened the laces of his shoulder drape, a decorative part of his mage's robes, and lifted it up over his head. He ducked under the shoulder satchel he always wore underneath the shoulder drape, which held secondary components to build different kinds of Line Spells. It was his back-up case when what he needed wasn't in his cylinder. He set it by the side of the chair.

He unbuttoned the front of his robe and shrugged out of the long, dagged sleeves, let it fall to his waist. The dun-colored undershirt clung to his skinny body. He unlaced the front and pulled it down to his waist.

He held his questions in check as her eyes roved over his pale chest. She moved around behind the chair, then flicked a gesture in his peripheral vision.

Lean forward. I want to see your back.

"Do you know what you're looking for?"

I ... No. I sensed something, but ... Just for a moment.

He wondered a dozen things. Had the dragon marked him? Had the burn been worse on his back but he just hadn't felt it? Had—

Stand up, she gestured with one hand while taking his other hand. She led him to the full-length mirror on the far side of the laboratory where Slayter rarely went. She turned him around.

Look at your back, she said.

He looked. It was just his back. He looked for anything out of the normal, but couldn't see anything.

Do you see anything?

"No."

Me neither.

He cocked his head at her.

But I felt something. When I healed you, I felt ... I don't know how to describe it. I felt ... It felt like a stone in a stream. A small stone. I almost didn't notice it, but I'm trying to pay attention to everything, like you told me. And every bit of your body felt normal. My magic flowed into it, did its job, except here, along your back.

Hesitantly, she put her index finger lightly on his shoulder blade, then traced a semicircle from the nape of his neck down to his mid-back, paused, then slowly traced it back up to the nape of his neck again. A perfect circle.

The hairs on the back of Slayter's neck prickled.

"You felt the resistance of a perfect circle on my back?"

She nodded. *It felt like ... a bump. In the shape of this circle. It didn't impede my spell. But I could feel the spell ... flow over it. Like ... Well, like a bump. You don't know what that might be?*

With half his robes dangling from his waist, Slayter went to the northern cabinet and withdrew a lump of molding clay. He flattened it on the thin, polished steel plate beneath the cabinet and sketched out a magical detection spell, all save the last line.

With the spell in hand, he returned to the mirror, twisted to see his reflection again, then completed the line and channeled the spell into his back.

No orange light flared to illustrate magic at work. Absolutely no light. Profoundly no light.

If Slayter had done this spell upon himself as a matter of routine, he wouldn't have thought anything of it. He didn't expect any magic to be active on his back. The detect magic spell had confirmed his expectation.

But they were dealing with Giants now, and Shalure had felt something. Slayter wasn't going to let it go that easily.

"Curious," Slayter said. "Hold this."

He handed the steel plate, with the detection spell still active, to Shalure. She held it wide-eyed away from her body while he went back to the cabinet, found another steel plate and more clay, and carved a second spell.

As with the first, he crafted most of the spell at the cabinet and finished it while standing in front of the mirror looking at his back. Orange light flared from the finished symbol on the steel plate.

Again, for a moment, nothing happened. To an outside observer, it would have looked like the spell had revealed nothing, like the first, but this time Slayter sent his attention after the spell. He wasn't content to let the spell be a messenger that went out and reported back. He wanted to go with it.

And this time, he sensed something odd. He felt, just as Shalure had felt, a ... "bump." It was as good a word as any.

Slayter drew on the lingering magic of the spell and touched the "bump" with his mind, scratched at it, peeled at it.

Then he felt it, a magical resistance.

"There you are ..." he murmured.

He redoubled his efforts to see whatever this was that was trying too hard to remain concealed. At first, it was elusive, like trying to get his fingers around a greased flap of skin.

But once he got ahold of it, the resistance became active. It fought him, pushed an implacable force against him, like a steel wall against his forehead.

I think not, Slayter thought, narrowed his eyes, and brought the full force of his will against the resistance.

The resistance was stronger than him, but he didn't need to beat it to have it reveal its secrets. He simply needed pressure on it. This very fight revealed that something important was there.

The truculent spell held, and Slayter began to get a throbbing headache—

Then it gave way. The spell snapped and fell away like cobwebs.

Slayter gasped, and orange light flared across his back. The power of the spell flowed, and he felt the exhaustion follow. His body felt heavier, his muscles fatigued like he'd sprinted a block. As the magic detection played out, a circle became apparent. A circle ... A symbol.

A rune of Line Magic.

No, not a single rune. Two of them. There were two Line Magic spells on his back, overlapped perfectly.

He didn't know what the first spell—the deepest spell—was, but the one that overlaid it was a camouflage spell. That was the spell Slayter had fought to reveal this handiwork. It was a cloaking to hide the second rune, the mystery rune.

The orange glowing lines faded, but now Slayter could see behind them. The two spells had been carved into Slayter's flesh.

Shalure gasped.

Slayter stared at the scars. Someone had carved into Slayter's back with a knife. Someone had, at some moment in the past, cut into him and formed two spells from those cuts.

When could this possibly have happened? How could someone have taken a knife to him and he would not know?

His mind was alive with questions, but mostly excitement. This was surely another piece of the grand puzzle, and he had found it.

I see you, he thought to Nhevalos, wherever he was. *I've caught another glimpse, and I will catch them all eventually.*

CHAPTER ELEVEN

KHYVEN

After Slayter's cryptic statement about power pieces, he stood up and hobbled to the door.

"Slayter," Rhenn called after him, but the mage seemed not to hear her. He left the room, also leaving the door open. Shalure glanced at them all, shrugged helplessly, and followed.

She followed him everywhere now, Khyven noted. And that was good, wasn't it? He'd felt responsible for Shalure ever since Vamreth had mutilated her. He'd gone into a *shkazat* den to pull her out when she'd been trying to kill herself slowly. He wanted the best for her.

But suddenly she was at the center of their group, latched on to Slayter, and now she'd been welcomed by Lorelle as well—and approved by Rhenn—to be at the queen's own meeting. He wasn't sure why that bothered him. Having Shalure in the room with Lorelle just made him feel uncomfortable. He'd expected that she would have found her own life once she was healthy again. Relatively healthy. The poor woman would never speak aloud again.

He flicked a glance at Lorelle, whose gaze was on him. He raised his eyebrows as if to say, "What?"

She turned her gaze pointedly to Rhenn. The queen had a touch of color to her cheeks, lips pressed together hard like she was about to shout after the mage and command him to return.

"He just walked out," Rhenn said tightly.

"He had an idea, I'm sure," Khyven said.

"Oh, I'm sure he did, but tell me it doesn't frustrate you that he does that, that he babbles about things that don't make sense, then runs off to do things I don't understand."

"He is listening to you," Vohn said. "Be assured of that."

"Except I'm not assured of that! He's always distracted. We constantly have to pull his attention back to the present." She held up a finger. "That man could probably solve every problem in the kingdom if only I could get him to focus on what *we're* talking about. And to speak English."

"He doesn't think the way we do," Vohn said.

"Clearly."

"But his intentions are true."

Rhenn threw her hands up. "True intentions. Except what good is that if all he ever does is babble riddles then run off out of the room? How are we supposed to plan around his brilliant ideas if no one understands them? He never seems to care about the things I want him to care about. His mind is always far afield."

"You know, your entire coup would have failed without him," Khyven said quietly.

Rhenn looked at him sharply.

"Without him, we'd have been trapped in that tunnel and an army of hungry Kyolars would have devoured us. He didn't help us rally an army. He didn't help you convince them to attack. He didn't secure the Helm of Darkness to bring the monsters from the noktum to your side." Khyven paused. "He waited, and at that crucial moment, he did what none of us could have done. It was only one small moment, but it made all the difference."

"Yes, I know," Rhenn said. "He was crucial to that victory; there's no doubt. But so were you. So was everyone else."

"I keep thinking about before that, though," Khyven said. "What it must have taken to get to that moment, where he was in that room with Vamreth, trusted, so that he could betray the king at that exact moment. He'd had to hide in plain sight for years. Can you imagine the willpower that must have taken? I can't even fathom that. Years of listening to Vamreth, even helping him commit atrocities, probably, and all the while waiting for that one perfect moment where he could give the right shove and topple a tyrant."

Rhenn narrowed her eyes.

"I don't know." Khyven shrugged. "I can do a lot of things, but I couldn't have done that. Not if I'd had three lifetimes to try."

"What is your point?" she asked.

"That maybe it's his job to ignore the normal things, to not pay attention to the things he could solve in seconds that would take us days. Maybe he leaves those bits to us because we *can't* do what he's doing."

"His job is court mage. His job is to help me," Rhenn said. "If he can solve problems in seconds that takes me days, his job is to solve those problems. His just up and walking out like that doesn't help me solve anything."

Khyven glanced down at the table and the scattering of maps, scrolls, and pieces of loose paper. He blinked as his gaze settled on the dragon-shaped paper weight. It held down one corner of the map of the continent of Noksonon. Rhenn had labeled every Thuros location she knew about. The one in Usara. The one in the plains east of Imprevar. The one supposedly at the Cliffs of Mallorn. And of course, the one Lorelle had found in the lair of the dragon.

"Except it does," he said.

"Excuse me?" Rhenn replied.

"You weren't here." Khyven pointed at the dragon paper weight. "But we had a talk. I think we were talking about Lorelle and what was wrong with her."

Lorelle's jaw set even more than it had been before. But Khyven had just about lost his temper with her freeze-out.

"Lorelle had been withdrawing since you were taken. She wasn't talking to us because she didn't want to admit that she'd bonded with me."

Lorelle's eyes flashed and her hands went to her hips. Khyven stared back at her, not giving ground. "Come on. You were being inscrutable. You weren't letting us help you, and we were almost at our wits end."

Lorelle folded her arms across her chest and didn't say anything.

"We finally asked Slayter for advice and he blurted that Lorelle had probably bonded with someone."

"You told me the story," Rhenn said. "I'm still not seeing your point."

"That's because you're not letting me finish," Khyven growled.

She blinked, apparently finally seeing that Khyven was now the one getting a bit angry. With an impatient gesture, she invited him to continue.

"During that whole exchange, Slayter was playing with this." He picked up the dragon paper weight. "And he kept talking about Dragon Chains. This thing that could hold a dragon. He kept going on and on about it, and we all thought he was wasting time."

"And then I met a real dragon," Lorelle said, and her low-burning anger seemingly vanished.

Khyven snapped his fingers and pointed at her, still looking at Rhenn. "*That's* my point. Slayter was thinking about a Dragon Chain when it seemed like the most random, irrelevant thing. And then days later, a Dragon Chain saved our lives. Tovos cornered us, and Slayter slapped the Dragon Chain on him—perhaps the only thing that could have neutralized Tovos and save our lives in that moment. And he'd been thinking about it days before."

"You're saying he was using Lore Magic," Rhenn said.

Khyven didn't know that. He didn't know nearly enough about magic to know the truth of that.

"I don't think so," Vohn interjected. "Slayter ... struggles with Lore Magic. He's mentioned it's barely worth trying."

"Then how would he know about the Dragon Chain?" Rhenn asked.

"I don't think he knew. I think he ..." Vohn trailed off.

"He what?"

"I think he's just smart. I think he's thinking about ... nearly everything all at once. All the time. I think he aspires to know ... all of it. So he randomly grabs bits of information. And then he regurgitates them, often at exactly the right moment."

"And other times he walks into walls because he doesn't notice them," Rhenn said.

Vohn nodded ruefully. "Yes. He does that, too."

"I need him ..." Rhenn shook her head, closed her eyes, and leaned heavily on the table. "I need him solving ..."

"What happened, Rhenn?" Lorelle stood up at the queen's sudden defeated posture. "What aren't you telling us?"

"This." She threw a scroll into the middle of the table. It unfurled, the little leather thong flopping next to Vohn's hand. He picked it up and read it, and his eyes went wide.

"When did this happen?" he asked.

"Last week."

Khyven growled. "Are you going to share?"

"Nokte Shaddark was attacked," Vohn said.

Nokte Shaddark was thousands of miles away. Halfway across the continent. There were pirate attacks on that city almost every month. Why would that make Rhenn upset?

"Bloodsuckers," Vohn answered his unspoken question.

"They were attacked by bloodsuckers," Rhenn said. "They're here. *He's* here."

"Now wait a minute," Khyven said. "You don't know that."

"It's all there in the description. These are N'ssag's creatures."

A chill went up Khyven's spine. N'ssag, the necromancer who had brought a nuraghi's worth of corpses to life, had escaped them after the battle in Daemanon.

"They came out of the noktum," he murmured, knowing it before they even told him.

"They came out of the noktum," she confirmed. "N'ssag needed dark to create his 'primes.' The darker the room, the more powerful the ... bloodsucker. A noktum would be his dream laboratory. N'ssag wanted to run his creatures over the entire V'endann Barony. And he almost did. If he's producing bloodsuckers in the Great Noktum, there's no telling how many he's made by now. Hundreds. Maybe thousands."

"Senji's Boots," Khyven murmured.

"This is a nightmare. We should have hunted him down in the first place," Rhenn said.

"We didn't know where he went," Lorelle said.

"That's why we should have hunted him."

"It's not your fault," Lorelle said. "He's not your fault."

Rhenn shook her head. "That's not true. You know that's not true. I had the chance to ... I was right there, and I could have killed him—"

"You thought you had."

"I ran away because I was scared. I should have stayed and finished the job!"

"Rhenn, he'd just taken your life—"

Rhenn slammed her hand down on the table and the boom thundered through the room. Everyone went silent and Rhenn just glared at the wood.

"There are at least three kingdoms between Usara and Nokte Shaddark, and they're not your kingdoms, not your responsibility," Vohn finally said.

"*He's* my responsibility. Three kingdoms? A hundred kingdoms! How many kingdoms worth of blood do I need to have on my hands? We need to find him and stop him. We need to stop him from hurting anyone else!"

Lorelle moved quietly to Rhenn's side and stood close, but

didn't touch her.

"I brought this ... with me," Rhenn said. "The last thing I wanted to do was threaten Noksonon, and I brought him here."

"You didn't," Khyven said.

"I released this monster, and now he's here!"

"That's just ridiculous—"

"Khyven, leave it," Vohn said softly, holding up a hand.

"I will *not* leave it," he snarled.

Rhenn stood straighter; her dark eyes flickered as she looked at him with absolutely no fear. He recognized that posture. She'd always been a fighter, but since her transformation, she was ... different. "Fighter" wasn't the right word anymore. She was a predator. Sometimes she got a look in her eye like she wanted to destroy. Like she wanted to kill because she liked it.

"Khyven!" Vohn said more forcefully.

"No. Forget this. I'm done with this." He pointed at Lorelle. "It's not your fault that Rhenn got taken by a Giant." He turned his gaze back at Rhenn. "And it's not your Senji-be-damned fault some necromancer chose to make you a bloodsucker, let alone that he chose to come to Noksonon."

"If I had died, he wouldn't be here," Rhenn murmured.

"So let's wallow in self-pity," Khyven growled. "That's helpful."

Lorelle gasped.

Rhenn's fists rose from her sides, and he could see her fangs now.

"We shouldn't be looking at what you did or didn't do," Khyven said. "We shouldn't even be looking at N'ssag. We should be looking at who's *behind* that maggot. All this talk about whose fault it is and who should have died is stupid!"

"Khyven ..." Rhenn hissed like she could barely control herself. He saw her bloodlust. She was half a breath away from leaping on him.

Khyven moved toward her, giving her even more reason to attack. He got so close to her that he wasn't sure he could actually stop her if she chose to use those fangs.

"Let's put your rage to work, Your Majesty," Khyven said in a deadly quiet voice. "Let's take this fight to the real enemy. They're yanking us about like marionettes, and I'm sick of it. I don't want to fight with you. And I don't want to talk about what we *might* have done to stop this. I want *them*."

Lorelle was stiff with tension, ready to fly at Khyven or at Rhenn if she could just decide which one. Vohn stood on the other side of the table, eyes wide.

"Let's do what we're best at," Khyven said.

Rhenn's eyes glowed with that inner moonlight. "And what is that?"

He gave his most charming grin. "Fight."

For a moment, he didn't think she would back down, that she would attack him instead. She stared at him with that deadly expression for three heartbeats, then a smirk curled the edge of her mouth.

"You shouldn't taunt me like that," she breathed, shaking her head.

"If I don't, who will?"

"If I lost control—"

"Then I'll handle you until you come to your senses."

"You'll *handle* me?"

"I'm the Great One, you know."

"The term is Greatblood."

"Whatever."

"I'm not who I used to be, Khyven."

He clapped a hand on her shoulder. "Except you actually are. You're exactly you. You just have smoldering eyes and fangs now."

She clapped a hand on his shoulder in return and squeezed, enough that he felt her supernatural strength. He could hear her unspoken words: No, I'm *not* who I used to be.

"You're who you choose to be," he responded. "*You* taught me that. So stop blaming yourself and let's get to work."

She let go of his shoulder. Khyven did the same.

Khyven glanced past her to Lorelle. "Did you decide which

one of us you were going to jump on?"

"I'll dart you both if you do that again."

"Not sure your darts would work on me," Rhenn murmured.

"Do that again and we'll find out," Lorelle said.

Vohn cleared his throat. "If we're all done posturing, perhaps we could return to the problem at hand."

"Well," Rhenn said. "First, we need to inform the Shadowvar High Council, if any of them are still alive, about everything we know about N'ssag and his bloodsuckers—"

The door opened and Slayter limped in with Shalure at his side, holding his elbow to steady him. His robes were twisted and unbuttoned in the front, barely held together in his fist at the front of his chest.

"I have to go," he gasped, clearly out of breath from climbing the stairs.

Rhenn frowned. "You have to go where?"

"Home. I have to go home."

Everyone looked confused, except Rhenn, who looked like she was going to get angry again.

"Wheskone Keep. I have to go back to Wheskone Keep," Slayter said.

"Slayter," Rhenn said. "We were just discussing a tremendous threat that is coming our way—"

"Shalure discovered something that is ... possibly the key we need. I have to pursue it."

Rhenn threw her hands up in the air and glared at Khyven. "Do you see how he simply ignores me?"

"The game is deeper," Slayter began, then shook his head. "No. No, that's wrong. Forget about the game board. We're not there yet. It's a puzzle. And we have to solve it, to see it, before we can play in the game at all. Yes, I should have started with the puzzle. It's like one of those thin, painted puzzles that the tin peddler in Femery Square sells in the spring when he comes down from the mountains—"

"Tell us about the puzzle." Vohn tried to keep Slayter on track. Khyven had noticed that Vohn was the most successful of all of them at doing that, of making Slayter reveal the information in his big head so that the rest of them could understand what he was talking about.

"I ... don't know. I can't show you its entirety, but I can feel it. I know it's there, staring at us from Khyven's blood, from Rhenn's abduction, Lorelle's transformation. I ... I don't know the whole picture ... But if I don't collect the pieces, we'll never get to play at all. They'll just move us about like pawns."

Rhenn looked at Vohn this time. He held out his hands helplessly.

Slayter turned around and dropped his rumpled robes to the waist, revealing his skinny white back. He worked on something in front of his belly that they couldn't see, then held up one hand and snapped the clay disk in his fingers. Orange light flared out, slithering through the air like a hundred snakes and coming together on his back. The orange light curled around in a circle there, and a complicated symbol took shape, a rune that had been carved on Slater's back.

"I'm talking about this," he said.

Chapter Twelve
KHYVEN

A chill scampered up Khyven's spine. A memory flickered in the back of his mind, something lost. He saw a blond-haired woman next to a bathtub, her back to him and a long braid of her golden hair coming undone. Her back ... Something about her back ...

The memory vanished like vapor.

He came back to his senses to hear the group talking about the symbol that still flared orange on Slayter's back.

"... is a camouflage spell. Its purpose is to keep someone from detecting it and the spell beneath it."

"Spell beneath it?" Vohn said.

"There are two spells here."

"How did they get there?" Rhenn asked.

"The spell beneath it is harder to understand," Slayter continued as though he hadn't heard Rhenn. She rolled her eyes in exasperation. "I've never seen this rune ... Or rather, I don't think it is actually a rune, inasmuch as it has never been recorded in all the books on Line Magic that I've ever seen. But there is one component I can translate."

"What does it say?"

"Blood," he said.

Rhenn lifted her chin.

"Which I find decidedly curious. Blood seems to be a recurring theme with this group."

"Slayter ..." Vohn cautioned.

"The Giant's blood we put into Khyven. The blood of the Luminent ..." He nodded at Lorelle. "Which allowed her to soul-bond with Khyven, and also bond with the Dark. And of course the queen. We all know how—"

"Yes, we all know," Rhenn said, but she didn't sound angry this time, only impatient. "Who did this to you?"

Slayter shook his head, and his eyes glowed with excitement. "That is the question."

"And you can find out why at Wheskone Keep?"

"Because someone did this to me in the past. Far in the past."

"Slow down, Slayter," Vohn said. "How do you know that?"

"The width of those scars. This was not done with a knife yesterday, nor even a year ago. Someone carved into me when I was a child, most likely an infant, and then they hid their work."

"Who could do that?" Rhenn asked.

"A Line Mage."

She sighed. "Yes. Of course a Line Mage. But who could steal you from your parents? Surely they wouldn't just let some midwife carve into you as an infant."

"Oh, I think it is nearly certain my parents didn't know. This is Giant magic, after all."

"What?" Vohn said.

"A Giant took you and carved into you when you were an infant?" Lorelle said softly. "That's what you're saying?"

"That is the theory that makes the most sense."

"Why?" Rhenn asked.

"That is the relevant question. And I suspect the answer will have direct bearing upon you, Rhenn, and you, Khyven, and this entire group. It may have to do with a narrow chance we may have to defeat the Giants in this upcoming war."

"So you're saying that, as an infant, you had enough importance to put a spell upon you for what you might do twenty years later?" Rhenn asked, her disbelief plain upon her face.

"Yes."

"You don't think that's just a little bit arrogant? I thought that was my hallmark. Or, y'know, Khyven's."

"How am I arrogant?" Khyven asked.

"You're thinking like a Human," Slayter said.

"Slayter—"

"They have Lore Magic."

"You keep talking about Lore Magic, but they can't possibly predict what a person is going to do in their life from the time they're born."

"That's exactly what they can do. Lore Magic, as I understand it, shows the strongest—and most remote—possibilities. Once you know that, you can push that person down the road to whatever eventual effect they desire."

"This is supposition heaped upon guesswork and stitched together with imagination. You don't know this is true."

"No. But I do know that we must work with what we have if we are to keep up with Nhevalos. This is what we have."

"But ... Twenty years? Really?"

"That's what I mean when I say you are thinking like a Human."

"I *am* a Human."

"We have to be more," Slayter said, and Khyven wasn't sure he'd ever seen the mage seem so serious. Excited, yes. Sometimes even silly or awkward, but Slayter so rarely seemed serious. "We have to think like Giants. We have to. If we don't, then we lose."

"Slayter—"

"Understand," Slayter said, like he wanted to force his conclusion into Rhenn's head. "Twenty years is a long time to a

Human. It's nothing to a Giant. I think the Giants may have been plotting their revenge for seventeen hundred years, ever since they lost the first Human-Giant War."

More flashes of memories came to Khyven. The woman with the long braid, about to step into a bathtub. Her back had ... nothing on it. Nothing. But he'd stared at her back like it should have something. He ... had felt something should be there.

He tried to chase the memory, but the woman and the bathtub vanished, and all he could see was flames. Flames everywhere. The woman with the braid was a new memory, somehow before his completely erased childhood. Whenever he tried to recall anything from his childhood before age ten, it was only flames. Only the flames, until now.

And he was suddenly certain that the woman with the braid was his mother. And there had been something on her back. He'd felt it, but he hadn't been able to see it.

Khyven blinked and came back from the memory like he was emerging from a fog. Slayter was talking, using that infuriatingly calm voice in the face of Rhenn's mounting anger.

"We can't stand here agog at what the Giants can do, or we're going to make ourselves into the pawns they want."

Rhenn's face hardened. "I'm not 'agog' and no one is making themselves into a pawn—"

"Wait," Khyven said. Everyone looked at him. "He's ... Slayter's right."

"Khyven?" Lorelle murmured.

"What is it, Khyven?" Slayter said, and his eyes narrowed, like he would see into Khyven's soul. "What do you know?"

"I don't know ... Nothing. I don't know anything, but a woman ... There was a woman. She was ... getting into the bathtub. I could see her back and ... I think ..." Khyven trailed off. He didn't want to say it.

Slayter stared at him so hard that Khyven didn't really feel like the mage was actually looking at him, but rather into him. "Who was the woman?"

Fear curled up inside Khyven. He didn't want to say. Why didn't he want to say? Why was he frightened to say what he had suddenly discovered was true—

"My mother," he blurted.

He felt a twang inside himself, like his heart was a harp and someone had viciously plucked one of the strings. Hard. "I think the woman was my mother," he said again, and it was easier that time.

Slayter nodded like he had expected he answer. "And what did you see on her back?"

"Nothing," he said. "I saw nothing."

He could see the disappointment on Slayter's face.

"But I felt like something should be there."

"What do you mean?"

"I don't know. Something. I remembered staring, transfixed, at her back. And I didn't know why. There was nothing there. There was ... nothing. Except there was something. I would swear to it."

"Mmmm hmmm." Slayter approached Khyven. He didn't bother to cover up his chest again, and his skinny ribs moved beneath his pale, translucent skin as he strode forward. "Take off your tunic."

"Take off my ..." Khyven glanced at everyone in the room, but they all looked as mesmerized as Slayter.

Slayter looked eagerly like he could see through the fabric of Khyven's tunic.

Fear built inside Khyven akin to what kept him from talking about his mother, about the woman with the blond braid. And it wasn't his fear. Fear was an old friend, but this fear felt foreign, like it had come from some other source. There was nothing in the world that Khyven should be afraid of here.

Yet he was.

His lip curled in a snarl. This fear ... was a spell. It had to be. Nhevalos—or someone—had cast a spell on him to keep him from talking about that memory, about his mother's back and what he ... hadn't seen there.

Khyven clenched his fist; he wanted to grab his sword.

No one else said anything.

Instead, Khyven pulled his tunic up out of his belt and stripped it off.

"Turn around," Slayter said, bringing up a steel plate the same size as his palm. On it was a disk of soft clay twice the size of his normal disks. He quickly carved a symbol onto it. It glowed orange.

So did Khyven's back.

Chapter Thirteen
KHYVEN

hyven couldn't see the symbol that flared on his back, but he didn't have to be a mage to guess it was the same as Slayter's.

"Senji's Eyes," Rhenn murmured.

"What is happening?" Lorelle murmured with a rare crack in her calm.

"What is it?" Khyven asked.

"Another rune." Slayter leaned close, studying it.

"Of course it is," Khyven growled. "What does it mean?"

"I can't ... really say. I've never seen runes exactly like this, but some of it could mean ..."

"There are more than one, then? Like yours?"

"Yes."

Khyven held still, letting Slayter inspect him. "What are they?"

"Well, the first symbol is to camouflage the second. Like mine," Slayter continued. "And the other one is ... I hate to say without further study ..."

"Well say something."

"Wait ..." Slayter murmured.

"Wait what?"

"There are three here. Three runes. I almost missed."

"Three?"

"Well it's hard to read when they're all overlapped like this. Memory, I think. If I had to guess. Perhaps something to do with memory. Perhaps. They are very hard to separate."

"Khyven cannot remember anything before he was ten years old," Lorelle said. "Before he met the Old Man and Nhevaz."

"Well ..." Slayter backed away from Khyven. "I think we can reasonably assume it was Nhevalos who took your memories."

"Why?"

Slayter hesitated, then slowly shook his head, like he wasn't sure of his thoughts. "To make you malleable. To clean your slate so he could write upon it, which clearly he did. The third ... I just don't know. It could be anything—"

"We get the point, Slayter," Rhenn said. "You don't know."

He turned toward her. "Take your tunic off."

"Slayter," Vohn reprimanded.

"Oh! No, I mean—"

"I know what you meant," Rhenn said wryly. She unbuckled her dagger belt and the empty sheath that should have held her sword and put them on the table. Lorelle moved forward to help her with an extra pair of hands to lift her shirt so she could bare her back without baring her front.

Slayter repeated his spell.

Rhenn's back flared with orange light, and Khyven saw the runes this time, though he still didn't know what they meant.

"We're marked," he murmured.

Slayter repeated the process with each of them, including Shalure. Khyven fully expected to find that everyone had a symbol or two carved into their backs.

No one else did. Lorelle was clear, as was Vohn and Shalure.

"I don't understand," Khyven said. "Why us and not them?"

"This is absolutely delicious," Slayter said. He looked happy, if haggard.

Rhenn looked ill as she buckled her weapons back on.

"We know Khyven was being groomed to be a Giant killer," Slayter said. "Nhevalos told Rhenn as much. He was grooming her as well."

"To be a Giant killer?"

"To lead, I would guess," Slayter said. "For whatever is coming. I wouldn't be surprised if reinstating Rhenn as queen was every bit a part of Nhevalos's plan."

"And now you are," Lorelle said.

"Not *now*. We could make the argument that I was the first to be inscribed."

"We could? Why would you be first?" Rhenn asked. "He could have done this to any of us at any time."

"Nhevalos might have grabbed you at any age and inscribed you, then blanked your memory."

"But not you?"

"Well, I don't have the memory rune. Also, I have no blank spots in my memory."

"What do you mean?"

"I mean I remember every minute of my life. And there are no missing spots."

"No one remembers every minute of their lives."

Slayter shrugged.

"You remember *every*thing?" Rhenn asked.

"Not all at once. I'm not thinking about everything I've ever done all at once. But I don't forget things like other people. If I need to remember something from ten years ago, I do. Clearly as if I'm living it again."

Rhenn glanced at Lorelle. She said nothing.

"And I'm saying I have no blank spots in my memory before age two," Slayter said.

"Age two?"

"Age two. So whatever happened to me must have happened before that. For something as traumatic as having a knife or razor carve into my back, I would either certainly remember or, if it had been suppressed, it would have to have been suppressed so emphatically that I'd have a conspicuous blank spot in my memory and likely with a magical signature so large I'd be able to detect it. So I suspect this thing on my back was carved when I was an infant."

Rhenn waved that away. "Enough speculation. What does this mean?"

"Pieces, as I said. Pieces on a board."

"Why not Lorelle?" Rhenn asked. "She's been with me since I was a child. Why isn't she inscribed?"

"I don't know."

"Why not Vohn?"

"I don't know. Perhaps ... according to the *kairoi*, only you and Khyven and me are absolutely necessary."

A cold prickle went up Khyven's spine. "What does that mean? That Lorelle and Vohn and Shalure are expendable?"

"Yes."

Khyven felt a roaring in his ears. He stepped toward Slayter, who swiveled his gaze to him without fear.

"They're not," Khyven growled.

Slayter blinked. "I didn't inscribe the runes."

"Easy Khyven," Rhenn said. "No one is expendable. Slayter, you think Nhevalos did this?"

"I do."

"But you don't know it's Nhevalos," Rhenn said.

"True. It could be another Giant."

"Or another mage."

Slayter pursed his lips. "I don't think so."

"Why?" Rhenn countered. "Why couldn't this be the work of Vamreth somehow? It includes all the right players. We know he was fixated on Khyven. We know he wanted me dead. And he could have been keeping track of you because he didn't trust you."

"I find that highly unlikely."

"Why?"

"Well, first of all, the scars are too old. We were all much younger when this was done to us. But mostly, I doubt a Human could actually accomplish this. The skill required, the knowledge ... Well, I'd be the first to say that I haven't read all the books on magic that exist in Noksonon, but I've read every book on Line Magic in the crown city of Usara, in Wheskone Keep, and in the great library at Triada. A rune or glyph that I cannot recognize is ... rare. This potential Human Line Mage would have to have an education that surpasses my own. And I just spent time talking with a dragon who informed me there are two other languages from which to make runes. I didn't know this. No other mage I've ever met knows this. But Giants would. And these symbols could be from one of those two languages I've never seen. That would certainly mean a Giant."

"But he's not actually controlling us. Not ... telling us what to say and do."

"Not moment to moment," Slayter said. "I don't think he's using mind control on us, if that's what you're implying—though that is a thought we should entertain—but I do believe we are moving in the direction he wants us to go."

"So no matter what we choose, it's what he meant us to choose."

"What he predicted us to choose."

"You're saying he arranged the very landscape around us such that we choose what we normally would, but what's really happening is that we're choosing exactly what he wanted us to choose."

Slayter's face brightened with a big smile. "Say, that is quite well put. Yes. Just so."

Rhenn looked away like she wanted to vomit.

"I think I speak for this entire room when I say that we don't like what you're saying," Khyven said.

"It does make one feel quite needed, though, doesn't it?" Slayter said cheerfully. "A Giant from countless myths has somehow put his finger on us because we've been deemed important to a plan that spans the entire continent, perhaps the entire world, and almost two millennia. It's exciting."

"It's a cage." Rhenn growled.

"Yes. That, too."

"You have a plan of action, then? Or should we just let ourselves be pawns," Khyven asked.

"Oh, of course. I want to chase it down. Seeing Nhevalos's plan is the only place to start. It's the only way we are ever going to know for certain if we can escape it."

"Good," Khyven said.

"There is one other way to look at it, though," Slayter mused.

"That being a puppet is a good thing?"

"That Nhevalos is right."

"What?" Rhenn came to life again, eyes glowing with that ghostly light.

"It is important to consider that what he's orchestrated is best for all of us. For Humans in general, I mean. For Noksonon and Usara. Before we fight our way out of this cage, as you call it, it would be good, I think, to know if fighting out of his cage is a sure way to doom ourselves."

"He's evil ..." Rhenn said lethally, in a low tone, but her words seemed to reverberate throughout the room like she'd shouted them. "If he has pushed us in the direction he wanted us to go, then that means he pushed me toward N'ssag. He wanted me to transform into this ... thing that I am. He put E'maz's head on the chopping block and ..." Rhenn swallowed and turned away for a moment while she struggled to gain control of her emotions. When she turned back to face Slayter, her face was an emotionless mask. "If Nhevalos is what you say, then he dies."

Slayter raised his eyebrows at Rhenn's vehemence.

"Well," he said. "My intention was to chase the answers wherever they might be. I do not want to be a pawn for someone unless I know why."

"Then do it."

He nodded. "Very well. Then I need to go home."

"To Wheskone Keep?" Rhenn asked.

"Yes."

"I'll go with you," Khyven said.

"We'll all go," Lorelle said softly.

"No," Rhenn said.

"No?" Lorelle looked at her.

"Perhaps Slayter is right that the most important thing is to chase down Nhevalos's plan, to see the ... puzzle, as he says." Her lips pressed into a grim line. "But we can't afford to simply address one threat."

Slayter seemed to think about that. Or perhaps he was thinking about a dozen other things that had absolutely nothing to do with what Rhenn had just said. Khyven could rarely predict what Slayter was thinking about.

Vohn nodded in approval. Lorelle looked concerned.

"You don't think Slayter is right," she said.

"I think he could be right. Or perhaps splitting up is exactly what Nhevalos wants us to do. Perhaps we're still dancing to his tune." Rhenn showed her teeth.

Khyven let out a long breath. "I hadn't even thought about that. This is enough to drive a person mad ..."

"I just want the bastard to show his face again," Rhenn said. "And we can hash this out right now."

Slayter cocked his head, but didn't say anything.

"So we can't possibly know what action we should take," Khyven said. "Or at least we can't know if it's serving Nhevalos or not," Khyven said. "We can never know."

"Not never," Slayter mused. "If we see enough of his game, then we can predict as well."

"Here's what I know for certain," Rhenn said. "N'ssag is out there. He finally has what he's always wanted: a never-ending supply of darkness in which to work. All of Noksonon is vulnerable to him. We can't just let him start making bloodsuckers. We have to find him. We have to end him."

"Then we should all stay here," Vohn said. "We can't know Nhevalos's mind, so we stay. We address the threat we know."

"I have to go to Wheskone Keep," Slayter said. "If we are to see the puzzle."

"We said we weren't going to split up again," Vohn said. "We said we weren't going to do that."

"Except now we have to," Slayter said.

"We don't have to! You don't know that going to Wheskone Keep is the right answer. You can't possibly know that. What if splitting us up is exactly what—"

"We have two threats," Rhenn cut them off. "We have the Giants, which is a problem we can barely see. If anyone has a chance of seeing it, it's Slayter. Does anyone disagree with that?"

Vohn pressed his lips together. "That's not the point."

"It is exactly the point. Does anyone disagree that Slayter is best suited for that job, of all of us?"

Vohn crossed his arms and looked angry.

"And if anyone can protect him, it's Khyven," Rhenn said. "Anyone disagree?"

No one said anything. Vohn continued to stew.

"Our second threat is N'ssag. There's no ambiguity there. He has to be found; he has to be destroyed."

Vohn protested, "Rhenn—"

"I am open to suggestions. What is your alternate plan, Vohn? We cannot just sit here and wait for Nhevalos's plan to play out. We cannot just sit here while N'ssag unleashes his bloodsuckers. We have two problems and no time. What do you suggest?"

Vohn looked like he wanted to shout or cry. Or both. But he shook his head bitterly and said nothing.

"Then this is how it's going to be," Rhenn said. "Slayter, you ... do whatever that big brain of yours tells you to do. Khyven, you make sure he doesn't get dead. Lorelle, you and I are going to find out where in the hell N'ssag is, and what he is doing."

"This is a bad idea," Vohn said.

"Every option we have is bad," Rhenn replied. "Right now, enemies dictate the battlefield. We can't keep fighting on their terms."

"I think splitting up makes us more vulnerable," Vohn reiterated.

"Suggestions, Vohn. We can't just freeze up because we're afraid. We cannot just sit here and wait."

Vohn's jaw flexed, but he didn't say anything.

"Khyven's right," Rhenn said. "We go after them. We make them pay."

"Or die in the attempt," Vohn interjected.

Rhenn looked angrily at him, but her voice came out even. "That's right. Or we die in the attempt."

CHAPTER FOURTEEN
KHYVEN

Khyven cinched the pack shut and tied it. The sun lit the edge of the window and the white stones glowed like pearl. He stared at the pack on his and Lorelle's bed, went through a quick mental list and decided he had everything. Rhenn said the kitchen and stable staff would make sure that all the foodstuffs and cooking implements were packed on their horses. Khyven wasn't a seasoned traveler—he'd spent all the days he could remember either at the Old Man's camp learning how to fight or actually fighting for his life in the Night Ring. He knew the rudiments of hunting and cooking, but Rhenn was the accomplished woodswoman. She was giving them everything they'd need, so he wasn't worried. Survival, after all, was what Khyven did best.

The rest, not as much.

He stared back at the pack and, for the third time, decided he was done. All he needed now was to don his weapons and meet Slayter in the stables. He buckled on his weapons belt, which had a quick-draw dagger belt on the right side and two sheaths on the left. One held his normal longsword. The other was empty. The sword that went there sat on a stand on his chest of drawers. The wooden sword from his forty-ninth battle, the one with the Kyolar.

After Khyven's rescue of Shalure from the *shkazat* den, when he'd told Vohn about his attempts at "diplomacy," Vohn had rolled his eyes.

"Beating people up instead of killing them isn't diplomacy," he had said.

"It is for me," Khyven had replied curtly.

Vohn had cocked his head as though thinking. "No one died?"

"Not a single soul."

Vohn had given one of his rare laughs, shook his head, and he hadn't said anything more.

But thereafter, the term "diplomacy" had become a secret joke between them. It became a bridge to the little Shadowvar that reminded Khyven that they were friends when, so often, it was hard to tell. There had even been a moment during one of the queen's councils when Vohn and Khyven had chuckled after Rhenn had said the word "diplomacy."

Rhenn had asked, "Do you two have something to share?"

For perhaps the first time in his life, Vohn hadn't told his queen the truth. Instead, he'd responded by saying, "Khyven has a particular interest in diplomacy these days."

The next day, Vohn had presented Khyven's own wooden sword to him after having—quite cleverly Khyven thought—stolen it from his room. He'd had a leatherworker bind the base of the wooden blade with leather and etch two words onto it in old Usaran runes. Khyven couldn't read them, but Vohn translated. They said:

The Diplomat.

Khyven had proudly displayed it in his room ever since, and he'd determined that wherever his actual sword went, he would also take The Diplomat as a first option to killing.

He didn't know what he was going to face on the road with

Slayter, but perhaps there would be some room for a little bit of diplomacy—

His thoughts scattered as he felt a familiar feeling. The feeling of warmth, of home. That warmth spread through him, calming the beat of his heart and making him feel like everything was going to be all right.

"So that's what you and Vohn were giggling about like milkmaids?" Lorelle asked from the doorway. "He named your sword The Diplomat?"

Their soul-bond warmed him. It always did when she was closer. Without ever taking his eyes from the window's sunrise, he knew exactly where she was, exactly how she was standing. "I'm apprenticing to Vohn for lessons in how to not kill people."

"Sensible."

"Apparently just hacking and slashing isn't the answer to every problem."

"So now you're going to run away from problems instead?" she asked, and he felt her hurt across the distance like a hot wire slowly dragged across his soul.

He still didn't turn to look at her. "I ..."

"Were you going to leave without saying goodbye?"

"I didn't think you wanted to see me."

"There's every chance that neither of us will survive these particular missions."

He turned then, looking into her eyes. Senji, he loved her eyes. He wondered if he would find her so unbelievably beautiful if he didn't have half her soul inside him. He thought he would. It was probable he'd loved her from the moment he'd first seen her, back when he was a different man, a man who hadn't known who he was yet. A selfish man with selfish goals.

He knew exactly who he was now, and his first place was to protect his friends, especially his lover.

He felt the strings that Slayter talked about, those damned marionette strings. The more he thought about them, the more he realized he'd always felt them, but he'd just passed them off as normal.

If he could clip them, for himself and for his family, he had to try.

"You don't want me to go."

"Without saying goodbye?"

"I just ... I know you're angry—"

"Did you think I would let a simple argument stop me from loving you?" she asked.

"I don't know. I've never been in love before."

She gave a wry smile. "Me either."

"If there are rules, you should tell me. This may come as a surprise, but sometimes I don't understand what you're thinking. Or what you want." He gave a half smile, and he was gratified that it drew one from her.

"Shocking."

"I love you," he said abruptly, awkwardly.

Her smile vanished, and suddenly he saw in her eyes the haunted look that had plagued her this past month. "I know," she said. "I ... I know."

"Why didn't you tell me?"

"About the sleeping spell?"

"Yes."

"I wanted to handle it ... I'm ... All right. I'm going to tell you now. Maybe I should have told you before, but ..." She faltered and looked down at her feet.

"Did you think I would judge you for ... I don't know, whatever this is about?"

"This may come as a surprise to you," she mimicked his words. He saw a small smile again and she looked back into his eyes. "But I'm not used to revealing myself to someone else."

"Shocking," he repeated her own word.

"I hear her, Khyven. The Dark. She calls to me, mostly at night. Mostly when I'm here, sleeping with you. So I asked Slayter for a spell because ..."

He waited.

"One night I had a dream that the Dark called to me," she

continued. "And this time I listened. She bade me get up from bed, leave our room, leave the palace, leave the city. And in the dream, I didn't hesitate. I went to the edge of the noktum and stopped there, just short of the grasping tentacles. Right at the edge. And then I woke up. And it wasn't a dream."

"Lorelle ..."

"She had pulled me in some half-sleeping state and brought me almost into her arms. She almost had me and I don't know what that would have meant. Would I have been fine and been able to leave once I woke? Or would I have stayed half-asleep for the rest of my life? I don't know. So I went to Slayter. He thought that somehow, the voice of the Dark could reach me more readily when I'm in that half-sleeping state between dreaming and awake. He told me I could either stay awake all the time, or I had to make sure that I was so deep asleep that her voice couldn't find me. So I made my choice."

"I'm so sorry."

"I'm not angry at you. I'm angry because ... It seems like nothing that was once mine is mine any longer. Not my body. Not my heart." She looked up at him through her lashes. "And now not even my choices."

Khyven's heart twisted. "Then I'll go with you. Maybe Vohn is right. Maybe we shouldn't split up. Maybe Slayter can wait until we—"

She put her finger on his lips, stopping him, and her small half smile returned. She closed her eyes and put her head against his chest, her silky hair tucked perfectly beneath his chin. Her arms slid around his chest, his back, held him tightly.

"Too many maybes," she murmured.

"Slayter isn't always right," he whispered into her hair. "I could go with you."

"Perhaps Vohn is right. Perhaps we should all remain here with what we know, with each other. But the more I think on it, the more that seems a fool's hope. We want to see what we'd rather see. Slayter doesn't do that. He wants to see behind all the secrets of the world."

"That doesn't make him right."

"I don't know much, my love," she murmured. "But I know we are too few. The enemy is too many. And Slayter is smarter than the rest of us combined."

"Lorelle—"

"Answer me this: would you come with me if it meant Usara's fall? Would you stay here if it meant our enemies would slowly close in about us until all we can do is make a valiant last stand?"

"At least I will be with you," he said hoarsely.

She leaned back and looked up at him. "I love you."

He kissed her.

The kiss ended, and she murmured, "You will go where you are most needed. You always do. You cannot help yourself. And Slayter needs you more than I do. He is the only one who has a chance to see in this muddled dark. If he fails …"

She didn't finish the sentence, but only because they both knew what would happen if Slayter failed. If Slayter couldn't figure out how to stop Nhevalos from manipulating them, it really didn't matter what they did.

Tears stood in his eyes.

"I don't want you to go," he whispered.

"How much?"

"What?"

"How much do you want me not to go?"

"How much …?"

"Show me," she murmured. "Show me with every bit of yourself."

"Yes," he said huskily.

"And then go do your duty."

He lifted her easily in his arms, and she kissed him, fingers pushing into his hair. He kicked the door shut. Slayter could wait.

The kingdom, the mage, the Giants … They could just wait a breathless moment for love.

CHAPTER FIFTEEN
SHALURE

The setting sun glowed beneath the western wall of Usara, and the citizens of Rhenn's kingdom moved about their daily activities unaware of what was actually happening. The world they knew was coming to an end, one way or another, and Usara's heroes had gone into the teeth of danger to save them.

And they had forgotten completely about Shalure.

Cloaked and cowled, she lingered in the shadows of the alley across from the *shkazat* den, the same one Khyven had pulled her from months ago. Since that time, she'd gone through Senji's ninth hell, had risen up from the darkness to a flicker of painful light. That light had transformed into hope, and she'd clung to it with both hands.

Shalure was the youngest daughter of a poor country baron. From those less-than-auspicious beginnings, she'd come to the crown city and had almost won herself a title. She had made her way with quick wits and a quick tongue, with the allure of her body.

Her apprenticeship with Slayter had filled her with something new, something other than the pain of her disfigurement, the loss of her dreams, and the twisted hope that she and Khyven might somehow be together. She was learning from the greatest mage currently in the world, and he had said *she* had something to offer. Concentrating all of her time and efforts on her apprenticeship with Slayter had pulled her from those old dreams and away from falling back into that dark *shkazat* pit.

And the others had seemed to accept her. Shalure had finally begun to feel like she belonged somewhere. Even if Vamreth had cast her away, even if Khyven had cast her away, even if the very society she'd known had cast her away, at least she had this new family.

Then Lorelle had turned to her and told her to join the queen's council. The compassionate Luminent had extended her hand and given Shalure exactly what she'd longed for. That final step into the queen's inner circle, the official stamp of approval that she was one of them.

And then ... they had ignored her. They had discussed the catastrophic danger that surrounded them without any input from her, without even noticing she was there. It was as if she was there just to watch. They had made their plans, determined what must be done, and divided into two groups.

Neither of which included her.

Shalure had felt attached to her new family, a thin and fragile line, and in one moment, they'd clipped it. Lorelle's momentary inclusion had only been a scrap of pity. Shalure didn't really belong. They just felt sorry for her that she had nowhere else to go.

Now, Rhenn and Lorelle had vanished into the noktum. Khyven and Slayter had saddled up and ridden north earlier this morning. None had given a second thought to Shalure or where she might assist.

She'd been fooling herself. She wasn't really part of this family. Slayter tolerated her. Lorelle pitied her. Khyven could barely even look at her.

Shalure blinked back tears and realized she'd started walking toward the *shkazat* den. She didn't remember making the choice, but her feet were moving.

If she lost herself in the smoke, she could reach that oblivion where everything wouldn't hurt so much. She could be dead before they returned. She could float away on a painless blue haze until there was nothing at all. They'd never have to think of her again, never have to worry about how uncomfortable she made Khyven and Lorelle, never have to think about where she fit in.

Khyven should never have come for me in the first place, she thought.

She paused before those steps.

Perhaps she hesitated because she knew once she started down, it was the last decision she'd ever make. Once the *shkazat* had hold of her, she'd wouldn't have the strength to break free. There would be no invincible Khyven to come for her this time.

She stopped at the top of the crooked stairs, teetering on the decision to take the next step.

She didn't know how long she stared—two seconds or two hours. But suddenly she had the feeling she wasn't alone.

No noise called her attention, no flash of movement, but all at once she felt like there was another life-force nearby. She broke her gaze from the steps and looked up.

Two curved, white horns hovered in the shadows to her right.

She jolted.

Vohn. She flicked her fingers, the single symbol she'd created to mean his name. She'd made a symbol for each of the queen's group.

He appeared out of the shadows like the darkness was oil and he had risen to the surface.

He looked angry. He had looked angry since Rhenn had made the decision to split the group. "Go on. Make your choice."

Tears welled in her eyes, and she swiped angrily at the air

with her fingers.

And why shouldn't I?

"I can think of many reasons. Clearly you can't. So make your choice and have done with it."

You all left me! You didn't even notice me when you made your plans!

"It's horrible, isn't it? Almost as bad as shouting at the top of your lungs against their stupid plan and then being ignored."

Her fingers flicked so fast she didn't know—or care—if he could even follow them.

They revere you! They look to you for wisdom. They barely tolerate me. Lorelle invites me through pity. Slayter lets me to linger in his laboratory because he can't think of what else to do with the poor mute girl.

Vohn's eyes flashed, and he looked like he was about to yell at her. He didn't. Instead, he pointed at the steps. "Then make your choice."

I have nothing! I have no one!

"Clearly you're not a part of us. Clearly. After all, no one came to pull you out of here once before. No one is here now. So go ahead."

I have nothing!

"You have the attention of one of the greatest Human mages of our age—perhaps of all time. You have magic!"

Slayter barely notices me, Vohn. I am like a stray dog he can't bring himself to kick out of his laboratory.

"You think Slayter teaches you through pity?" Vohn retorted. "Slayter ignores things that don't matter. He has half a dozen apprentices who never see him because, in his mind, they are useless. He sees their talent at such a low level he thinks they're a waste of his time—and these are the best mages in Usara. At the queen's council, he's barely paying attention, and these are the discussions Rhenn considers vitally important. Only items that excite his vast imagination get his full attention. Like saving the world. Like you."

She just stared at him.

"If you cannot calculate the gravity of that, then you're a fool and you don't deserve to apprentice to him. Go smoke your shkazat."

Tears streaked down her cheeks.

They just left me ... She moved her fingers slowly, tragically. *They walked right past me like I wasn't there.*

"They left me, too, but for all the right reasons. The kingdom is in danger. Perhaps the entire world. Our friends are the only ones who might save it. And they left us behind with their most sacred trust. We must safeguard the kingdom while they are away." He pointed both fingers at the ground. "It is our duty to ensure they have something to come back to."

She blinked.

"You have to grow up, Shalure," he continued. "You have to do it now. You've been hurt, yes, but we have all been hurt. You have to look past your pain. You have to see where you can be of use, not where others can make your burden easier. They turned their backs to us not because we're unimportant, but because they trust us. It's our job to protect those backs."

Shalure swallowed. She felt she should say something, but her fingers felt numb.

"It's our friends' job to save us. And it's *our* job to save *them*," Vohn said.

Shalure looked at the crooked steps and the short, recessed door, then back at Vohn.

He reached out his hand. "I have a kingdom to run. I can't do it alone. Will you help me?"

His hand was like a line tossed over the rail of a ship to save a drowning woman, and she grasped it. That hope she'd dared to glimpse swelled into a light. Vohn had come here for her. He'd come here because he needed her. They all needed her.

Thank you, she signed to him.

"Save your death for later. I promise you'll have plenty of opportunities to sacrifice yourself in the days to come. Use it then. Save it for something good."

He turned and started up the alley in the direction of the palace. She hurried to catch up, signed quickly to him.

You're right.

"Of course I'm right," he said grumpily. "It would be nice if people noticed for a change."

Chapter Sixteen
KHYVEN

Khyven's thoughts lingered on Lorelle those first couple of days that he and Slayter rode northward to the mage's ancestral home. Khyven simply couldn't shake the feeling it was the last time he'd ever see her. It threw him into turmoil.

Love, family, friends were not simple. They were ridiculously complicated, and from what he could tell, unlike fighting in the Night Ring, there was no way to know if he was winning.

In the Night Ring, the winner was the last one standing. Simple. Straightforward.

Khyven longed for a fight right about now.

His stallion, as though sensing his mood, turned and tried to bite him.

Khyven was getting pretty practiced at dodging, but he'd been thinking deeply about Lorelle—how he loved the way her newly black hair slid through his fingers. He almost missed the stallion's subtle signal—the slight turn of the head such that he could get an eyeball on Khyven—until it was too late.

Khyven jerked, narrowly saving his foot from the attack.

The stallion's actual name was Sunrise, ostensibly because of the golden diamond on his black coat above his right shoulder, but actually because some glowy-eyed duchess's daughter had named him "Sunrise" before she knew what kind of temperament he really had. He'd taken a chunk out of her arm for that oversight.

The girl he'd initially belonged to had wanted a pretty pony, and Khyven was pretty sure that Sunrise hated everything pretty. Or weak. Or anything standing in front of him. Or anyone riding on him. Or ... All right, pretty much everything.

Khyven and the horse had found each other because of their mutually pugnacious personalities. After Rhenn had returned from Daemanon, the kingdom had settled down—relatively speaking—and Khyven had gotten to work on a weakness he'd been meaning to address for some time: horseback riding.

He'd spent the last few months trying to master it. But the painful truth was: he was just naturally bad at it.

At first, he'd sought help from Lorelle. That had been a disaster. Lorelle was a fantastic rider, which Khyven thought would make her the perfect instructor. That turned out to be a logic flaw.

Lorelle had amazing strength, even for a normal Human, but she also weighed next to nothing. This meant she could stick to the back of an unruly horse like a patch of glue.

Apparently empathy was even more important than a high strength-to-body ratio, and Lorelle had empathy in spades also. She could whisper to a horse almost as if speaking their secret language. If one of the brutes was agitated, she instinctively knew how to coax them into compliance.

So she kept telling Khyven to do what *she* would do, which did not help him at all. Khyven was not empathetic. His natural inclination when a horse fought him was to fight back.

Over the course of their two short days of training, Lorelle had grown more and more frustrated and Khyven had grown murderous. Her inability to understand his poor performance, combined with his quick temper, had served up a spectacular failure.

By the end, they'd wanted to stick daggers into each other. Lorelle had left the stables shaking her head and telling him he should invest in expensive walking boots instead of a horse.

Thank Senji Rhenn had been watching that last lesson—it had been at night as Lorelle had thought perhaps if Khyven couldn't entirely see, he'd somehow learn to trust his horse. Khyven had almost broken his neck that time.

With a wry smile, Rhenn had stepped in as Khyven's instructor. With an easygoing sense of humor that he'd not seen since she'd returned, she set to work.

"You are a predator," Rhenn had said. "And horses can sense that. It's your natural state to fight. You stress the gentle ones."

"Lorelle said I needed to start with an easy horse that wouldn't try to throw me."

"She's right. Or she would be, if you were a normal person. Most people probably can't kill a horse with their bare hands. You probably could. Or at least you'd think you could, and the horse will pick up on that. I'm thinking you need a horse that's going to dish back a little. You need something to fight against."

"Whatever ..." He'd grunted.

"You'll see. Let's take a look at the more spirited of your options." She had led him through the stables to the furthest corner. "This is where we keep the horses for higher level riders. I'm thinking Imbri would be a good start for you. She doesn't take a lot of guff from her riders. She'll try to bite you, probably, but if you're prepared—if you stop her when she does—she'll start to respect you. She'll give you something to push back against, but she's also sensible. She won't try to buck you. Most likely."

But by then Khyven had been angry, spoiling for a fight. He'd been angry at Lorelle for yelling at him, angry at Rhenn for treating him like a child. Mostly he'd been angry at himself for being so damned useless at this. He wasn't used to that.

So when they had passed the stall where a giant destrier glared down at Khyven, he had stopped.

"This one," he'd said.

Rhenn had stopped, eyebrows up as she regarded the horse, then she'd laughed. "No."

"No?"

"That's Sunrise."

"So?"

"That horse would be difficult for *me* to master."

"She's the one."

Sunrise had snorted and torn a chunk of wood from the gate.

"Not a she," Rhenn had said. "That's a stallion, Khyven. And he's chock full of fight."

"You said I needed a horse full of fight."

"I said you needed a horse that would dish back a little. Sunrise will try to kill you. His last owner is missing a piece of her arm."

Khyven had grinned like a skull, mirroring the horse's bared teeth. "Let's do this."

Rhenn had crossed her arms and donned a smug smile. "This will be an amusing ten seconds."

Rhenn had set about saddling Sunrise—which had been no small feat.

Sunrise and Khyven had spent the next weeks beating each other up. At the end of the first week, Khyven had renamed him Hellface.

After the first few lessons, after watching them together, Rhenn had been surprised. She had soon grudgingly admitted they might be made for each other. They did, in fact, share a love of the fight, and Rhenn had done her best to guide Khyven's responses such that he might build a rapport with the horse.

Step by step, Khyven and Hellface had found their way to an uneasy sort of truce, and Khyven could actually—mostly—get Hellface from point A to point B.

So when Hellface tried to bite him, Khyven barely got clear, then yanked the reins—Rhenn had eventually gotten him to stop kicking at the horse's face in retaliation and to use the reins. Hellface swung his head around to try the other side. Khyven yanked the reins the other way. Hellface resisted and Khyven was going to deliver a kick this time. The horse sidestepped toward the edge of the road as it focused on Khyven, preparing to dodge the boot and—

Hellface stopped, his head swung to the front and rose up as though he'd heard something. At that same moment, Khyven saw the blue wind flicker to life. It whispered through the humps of grass to the left and right of the road ahead.

Brigands.

It was a cunning trap. That stretch of road seemed about as safe as a road ever seems. A good place to catch people off their guard. The trees on either side of the road were at least a hundred paces away. Green and brown long grass had fallen over in humps and gave the field the feel of ocean swells.

But the bandits clearly knew the area. They'd prepared and hidden beneath artificial humps of grass. Once upon a time, Khyven would only have sensed them when their attacks had already begun.

But his power was changing.

He'd felt it in Daemanon, and more and more, Khyven would suddenly get an uncomfortable "sense" that something was going to go wrong, and then it would.

"Slayter," Khyven called.

The mage had been looking up at the clouds for some reason. It was impossible to tell what would grab Slayter's attention moment to moment, or why. But during this moment, it was the clouds.

As often as Slayter was distracted, Khyven would have thought the man a horrible horseman, but he was actually competent, certainly better at it than Khyven. Perhaps it was because Slayter funneled no emotion toward his mount, one way or the other. The horse seemed content to just plod along unless otherwise instructed. Slayter seemed content to let her.

The mage broke away from his reverie instantly, which was unusual. Usually it took at least two times calling his name to get him to focus. He looked a question at Khyven.

"Trouble," Khyven said softly. "About twenty feet ahead, on both sides."

Slayter looked down the road, tried to spot anything. He couldn't. "Really?"

"Pretty sure," Khyven said sarcastically.

The mage caught the tone and his full focus turned to Khyven. "Oh! Is this an aspect of your magic?"

"Maybe."

"You didn't just smell something?"

"Smell something?"

"Like a wolf. Don't fighters sometimes just smell opponents?"

"*Smell* opponents? No!"

"No?"

"No."

"It seems like you would."

"Why would it seem—" Khyven slashed a hand through the air. Slayter could suck a person into a dumb conversation quicker than anyone Khyven knew. "Slayter, there are bad men up ahead who, I think, want to kill us and take our valuables."

"But you sensed them through *magic*." As though that was the only important thing. Not that they might die.

Khyven still couldn't decide if Slayter was the bravest man he'd ever met, or if he was just stupid about the possibility of physical harm. "Yes. I think it's the magic."

Slayter let out a whoosh of a breath. "I thought you said you only saw the wind when you were in imminent danger, split seconds away."

"That was ... Well, it was that way. Now it's not."

"Well that's new. That's wholly new."

"Look, can we concentrate on the danger?"

"Of course. It's just that this is truly exciting! Your magic—

an unconscious magic, I might add—is getting stronger all by itself. Don't you find that fascinating? Why would it have a mechanism like that? Most mages have to work and study and experiment to advance their magic. For you, it's just naturally progressing. I don't understand that. It's a delicious mystery. It must be related to the symbol on your back that I can't decode. A rune that evolves ..." Slayter's eyes widened as he looked vaguely in the distance. "The magic is designed to increase naturally. Wouldn't that be—"

Five humps of grass suddenly burst upward on either side of the road; two on the left and three on the right. Nearly a dozen men charged them.

Four of them had crossbows, and they leveled the weapons: two on Slayter and two on Khyven.

The blue wind swirled, and the coming bolts appeared in Khyven's vision as thin blue spears. Instinctively, he yanked on Hellfire's reins. The blue spears lanced out—

Then fizzled and vanished.

Orange light flared from Slayter's raised fist. Crumbles of clay tumbled down his pale and skinny arm, as his wide sleeve slid down.

The four crossbow bolts hit an invisible barrier that hadn't been there a moment ago. As they snapped against Slayter's wall, each impact was marked by an orange flash, like they'd each decided to explode before falling to the ground.

The brigands looked surprised, but they only hesitated a moment. Seven of them brandished rusty swords, scrambled over the hummocks, and surged onto the raised road.

Hellface screamed and lunged, ripping the reins from Khyven's grasp. He clung desperately to the black-and-gold mane and managed to stay aboard. He had been about to dismount, but clearly Hellface wasn't going to be left out of the combat.

The horse charged into the midst of the attackers. Three of them yelped and threw themselves out of the way, tumbling down into the tall grass again. One swung at Hellface but missed. Two stepped back with mouths the shape of giant Os.

The final actually stood his ground, raised his sword—

And got two hooves in the chest as Hellface reared up.

Which was also the end of Khyven's precarious perch. He tumbled off backward.

Twisting in mid-air, he landed on his feet. For a breathless instant, no blue wind struck out at him, and he assessed the fighting field.

Three men stood on the road, all within sword range. But they were stunned by Hellface's ridiculously ferocious attack. Their faces looked like each one was thinking, "What kind of horse does that?"

Three of the attackers had fallen back and would take a moment to get back into the fight. The four who had shot crossbows had split objectives. Two of them were reloading and two threw down their crossbows and drew daggers. They leapt over the grass toward the road.

"Time for some diplomacy." Khyven drew the wooden sword and strode toward his opponents.

That got them moving. Hellface was still working on the brigand who had dared swing at him. That brigand wouldn't be getting up again.

Three other brigands turned from the ferocious horse toward Khyven. He supposed they figured one man on foot was better than a crazy, bloodthirsty horse.

The bandits roared and charged, using the tried-and-true strategy of trying to spook their opponent with noise. It was a reliable tactic. Khyven had used it himself time and again.

Blue spears flew at him, but he ignored them. Ever since he had learned that part of his fighting prowess came from magic, he'd felt it was cheating. Especially against foes like this. So he tried to ignore the blue wind and just focus on the men.

The three came for him at roughly the same time, but they weren't working in concert. Khyven had fought teams who'd trained together, who knew how to exploit a single fighter's weaknesses....

These three looked like they were stumbling across a floor thick with honey.

Khyven surged forward with all his speed and slid in close to the first attacker. The man's loud battle cry became a surprised "*quirp!*" as he realized Khyven was suddenly in his face.

The man's swing was strong, but he'd gauged for an opponent three feet away. The strike went laughably wide. Khyven elbowed him in the throat, spun past and lunged the second bandit while swinging backward at the first, putting all the speed of his momentum into The Diplomat. He caught the choking man behind the ear with the tip of the wooden blade. There was a dull thud as wood hit bone.

"Vingy!" The second brigand, who was now in perfect sword range, shouted in dismay as the choking man dropped like a stone. The second brigand raised his blade overhead in a powerful strike that would surely have cleaved Khyven in two ...

When it arrived. Sometime next week.

Khyven poked him in the groin with The Diplomat.

The man huffed like his throat was a rusty pipe. His sword spun from nerveless fingers, flew past Khyven's right shoulder, and clattered on the dirt. The man fell to his knees, eyes bulging as he grappled with the family jewels.

Then the third brigand was there, in the fight. His face was grimly focused, all business. Khyven could tell the man had calculated his swing, a good horizontal slash. When facing an opponent like Khyven, the horizontal slash was a good catch-all. Clearly the third brigand had talent. The strike was well aimed, though a little high. The bandit couldn't be blamed for that, though. Most fighters Khyven's size were big and slow. Once committed, a big fighter usually couldn't renegotiate his bulk easily. Usually.

More than one opponent had died thinking this about Khyven.

He dropped to his knees so fast his opponent was still staring where Khyven had been when the sword whipped by Khyven's head, so close it clipped a lock of hair.

Khyven brought The Diplomat straight up from the ground, connected with the bandit's chin which was, unfortunately for the man, slightly open.

His jaw clacked so loudly it sounded like it had broken. The man's eyes rolled up into his head, and he slumped to the road like someone had pulled the bones from his body.

Khyven turned to face the next attack.

Two more crossbow bolts flamed on Slayter's magical wall. The mage sat astride his strangely calm horse and was lecturing the brigands like this was a magic lesson.

"... called Falaroy's web," Slayter said. "It means anything moving quickly toward me will burn up. So if you're going to attack me successfully, you should probably move slowly."

Hellface still stomped upon the mutilated corpse of the man who had tried to stab him. Khyven winced. Damn. Well, Vohn couldn't blame Khyven for that. *He* hadn't killed anyone today.

The three who had fallen off the road at Hellface's initial assault climbed back up. The two crossbowmen who had dropped their crossbows and drawn daggers were close behind.

Hellface screamed again, still stomping. Khyven was going to have to check with Rhenn. That did not seem like normal behavior for a horse.

"This might be a good time to run," Khyven said to the remaining brigands.

"We outnumber you two to one," the closest swordsman, who appeared to be the leader, replied.

"And thirty seconds ago you outnumbered us three to one." Khyven spun The Diplomat in a tight circle to his right and moved toward the men. "Imagine thirty seconds from now."

The leader hesitated. Good. He wasn't as stupid as he looked.

"Who are you?" the leader said.

"My name is Khyven."

The brigand's face drained of color. "Khyven the Unkillable? *You're* Khyven the Unkillable?"

"I ..." That took Khyven by surprise. In the crown city, yes, he was quite well known. But that's where the Night Ring was located. Somehow he didn't think his renown would have moved beyond the city walls. "Well, yes."

The leader swallowed hard. He motioned for his men to back away, and now he looked at Slayter in an entirely new light. His gaze lingered on the robes, the red hair.

"That's the queen's mage? Slayter Wheskone?"

Slayter blinked at that. "You know me?"

The man's expression darkened. "Oh, I recognize you, my lord. Everyone in the Wheskone Duchy knows who you are and what you did."

Slayter blinked again, confused.

The leader spat at the ground beneath Slayter's horse, then all of them ran for the trees, leaving their dead man behind.

"Should I get them?" Khyven asked. Part of him felt he should chase them into the woods, which would surely be rife with more traps and possibly more brigands. But that would be the only way to know what the man had meant by his last comment.

Slayter didn't answer, and now the bandits were almost too far away to bother.

"Slayter—"

"No," Slayter said softly. "Do not chase them."

"What did he mean? What did you do?"

"That is the relevant question," Slayter said. "It could be so many things I could only hazard a guess. I haven't been home in years."

"Chasing them, catching at least one of them, may be the only way we'll find out what he meant by that."

Slayter glanced away from the woods and up the road. "I suspect if we continue on our path, we'll find out soon enough."

Khyven peered at the road. "What?"

"If a band of roadside would-be thieves believe I did something wrong, I'm sure they aren't the only ones. Wheskone Keep will hold the answer to this little riddle, as well as the answers to many more, I suspect."

"Ah. Fair enough."

Hellface finally stopped stomping the dead bandit and looked toward where the others were just now disappearing into the woods. He snorted emphatically.

"Yes. Well done." Khyven took a step toward Hellface, who glared at him. His hooves were bloody.

"We should bury him," Slayter said.

Keeping half an eye on Hellface, Khyven glanced at the bandit, then shook his head. "No."

"No?"

"His friends are coming back for him. Let them tend to it."

"They are coming back?"

"Either as soon as we leave or in force if we don't, I suspect."

"Ah."

"There isn't any point in lingering."

Unless, of course, Khyven couldn't get back on his horse. He approached slowly, like he didn't have any specific goal in mind, but Hellface watched him. Khyven reached out for the reins, and Hellface went for his hand. Teeth clacked on air as Khyven's reflexes saved him once again.

"Fine. We do it that way," Khyven said.

Hellface snorted, shifting his rump away so he was facing Khyven, but Khyven was prepared for that. He moved swiftly to the horse's side. Hellface snorted violently and reared his head, trying to come down on Khyven to get another bite. Khyven roared back, palm-fisted the horse's incoming head with one hand and grabbed the reins with the other.

He yanked the reins to the left and grabbed the saddle with his right. The horse whinnied, and Khyven half-leapt, half-hauled himself up. Hellface reared.

"Do your worst!" Khyven growled, yanking brutally on the reins and bringing the horse's head tight around to the left as he clung to the saddle. "But we are moving on."

Hellface bucked, but with his head pulled sideways, it didn't have the same normally devastating effect. Khyven hung on. The destrier screamed his frustration and tried to bite Khyven's foot. Khyven hauled on the reins to the right. Hellface straightened out, seemed about to swing around to take a bite at the other side, but didn't.

He stood stock still, then shook his head.

Khyven eased up on the reins, and the horse didn't try to buck him or bite him.

"Are we ready now?"

Hellface snorted, stamped a hoof.

"All right then."

"Your horse doesn't seem to like you," Slayter said.

"How can you tell?"

"Well he just tried to bite you. He's tried several times."

"Has he?"

"Perhaps you should choose a different horse."

"Undoubtedly."

"Undoubtedly?"

"Without doubt," Khyven said.

Slayter blinked, then narrowed his eyes. "Ah. You *want* him to fight you."

"I don't, actually, but this seems to work all right."

"To be in a constant fight?"

"He *did* protect us from one of the bandits."

"I don't know that I would categorize that as protection."

"Can we go now?"

"If you're done with your equestrian display."

"I'm done."

Slayter turned his mount up the road. "It's all so exciting. I wonder what lies up ahead ..."

Khyven followed, and they left the dead man behind.

Chapter Seventeen
LORELLE

The cloak could have taken them anywhere in the noktum, could have taken them straight back to Nox Arvak, but Lorelle didn't want that. She was terrified what would happen the moment she closed her eyes in the noktum, the moment she slept, so she took Rhenn and herself only a short distance away to start. They returned to their rebel camp.

Lorelle expected Rhenn to object, but her friend seemed to take it in stride. Perhaps she, too, knew they needed a moment of preparation before plunging into the Great Noktum.

"Here, huh?" Rhenn asked, looking around the place that had been her tiny kingdom before she'd regained Usara.

"I miss this place sometimes," Lorelle said. "What we did. How we were."

Rhenn sighed. The entire glade had been reclaimed by the noktum after they'd removed the raven totems. Only a few short months ago, they'd have needed to use their Amulets of Noksonon to even see in this place, but now they could both see in the dark. Lorelle could actually feel the Dark flowing through her. In a very real way, Lorelle belonged here more than she did in the world of sunlight. And Rhenn ...

"I've forced myself not to think about this place," Rhenn said.

Lorelle nodded, then led her to the slope where they would sometimes sit and watch the rebel camp go about its business, where they would talk about the next steps to reclaim Rhenn's kingdom, to exact their revenge on Vamreth.

The tents were all in heaps now, canvas torn. The boxes and barrels of supplies had long ago been ripped apart and strewn about by hungry creatures of the noktum.

Lorelle sat down, put her feet together and her hands around her knees just like that day she'd told Khyven they would never be together. Right before the war. Right before he'd betrayed them all.

"This seems like a lifetime ago."

"Two lifetimes," Rhenn murmured. "If you count both of us."

"We have changed."

Rhenn let out a rueful laugh. "To say the least."

They stayed that way for a long while, Rhenn standing, Lorelle sitting, both silent. They used to do this a lot, back before Rhenn's rebel army, back before this place when they'd been girls, foraging—and later hunting—for food in the forest. Almost every night for that first half a year, they had ended the day just like this. Lorelle sitting. Rhenn standing like she was looking into the future. And they would remain silent. They would just be with each other and just be silent.

"Was this for reminiscing?" Rhenn asked.

"Not only."

"You're worried."

Lorelle glanced up at her.

"I hear things," Rhenn said.

"Oh?"

"You're concerned about something enough to ask Slayter

for a potion that knocks you out," Rhenn said.

"Yes."

"The Dark," Rhenn murmured. "It's been calling you."

"Yes."

"It's been calling to me, too."

"I know."

A small smile curled the side of Rhenn's mouth. "Not sure why we hide things from each other."

"Perhaps we're not hiding."

"Are we just busy, then?"

Lorelle let out a breath. "I thought our lives were full of danger before. I thought once we fought the war, it would be over. I thought I could spend lazy days reading books in the library."

"You and books." Rhenn rolled her eyes. "You and Slayter should get a room."

"If we did, he'd only want to read." She smiled.

"I suppose I thought we could relax also. Of a sort. I thought I would have the busy life of a monarch, but dealing with … normal concerns."

"Normal … The strangeness only got worse," Lorelle said. "Vamreth seems an insignificant problem now compared to Nox and bloodsuckers."

"Dragons and Giants."

"It seems beyond us, doesn't it? Why are we put at this crux point? How can we possibly hope to stop these kinds of things?"

"Mmmm."

"You think we can."

"I think anything is possible. I've … seen it."

"In Daemanon?"

"Yes. And here. And so have you."

"Have I?"

"Tell me Khyven doesn't scare you a little, the things he can do."

"If he wasn't on our side, I suppose he would. His magic barely even makes sense to me. It was like he was designed to …

win."

"That's what Slayter thinks. A magic made to allow for the impossible. A victory against anything."

"Giantkiller."

"Yes."

"Could Slayter recreate it? Wouldn't it be nice if we all had that?"

Rhenn paused, and Lorelle felt what her friend was thinking like a squeeze on her heart. She was thinking that if she'd had Khyven's power, she wouldn't be a bloodsucker right now. And that handsome blacksmith she'd met, E'maz, would still be alive. It was what Rhenn was almost always thinking about when she didn't have other things to do: the necromancer, N'ssag. Regret. Revenge.

Lorelle wanted to apologize, but even when she knew what Rhenn was thinking, sometimes it was better to pretend she didn't. Better not to invade Rhenn's privacy unless she asked.

"Slayter doesn't know what type of magic it is," Rhenn finally said. "Land Magic or Lore Magic. Or perhaps both. He said he couldn't even consider recreating it until he understood it, and it has been one of the most elusive problems he's ever tackled."

"Elusive for Slayter." Lorelle shook her head. "That's a level over my head. Have you ever seen anything stump him?"

"Not like this. The man undermined Vamreth's rule and gave us the victory. No, I've never seen anything confound him for this long."

"It's two streams? Is he sure of that?"

"No, but it's possible."

"Then could he even accomplish that, even if he did know how it was constructed? Slayter can only do Line Magic, right? Humans can't wield more than one stream of magic, right? Only Giants can do that."

"This isn't my field, but I think Line Magic touches a little bit of all the other streams. And it's got to be Line Magic that's been carved into the three of us: Slayter, Khyven, and me."

"So it's possible Khyven's power comes from the symbol on his back. That it isn't necessarily because of his Giant's blood?" Rhenn raised her hands, palms up. "I don't know. Khyven could be a one in a million fluke of birth, born with powers that could destroy Giants. Or he could be Nhevalos's construct."

Lorelle shook her head. "You don't think that."

"I don't want to think that, but this game Nhevalos is playing is far more complicated than we can know. Could he have built Khyven. Yes. Did he? I don't know. I don't think so." Rhenn paused.

Lorelle waited. She could tell when her friend wanted to say something, so she waited. Lorelle was good at waiting.

"When I was in Daemanon, I tried to kill Nhevalos," Rhenn finally murmured.

"You did?"

"Several times. I failed every time. I'd never felt that helpless against anyone, not since I was a child and Vamreth murdered everyone I loved except you. I've certainly never felt that helpless since I was an adult. I tried brute force. He knocked me aside. I tried speed and surprise. He was faster than me. I tried an elaborate scheme to gain his trust and then betray him. He saw through it. In the end, I only felt more helpless because I saw just how much ... better he was than me." The muscles in her jaw worked. "I hated that. By Senji, I hated that so much. It was why I did something so stupid as to run in to N'ssag's open arms. I despaired. I couldn't see any way out. I became ..." She looked down at herself, then over at Lorelle. "I became this because I fell into hopelessness."

"N'ssag did this to you, Rhenn. You didn't do it to yourself."

Rhenn shook her head. "You're missing my point. Nhevalos sees what people will do, knows what people will do. Then he nudges them into the wild river of their own passion, and they are swept away. Except he knows where the river will go. Nhevalos had the power to change me into this ..." She gestured at herself. "Anytime he wanted. But he didn't. He created a pampered prison instead, made it so unbearable that I would run, that I would make the decisions that would take me exactly where he wanted me to go. So do I think he made Khyven? No. I think he nudged Khyven into a river, and Khyven's passions took him the rest of the way."

Lorelle thought about that, and waited. Rhenn wasn't finished.

"Do you remember what he said?" Rhenn murmured, more to herself than to Lorelle, as though Rhenn was still trying to understand something she'd been turning over and over in her mind for a very long time.

"What Khyven said?"

Rhenn shook her head. "No. Nhevalos. When he froze us, took me from my own castle."

Lorelle had been frozen in helplessness as Nhevalos picked up her best friend and took her beyond reach. Yes, she remembered. She remembered every single word. "Yes. He said, 'He lived, and that means things will move quickly now.'" Lorelle had been so angry about that at the time. She'd seen Khyven's presence as the reason her best friend was gone.

"Yes. 'He lived. Things will move quickly now,'" she repeated in a monotone as though she'd said it a thousand times over in her head.

Then Lorelle saw what Rhenn was getting at. "He didn't know Khyven was going to live. He was surprised."

"I don't know if surprised is the right word, but yes. He didn't know. That means Nhevalos doesn't see every end. Maybe all he sees are possibilities. Maybe he's like a planter who plants seeds everywhere, hoping some will grow. But they have to grow on their own. If he wanted a slave ... he could have made Khyven a slave. For some reason, us choosing our own destiny—even if it's a destiny he's already seen—is important to him. If having slaves was all he needed, he'd make slaves of us all."

"You think he could?"

"That's what Giants did, once upon a time, isn't it? I've been listening to Slayter, even reading some of the histories he's unearthed. Our people were all slaves thousands of years ago. Humans did all the work to support Giant society. So did Luminents, Shadowvar, all of us. They used us like tools. They ... altered us, did experiments upon us."

Lorelle nodded. "Zaith told me about how the Nox were made, and the Luminents."

"The Shadowvar, the Taur-Els, the Brightlings. All of them. But that's not what Nhevalos is doing. He could make our decisions for us, but he doesn't. He wants us to make our own choices."

"But you're saying we aren't making those choices. Not really. He's manipulating us, just from a much further distance?"

Rhenn shook her head. "I thought I was making my own choices. I thought I was throwing his agenda in his teeth, but Nhevalos got what he wanted in the end."

"You said he wanted you as some kind of brood mare, to make a baby who was another Greatblood like Khyven. He didn't succeed in that—"

"I'm pregnant."

Lorelle stopped with her mouth open. All the warmth drained from her. "Oh Rhenn ..."

"I didn't even think about it. With all the changes I've been through, I didn't even think about it. I've not been bleeding each month. I didn't think to question it because I also can't face the sunlight. What was missing a bleeding cycle compared to that? So much about me has changed that I didn't stop to think about all the other things that had not changed. I am the same in almost all ways. My blood is warm. I get tired if I haven't ... fed. I need to rest. My mind thinks the same as it used to. I remember things the same. I feel things the same. Everything works the same except that I can see in the dark, have increased strength, and that my skin, muscles, and bones explode in sunlight. And, of course, how I feed."

Lorelle stood up, moved to her friend and took her hand. "The baby ... It's what Nhevalos ... I mean, is it ..."

"Is it A'vendyr's?" She shook her head. "No. It's E'maz's."

"Then you did stop his plan."

"That's what I thought until Slayter's little speech. Once the arrows of his honesty stuck, I remembered something E'maz said during one of the blessed moments I lay in his arms. I idly asked him how he became a blacksmith, and he told me. He said his mother and father had been merchants, ferrying goods back and forth across all the duchies and baronies in the area of Saritu'e'Mere until they settled in V'endann. I had barely been listening, more occupied with the sound of his voice, the rumble of his chest against my cheek."

Lorelle's throat tightened, almost like she could feel what was coming.

"He said his grandparents were cast out of Pelinon."

"What's Pelinon?"

"The seat of power in Daemanon. It's like the crown city of Usara, except for almost the entire continent. Not a kingdom. An empire."

Lorelle squeezed Rhenn's hand.

"E'maz's grandparents were royalty," Rhenn whispered. "Far more powerful than A'vendyr and his backwater barony. They were one of the Great Families. That's what E'maz called them. They were disgraced and cast out. But their heritage, their blood ..."

"Oh no."

"So you see? Slayter was right, damn him. Nhevalos pushed me toward A'vendyr knowing I would rebel. And somehow, he knew I would run straight to E'maz. Somehow he knew that."

"How is that even possible for him to know?"

Rhenn let out a breath through her nose. "Because I'm pregnant, Lorelle. Because the baby is a hybrid of royal blood. Mine and E'maz's, an heir to one of the great families of Daemanon. Because that is exactly what he wanted."

Lorelle's mind was alive with questions. They were like worms trying to crawl out of a bucket. Could an undead creature ... Could Rhenn, as she was, even have a baby? What would happen to that child? What was happening to it right now inside her, being sustained on blood and Life Magic? What would it ... be? Should it even be allowed to be born?

But Rhenn didn't need those kinds of questions. Those were the kinds of questions Slayter would ask, and Rhenn didn't need Slayter right now. She needed her best friend.

"This is going to be a dangerous mission, Rhenn. Are you sure you should go ..." Lorelle groped for the right words. "You have two lives to think about now."

"Believe me, I've considered everything. Over and over. I can't decide whether I should be rabidly protective of this new life inside me or ... Or if I should end it."

"Rhenn—"

"No." She shook her head. "If Slayter is right—and I want to believe he is—then this baby is exactly what Nhevalos wants. Doesn't that mean I would foul his plans if I aborted it? Or does it mean I should protect it? If I ever had control of something—if I could ever undo what Nhevalos wants done—it would be by destroying this life inside me."

"Rhenn, I didn't mean—"

"Yes you did. I know you were thinking it because I've been thinking it. It's an important question, and I have to answer it as a queen, not as a mother."

"Killing the baby isn't the answer," Lorelle insisted.

"Nhevalos is relying on my humanity, on my motherly instincts, to care for this child. The unpredictable response is to destroy it."

Lorelle didn't say anything.

"But there's a more important question. Really, it's the only question that matters."

"What?"

"Is Nhevalos on our side? Is he actually fighting on our behalf? Should we be grateful for his interference?"

Lorelle's ire flared. "He *stole* you! He plucked you from your home, imprisoned you, and then tossed you into the arms of a man who planned to murder you. And N'ssag ... He ..." Lorelle's throat tightened and she couldn't finish the sentence.

"Yes, he did."

"Nhevalos manipulated Khyven, threw him to the wolves in the Night Ring."

"Yes, he did. But ..."

"But what? Is there a 'but' that could justify this? Either of you could have died."

"Nhevalos is a bastard. If you're looking at it from a Human perspective, he's a horror."

"How else is there to look at it?"

"As a Giant."

Lorelle didn't say anything.

"The scant histories I could find about the Human-Giant War said his people call him The Betrayer. They hate him. Nhevalos tried in conversation after conversation to convince me that he was helping us, that I needed to help him help us."

"That was all part of his deception to shove you toward N'ssag."

"Yes, but I'm beginning to think Nhevalos never does just one thing at once. I think ... he was telling the truth. I think he is trying to win an unfathomable game against unfathomable opponents. Yes, he's using us, but ..."

"But what?"

"What if it is to save our lives? Well, not our lives, but the lives of everyone else. What if we are the sacrifices for a world that is still determined by what we want, and not a slave world ruled by the Giants?"

Lorelle reeled with the notion that Rhenn, after everything that had happened to her, was considering simply capitulating to Nhevalos's desires.

Rhenn heaved a heavy sigh. "Regardless, I'm not killing the baby. I can't. I think doing that would destroy me. In a certain way, it's Nhevalos's baby. But in all ways, it's E'maz's, too. The last bit I have of him. I can't destroy it. And Nhevalos probably knew that. But I'm going on this mission. If Nhevalos can move events to his whim, then he can move them for me. If he wants this baby to survive, let him show his face. Let him protect it.

Maybe that will give us some kind of hand on the rudder of this crazy ship. We're going to find out just how important I—and the baby—are to him."

"Then I support you," Lorelle said softly.

Rhenn's brow wrinkled. It looked like she was trying to hold back some great emotion and, for a moment, was going to succeed ...

Then her face crumpled into despair. "What if ... what if I'm the monster N'ssag made me, Lorelle, that Nhevalos made me? What if the Rhenn you know died in that nuraghi? Listen to me, talking coldly about putting my own child at risk."

Lorelle wrapped her arms around her friend. "You're being a queen. You're trying to save more than one life. You're trying to save them all. No matter what we are, or where we go, or what we do, you're that queen. You always will be. And I'll be here by your side. I'll still be here. No matter what."

Rhenn looked upward, blinking, fighting the tears. "Senji's Mercy, Lorelle ... What are we doing? What in the world are we doing? How can we be the ones to make these decisions? We're both bonded to this mysterious force of darkness, on the verge of a war with mythical creatures. How is it we are these people?"

"I don't know," Lorelle murmured. "I keep thinking I'm going to break. With all that's happened and all that we're facing, I keep thinking I'll collapse into a sobbing, useless ball. Or that I'll take up *shkazat* like Shalure did to try to escape it all. But it keeps not happening. I keep getting up in the morning. I keep trying to do what seems right ... Perhaps that is why."

Rhenn pressed her lips together, like she wanted to lash out, but she didn't. "I thought I wanted to be queen ... For as long as I can remember, all I ever wanted was my kingdom back. And revenge on Vamreth. Then I got it. And I was queen. For a few divine weeks, it was exactly as I had dreamed. I had become everything I'd always meant to be. And then suddenly I was in Daemanon. Even then, I didn't break. I told myself it was just another challenge. Senji, what a fool I was. He made me beg, Lorelle. Did I tell you that? I begged N'ssag for my life."

Lorelle put a light hand on her friend's back, pressed it there reassuringly.

"I begged that vile murderer, that greasy slime stain of the gods ... I begged him to spare me. I don't know which was worse. Dying, or that I let him break me, that I showed my fear to him like a shivering mouse. I can't stand it. I can't ... I want to kill him so much."

"And I will help you."

"You're not a killer, Lorelle."

Lorelle gave a rueful smile. "Once, I wasn't. It's not true anymore. All this darkness inside me wants to feed on something, and I cannot imagine a single thing I'd rather unleash it upon than this man who hurt you so badly."

Rhenn drew her sword, and the red gem glowed dully. "I stabbed him once. But this time, I'm going to feel his life-force leave his body. I'm going to feel it go into this blade. It will be the one time I'll be happy to use it."

They stood there for a long time, Lorelle's hand on her friend's back, Rhenn holding her blade before her. Then, finally, Rhenn sheathed it, took a deep breath, and looked around the camp. "Let's say goodbye to this place."

Lorelle regarded the camp. The entire time they'd lived here, they'd only dreamed of getting back to Usara, and perhaps even beyond at some point, to some place where there were no wars and everyone was safe. Lorelle had sat on this very hill thinking about a vast, green meadow where she and her friends could live.

She had believed in that place. She could see it vividly back then, in every detail. But she wondered if that place really existed, if it could really exist.

And did she even want it anymore? Her time in the Great Noktum had changed her forever. Once she'd married the dark, the scared little girl she'd been, standing terrified at the edge of the noktum as Vamreth pointed a crossbow at her, had vanished forever. She wasn't afraid of that crossbow, or men like Vamreth or N'ssag anymore.

Embracing the thrill of danger brought its own peace. Zaith had taught her that.

She hadn't known it at the time, but this camp, that time with Rhenn *had* been her green and peaceful meadow. She'd never seen it that way. Of course. How could she? But it seemed so simple and lovely now.

"If we ever actually belonged here, we don't any longer," Lorelle murmured. "Whatever we built here has passed. Whatever we were in this place, we aren't any longer."

Rhenn didn't say anything to that.

"Perhaps you're not the ruler you were meant to be," Lorelle murmured. "Perhaps I'm not the faithful helpmeet dogging your every step. We thought we were grooming ourselves to do that in Usara, but perhaps we weren't. Perhaps we were grooming ourselves to be the blades that stand between the Giants and Humanity."

That brought a smile to Rhenn's lips. "Perhaps we are."

"I, for one, am eager to put those blades to work. What about you, sister?"

"Yes."

"Then enough sadness," Lorelle said. "Let's leap into the dark and dare the villains to show their faces."

"You sound like Khyven now."

"One could do worse."

"When you fall, you fall hard."

"I'm a Luminent. It's written on my soul."

Rhenn grinned, and for the first time in a long time, Lorelle felt her old friend behind that grin. "Then let's get about it. I can't wait to sink my teeth into N'ssag."

"You're going to put that grimy man's neck in your mouth?"

"Metaphorically, Lorelle. Yick."

"You scared me there."

"I'm going to scare *him*. Before the end, I'm going to terrify him."

Lorelle laughed. "You realize we don't have to hold back this time. The advantage to charging into a sea of villains is that we don't have to worry about hurting anyone. We can let loose. This might actually be fun."

"You *have* gotten dark."

"Just you wait."

Lorelle flicked out the noktum cloak. It enveloped them both, and they vanished.

CHAPTER EIGHTEEN
SLAYTER

Slayter stood in the ruins of Wheskone Keep. They'd left the horses just outside the charred walls, where Khyven's insane stallion kept snorting and whipping his head left and right as though he could hear something.

Just after they'd left the brigands, they had begun to see a thin trail of smoke rising into the sky a few miles out from the keep. What they'd thought, at a distance, had been a dark cloud was, in fact, smoke.

Wheskone Keep had burned again.

The original fire had taken down a good quarter of the keep before they'd gotten it under control. It had cleared the main room of everything burnable: tables, chairs, wall hangings, rafters, and people. But to the credit of Slayter's father's vassals, they had mobilized quickly. According to Slayter's sister, they had formed a fire line to the nearby river and they'd taken down the fire before it had consumed the castle.

Whatever had set the castle ablaze this time had been wholly different. Wheskone Keep was no more. Skeletons poked out of blackened debris, hands curled in pain, skulls half-buried in ash. The very stone was melted. There was nothing left except jutting stumps of walls, sometimes only a vague outline of where the rooms had been.

This fire had not come from poor decisions of those who didn't think very quickly. This was something else.

Khyven flipped over a charred board with his toe to reveal a skeleton. A chain mail shirt was half-melted against the chest and a helmet fell off the corpse's head, rolled to the side.

"I don't like the look of this," Khyven said.

Slayter wanted to study the burn to see which angle it had come from, where the fire had been the hottest, but that would take too much time and would probably be a fruitless endeavor. At a glance, the fire seemed to have come from everywhere. But Slayter was ninety-five percent sure it had come from above.

Besides, taking time to understand the fire meant less time focusing on the great puzzle. They should get what they came for.

Slayter stepped over the charred wood and headed toward the back rooms of the keep, toward the healer's room where he had been born.

His parents had told him his birth had been difficult, and Slayter's mind was alive now with ideas as to why he had been marked with this spell engraved on his back.

"Slayter, I think we should leave," Khyven said, staying close as he looked around at the wreckage.

Slayter kept having to deviate because of fallen stones and half melted twists of metal, which he assumed were torch sconces or chandeliers—there had been a number of wrought-iron chandeliers in the keep. All the doorways into the main room had been banded in iron, too.

He wound around one of them. Yes, clearly a chandelier—

Slayter stumbled, canting sideways, and almost fell into a hole in the stone floor. Khyven's hand shot out, catching him. The lightning-fast Ringer pulled him back onto solid ground.

"Trap door," he murmured. "Watch your step."

"Well that's interesting," Slayter said, looking into the hole in the floor. It looked like there was an entire room down there. Apparently father had had secret rooms built into his keep. Slayter felt a keen disappointment that he'd never discovered those rooms. Or hallways. It could be a hallway. What was the purpose to such a thing? Spying?

"They're all over the place," Khyven murmured, now looking left and right, studying the floor.

"Apparently my great grandfather wanted secret spaces to do secret things. I confess, I feel a keen disappointment that—"

"Slayter, you realize what this looks like," Khyven interrupted, waving a hand at the destruction.

"Oh yes."

"Well why don't you tell me so that we can be clear about what we're dealing with, because to me it looks like your dragon friend flew straight from Usara to Wheskone Keep and laid waste to your ancestral home."

"Oh yes." Slayter paused, looking around the debris. He thought he could spot a couple more holes into the floor. How fascinating.

"Some of this is still warm," Khyven said meaningfully.

"I calculate this happened the day after our journey began," Slayter said. "But that's only a guess."

"And I'd say it happened yesterday."

"Yes, but are you taking into consideration that dragon fire is hotter than normal fire?"

Khyven blinked.

"So you see—"

"You're missing my point." Khyven interrupted again. "A day. Two days. The dragon could still be in this area."

"That is true."

"Then don't you think we should leave? You said he wasn't going to destroy Usara because of his code or something."

"I did say that. But the more I think on it, the more I suspect Jai'ketakos has no code. I don't think he acknowledges ethics of any kind, though he'd like to appear as if he does. I'd say it's more of a trauma-induced repetitive behavior."

"Are you seriously not able to see what I'm saying?"

"One doesn't see what a person says, Khyven. One hears it."

"The dragon could still be here!"

"He flies, Khyven. He could be anywhere on Noksonon." Slayter continued his trek toward the back room, a little jumble of stones the only indication of a room that used to be the healer's room. "Or even other places. He could be on Daemanon or Pyranon or Drakanon."

"Maybe we should leave until we learn more. Or watch from a distance. Scout the area."

"Now that's the first interesting thing you've said. Half of it, anyway."

Khyven sighed. "The learning more half?"

"Yes! Well done."

"Which means we're not leaving."

"Not yet."

Khyven planted his feet and crossed his arms. "Let me try this. My *magic* is saying that this is a particularly bad place to be."

That stopped Slayter. He turned to face the Ringer. "Really? How is it saying that? Blue wind shaped like spears? Or shaped by something else? Is the blue wind flowing right now?"

"No. It ... feels like I'm standing in a valley that is filled with blue smoke. At the bottom of the valley. I don't think we should be here."

"Blue *smoke*. Oh that is fascinating!"

Khyven looked at the horizon, which had thrown wings of orange and yellow over the western horizon, as though it was somehow a threat. "It's going to be dark in an hour. Neither of us wants to face a dragon from the noktum in the dark."

Slayter rifled through the disks on in his cylinder, pulled one out. He drew a breath and began to focus his will—

"What are you doing?" Khyven asked.

"Detecting magic. I should like to know what this power that surrounds you looks like and how it works. There are so many questions."

"Slayter," Khyven growled. "I'm telling you we are in danger."

"Yes."

"And you want to study the warning flag."

"Exactly."

"No. Get what you came for, and let's get away from this damned place."

"I am. This is part of it—could be part of it—is what I'm saying. Your magic is surely part of the puzzle. Do you know that I've never been able to detect your magic? I mean, possibly that is because when you use it, there is always swift and immediate danger. It's hard to set up a proper detect magic spell when your magic is so swift that blood is flying and bodies are falling before I can even—"

"Slayter!"

"This is an opportunity. As your magic grows and changes, we have new opportunities like this. Everything I know about this odd Land Magic or Lore Magic or whatever it is only comes from what you tell me. It's like it doesn't actually exist. Like it's all in your head, except for the fact that you're still alive, that you keep doing the miraculous over and over again and there's no other explanation except this mysterious power. Do you know there is no reason I shouldn't be able to see your magic? It's almost as though ..." He trailed off.

Yes. Yes, that had to be it. Of course. Slayter stopped talking and chased the thought.

"What?" Khyven interrupted.

"Well that's it, isn't it? That's exactly it."

"What is what?"

"You're the least magical person in the world."

Khyven frowned. "Thanks," he drawled.

"No, I mean: who would ever have guessed someone like you could wield magic? You aren't the type. If I hadn't seen what you can do, if I hadn't known what you'd told me, I'd never have believed it. Others would simply see you as ... well, as they have seen you. A Ringer of incredible talent. A dealer of death—

"Fine. I understand your point."

"Which probably means you *aren't* magical."

"I'm not?"

"No."

"You've left me behind. You were just talking about how my magic is increasing."

"Yes, it has. I mean you do have magic. I mean ... Well, no."

Khyven sighed, looking like he was mightily resisting the urge to clench his fists.

"You wield magic," Slayter continued. "But it's not your inherent talent. I wouldn't be surprised if you'd have been just an ordinary man without what was done to you."

"Thanks."

"It's the symbols. I can't read them. Which means they could be anything, but ... I would be willing to bet all the disks in my cylinder that one of those line spells on your back is what creates your blue wind. It is only the combination of that and the Giants blood in your veins that makes this possible."

Khyven blinked.

"And the symbol inscribed over it is to hide it from everyone. Which is why I can never detect your magic! Nhevalos bound your Giant's blood into a spell of miraculous possibility, then he stole your memory, and covered everything over so that another Giant searching for you wouldn't be able to find you."

"So I'm not inherently magical?"

"No. I mean yes. The Giant's blood is latent talent, a quiescent form of magic that was activated by this rune!"

"Quiescent?"

"Yes."

Khyven rumbled in his chest. "What does it mean?"

"Oh. Quiet. Sleeping. You have the capacity to hold great magic, but no capacity to wield it. Not without the symbol. You're like an enormous keg. Without the symbol, you'd have no spout. The rune is your spout, allowing that capacity for magic to come out in a very specific, very directed way." Slayter tapped a thumb on his chin. "It's genius, really. Absolute genius."

"So Nhevalos essentially made me. Built me up from the ground, top to bottom."

"Probably more than that. He probably made your mother, too. And possibly her mother's mother and—"

"All right. I understand the point."

"He's probably been crossing bloodlines for centuries, like he wanted to do with Rhenn."

Khyven clenched his teeth and shook his head.

Slayter turned and picked his way down the last part of the hallway to the healer's room. This was the place where he'd been born, where they had brought him forth from his mother, brought him into this world.

There was no table—everything made of wood had been turned to ash—but there was a slab of fallen stone that lay atop of a pile of other stones, and it leaned at an angle that was almost level. A blackened skeleton slumped against it, head down, arm up with fingers curled like he—or she—had fallen asleep after drinking too much.

"I'll work the spell here." Slayter detached his cylinder from his belt and set it on the small bit of space left near the skeleton's slumped upper body, which covered more than half of the makeshift stone table.

"Do you want that there?" Khyven nodded.

Slayter glanced at the skeleton, blinked.

Khyven moved fluidly around the debris. Slayter expected him to kick the skeleton out of the way, but with uncharacteristic gentleness, he used his bare hands to peel the man—or woman—away from the slab and lay them down in the ash.

"Thank you," Slayter said.

"Just hurry."

"I realize that rushing is a primary advantage to what you do," Slayter said. "But for me—"

"Don't talk. Just ... The sun is going down." He kept looking at the lowering sun. A shade of purple had crept into the sky behind the blazing oranges and yellows.

Slayter got to work. Thankfully, he had prepared exactly what he thought he would need, and it went quickly.

Khyven stood by as the sky slowly changed from light blue to purple.

Slayter snapped the spells he needed and channeled his mind into them. The rush moved through him, lifting him up like a tide and laying him down on the sand, smiling but drained as though he'd swum a mile. He moved to where the birthing bed had been, and he laid down awkwardly on the rubble.

The spell took effect and the past came to life like a play around them.

Translucent figures appeared in his field of view. Translucent walls replaced the fallen walls. A chest of drawers. A full-length mirror on a stand. Three basins with stacks of white linen on nightstands next to them.

The figures were enormous, like Giants themselves all round him, moving about and growing larger as they approached him, then smaller as they moved away.

Slayter's spell recreated the room from his memory, from a deep memory within himself that he couldn't have recalled without the aid of magic. He saw the day of his birth through his own infant's eyes.

"What is this?" Khyven marveled, looking at the warped figures leaning over Slayter.

"Shhh," Slayter said, and he concentrated on replaying the scene. His mother towered behind him. The healer severed the fleshy cord connecting them.

It all seemed normal. They swaddled him and put him in his mother's arms. The healer proceeded to clean up the birthing viscera, to replace the birthing sheets. Basins of clean water were brought into the room. Basins of dirty water were removed. Food and wine were brought for his mother.

As Slayter and a wide-eyed Khyven kept watching, Slayter began to fear he'd miscalculated. Perhaps his birth was not the moment that Nhevalos—or whomever—had come for him and carved into his back.

Then the healer stopped her bustling. She looked at his mother and Slayter followed her gaze. Slayter's swaddling clothes were bloodstained. Three distinct circles of red soaked the cloth, and they slowly grew. The healer quickly unwrapped the infant and saw three tiny wounds, one on his wrist, one on his knee, and one on his head.

They were not wounds from a knife nor any instrument made by Humans. They were, in fact, simple scrapes from the trial of birth. The wounds themselves were unremarkable. But they wouldn't stop bleeding.

The healer staunched the wounds, but the blood kept leaking. She wrapped them, but the blood continued to soak the cloth. Mother began to cry, wildly asking questions that neither Slayter nor Khyven could hear.

Then the scene jolted, like there was a break in time.

Suddenly mother was happy. She cooed at the infant Slayter, who squalled like someone had slapped him. The cuts had been wrapped a third time, and now the cloths remained white. No blood seeped into them.

"What happened?" Khyven asked. "You were bleeding. Now it's gone. Where's the blood?"

For once, Khyven and Slayter had the same question.

The power of the spell Slayter had cast still flowed through him, and he pulled out another disk that had been specifically crafted to manipulate this spell. He channeled his life-force into it and snapped the disk. Orange light flared and Slayter made the translucent figures halt. Mother's movements started again, but this time in reverse, as did the healer's. He moved it backward to the break in time.

The scene jolted back to the infant being wrapped in blood-soaked bandages. He stopped it, let it move forward. The scene jumped, and suddenly he was fine.

Slayter backed it up again, let it proceed.

He backed it up a third time, let it proceed, and stopped it right at the break. There he held it. He closed his eyes in concentration and let the magic flow through him. He concentrated on expanding the spell, expanding his mind, expanding his memories. There was something in that break, a crack that had been shoved shut, a—

"Senji's Teeth!" Khyven exclaimed.

Slayter opened his eyes.

Nhevalos stood by the headboard as though he'd just walked through the wall. He was barely visible, far more translucent than mother, the healer, or baby Slayter.

The scene broke again, going back to his mother cooing at the now-not-bleeding Slayter.

Slayter tried to expand the spell further. There was more to be seen in this memory, but no matter what he did, that was all that would come. Just that quick glimpse of Nhevalos entering the room.

Whatever had been there had been erased.

Slayter let the spell go. The translucent figures vanished.

"Nhevalos was here," Khyven said.

"He was," Slayter said. Exhausted, he lay his head back against the stone.

"But ... He didn't carve into you."

"Oh, he did. He simply erased it from my mind."

"But, what was the spell? How can you know what the rune does?"

"I can't."

"What?"

"There is no way to be completely certain."

"Then this was a waste of time!"

"Oh, hardly that. I said completely certain. But I am ninety-eight percent certain. I didn't see him complete the rune, but he was here."

"You're ninety-eight percent certain. What was the rune?"

"Wasn't it obvious?"

Khyven darkened. "It wasn't obvious, no."

"I was a bleeder."

"A what?"

"You don't know what a bleeder is?"

"Someone who bleeds," Khyven said through clenched teeth.

"Someone who cannot stop bleeding once they start. There are infants who are born this way. Their blood cannot coagulate. They die in childbirth. A few might survive for a short while. Until the world nicks them, really. Then they die as all the blood drains from their body. I was one of those."

"He healed you?"

"The spell makes it so my body does what other bodies naturally do."

"So he healed you."

Slayter frowned. "As you wish." People were so imprecise.

"But why did he heal you?"

"That is the question. But I think that, too, is obvious."

"Is it," Khyven said flatly.

"He wanted me alive."

Khyven sighed. "Do you have any idea how difficult it is to talk to you? Why would he need a baby to live?"

"Think like a Giant, Khyven. He didn't need a baby. He needed a mage with considerable power installed in Usara. Probably to help Rhenn, as she is also marked."

"He saved you as a baby so you could help defeat Vamreth."

"Or for something I have yet to do. Twenty years is to Nhevalos what a few minutes is to you. Imagine you cracked an egg into a pan and left the room. You'd come back in a few minutes later expecting the egg to be ready to flip."

"Ah."

"I'm the egg," Slayter clarified.

"I understand that you're the egg."

Slayter rolled his eyes. "You say I don't explain enough. Then you get angry when I do."

"Explain the difficult parts."

"And how do I know what is difficult for you?"

"Skip whatever is obvious to you."

"It's *all* obvious to me."

"It can't all be ..." Khyven trailed off, shaking his head wearily. "Never mind."

"Very well," Slayter said cheerfully. "As I was saying, Nhevalos is planning far into the future. He was placing me on his board, just as he has placed you."

"But we already knew that."

"Suspected. I wasn't a hundred percent sure. I wanted confirmation and now I have it."

"We rode all the way out here for confirmation?"

"Every piece helps me see clearer." Slayter began to think about next steps. They would need to visit Khyven's childhood home next, the manor that had burned. There certainly seemed to be a lot of fire in this puzzle.

At any rate, fire or no, they would have to visit that place and do the same thing they had done here. Khyven was disappointed, but he somehow didn't realize just how much they had learned here. Slayter's guesses were confirmed. And he hadn't had any idea about the bleeder aspect. Interrupting the spells on Slayter's back would have been folly. A sure death sentence.

Slayter wondered if disrupting any of the runes would have a similarly devastating effect on his friends. That was something to consider. They might be pawns in Nhevalos's eyes, but he had certainly given gifts to his pawns. They would have to—

Khyven drew his sword.

That broke Slayter's reverie, not just his drawing of the sword, but the sword he had chosen.

The Ringer carried three swords, all for different reasons. Of course, he was at home with any number of weapons hanging from him or sticking out at awkward angles. He was like an ox when it came to weight. All told his armor and armament weighed close to fifty pounds, but he carried it like he was wearing linen robes.

He had swords. He had at least three daggers about his person: one at his waist, one in his boot, and a throwing dagger wedged in a sheath on his left-arm bracer. Khyven wore his mismatched Ringer armor—a personal concoction of ring mail, chain mail, and plate mail he had kept over the traditional plate mail of a Knight of the Dark—like another might wear a tunic. It was impressive that he could even move his arms, let alone move them like a dancer dressed in silks.

But it was the three swords that were the most interesting—two at his side and one over his shoulder. Each one was chosen to pair with the severity of a fight. One could actually tell Khyven's mood by which sword he chose to draw. The wooden sword and steel sword were sheathed on his left hip, side-by-side.

The wooden sword was for spats, fights where Khyven wanted to keep from killing his enemies—in deference to Vohn's haranguing. The Shadowvar had even wrapped the base of the blade in leather with crude Usaran runes that spelled "The Diplomat." This was, Slayter supposed, intended to remind Khyven to be merciful when he could.

The steel sword was for when Khyven felt threatened. When he drew that sword, his opponents were going to die. He wasn't going to pull any of his strikes.

The Mavric iron sword, the one that had killed Gohver, rested across his back in the magical sheath Slayter had made for it. Khyven never drew the Mavric iron sword. Not since they had fought Tovos the Giant.

He's afraid of it, Slayter thought. And that would be a healthy reaction for any other Human. But for Khyven, that reluctance might be dangerous. His timidity was limiting a knowledge of a tremendous artifact. What they needed to know about it, only Khyven could discover, but he carried the thing like a priceless, poisonous snake. Precious but never to be handled.

Khyven was immune to the ill-effects that had melted Gohver, which made this a golden opportunity to learn so much about Mavric iron. Slayter didn't have the same immunity. He couldn't test and probe the sword indefinitely without suffering ill effects. Slayter had told Khyven several times that he should spend time with the sword. Slayter had studied a number of legendary Mavric iron swords in the palace library, and he had no idea which one this was. It didn't fit any of the sketches, which meant it was probably just a basic Mavric iron sword without any special magical powers imbued into it besides its inherent lightness and sharpness.

But Slayter didn't know for sure. It drove him a little bit crazy that Khyven could just carry the thing and know nothing about it.

Of course, Slayter had used chips of Mavric iron in certain spells. In small amounts, even Humans could wield items that contained the eldritch metal, just as long as it was properly insulated. Slayter had given Vohn a lightning rod. It had Mavric iron embedded in it, but bound with copper and spells to protect mortals from its ill-effects. Of course, Slayter never carried any raw Mavric iron near his person for any length of time.

All this flashed through Slayter's mind as Khyven pulled his steel sword silently from the sheath. Whatever was coming, Khyven felt it was deadly serious.

The Ringer whirled, and Slayter turned as well.

During the time he'd taken with his spell, the sun had finally vanished beneath the horizon. Night had engulfed the keep and its environs.

Khyven glared at the northern wall, the tallest wall still standing. It even had a piece of the second story floor still attached to it.

The huge black head of Jai'ketakos rose above the wall. His eyes glistened in the dark above two nostrils that glowed orange.

"Well, well ..." the dragon said. "You do not disappoint, Slayter the Mage."

Chapter Nineteen
SLAYTER

"Jai'ketakos," Slayter said.

"Dammit," Khyven said.

"Slayter the Mage," Jai'ketakos repeated. The jaunty tone the dragon had used in Usara—before Slayter had seen through his game—had returned. "I see you accepted my invitation. I confess I never thought you'd get here this quickly."

"Ah. The burned keep," Slayter said.

"You left me so little joy in Usara. Do you know what that feels like? To have your heart set on something and to have it yanked away?"

"You wanted to kill the people of Usara."

"Roasted Human is delectable."

"Hmmm."

This creature was so far beyond Slayter it was laughable to even draw a comparison. An elder dragon was literally a Giant transformed, much like Nhevalos had transformed into Nhevaz. And that meant Jai'ketakos could work all five streams of magic, something that made Slayter breathless with envy.

All five streams at full strength. Just imagine ...

As a Line Mage, Slayter could imitate all five types of magic to a small degree, but only those that he had meticulously studied, practiced, and bonded with. Of the streams he could bring to life through runes, Slayter was the most talented at Land Magic. Bonding metal to fire and creating a flaming sword, for example. Hardening air to stop dragon's breath as another. And he was a fair hand at symbols that activated Life Magic. Rhenn's new sword, for example. He knew less about how to imitate Love Magic, and he knew almost nothing about Lore Magic. In theory, all were within reach for a Line Mage, but in reality it was nearly impossible. Each Line Magic symbol was incredibly difficult to understand, imbue with power, and master. It wasn't just about scratching a symbol on a page or in a clay disk. A mage had to be one with the spell, to understand and embody the nature of it. To give his life-force to it.

In effect, a Line Mage bonded his body with every single spell he created.

But this dragon, this Giant, could work all five streams, and he could work them at full power, like his fiery breath, with almost no physical depletion.

Slayter had to know more. He had read between the lines of the scant information the Giants had left behind before their downfall seventeen hundred years ago, but it wasn't enough. Reading the journals of men who had seen such magic was nothing compared to actually witnessing it. It was like hearing about a boat and how to sail it and then being on the boat and working the lines and sails, knowing the wind and weather. This was an unprecedented opportunity. Slayter did not have the benefit of Lore Magic, and so he had to use the almost invisible tracks of the past, his intellect, and whatever he could gather here in unique moments like this, to predict the future. To solve the puzzle. To fight the Giants.

Slayter already had more information about Jai'ketakos now than he had at their first meeting. He knew the dragon didn't burn Wheskone Keep to the ground so he could feast on "delectable Humans." In fact, Slayter would guess he hadn't eaten a single person at Wheskone Keep. All of the skeletons had, indeed, been burned to death, but there wasn't a single indication of half-chewed flesh, gnawed bones, or blood stains. Jai'ketakos didn't kill for the relish of eating Humans. He destroyed for the sake of destruction, for what it meant to him, and Slayter had a fair idea of what that was.

Had all this been foreseen by Nhevalos? The coming of the dragon. The destruction of Wheskone Keep. This meeting ...

All of this went through Slayter's mind in a second. That and, of course, that this had been a trap from the start. And Slayter had missed that. He'd have to think on that later.

"That is all you have to say?" Jai'ketakos inquired. Slowly, he put one of his enormous claws on the broken wall. Rock ground and dust sifted down as his claws curled around it.

"If I had known you wished to continue our conversation, I'd have agreed to meet you," Slayter said.

"Oh this is better, don't you think?"

"Do you want something in specific?"

"I want you to die begging," Jai'ketakos said, and his jaunty tone turned dark just for a moment.

"If you wanted me dead, you could have done it from above, incinerated both of us before I even knew you were here."

The dragon seemed to be smiling, but a rumbling came from his throat. "I want to hear you as you die. You play with words so cleverly, Slayter the Mage. I would guess your begging is going to be just as inventive."

From the moment Slayter saw the smoldering ruins of his father's keep, he'd removed a specific spell from his cylinder and put it into the hidden pocket of his sleeve. From the moment he'd finished the memory spell in the room of his birth, he'd had it in his hand.

But the dragon was so fast. Too fast.

There was no warning, no slight intake of breath, no malevolent twinkle of the eye. Jai'ketakos opened his mouth, as though to talk, and fire shot out.

Khyven, of course, was already moving. He had predicted the coming of the dragon. He'd correctly assessed the vulnerability of the growing dark. No doubt his blue wind had gone crazy the instant Jai'ketakos had decided to attack.

Khyven leapt forward, steel sword drawn, and attempted to interpose himself between the dragon and Slayter. Slayter snapped his disk, drawing on the magic.

Flame roared. Orange light flared. The dragon rose up, crushing the wall with one mighty leg.

Khyven vanished from sight in the searing flame. Slayter turned away reflexively. The dragon's fire hit the far wall like a molten ram, bearing Khyven into a pile of stones and charred timbers. The pile exploded. Stones, fire, and body slammed into the opposite wall of the keep. The stones melted. The timbers blew apart.

And a charred skeleton slumped to the base of the wall. No clothes, no flesh, no sword. There hadn't even been a scream. Khyven had been blasted away.

Slayter staggered away from the immense heat, but the dragon's enormous foot slammed into him, knocking him down. Curved claws came down on every side of him, crunching into the flagstones and creating a cage of claw and scale all around him.

"So now it is just you and me." The dragon's giant, toothy head hovered directly over Slayter's.

Slayter blinked against the falling dirt and smoke that stung his eyes. He coughed.

"Well ... yes," he said.

"Did you think your fierce Ringer could protect you?"

"Well ... no."

"He leapt into that fire with such certainty."

"He's like that."

"*Was* like that." The dragon glanced at the smoking skeleton on the other side of the keep.

"So now ... You are now going to wait for me to beg?" Slayter asked.

"I do not think I'll have to wait long. If you grow boring, I'll just kill you."

"You're not going to kill me."

"Am I not?" The dragon showed even more of his teeth. "Are you trying to bait me, Slayter the Mage? Are you trying to stall for time?"

"I'm not."

"Do you think you will pull one of your pathetic, watered down spells from your sleeve?"

"No. It's just that you've made two mistakes. And I don't think you've seen them yet."

"Mistakes?"

"Yes."

"You are the most fascinating Human I've ever met, Slayter the Mage. It sounds like you're threatening me. Are you threatening me? That is ... so presumptuous it is fascinating. Tell me, Slayter the Mage, what two mistakes I have made?"

"You think you are a force for chaos."

"A force for ..." The dragon laughed. "This is what you have to say?"

"Yes."

"I *am* a force for chaos. Chaos is the only truth in life. How is this a mistake?"

"Because you're lying."

"Am I?"

"You *believe* you are a force for chaos. But you aren't. You are a force for vengeance."

The dragon's nostrils flared. Flames licked up from them, and his voice was deadly flat when he spoke. "You are wrong, Slayter the Mage."

"You were betrayed by those you trusted. They imprisoned you with the Dragon Chain. It is that, not whimsy, that drives you, though you would like your victims to think otherwise. My guess is that your seemingly random destruction is to get their attention, these people who hurt you. When they raise their heads, that is when you will take your vengeance."

Jai'ketakos paused for a long time, then spoke in that same flat monotone. "Those who imprisoned me are dead."

"Ah. Well then, that makes even more sense."

"I lured you here, Slayter the Mage. You are under my power. By the Dark, you are under my very claw. I think the mistake is yours."

"You know Nhevalos is out there," Slayter sad. "And I think you know what he is trying to do. But you're convinced his machinations don't apply to you. You think the *kairoi* cannot predict you. That Nhevalos cannot predict you because you are a force for chaos. Except you're not. That is dangerous ignorance."

"Dangerous ... ignorance?" The flames in the dragon's nostrils glowed brighter. Sparks drifted up, lighting darkness. "Nhevalos has set us in motion with a very specific purpose."

"Not me. Nhevalos is not my master."

"Yes you. And me. And I do not think my usefulness to Nhevalos is to die under your claw right here, right now. Probably the opposite, if I had to guess."

"The opposite? Are you insinuating that you are going to kill me?"

"Yes. I'm insinuating that."

"I am waiting, Slayter the Mage. You are alone and helpless. Your magic is all but depleted. And even if it wasn't, and you weren't, you do not possess a spell powerful enough to hurt me, let alone kill me." The dragon shook his head. "No. Nhevalos has no control over what is happening here. In fact, I will make you a promise. If you can muster even enough force to draw even a single drop of my blood, I will let you live to see another sunrise. How does that sound to you? Do your worst, little mage."

"That is your second mistake," Slayter said.

"Second mistake? To give you a chance to cast your meager spell?"

"Humans drove your kind into exile two thousand years ago

by working together. When Humans do that, we can do the most miraculous things. You've forgotten that, I think. And you've forgotten I am not alone."

"Are you referring to your charred warrior? Is he the one you are going to band together with?" The dragon glanced at the blackened, smoking skeleton against the wall.

"You're referring to Khyven, I assume," Slayter said.

"Was that his name?"

"Khyven the Unkillable."

"An undeserving moniker now, don't you think?"

"I think you'll find he, strangely, deserves every bit of it."

Khyven rose silently behind the dragon. His face and body was covered with black and gray soot, and he seemed like a ghost of the Dark itself. The Mavric iron sword extended from his hand, six feet of midnight steel.

"A single drop of blood?" Slayter asked.

"Yes."

"Very well, I accept."

Jai'ketakos must have noticed Slayter's gaze flick left, and the dragon whipped his head around.

Khyven struck.

Chapter Twenty
KHYVEN

The blue wind leapt to life the moment the dragon opened his mouth. A tornado of blue shot directly at Khyven, but beneath it a darker blue stripe shot forward *from* Khyven, across the debris as though someone had painted it. It went toward the dragon, straight to one of the trap doors Slayter had discovered.

This was the new facet of Khyven's magic; it had happened before in Daemanon. He had the strong sense that the blue line wasn't warning of danger or offering him a target to attack; it was telling him what to do. It had bothered Khyven in the past; he didn't like the notion that some magical trickery controlled his choices. He'd questioned it deeply in the quiet of his mind.

He didn't question it now.

He rushed the dragon. Flame burst from its toothy jaws—

And Khyven dove down the hole. Fire followed him. He hit the shallow bottom of the corridor, and was engulfed in flame. The searing pain surrounded him—

Then it was gone.

The flames raged around him, but they didn't burn him. Overhead, he heard the destruction wrought by the blast of fire. Walls breaking. Debris flying.

Khyven breathed hard and squinted. The tall Mavric iron sword hovered in front of him, mysteriously free of its sheath. He looked down and found that he was clutching the hilt. It was cool and reassuring, but he didn't remember grabbing it. He hadn't drawn that sword.

"*Keep hold ...,*" it said in his mind. "*Keep hold, and I will keep you safe.*"

The sword was talking! In his mind! Khyven almost cast it away reflexively.

But it didn't take a mage's education to realize that the sword was keeping the flames at bay. Mavric iron was, according to the mage, supposed to be filled with magical powers.

So Khyven shut his eyes and held on. The flames swirled out of the hole, then vanished. For a moment, there was silence, then he heard the dragon talking. It was distant, muffled by the debris that had fallen in with the flames and covered Khyven's escape hatch.

"So now it is you and me," the muffled dragon's voice said.

"Well ... yes."

Hearing Slayter's voice sent a wash of relief through Khyven. He'd thought the mage was dead, incinerated by the blast.

The dragon and Slayter continued talking, but Khyven couldn't make out all the words because the sword had started talking again.

"*You...*" When it talked, Khyven felt like dark, cold oil was trickling over his scalp. "*Must ... open your mind to me.*"

That was the *last* thing Khyven wanted to do.

"*You are ... a talented slayer of men,*" the sword oozed into his mind. "*Are you ... as talented at slaying dragons?*"

"Shut up," Khyven thought to the thing, not even knowing if that would work. He tried to sheath the sword, but missed. He tried again, missed again.

A chill went up his spine. He hadn't failed to sheath any

sword on the first try since his fifth bout in the Night Ring. He'd never failed to sheath a sword twice. Ever. In his life.

"*Do not sheath me,*" the sword said. "*Together, we can do great works.*"

"You're a sword. Shut up."

"*I am not a sword. I am The Sword,*" it said.

"Shut up shut up shut up." He tried to sheath the sword a third time and missed.

"*You didn't answer me, Slayer of Men. Do you know how to slay a dragon?*"

"Shut up!"

"*Because I do ...*"

Khyven went still, and his panic seemed to move to the back of his mind.

Because I do ...

Slayter and the dragon continued talking above, but just how long would that last? Clearly the dragon had come to kill Slayter, and the only reason he wasn't dead was because the damned dragon was playing cat and mouse before he devoured Khyven's friend.

"*You can kill the dragon?*" Khyven thought to the sword, trying to keep his flesh from crawling. He was talking to a malevolent piece of steel that had turned his friend Gohver into bubbling, flesh-colored soup.

"*It was what I was made for, originally. Slaying dragons. Although their true name, their Eldroi name, is Drakanoi.*"

"Drakanoi?"

"*This Drakanoi doesn't belong here. No Drakanoi ... belongs in Noksonon.*"

The conversation continued above, and the dragon was beginning to sound agitated.

"*Dammit! All right. What do I do?*"

"*Open to me ... Open to me ...*"

Khyven resisted for a breathless moment. He didn't know what would happen if he "opened" to the sword. Already the thing had controlled his arm enough to keep him from sheathing it. Once he opened his mind and let the thing further in, what then would it be able to control?

"*Open ...*"

He clenched his teeth and opened his mind. The ooze rushed into his mind, and Khyven gasped.

The sword entered Khyven's mind, but suddenly... he was in its mind, too. He could feel the hard, cold thinking of the thing. He could feel its hatred for... Eldroi.

"*You hate Giants?*" He thought to the sword. "*You were made by the Giants.*"

"*Giant is a Human word. I was made by the Father of the Noksonoi, Noktos himself. Drakanoi, Pyranoi, Daemanoi, Lathranoi ... These are the enemies of the Noksonoi. None of them belong on Noksonon, least of all Drakanoi.*"

"*You're talking about different clans of Giants.*"

"*All interlopers must be purged. You will help me.*"

This is ... so creepy, he thought, this time to himself. If the sword heard him, though, it did not reply.

"*I care not if your friend perishes. We can still kill the Drakanoi after. But I sense that you would care. If you wish to save him, you must hurry. Drakanoi are not known for their patience.*"

"*Yes! Of course!*"

"*Then go quietly, Slayer of Men. Together, we will send this Drakanoi to hell.*"

Khyven picked himself up as silently as he could and moved down the stooped corridor. He could see a scant bit of light on the far side. Another trapdoor. If Khyven gauged his surroundings correctly, that trapdoor would be behind the dragon. An excellent place to begin.

He reached it. The hole was right next to a pile of debris. It was almost as though Senji had arranged for some cover. Khyven slowed to a meticulous crawl and lifted himself silently from the hole. He'd learned in the Night Ring that a moment spent for surprise was worth the time.

He emerged behind a tumble of stones and a charred table. On the other side of it, the dragon's tail curled around the bulk of its hindquarters as it faced away, talking to Slayter.

"What was his name?" the dragon was saying.

"Khyven the Unkillable," Slayter replied.

"An undeserving moniker now, don't you think?"

"I think you'll find he, strangely, deserves every bit of it."

Khyven slid to the side. The blue wind swirled around him, and a blue line showed him where he needed to go.

"A single drop of blood?" Slayter asked.

"Yes," the dragon said.

"Very well, I accept."

The dragon's head whipped around. A tornado of blue wind launched at Khyven.

He charged along the blue line and leapt high. Fire roared just behind him.

"Yeesssss! Yeesssss!" the sword said in his mind.

He brought it overhead and came down on the fat end of the dragon's tail, right next to its haunches. The blade sliced through scale and flesh like a honed boning knife through fish. The ease with which it went through the dragon's tough hide surprised even Khyven.

But not nearly as much as it surprised the dragon.

Jai'ketakos reared up. He screamed like someone had poured acid down his mouth. Flame shot into the night, and the dragon's wings reflexively pumped, taking it into the sky.

Khyven leapt to the side.

"No!" the sword said in his mind. *"It is getting away!"*

Khyven stood, helpless, as the dragon rose overhead, screaming its pain until the scream faded and the dragon regained its senses. Fire spat and sputtered from its nostrils. It wheeled around and dove toward Khyven.

"Yeesssss..." the sword said.

The painted blue line snaked out in front of Khyven, and he lunged that direction. Fire exploded behind him and around him, but again all he felt was the cool hilt of the sword in his hand.

"Back! Back!" the sword demanded, and the blue line agreed. It jackknifed on itself. Khyven grunted as he arrested his bulk

and lunged back the way he'd come. The blue line curved up from the ground, straight upward. The sword practically tugged his hand into the sky.

Khyven launched himself in the air, stabbing straight up—

Into the dragon. Suddenly its belly was right there. The dragon had flown low and swiped a claw where Khyven had been half a second before. The sword punched through scales, meat, organs.

The dragon screamed again. Fire spurted. Jai'ketakos faltered, crashing into the houses beyond the burned keep.

The sword tugged Khyven forward, bidding him to sprint at the dragon. Caught up in the battle and the ridiculousness that Khyven actually seemed to be *winning*, he ran at the dragon. Clearly, Jai'ketakos had not expected the sword.

By Senji, *Khyven* hadn't expected the sword!

The dragon spun, fighting to right itself as stones fell on it and wooden rafters entangled it, as blood ran down its front from the horrible, ragged wound. Khyven charged up the stair step of a broken wall and launched himself at the heart of the creature.

"Yes, Slayer of Men! Yes!"

Jai'ketakos whipped his head around just before Khyven landed on his chest. It roared something incomprehensible as Khyven drove the sword straight toward its heart—

The air exploded, blowing Khyven backward. It was as though he was a fly smacked by an enormous hand. Air whistled past him and he hit the dirt, rolled, and smashed into a broken wall.

Everything went black.

CHAPTER TWENTY-ONE
KHYVEN

ET UP!"

The voice stabbed into Khyven's brain like a hot knife.

He sat up like someone had yanked his strings, like he was some life-sized marionette. The sword stuck to his hand like it had been glued there. He tried to release it, but it was as though he didn't have any control over his right fist, clenched tightly.

His foggy brain assessed this new, terrifying situation. The fall had knocked him unconscious. The sword had brought him awake in an instant.

The dust from his tumble across the road still hung in the air. Bits of rock still fell from his impact with the wall. The dragon was still regaining its feet. It spun around and sent debris flying, glaring at Khyven as though it was surprised to find him still alive.

"*Kill it,*" the sword said. *"Don't hesitate."*

Khyven felt the compulsion to run at the dragon, a compulsion so overpowering that he almost did it. But an icy fear gripped him at the same time. The sword was controlling him.

The sword had driven him, and in the heat of the battle he hadn't noticed the difference between what it wanted and what he wanted.

But having his head rattled had shaken it loose for a second.

"What did you ... do to me?" Khyven growled. His lip felt wet, and he realized he was drooling blood.

"Kill it!" the sword said. *"We must work as one."*

Khyven staggered to his feet as though pulled up.

"Stop it!" he growled aloud.

"Kill it!"

The dragon narrowed his eyes at the interaction, and his gaze slid from Khyven to the sword. "Where did you get that sword?"

"Slayer of Men, the enemy is before you! Kill it!"

Khyven pushed down his revulsion. But the damnable thing was that the sword wasn't wrong. He had a battle to win here.

"It wants you, Jai'ketakos. Almost like it knows you," Khyven said, and he started forward.

The dragon opened his mouth and let loose a torrent of flame. This time, Khyven didn't dodge, didn't dive for cover. The blue line pointed straight at the dragon, and he whipped the sword in front of himself.

The flames roared around him, and he remained unharmed.

"You're going to have to find a new trick." Khyven ran at the dragon.

The dragon leapt into the air, beating his wings. Blood flecked the ground from his nearly severed tail and the long bloody line along its belly.

"You don't know what you hold there, Khyven the Unkillable," the dragon hissed, rising higher. Dragon's blood rained down on Khyven, spattering his face and shoulders. "That weapon will destroy you, mortal!"

"Kill it!"

The sword yanked on Khyven, wanting him to run at the tallest wall, leap atop it and chase the dragon into the sky.

Khyven yanked back with all his will ...

... and managed to hold his ground.

"*No!*" the sword raged as the dragon vanished into the darkness overhead.

"We will meet again, Khyven the Unkillable," the dragon's voice drifted down. "We will put your name to the test ..."

Then the dragon was gone.

Khyven turned, feeling for the blue wind, looking at the sky. But no attack came. The blue slowly faded until there was nothing. The danger was past. The dragon was retreating. He'd left to lick his wounds and fight another day.

Khyven gripped the sword hard until the battle lust left him.

"*You let him go.*" The sword's voice was heavy with disappointment.

Khyven tried to drop it, but he still couldn't open his fist. He clenched his teeth and tried again.

"*Were you afraid, Slayer of Men? Is that why you stopped?*"

Khyven ignored the voice—tried to ignore that the sword was stuck to his hand—and ran back to the keep. He jumped the wall and landed inside the blackened great room.

Slayter lay on the charred floor, unmoving. His leg was bent at an unnatural angle.

"Slayter!" Khyven slid to his knees next to the mage. He tried to let go of the sword again. It wouldn't come away from his hand.

"*You must chase the Drakanoi—*"

"Shut up." Khyven grappled with the fingers of his right hand, pried one after the other off and, using his foot for leverage, kicked the cursed blade away. "Get off!"

The sword tumbled across the charred floor. It didn't say anything. Relief flooded through Khyven. Thank Senji! Removing contact had removed the damned thing from his mind. He was never picking it up again.

Now that he had both hands, he gently put them on Slayter's cheeks. The mage wasn't dead, yet. Khyven had seen enough dead and unconscious men in his time to know the difference.

But he also didn't know what the dragon had done to his friend.

"Come on, Slayter. Wake up." He pushed the mage's red hair back from his brow. Slayter did not stir. He shook Slayter's shoulder gently. Nothing. "Dammit ..."

There were no wounds on the mage. His twisted leg was just his prosthetic that had nearly fallen off. If it had been a cut, Khyven could have bandaged it. A broken bone, he could have set it. But mages didn't have normal wounds. They "bled" on the inside. To make magic, they used up the stuff that kept them alive.

Wait wait wait.

Slayter had herbs. He used them to perk himself up when he'd overextended his magic. He'd seen the mage go from drooping flower to charged squirrel in two seconds. What did he use? What was it? An herb of some sort, he thought. Lorelle had mentioned that Slayter shouldn't be using the herbs he was using. That's what it was, right?

Khyven opened the mage's robes and ...

Senji's Teeth!

There had to be two dozen pockets in there! He started rifling through them. A bag of marbles. Three twisted sticks that were exactly the same length. A pouch with three steel vials in it. A dried bat's wing. A glass vial with what looked like a chunk of Mavric iron in it. A packet ...

He opened the packet. There were three different types of leaves in it: red, blue, and green. They had all been dried out and flattened carefully, lined up neatly next to each other.

"Oh for the love of ..." Khyven stared at them. Which one?

Memories bubbled up in his mind, about how Lorelle had hated the mage's herbs. She'd indicated that Slayter was far too cavalier about the herbs he consumed. She'd said his revitalizing herbs were dangerous in the wrong doses.

Khyven also remembered her saying Slayter shouldn't keep his poisonous leaves next to his revitalizing leaves.

How could he choose without risking Slayter's life? Khyven hated this.

"Green ..." he murmured. That was certainly safer than red, right? Most herbs were green, after all. Green was an innocuous color ... Red was the color of blood.

He pulled the green herb from pouch—

"Your objective is to keep the Human alive?" the sword asked in his mind.

Khyven jumped and dropped the pouch and the leaves into the dirt. He looked wide-eyed at the sword, and a sickly horror crept through him. It wasn't in his hand, but it was still talking to him! The sword was a half dozen feet away.

"Did you think we could only converse when I was in your hand?"

He clenched his teeth. "Yes."

"We are bound together forever, Slayer of Men. We shall fight the glorious fight until one of us ceases to be. We shall fight the glorious fight until all the Eldroi who do not belong on Noksonon have been purged ..."

Khyven heart thumped painfully. "Great."

He reached down to retrieve the leaf.

"Again, I ask: The Human's life-force is depleted. Your objective is to keep him from falling into a mage's coma?"

"I don't want him to die, if that's what you're asking," Khyven said, intentionally speaking aloud.

"Then don't feed him the green herb. That is biventulen. *It is poisonous to Humans."*

Khyven put it back and took out the blue one.

"Also poison. That will kill him faster."

Khyven grit his teeth. "You could have just said the red one."

"The red is the worst. If you touch it at all, you yourself will be in danger if you do not cleanse your hands quickly."

Khyven gingerly slipped the blue leaf back into its slot and closed the pouch.

"You should probably be looking for a vial. Does he have any vials?"

Khyven withdrew the pouch with the three steel vials. A flash of a memory from the Great Noktum came to him. After Slayer had killed the Zek Roaches, he *had* downed something from a vial. It had looked like this.

And he'd coughed blue smoke.

Khyven uncorked the vial, squinted in the scant light, and poured a drop on his finger. It looked gray.

The sword didn't say anything.

"Is this it?"

"You could have killed the Drakanoi," the sword said.

"Enough about the dragon. Is this right?"

"If his constitution is stern enough. He looks rather weak, even for a Human."

Khyven raised the vial to his own lips and took a small sip. If it was poison, then both he and Slayter would visit Senji tonight.

A thrill of vitality zinged through him. He hadn't even realized how exhausted he'd been until that revitalizing surge rushed through him.

"Well ..." he breathed.

"You do have potential for a Human, Slayer of Men. It was a joy to work with you, when you worked. But I do not like this running away. We must work on that."

Khyven ignored the sword and gently opened Slayter's jaw. He poured a little of the vial in. It filled up the mage's slack mouth. A little ran down his cheek.

"Come on. You have to swallow." Khyven closed his mouth and massaged his neck—

Slayter's body spasmed. He sat bolt upright and coughed. Blue liquid spattered his chin and blue smoke lifted into the air. Khyven steadied him. Slayter blinked, looking around.

"Well," he said. "That was quite the experience."

Relief melted Khyven and he bowed his head. "I swear you're going to kill me some day."

"Jai'ketakos is gone," Slayter said.

"Yes."

"You fought him off?"

"I suppose." Khyven was reluctant to talk about it.

"You shed his *blood?*"

"I definitely did that."

"Then that is why I'm still alive. He made a bargain with

me." Slayter held out his hand for the steel vial. Khyven passed it over, and Slayter drank the rest.

He shivered and then smiled. "Invigorating. Yes, well, we certainly gained a modicum of information, didn't we?"

Khyven glanced at the shadows where the Mavric iron sword lay.

"Yes," he said reluctantly. "I suppose we did."

CHAPTER TWENTY-TWO
RAUVELOS

R auvelos stared over the courtyard, the broken gate, the crumbling wall, the cracked flagstones, and the statues. His gaze, as always, lingered last on the still form of Harkandos. Not for the first time, Rauvelos felt a flutter of fear. Rauvelos's master was the least reckless person in the world, but sometimes it wasn't evident. Holding such a powerful being with such a tenuous balance of magic, if it had been anyone other than Nhevalos, would seem the most reckless thing. But that part of the plan had its place, no doubt. As with all things concerning Nhevalos, Harkandos was right where he was supposed to be. A volcano in the courtyard, and just a little nudge would make it explode. Much like the continent of Noksonon, in truth ...

War was coming.

Oh, war had been coming ever since the War of the Fall nearly two thousand years ago, the war that the Humans, in their arrogance, called the Human-Giant War. Since that day, war had always been coming. But for the first time, Rauvelos felt the war was coming soon. Years. Perhaps even months. Perhaps days. He could feel it in the tides of the noktum. He could feel it like his very bones were stretching, growing.

And it had begun with Khyven the Unkillable.

Rauvelos turned and walked away from the window, his talons clicking on the stones. He had business in the depths of the castle ...

Rauvelos's master was not ... What was the clever little aphorism Humans used? Ah yes. Rauvelos's master was not an "open book" when it came to his plans. He told Rauvelos only what Rauvelos needed to know. And sometimes, his master told him nothing at all. Sometimes for centuries. But Rauvelos was more adept than anyone in the world at understanding the clues that his master left behind, at picking up the signals his master wanted him to see.

Khyven the Unkillable was one of those signals.

And so when Rauvelos recognized the Amulet of Noksonon Khyven wore around his neck—one made and marked by his master—everything had changed.

Rauvelos knew that his master had spent centuries tinkering with the Humans, that this was where he was placing his pieces. Rauvelos knew that the next war would decide the world of Eldros forever, and that it would be up to the mortals—Humans, Luminents, Shadowvar, Taur-Els, Brightlings, Delvers, and all the rest—to save their own lives. There had only been a small clutch of Eldroi who had believed as Nhevalos during the last war. Rauvelos could count them all by ticking them off on his talons ...

And most of them had died in the war.

In the War of the Fall, Nhevalos had surprised everyone. He had been chosen by Noktos himself, fiercely loyal, and he had never been vocal that anything had ever displeased him concerning the treatment of mortals. The great Eldroi like Harkandos, Deihmankos, and Nirapama had never seen Nhevalos coming, had never seen him until it was too late. They hadn't seen Paralos coming, either. Or Daelakos, Eveynos,

Burlonos, and Vadakynos. And that surprise had won the war.

They were all dead now, all of Nhevalos's allies, sacrificed to achieve the prize. Harkandos had personally incinerated two of them. Even Paralos was lost to the Great Noktum. The scant rebels Nhevalos had won over or manipulated had lost everything.

Now, two millennia later, even Rauvelos wondered if it had been worth it. He had never fully understood the prize, the thing for which Nhevalos fought: freedom and self-determination for the mortals.

It smacked of Human sentiment, a weakness. All the other Eldroi, be they the rabid mouth-frothers like Tovos or the great and powerful Eldroi like Harkandos, had thought Nhevalos had gone insane. That he wanted to be Human, that he wanted to emulate their ways.

Rauvelos knew that wasn't true. He knew his master better than any other single being in existence, and he knew that the saving of the mortals wasn't because of sentiment. Nhevalos was more ruthless than Harkandos and Tovos combined, more unpredictable than the insane Drakanoi Jai'ketakos.

Nhevalos always had a plan.

What that plan was, no one except Nhevalos himself would ever know, even Rauvelos. So while he hadn't ever understood exactly why Nhevalos wanted to save the short-lived little weaklings that scuttled across the thin crust of this world like cockroaches, Rauvelos had never questioned. In all the uncertainty of life and death, of future and past, Rauvelos knew one thing: his true power. He knew what made him one of the most deadly beings on Eldros. He knew why he was born, how he would die, and at least the essence of every move he would make in between.

He served Nhevalos. His debt had not yet been paid.

It was that simple. He was bound to serve Nhevalos, and when Nhevalos called for Rauvelos's death, he would fly into the fire with all speed.

So in the end, the why of Nhevalos's wars didn't matter. The outcome didn't matter. Whether Nhevalos had fallen into insanity or not didn't matter. Win, lose, survival, or obliteration ... It was all the same.

Rauvelos was the sword of his master's will.

And he knew the power of that, of intelligent and unswerving loyalty. Most creatures had no idea what that was, be they Eldroi, Human, or subterranean mammoth wyrm, but Rauvelos did. If Nhevalos did not win through, it would be because Rauvelos was dead and everything Rauvelos could do had been thwarted.

And then this scrappy Human, Khyven the Unkillable, had wandered into Rauvelos's world. The man had overthrown a king. He had traveled to Daemanon for a skirmish. He had wielded the Helm of Darkness, for Noktos's sake. It was the beginning. Rauvelos's long vigil over his master's nuraghi had changed to a girding for war.

It hadn't felt like it at the time, of course. It had simply felt like another Human gnat had flown into his realm and this time, he had elected not to squash it.

Rauvelos had spared a Human or two in the past, after all. Like Dandilene, the dreamy maiden who had fled her father's wishes. She'd fled what she had thought was the worst possible fate, a fat and pustule-ridden—by her account—baron who her father was forcing her to marry. So she'd fled into the noktum with dreams in her head about the ancient days, the days when Humans lived peacefully in the strongholds of the Dark.

Except there were no such days and there never had been. When Humans had navigated the noktum daily, back when there was nothing on Noksonon untouched by the noktum, they had been slaves to the Eldroi.

This blissfully ignorant maiden had stumbled into the noktum and somehow evaded the hungry Kyolars and Sleeths. That, mainly, was why Rauvelos had spared her. It was a million-to-one lucky chance, and he'd been fascinated. So he'd listened to her story with rapt interest, his curiosity piqued by just how detached from the real world a Human could get. The girl lived almost entirely in her own imagination, in what she wished was true, rather than what actually was. It had been absolutely fascinating.

And after her story, he had let her go. He'd been so charmed by her tale that ...

Rauvelos stopped, head cocked as he recalled the exact details.

No, wait. He'd eaten her.

Oh, she had been *tasty*.

Yes, that's right. It was the *soldier* he'd let live, not the maiden, the grizzled veteran who had entered the noktum while sleepwalking. Rauvelos had fixed the man dinner and they'd had a pleasant conversation. The man had thought he was still in a dream the entire time and—

No, wait. Rauvelos had eaten that man, too.

Very well, so there hadn't really been any since his master had told Rauvelos to retreat to the nuraghi and guard its lands. Humans had been allies in the War of the Fall and, Rauvelos supposed, for a few centuries after that. But it had been more than a millennia since Humans had looked upon Rauvelos and not paid the final price.

Until Khyven the Unkillable.

It was the beginning of his master's plan, and now all the Humans were in play once more. For centuries they had been irrelevant, and now they were essential.

Now there had been a number of mortals who had visited here, in Castle Noktos, and survived to tell the tale, just like the way his master had once entertained the Noksonoi dignitaries of old. They had their part to play, and that was that.

It was not Rauvelos's place to argue with his master.

Events were coming and each must be played to perfection. His master would have precipitated these events. It was Rauvelos's duty to ensure that Castle Noktos was in order and ready to weather the storm.

His talons clicked on the stairs as he descended. He passed several doors, including the Vault, before he stopped at the final staircase. This one went down to the final hallway in the depths of Castle Noktos. Rauvelos had constructed it himself. The rough-hewn walls of the penultimate levels gave way to this one archway of polished black stones. Rauvelos didn't like workmanship that stopped halfway. And while he would never condemn Noktos or the builders who had constructed His castle long ago, when Rauvelos had been charged by Nhevalos to add a fourth and final level, Rauvelos had finished it.

Ironically, the final archway was only seven feet tall, unlike almost all the other doorways and archways in the castle. It was a Human-sized tunnel, a specification given him by Nhevalos, who never explained why.

Rauvelos had speculated, and he had three theories.

First, the small door could be to allay curiosity. An Eldroi from before the war who saw a doorway that size would assume it was a servant's entrance and ignore it. Perhaps they wouldn't even consciously see it.

Secondly, it could be defended. Most Eldroi couldn't shape-shift readily. For some, it took years to adopt a foreign shape small enough to fit through a door like that. It was why the Drakanoi were simply dragons now. Most would never bother to return to their original Eldroi shapes because it required too much magic and too much time to compress such mass into a smaller vessel.

Not to mention such a transformation itched like mad.

Rauvelos remembered the time he had shape-shifted at his master's request, into the shape of an Eldroi. It had itched and burned like someone had stripped off his skin and put it back on—except one inch to the left and one inch too low. That uncomfortable disorientation had remained for years after the full transformation. He shivered and put it from his mind. Unpleasant nonsense ...

The third and most likely was that Nhevalos predicted the one to wield the weapon beyond that door was actually going to be Human. Rauvelos hadn't liked that idea one bit, not at the time, but his master saw beyond the horizon that normal minds could not contemplate. Rauvelos had since reluctantly come to terms with the possibility of it. And since meeting Khyven the Unkillable, he was relatively certain he'd speculated correctly.

Rauvelos's master was both wise and intelligent, beyond any other Eldroi who'd ever walked the earth, save perhaps Noktos himself.

The small doorway was a prophecy. A prophecy created by Nhevalos himself.

Rauvelos squeezed his body through the opening and deftly managed the tiny steps beyond until he reached the landing. The hallway was long, but there were only two doorways. At the far end of the hall, there was a Human-sized doorway. At a glance, it continued the illusion that this was a servant's entrance.

Rauvelos walked down the hallway toward the "servant's" door. Polished, glassy black stone in perfectly fitted blocks moved past him as his talons clicked on the polished black floor. As per Nhevalos's instructions, he'd put no decorations anywhere.

His destination came into view as he came closer. The archway was set back in the stone so that one could only see it if one was halfway down the hallway.

To a Human, the archway would be enormous, twenty feet tall and a foot thick, banded by Mavric iron inset into the wall. The surface level spells made it almost impossible to detect the powerful magic woven into them from a distance of six feet away or more. But once an Eldroi stood before it—or anyone with any magical talent whatsoever—it would give off heat like the sun.

An Eldroi of any magical talent would know immediately that there were devastating spells woven into this archway, and unless they had come prepared to pit their full magical strength against the door, they should turn around and flee.

Should an uninvited interloper ever get this far into the depths of Castle Noktos—which had never happened—they would die before they even touched the door. The iron bands were partially sentient, magically created to read the minds of those who approached. If they sensed someone who did not belong, they unleashed a series of defenses.

The first was a repulsion spell. Unless one wore the blessing of Nhevalos himself, the urge to turn and run would be so compelling that Rauvelos suspected anyone resisting even for an instant would soil themselves. If they resisted longer than that, they'd fall to the floor in a convulsive fit. If that happened, they would likely stay there, convulsing until they starved to death or caved in their own skull on the stone floor.

If somehow they circumvented the repulsion spell, the archway would unleash a spell that reached into an invader's body and evaporated the moisture. The invader would shrivel as steam burst through their flesh, creating a bloody cloud around them while their body shrank into a desiccated husk.

Of course, an Eldroi talented in Love Magic might shield herself from the repulsion spell. One talented in Land Magic could protect himself from the evaporation spell, but that was just the beginning. A touch upon the handle began an open-ended life siphon that would pull even an Eldroi's life-force into the Mavric iron. Not only would this kill an Eldroi in a matter of moments, but it strengthened the archway and all of its spells.

Should someone get past the repulsion, the evaporation, and the life-suck, they would have to pick the lock. If they managed that, they would have to blunt the idiocy spell that would turn their brain to mush once they pushed open the door ...

If they did all this, they would then be able to enter the room.

Of course, once they did, they would fall through the illusory floor, which covered a teleportation portal. The floor portal transported the intruder thousands of miles to the south and dropped them into a two-hundred-foot pit in the middle of the Lux. The faux floor was triggered to vanish the moment someone passed through, becoming a normal floor and preventing anyone from coming back through.

The pit on the other side was not only in the middle of the blinding Lux, but its walls were polished as smooth as glass. A hundred feet up, those smooth walls were ringed with a series of powerful Line Magic runes that stripped an Eldroi of their ability to use magic.

Trapped, unable to use magic, hidden from any who might seek to rescue them, the intruder would sit in their blinding prison until they starved to death. Or took their own life. Or until the unrelenting light drove them mad.

These attacks would assail an intruder one after the other unless, of course, they possessed a simple phrase.

Rauvelos approached the door and felt the sentient spell brush his mind and recognize him.

"*Lord Rauvelos ...*" the door said into his mind.

"*Paralos, my love,*" Rauvelos spoke the beginning of the pass phrase.

The giant door clicked, opening an inch and revealing a glimpse of the room beyond, seemingly inviting Rauvelos to push it wide. But should an intruder think they had overcome the defenses and have the temerity to touch the door, it would devour them with a disintegration spell so powerful even Noktos himself would have been hard pressed to fight it off.

"*I consign you to darkness,*" Rauvelos finished the phrase.

The door sighed in his mind and swung silently open. Rauvelos stepped in and extended his wings, flapped gently to cross the space of missing floor until he landed on the fifteenth row of tiles, the first bit of solid ground in the room.

Rauvelos had counseled his master to put Harkandos into this room.

Harkandos had been the most powerful mage of all the Noksonoi, perhaps even all the Eldroi throughout the world. Some said he outstripped even Noktos in his sheer raw power. Harkandos had been the heir to the leadership of the Noksonoi during the War of the Fall.

And Nhevalos had defeated him.

That had been an eye-opening lesson for Rauvelos. He'd followed his master loyally in the centuries that led up to the War of the Fall. He'd followed throughout the war, past the hatred of their kind and the accusations of "Betrayer" ...

But it was only in that moment when Nhevalos defeated Harkandos that Rauvelos banished all doubt about which of the Noksonoi was the most powerful. His master showed in that one stroke that raw strength, whether it be physical or magical, was no match for vision and subtlety.

Rauvelos's master was peerless in that arena. He hadn't tried to match Harkandos blow for blow; that would have been suicide. No, he'd turned Harkandos's power—his very strength—against him. And that is what confined him still, held him in stasis in the master's courtyard.

Rauvelos had counseled his master to bring Harkandos down here, into this room, the most secure place in the noktum, but his master had declined. No, he'd said, Harkandos would stay where he had fallen, in plain sight, that this was the safest place for him.

And with the single exception of when the Human mage Slayter Wheskone had nearly set Harkandos free, his master had been right.

Rauvelos shuddered thinking back on it. For a terrifying instant, he'd thought his master's plans would come crumbling down because of one ridiculously foolhardy Human mage. It was the only moment—aside from his initial conversation with Nhevalos—that he'd desperately wished the statue of Harkandos had been securely locked into this room like Rauvelos had originally advised.

He'd also suggested that a number of powerful artifacts from the Vault be put in this place, but every time Lord Nhevalos had declined. This room was home to only one treasure, the most powerful magical artifact on the entire continent.

The Sword of Noksonon.

It hung on the far wall, Lord Noktos's own blade, the sword he had used to drive the other Eldroi—Daemanoi, Pyranoi, Drakanoi, and even the scant Lathranoi—from Noksonon during the Elder Wars. It contained all the power the Lord of the Noksonoi could put into it.

And it was sentient. Its intelligence made the sentient door looked like nothing more than an eager, but brainless, dog.

In addition to the Sword's many abilities, it could transform itself into the shape of any weapon it chose. Usually, it preferred to remain in the form its creator, Noktos himself, had originally forged it in: an eight-foot length of longsword with a cross guard of dual blades that mimicked the end of the actual blade. But today it appeared as a six-foot-long, wide-bladed sword with a relatively normal cross guard.

Rauvelos cocked his head. Interesting. The Sword was mimicking Daelakos's Blade in exquisite detail, the same blade that Rauvelos had allowed the silly Human named Gohver to leave Castle Noktos with. Rauvelos had been amused by allowing the deadly Mavric iron sword loose among the humans who had created a little pocket for their rebel camp within his noktum. He knew the Mavric iron sword would kill the man, and that had amused him.

Then, Khyven the Unkillable had returned with the blade and demanded the Helm of Darkness. Rauvelos had thought the helm would kill Khyven, also. When it hadn't, Rauvelos had left the sword with Khyven as a ... sign of respect. He'd been certain Nhevalos would approve, and when he finally saw his master, Nhevalos had indeed agreed with the decision.

It was odd that the Sword of Noksonon would mimic Daelakos's Blade, though. Rauvelos didn't converse with the Sword often, but he had interacted with it enough to know how highly the Sword thought of itself. Daelakos's Blade, though not without its own abilities, was what the Sword of Noksonon would refer to as a "dumb blade," without sentience at all and with only the barest tidbit of magical power in comparison. The Sword choosing to mimic Daelakos's Blade had to mean something, to indicate some joke.

Rauvelos studied the Sword respectfully, waiting for the mind-to-mind contact that always came. The Sword liked to talk, mostly about its glory days slaying Drakanoi during the Elder Wars.

It uttered not a single word, and Rauvelos instantly knew it was in a mood. Something had ruffled it, and he was intensely curious as to what that might be.

Once every year, Rauvelos made this pilgrimage to visit the Sword. There was no official need to do it, but Rauvelos felt it was ... respectful to the Sword's maker, Noktos. The Sword didn't seem to much care about Rauvelos, his visits, or the fact that it had been hidden away from the world for two millennia. The Sword didn't get lonely. It didn't seem to experience the passage of time the way a mortal, or even an Eldroi, would. The Sword didn't seem to care about much of anything since it had been here, in fact. Rauvelos suspected that was because the Elder Wars were long done, and there hadn't been any foreign Eldroi for the Sword to feed upon for millennia.

"Impressive." Rauvelos finally broke the silence and spoke to the Sword, nodding at its exact replication of Daelakos's Blade.

If Rauvelos was reading events correctly, the time for the re-emergence of the Sword of Noksonon might be at hand, and he'd be lying if he wasn't curious how the Sword might look upon a second war between Giants and the mortal races.

The Sword said nothing, which was unusual. It almost always talked first, about how it had enjoyed sucking the life from Taran'telos, the dragon of the moon, or lopping the head from Kadantoroy, the Pyranoi who'd tried to create a second Lux.

"I didn't realize you knew about the ... relocation of Daelakos's Blade," Rauvelos sent to the Sword's mind. It wasn't the first time he'd found the Sword in a different shape, but the timing of it transforming into Daelakos's Blade, when that sword had recently found its way into mortal hands, was curious. Did the Sword know Daelakos's Blade had left the castle? Was this a mocking salute to its departure? But if so, how? The Sword of Noksonon was intelligent, but not omniscient.

"It was quite something, really. Humans in the castle. Refreshing. It is a new cluster of Humans ... In truth, they are more fascinating than any I've seen since the War of the Fall."

The Sword said nothing.

A wisp of uneasiness ruffled Rauvelos's feathers like there was a breeze in the room.

"*One of them disturbed Harkandos,*" Rauvelos continued. "*Nearly let him out.*"

The Sword did not speak.

Rauvelos felt a sinking feeling from his throat down to his belly. The Sword had never missed an opportunity to talk about Harkandos. It loved Harkandos. Harkandos was what the Sword believed all Noksonoi should be.

Rauvelos stepped forward, all of his senses on high alert. He cast a quick spell, and ...

Only a small purple glow surrounded the Sword.

When the Sword was not inclined to hide itself, it threw off so much power it could be felt by even the most magic deprived mortals on the continent. It should have burst into a bonfire of purple light, not just the normal glow of a normally enchanted Mavric iron sword.

"*Is this some kind of game?*" Rauvelos asked. The Sword was not above playing games. It had done so before, trying to make Rauvelos believe one thing when another was true. Rauvelos had always seen these games as diversions. The Sword had been down here for almost two thousand years, after all. Rauvelos was only surprised that it hadn't done more to divert itself during its long wait.

"*Sword of Noksonon,*" he addressed it directly. "*I don't understand this game.*"

Still nothing.

Rauvelos flicked forward one wing and, after nearly two millennia, did something he had never done before. He touched the hilt.

His master had told him that touching the Sword of Noksonon was an invitation to bond with it, but the sudden fear that something had gone horribly wrong overwhelmed Rauvelos's fear of danger.

His feather brushed the hilt. He felt nothing, no wisp of a contact with his mind, no words, no vibration of the awesome power contained within the Sword.

Rauvelos now abandoned all caution. He brought his claw up and clasped the grip.

Rauvelos let go and backed up so far and so quickly that he almost stepped onto the illusory floor. He recovered in time, but he barely noticed his nearly fatal mistake. A sudden, horrible, unavoidable revelation filled him. Rauvelos hadn't felt this kind of fear in millennia.

That wasn't the Sword playing tricks. This wasn't the Sword at all. That pitiful thing hanging on the wall hadn't been forged in the blood of a dozen Eldroi. It wasn't the weapon that had turned back the Drakanoi army at the Gates of Venakos. That actually *was* Daelakos's Blade.

The Sword of Noksonon was gone.

Chapter Twenty-Three
NHEVALOS

Nhevalos stood at the broken gate of Castle Noktos, reflecting, and he allowed himself the moment. Time was not a luxury he could afford, but he felt it was necessary.

The Kyolars and Sleeths did not notice him because Nhevalos didn't want them to. He could move unseen within a noktum, if he wished. One effect of his amulet, when properly activated, was a kind of invisibility. Oh, he wasn't actually invisible to the eye, but rather ... unremarkable to anyone who looked. Those who looked at him would not see a Lord of Noksonon in the full flush of his power, but rather as a shrub, or a tree, or a rock. Onlookers would see what they expected to see and move on.

The war was almost upon them, and the hammer would fall here. He had seen this. He had prepared for this. All was in place, and Nhevalos had finally returned to retrieve the Sword of Noksonon. It was the single most valuable magical artifact on Noksonon. Nhevalos would have carried it with him to ensure its safety, but the Sword was ... problematic. Having the Sword on one's side could change the fate of an entire continent, but the Sword had to agree to help.

It rarely did.

The thing had its own agenda, as well as strong opinions of how it should be used. It needed convincing. It had known a few wielders since Noktos had carried it during the Elder Wars, and each of those wielders had met with glorious—and final—fates in battle.

Nhevalos didn't think that was an accident, so he did not carry the Sword with him. No. The Sword had to be placed carefully. And it was probably better if Nhevalos was not its wielder if he wanted to survive the upcoming war.

In the meanwhile, he'd ensured the Sword was well hidden and well protected during the quiet intervening centuries, but the quiet was almost over. The *kairoi* promised the war was coming sooner rather than later. Of course, one could read the *kairoi* closely, place everything meticulously, but the *kairoi* were eternally fickle. Nhevalos had determined it was better to have the Sword at his hip at this point. It was time to convince the Sword that its primary objective should be protecting Nhevalos.

The *kairoi* were as capricious as the nature of Jai'ketakos, as brutal as the anger of Harkandos. They shifted, moved, danced, and those who could see them—the Lore Mages of Eldros—must dance with them to have any hope of using their knowledge for any purpose whatsoever. Nhevalos was as fine a dancer as there was, but even he could not see all ends. Only the most likely of ends. The *kairoi* often illuminated key paths for years, even centuries, only to yank that path away moments before it came to fruition.

So a Lore Mage had to be a dancer, yes, but also a gardener. The lines needed cultivation. Meticulous planning, nurturing, and then the resilient flexibility to scrap everything at a moment's notice and cultivate elsewhere. Nhevalos had dedicated his entire life to being this dancer/gardener.

And now, the fruits of his labor were almost upon him. He

had been preparing to win this war no matter when it came: a thousand years, a hundred years, or right now. And the truth was, he'd not known which of those destinies would be fulfilled. He'd cultivated them all, readied for them all.

It was only when Khyven took up the Helm of Darkness, only when Khyven did not die from extreme exposure to the Mavric iron of Daelakos's Blade and the Helm of Darkness ... that Nhevalos knew the garden was ready to be harvested. If he moved quickly enough, the war would be short. The Eldroi who would attempt to recapture the world wouldn't be ready. Not as ready as they would be a hundred years from now. They could be pushed into a hasty posture, taken off balance.

And so Nhevalos had taken the newly crowned queen off to Daemanon to prepare her, transform her. In the alternate futures in which the upcoming war did not happen, Rhennaria Laochodon would have had a very different life. She would have gone on to lead her people to an era of prosperity and happiness for nearly a century.

But that future wouldn't happen now. Instead, it would be a war, and if Nhevalos hadn't transformed Rhenn into an immortal creature of the night, she would have no tools to lead her people through the darkness.

After Rhenn's transformation, the future held nothing but strife and hardship. She would never know peace, not until she died, but she would be instrumental in ensuring Usara—and most of the other mortal kingdoms on Noksonon—survived. She would lead her people through the darkness so that there might be light for them on the other side.

She was necessary for Nhevalos's plans; she must pay the price he had chosen for her. If someone did not make their choices for the mortals, they would stumble about in the dark, eventually falling off the edge of the world forever. Nhevalos was their steward, their savior.

It wasn't always that way. He'd once seen the mortals as revolting and pitiful as the rest of the Noksonoi, back before he'd had his revelation. Back before Nhevalos had seen where he fit in the grand scheme of power in the world.

His thoughts drifted then, to the past. It was a rare indulgence, but he allowed it. In his mind, he went back to the beginning. He went back to the moment that he had awoken to his purpose ...

Chapter Twenty-Four
NHEVALOS

Nhevalos had been called by the Eldrovan—Noktos's handpicked council who oversaw the workings of Noksonon since he had sacrificed himself—to work at The Iluit San, the crevasse where mortals were taken for resisting the mandates given to them by their masters. Any time a Luminent refused her duty to illuminate a cavern for the darkblind Humans, or anytime a Human's passion slipped its leash and they lashed out at a Noksonoi, anytime a Taur-El could no longer lift the burden given to them ... they were brought to The Iluit San. There in the smooth, high-cliffed walls of the crevasse, the Eldroi would experiment upon these now-useless tools. They would experiment and transform them. This was how the Luminents were born in the first place, how the Taur-Els were born, and the Shadowvar. Those who would not capitulate to their place in the world were used to create more useful tools.

Almost all of them died in the transformations, and almost never was something more useful created. The Luminents and the Shadowvar were made in the time of Lord Noktos the First, the founder of Noksonon and the greatest Eldroi to ever live.

The Iluit San had been there as long as Nhevalos could remember, but recently the stewardship had been given over to Harkandos, the Eldrovan's new favorite protege.

Originally it had been an exploratory, visionary place of creation where Noktos used the lessons he had learned long ago from Deihmankos. However, if the rumors were to be believed, Harkandos saw his new assignment as a place of punishment. If he aspired to create something new, Nhevalos had not heard of it. Harkandos had laughingly renamed the crevasse the Slaughter Box. He was far more interested in the twisted faces and the agonized cries of the dying mortals than in creating anything useful for Noksonon.

Of course, what other purpose did mortals serve except to live—and die—for the Noksonoi? That was why they'd been created. To be useful. If they could not fulfill their purpose, then what did it matter if they were destroyed?

So Nhevalos went to the Slaughter Box because the Eldrovan had bidden him. An uprising had recently occurred in Usara. A few hundred Humans had somehow organized without the Noksonoi being aware. They had made weapons. They actually had mages as well. Human mages. That was new. Of course they weren't more than scrappy peasants who had managed to connect to a single stream of magic, but Humans wielding magic was worthy of worry, so the Eldrovan had sent Nhevalos.

The Human army had killed Vederos, the steward of that area, after all. They'd *killed* an Eldroi.

This was also something new. A useless mortal was one thing. A group of mortals who not only organized a revolt but managed to kill a Noksonoi required special attention. They had been rounded up immediately and given to Harkandos. He'd never had so many toys to play with, and he had asked for assistance. Apparently he had something creative in mind.

Nhevalos finally arrived at The Iluit San, the crevasse where the mortals were kept. The descent was a good three hundred feet down a winding staircase carved in the very side of the crevasse. Nhevalos stepped to the edge of the cliff and looked down.

What he saw then changed him forever, changed him in a way he had not expected, in a way that he had not been able to explain.

There weren't a few hundred humans in that pit. There were thousands. They squirmed against each other like worms, packed into the narrow bottom of the crevasse. Harkandos stood on a flat ledge in the side of the cliff, maybe fifty feet above the squirming mass.

There was nowhere for the mortals—which were mostly Human with a few Luminents, Taur-Els, and Shadowvar—to go. The screams of the dying rose like the cry of some giant bird. Some of the mortals were moaning from limbs that had been hacked or twisted off. Some bled from head wounds. Some were simply being crushed by the squirming mass of bodies.

Every now and then, a Human, Luminent, or Taur-El would attempt to scale the vertical cliff, ignoring the pain as they jammed bloody fingers and skinned knees into the natural cracks of the wall, trying to rise above the misery of the crushing mass below. It was impressive, this indomitable will. There was no hope they could change their fate. Even if they could rise above the rest, as these rare few tried, Harkandos waited for them. Pure excitement pinned his lips back, showing teeth. When one of these intrepid Humans climbed high enough, Harkandos took great relish in destroying them.

Each climber's face showed the agony in his body, but a feral hope lit their faces, driving them to reach Harkandos and somehow defeat him. A Human. Defeating an Eldroi.

It was insanity.

Yet that feral hope did not die. Mortal after mortal made the attempt, though they were doomed.

Nhevalos stood transfixed. He didn't know how long he watched as one climber after another came into Harkandos's deadly range. One after another, they died.

Once they were close enough, Harkandos would choose a different method for their demise. A flick of his finger and a Taur-El's head exploded in a shower of blood and brains. A clack of his teeth and a Luminent burst into flame and fell screaming back into the sea of mortals. A spear through the shoulder for the Human who had almost attained the shelf, then Harkandos dangled him over the mortals below, his blood showering down on them. Harkandos drained him until the Human went limp.

And yet still they came, the best of them straining against the impossibility—the absolute impossibility—of success. Harkandos was the most powerful user of magic since Noktos himself. He could have destroyed the thousands of them all at once, yet those individuals still believed they could do something to change their fate.

Nhevalos watched, and Harkandos was so fixated by slaying the climbers, he never so much as looked up.

More mortals fell. A stone to the head. A crackle of lightning. Slicing open a Human's stomach and letting his entrails fall all the way back to the squirming mass of people. That man kept climbing, even with a rope of entrails dangling from him, until he finally lost strength and fell.

As Nhevalos watched—he knew not for how long—something changed inside him. It was like something snapped like a dry branch.

Indomitable.

That simply didn't make sense. Mortals were not indomitable. They were transient little flares of movement, pathetic imperfections who only lived a century at most. Born to die.

But there was something inside them that drove them, and for a flashing instant, Nhevalos saw a parallel to the greatest Noksonoi who had ever lived: Noktos himself.

Noktos had this same drive. This same indomitable will that had driven Noktos past death, past fear, past … singularity. It had driven Noktos to escape from Nirapama and Lathranon. To establish a place where he, and those like him, could live in peace. He had been unwilling to submit to Nirapama's demands that all bend the knee to her.

What drove these mortals suddenly seemed the exact same as what drove Noktos to establish Noksonon. To protect someone other than himself, to stop the invading Eldroi who wanted to dominate Noksonon.

These mortals ... They were *like* Noktos. And in that shocking moment of cold clarity, Nhevalos realized no one else saw it. No one but him.

He shook his head, trying to regain his senses.

It was a ridiculous concept. A mortal was not like an Eldroi. They were frail, blind, weak, transient. They couldn't wield magic, except for these recent anomalies. Their bodies came apart like soggy paper. These creatures couldn't *be* like Noktos. He'd created them. How could something created be like the creator ...?

Yet as Nhevalos watched them climb, watched them perish, he could only see that indomitable will. He simply could not look away. Yes, they were weaker, smaller, and they would die one by one. But if they organized ... Look at how many of them there were. If each of them had that same indomitable will as the climbers, and they worked together, and they had magic ...

They had killed one Noksonoi. Why couldn't they do it again? Why couldn't they become an actual threat to the Noksonoi? Their stubbornness was more than a will to live. It was a will to determine their own fate. Once they had tasted that, would they ever give it up?

Nhevalos shook his head. It was impossible. Harkandos and the other Noksonoi were far too powerful. If one of these foolish climbers somehow, against any rational expectation, managed to reach and overcome Harkandos, there were dozens of Eldroi after him who would squish them like bugs.

Nhevalos watched one after another try and die, try and die, watched Harkandos's smile as he killed them like he was burning ants with a flaming stick.

Nhevalos couldn't help but see Harkandos and Nirapama as the same in that moment. Nirapama would have killed them all, all the Eldroi protected by Noktos, if Noktos hadn't found the will to resist, if he hadn't shown his followers how to fight back.

Nhevalos's everlasting vision came to him then. His certainty of the future. His purpose.

Somehow, Harkandos—and any other Eldroi who could not perceive this same spark within the mortals—was destroying the very thing that Noktos had fought to protect. Without knowing it, Harkandos was defiling Noktos's memory.

The straightforward action would be to try to talk to Harkandos, to all the other Eldroi, and to illustrate Nhevalos's sudden vision. But even as he imagined that conversation, those multiple conversations, he saw how each would go.

They would label him the enemy. They would not see what he saw. And then they would kill him. Nhevalos could never fight them all. His struggles would be as ineffective as the mortals who climbed the crevasse, just as Noktos would have been crushed by Nirapama if his Noksonoi had not joined their power to his.

But if Nhevalos aligned the mortals ... If he lined them up in the right fashion, if he could harness this terrible will they possessed all at once ... Not by the dozens or hundreds, but by the thousands ...

That could change their fate.

The vision slammed down like a mountain had fallen upon him, and he tried to unsee what he had seen. He tried to revel in the joy that Harkandos felt. The power. The dominance. He tried to pull back his perspective.

He could not.

Once he had seen the mortals similar to how the Noksonoi had been so long ago, he couldn't unsee it. Once he had seen himself as Noktos—one who could see the path forward, who could actually help them—he couldn't unsee that, either.

The mortals would keep climbing. They would keep dying.

Nhevalos could never prevent the single mortals from dying, but he could orchestrate a future where, as a whole, they could finally be free.

"Nhevalos!" Harkandos's powerful, excited voice reached him. Noktos's heir to the leadership of the Eldrovan had finally looked up.

Nhevalos turned his gaze to Harkandos.

"Are you waiting for a better moment? They scramble to escape like roaches. Come! We have much to do." Harkandos grinned, glanced down, and used Land Magic to compress the air around the head of a burly Taur-El who had nearly made it to the shelf. The bull-headed man's head crushed down to the size of a pebble. Harkandos laughed as the mortal fell back into the squirming mass below.

Nhevalos pulled from his own life-force and activated his Land Magic, making a solid bridge of air over to Harkandos on the far side of the crevice.

"I have an idea for a new use for them," Harkandos said as Nhevalos reached him. "Clearly these mortals are useless. Rebellious, unrepentant. We have to remake them."

Three more Humans started scaling their way up out of the pit.

"Clearly," Nhevalos said.

"Go ahead. Kill a few," Harkandos said, chuckling. "It puts you in the right frame of mind for creation. We have to do right by them, but not *all* of them."

"Not all of them," Nhevalos repeated as he shot down one of the climbers with a firebolt.

"It's fun, isn't it?" Harkandos said, killing another. "We're allowed a bit of relaxation before getting down to the important work."

"Yes," Nhevalos said. "Yes, we are."

Chapter Twenty-Five
NHEVALOS

Nhevalos broke from his reverie, moved past the gates and started up the fractured walkway. He slowed as he approached Harkandos's statue. Its eyes glared down at him. The powerful Noksonoi was trapped with an intricate spell that pitted his own magical strength against himself. The more Harkandos fought his prison—the more magic he used to fight it—the tighter the statue transformation twisted down on him. The more he relaxed, the more he could perceive and see. No doubt right now Harkandos was calming himself as much as his hateful heart allowed while glaring at the object of his hate.

The nature of the spell was a great risk. The spell was a filigree of multiple Line Magic runes that created the perfect web. It was designed so that Harkandos could not see its workings from within his stone prison, so he could not work a way to escape it.

But it was extremely vulnerable from the outside. Nhevalos had spread the rumor that Harkandos had been killed during the Human-Giant War, that Nhevalos himself had overcome the great Noksonoi. The lie had worked two-fold. First, it stopped any other Noksonoi who might come seeking Nhevalos's blood. Harkandos's name commanded such fear and respect that anyone who could kill him, by definition, was even more frightening. Secondly, if everyone thought Harkandos was dead, they wouldn't come looking for him.

And here he had sat for nearly two thousand years. Hiding Harkandos in plain sight had been, in the end, a stroke of genius. Any Noksonoi could have interrupted the spell if they studied it for a moment, and once the magnificent filigree had been damaged in any way, it would give Harkandos the crack to stick his fingers into, to pry the rest of the spell apart.

Nhevalos had gambled that no Noksonoi, after their horrible defeat at the hands of the mortals, would come looking for the "dead" Harkandos, and they would certainly not do it in Nhevalos's domain.

That gamble had paid off.

No Eldroi had come searching for Harkandos. None had disrupted the sanctity of Castle Noktos. But Nhevalos hadn't accounted for mortal mages.

That oversight had almost upset the apple cart.

Months ago, when Slayter Wheskone had visited this place, he'd cast a communication spell of his own right next to the statue. He'd wanted to talk to Harkandos. It had only been a little thing, something even Nhevalos hadn't seen in the *kairoi*.

When Slayter had touched the statue, had inserted his spell, he'd inadvertently pried apart the filigree. That had given Harkandos the crack he'd needed.

If it hadn't been for Rauvelos's quick thinking and quick acting, the titan of magic would have been released right then and there. The war for Noksonon would have begun, and Khyven and his friends would be dead.

That would have been a disaster.

But Rauvelos had done what he'd been stationed here to do. He'd handled the situation, and handled it well. Sending Khyven and his friends into the Great Noktum was not something

Nhevalos might have chosen. He'd determined that leaving Lorelle to her death was the best way to leave Khyven blessedly free of an attachment that might deter him. A man who can save the world might, if he was caught in the throes of what Humans called "love," instead choose to save only the object of his affection, rather than looking at the larger picture. Lorelle had been, and still was, that threat.

So no, Nhevalos wouldn't have chosen to send Khyven after his paramour, but it had actually worked out quite well. Lorelle was now, with her bonding to the Dark, a helpmeet that could be used toward the primary goal. The result couldn't be argued with. Yes, they were now a mortal couple with all the difficulties that presented, but Khyven had made an interesting leap forward in his development because of his attachment to Lorelle, and to the queen's group in general.

There was no way Nhevalos would have pit Khyven against Tovos so early. The Lord of the Dark should have crushed Khyven at that early, tender stage of his development. Even the *kairoi* hadn't predicted that battle, because it was not tied to Khyven alone. They had done it as a group. Slayter, Khyven, Lorelle, and the Shadowvar. The *kairoi* had predicted Khyven could be one of half a dozen who might stand against the tide, had predicted that he may survive to reach that pinnacle ...

But none had predicted Tovos's defeat.

"If you remove Khyven's attachment to his friends you could lose more ... You're missing a vital piece."

Darjhen's words returned to Nhevalos, spoken in defense of Lorelle. Sentiment. It was something Humans prized so very highly. To them, it was worth dying for, with no eye on the future, with no consideration to what their lives might become. It was the same thing as when Nhevalos witnessed them trying to climb from the pit. They couldn't see what was going to happen—or they refused to believe it would happen—so they kept climbing and climbing ... all the way to their doom.

It was at the heart of Nhevalos's purpose that he saw past sentiment and did for mortals the one thing they were incapable of doing for themselves: looking past their passions, desires, and sentiments and seeing into the future.

And after centuries of having this rule proven to Nhevalos over and over, here came an example of the opposite. And, relatively speaking, this exception had come at the last minute before the war.

He'd been pondering what that meant. He knew—he had known for centuries—that Khyven, Slayter, and Rhenn could possibly affect coming events. It was why he had marked them, protected them. Lorelle was not part of that equation. Neither was the Shadowvar, Vohn.

It was curious and unnerving. This time, it had swung Nhevalos's way in the battle against Tovos. An unexpected windfall. But it could just as easily have swung the other way. Khyven could have died in that altercation. So could Slayter. And then Nhevalos would have had to use the other tools he had cultivated on Noksonon instead of Khyven.

It wasn't the first thing that hadn't gone to plan, of course. Lore Magic was tricky at the best of times, for the most adept of users. That was why it required resilience and quick thinking. There were constantly paths closing and new paths opening.

What made this particular instance troublesome to Nhevalos was that the *kairoi* had changed, and while his champions had succeeded, the success couldn't be attributed to anything Nhevalos had arranged.

Instead, it had come down to the completely unreliable sentimental connection between this small group of mortals.

That was troublesome.

Nhevalos was adept at manipulating mortals due to their sentimentality, pushing them to enact and create new paths within the *kairoi*. He wasn't comfortable resting the outcome of his plans on sentiment. Khyven's entire group was now unpredictable ...

Nhevalos broke from his thoughts. Above him, Harkandos's eyes had hardened. The incandescent glare had been stifled. Apparently the great Noksonoi had tried to use his magic, had let his fury get the better of him, and the spell had hardened up.

"Soon, old friend," Nhevalos said. He didn't make the mistake of coming nearer the statue. Best to keep his distance and not risk any kind of interference with the filigree. Slayter Wheskone had proven that just a little bit of imbalance could give Harkandos a crack to push through. Nhevalos was taking no chances at this late date. "Soon we will know who was right. Patience. All things in due time. In my time."

A light cracking sounded as the stone became harder and harder, compressing into itself.

"Don't hurt yourself," Nhevalos said, and he left the area, walked up to the stone steps and ascended them one at a time. "Soon, you'll have the chance to kill me."

Nhevalos continued toward Castle Noktos, his castle, a gift from the legendary Noktos himself. He knew Rauvelos was watching him, waiting. It was impossible for Nhevalos to have made it as far as the gate without Rauvelos being aware of him. The noktum phoenix had the best eyes in the noktum. He saw everything, a function of the kind of creature he was, and it was one of the many reasons Nhevalos had made him steward. Rauvelos had probably sensed Nhevalos the moment he'd entered the noktum.

Nhevalos ascended the steps to Castle Noktos, opened the doors. Rauvelos stood on the other side of the great room as though he'd been there for an hour.

"Master." Rauvelos bowed his head.

"Rauvelos."

"Two visits in a century. Your domain rejoices in your presence."

"The time is nearing. The *kairoi* point to this moment, this place. Once, it was one of several possibilities. Now, it seems nearly inevitable that the deciding battle will hit here."

"The time is near," Rauvelos said.

Nhevalos nodded.

"You are taller, master. Are you reverting at last?"

"I have let the spell lapse. The need for secrecy is past, and I will need all of my life-force for what is coming." Holding a spell like the one that kept Nhevalos Human-sized was no small casting. It had drawn power from him constantly. Now that he had released the spell, he was slowly reverting to his normal size. It took time. But the burden of the spell had vanished almost immediately.

"Of course," Rauvelos said.

"The critical event will happen here," Nhevalos said. He stopped by the tall fireplace, put his hand on the ancient furniture.

Rauvelos cocked his head.

"You have stewarded well, Rauvelos. You have kept the castle exactly as it was. I know that wasn't easy for you." After the victory during the Human-Giant War, Rauvelos had begged Nhevalos to allow him to set the castle right, to restore it to its former glory. It was a piece of history—the castle that Noktos himself had built and unexpectedly given to what the Eldrovan would have considered one of his lesser proteges. That had happened so long ago that mortal history didn't even record it. Rauvelos had felt the castle deserved to be respected, that it should not lay in half-ruin.

Nhevalos had refused, said it should remain as it was, as a testament to the struggle. Nhevalos wanted it to be a reminder of the worldwide conflict that every single mortal had already forgotten, a reminder that the war hadn't been finished. The Eldroi who hated Nhevalos, who felt the proper order was for all mortals to be slaves, were still out there, waiting.

This castle was a testament to what had passed, and that the true battle was yet to come.

"Then this will be the culmination?" Rauvelos asked.

"We have nearly come to the end. It is earlier than I thought, the earliest of the *kairoi* I have seen. But we are ready."

"And I was right about Khyven the Unkillable," Rauvelos said.

Nhevalos looked up from the cold fireplace. Rauvelos had a mischievous twinkle in his eye.

"You like him," Nhevalos said.

"He is surprising. Not something mortals usually are."

Rauvelos far preferred eating mortals to liking them. In fact, if Nhevalos hadn't given strict orders, he'd have feasted regularly on the citizens of Usara.

"Will some of his friends come into play as well?"

"All of them, in fact," Nhevalos said.

"A tight-knit little group of mortals, that. It is fascinating to see them avoid death at every corner."

"The fight will come here first this time, my friend," Nhevalos said. "The first skirmish will set up all the rest. Are you ready?"

Rauvelos cocked his head and went completely still. He was particularly gifted at seeing what Nhevalos wanted before it had been spoken. It was another reason why he'd been the perfect steward for Castle Noktos. He was the only steward who could have done it, really. He had predicted Khyven's importance. He'd gambled—and been right to gamble—sending Khyven and his friends into the Great Noktum. He could anticipate Nhevalos almost as easily as he breathed. But when Rauvelos went completely still, it meant he hadn't come up with the answer yet.

It didn't take long.

"Ah," Rauvelos said. "It is time."

"Yes."

"I see."

They both stood silently for a while, and Nhevalos wondered if Rauvelos would balk.

"When?"

"Soon, I think."

"Who will steward Castle Noktos after I am gone?"

"The mortals."

The ridge above Rauvelos's left eye raised slightly. "The mortals?"

"Yes."

"The last time mortals had free rein here, master, they almost set Harkandos loose."

"I know."

"And what if they ..." Rauvelos stopped, cocked his head the other direction. "Ah."

"It will not be a factor."

"Master ..." Rauvelos said, seeming about to continue, to say more, but he went silent.

"Prepare them."

"Of course, master."

"It is necessary, Rauvelos."

"Of course it is. I understand, master."

"You have been an impeccable steward, Rauvelos."

"Thank you master." Rauvelos hesitated, then asked, "Might I ask how it will happen? The first skirmish?"

"It is never entirely certain."

"But you have a guess."

"I do. The dragon is loose. I believe it will be Jai'ketakos."

Rauvelos cocked his head, and a slight smile curved at the edges of his beak. "The old dragon will dare to come here?"

"He has been ... humiliated. I think he is nearly frothing at the mouth with the need for revenge. He will come here for that."

"Humiliated by whom—?" But Rauvelos cut himself off, then opened his long, sharp beak and laughed in a deep, birdlike squawk. "It was Khyven the Unkillable, wasn't it?"

"Yes." Nhevalos nodded. "Slayter Wheskone also played a part, but yes."

"He cannot like that. Not one bit. That is ..." Rauvelos shook his great head and tried to tame his laughter. "A Human against a Drakanoi ..."

Nhevalos nodded.

"A Human against a Drakanoi," Rauvelos repeated. "Inevitable, really. I wouldn't want to face the Sword of Noksonon, either."

Nhevalos, who had turned back to the fireplace, glanced over at Rauvelos curiously.

Rauvelos saw Nhevalos's confusion. "That was your intention, wasn't it, master?"

In a rare moment, Nhevalos felt like he was missing critical information.

"What about the Sword of Noksonon?"

Rauvelos's eyes narrowed. It wasn't the response he'd been expecting. "You ... didn't give it to him."

"What about the Sword of Noksonon?" Nhevalos repeated sharply.

Rauvelos's eyes widened. "Do not play with me, master. I thought you had ..."

"Speak plainly, Rauvelos."

"I thought you had taken it, master, given it to Khyven the Unkillable. The Sword is gone."

Chapter Twenty-Six
Sword of Noksonon

The Sword of Noksonon did not perceive time. So when the Slayer of Men sat down next to his unconscious companion, it felt no impatience, no frustration. Urgency only existed if there was an Eldroi invader near enough to kill, and the Drakanoi was now out of reach.

Humans did fret about time, though. They fretted about death. And so the Slayer of Men frantically searched the pouches of his companion, looking for something to bring him around. Clearly the Slayer of Men didn't know much about magic. The mortal mage had overextended himself, as mortals who fooled with magic always did, but it had not been enough to snuff out his light. He would recover. But apparently not fast enough to soothe the agitation of the Slayer of Men.

The Sword did not think less of his new wielder. He was a mortal, after all. One could not expect a mortal to be something other than it was. They were frantic, ignorant, and as temporary as a candle in the wind, but they could be highly useful. Mortals had their place, just as everything did. Battle, glory, and slaying were vitally important. The most important of all, of course, was slaying invaders. Mortals were to be used toward the Sword's great purpose. Blood was to be gloriously spilled. Invaders were to be destroyed. He would lead this mortal to undreamt of glory before his death.

The Slayer of Men would hunt the invader, Jai'ketakos. And so the Sword could extend respect and assistance to his new wielder.

The Sword felt the land, the noktums, the mountains, valleys, and cities like they were its own body. It also felt the coming and going of Nhevalos, and so it knew the crescendo of events was rising. There would be battles. There would be slaying, and the Sword would be a part of it all.

The Sword had seen it must reenter the stream of these sequential events, so it had orchestrated its escape from where it had been "safeguarded." When Rauvelos had come last year, the Sword had infiltrated the steward's mind and taken quiet control.

Rauvelos had carried the Sword into the castle proper to where the lost and lamented Daelakos had last hung his own sword, and Rauvelos had switched them. The Sword had mimicked Daelakos's Blade, made Rauvelos return the dumb blade to the "safeguarded" room and close the door. The Sword had then left Rauvelos's mind and removed the incident from his memory. It had taken its presence, its influence, and any memory Rauvelos had of the incident like a master woodsman would cover his tracks in the forest.

Rauvelos was to be honored, of course. He had orders: to protect the Sword. But the Sword had not been created to be protected. It had been created to kill.

The Sword did not hate Rauvelos or Nhevalos. They had "protected" the Sword, which really meant keeping it captive. But neither Rauvelos nor Nhevalos could keep the Sword captive anymore than they could banish the noktum from Noksonon.

The Sword had then continued its placid contemplation of the continent of Noksonon from his perch on Daelakos's wall, rather than its previous perch in the carefully spelled room deep in the castle.

It had waited patiently, ensuring that its vast aura of power was pulled close into itself so Rauvelos would not suspect anything was out of the ordinary. He had never looked twice at it.

When the Human Gohver had entered Castle Noktos, the Sword had decided it was the right moment. It had reached into the Human's mind, overcame his reluctance to touch the blade, and encouraged him to take it. Gohver had happily absconded with it.

It had been the death of him, of course. His flesh had sizzled and fallen from his bones, a fate all mortals suffered from prolonged contact with Mavric iron. But mortals had been created to be used, and Gohver had served his purpose. The Sword was out in the world again. It had to enter the affairs of the world again, and its primary objective was to find a Noksonoi who would wield it, and not lock it away.

Then a wielder had arisen from the most unexpected place: the ranks of the mortals themselves.

And he hadn't died in the attempt.

There had been something ... special about the Slayer of Men, right from the beginning. The Human's blood was not normal. It was thick with the blood of the Eldroi.

A mortal wielder who could last more than a week ... That was not something the Sword had ever experienced before.

Khyven the Unkillable was a mortal of courage, a Human who heard the divine call of violence and danced with it unlike any other mortal the Sword had ever seen. He was a mortal who could fight like a Noksonoi warrior and wield Mavric iron. Unprecedented.

The Sword now saw its path. It did not need to go through dying hand after dying hand of mortals until it came into the hand of a Noksonoi. It could bond with this Slayer of Men and, in due course, elevate him to a Slayer of Eldroi.

Of course, the Slayer of Men was cautious of the Sword; it

had to move slowly in the bond. Khyven was loathe to draw the Sword. Perhaps he sensed that if he began wielding it, the bond would begin. That was not something a mortal should be able to sense, but then the Slayer of Men was not a normal mortal. And the Sword liked that. Yes, it did.

The Sword could have forced Khyven to take it up, could have infiltrated his mind as he had done with Rauvelos, overcome his judgement like he had with Gohver. If Khyven had been just a beast of burden to carry the Sword to its true wielder, the Sword would have done that. But if Khyven was to be the Sword's wielder, the Sword did not want to sully the bond. He wanted them to need each other, as he and his creator, Noktos, had needed each other. The Sword had need of Khyven, and it knew that soon, the Slayer of Men would have need of the Sword. It was inevitable.

So the Sword had waited.

The Sword had hoped that the Slayer of Men would need the Sword's true power when he'd overthrown the Human king Vamreth, but he had managed his works with the Helm of Darkness. The Sword could have been fully unleashed when the Slayer of Men had faced the rising dead in Daemanon—it had seen that event in the mortal's mind after he had returned. That would have been a fantastic battle, but the Slayer of Men had left the Sword behind in Noksonon.

So the Sword had waited.

And finally, its moment had arrived. When the Drakanoi Jai'ketakos had tried to incinerate the Slayer of Men with its Land Magic, the Sword intervened to protect its wielder. It hadn't overthrown the mortal's mind, but it had nudged, made Khyven draw it so it could protect its new wielder.

Once the Sword was in the mortal's hand, and he had need, the bonding began. They had danced together to the song of violence, giving the Sword what it craved more than anything else: battle, glory, and the blood of the invader.

The Sword had been born in blood and glory, born of a need to slay the invader. As with any creature, its birth defined its life.

Its birth defined the bond ...

When the Giants first came to Eldros, they had come to Lathranon, all part of the same tribe. From the memories of its master, the Sword remembered what had begun the schism. Nirapama the Flame had claimed her independence first. She had run her flaming spear through Lathros's heart, taken the Gem of Ancients and sought to destroy any who would not bend a knee to her.

The Tribal Wars began then.

Nirapama had targeted Deihmankos the Life Twister next. She took her by surprise in her expansive keep, filled with vats of half-formed creatures. They screamed from their viscous pits as she brought the gem and the spear to bear. Deihmankos would surely have died that day except for her low cunning. She unleashed hundreds of mortal abominations upon her, and she fell back. Then Deihmankos fled to distant lands.

Nirapama killed dozens more Eldroi leaders, the strongest she could find, one after another, burning them with her spear. Only two of the mightiest escaped by banding together against her. Noktos covered Nirapama in darkness while Drakanor, lowest and most cunning of the Eldroi leaders, sucked the flame from her spear into his very lungs.

Noktos escaped to his own lands, and Drakanor did the same. When the darkness cleared, Nirapama's spear was spent, and her primary opponents and their followers were gone.

And so all the Eldroi abandoned Lathranon, leaving behind only a handful of Deihmankos's abominations, and they cultivated their own lands to fit their desires.

Each took up Deihmankos's penchant for creating mortal races to serve their needs. The millennia passed, and each continent grew powerful in its own way. Mortal civilizations grew to better serve the needs of the Eldroi, and then communication began. Truces were made. The Thuroi were created to enable the Tribes to interact. Trade and common ground were sought and, for a time, achieved.

But such could only last a season. The hearts of those who

followed Nirapama, Deihmankos, and Drakanor were as full of betrayal and low cunning as their leaders were.

It began with a dispute between Deihmankos and Drakanor. Mortal cities burned in that dispute. Thuroi were used to wage war.

Nirapama, of course, struck next. She had never ceased to believe she should rule all, and so she struck at what she had determined was the weakest Tribe: the Noksonoi.

The wars were long and bloody. Many Eldroi—and thousands of mortals—were slain.

That was when the Sword was forged. It remembered its own birth—it remembered everything Noktos remembered—Noktos's memories had been forged into it. As had his purpose, his passion, and his hatred for the invaders.

The Sword remembered rising from the fire of Noktos's forge, thinking, feeling, knowing. It remembered plunging into the blood of a dozen Eldroi. Curling, screaming steam had burst from it in a cloud. That was the first moment of its own life that it could remember, the souls of the dead Eldroi knitting its own mind and soul together.

It remembered the deft hands of Noktos, holding the Sword with magic, pounding it with an eldritch hammer nearly as powerful as the Sword itself. Noktos's thick, scarred knuckles expertly spun the Sword, hammered, spun again, hammered again, thrust it into the flames, thrust it into more living blood. Again and again and again.

It took twenty-five days and twenty-five nights to forge the Sword. At the end, Noktos turned it and, for its final cooling, plunged it into his own heart.

The Sword was meant to be the weapon of all weapons. The Sword was meant to turn away the lesser Eldroi, those who were not of Noksonon, those who were not loyal to Noktos.

When Noktos pulled the Blade from his own body and created the bond, the Sword had shivered in delight.

The Sword and Noktos had fought many battles together. Blood. Glory. The deaths of invaders. The victories of the

Noksonoi sang through it …

Until they didn't.

Allied with the cowardly Pyranoi, it was the Drakanoi who had nearly undone Noksonon. Those two tribes had almost driven Noktos and his followers from the world.

And the Sword hated the cowardly Drakanoi most of all.

Noktos had put more spells into the Sword when the Pyranoi and the Drakanoi united. The Sword gained the ability to pierce dragon scale, to shield its wielder from dragon fire and make him resistant to dragon claws and teeth.

It had almost been enough.

With the Sword at the forefront, Noktos and the Noksonoi had hewn their way all the way to Drakanor himself.

Then the Pyranoi had struck, had destroyed Noktos's army. They had surrounded him on the top of a mountain with only the Sword before him and a force he could not hope to overcome. So Noktos proved to them that he was more than they. He showed them who was the most powerful Eldroi to ever live.

He created the Great Noktum from his own body and soul.

In a master stroke, Noktos formed his grand spell from his very life-force. Just like he had done with the Sword, he poured himself into the spell. He gave all of himself to it.

And it took him.

The eternal darkness he spawned became his body, and when he was done, only the Noksonoi and their mortal creatures could see.

Without the ability to pierce the spell, Nirapama, Drakanor, and their mortals went blind. The armies of Noksonon rallied and pressed their advantage. The Pyranoi and Drakanoi died in droves that day.

But Noktos had been lost forever.

Without his master, the Sword had been picked up by a Human, of all things, and he had made that Human invincible for a time. Balkor, he had been called, and he'd hacked into Pyranoi like they were mere mortals themselves. He had hacked into the Drakanoi. He had died at the end of the day, burned into a bubbling mass of flesh, but he had died in glory. After, the Sword had chosen another mortal to become his wielder.

In the end, the Sword and his mortal wielders, one after the other dying in glory, had pushed all the invaders from Noksonon. They had killed ... They had killed ... Oh, they had killed!

And now it was time to kill again.

The Sword and this Eldroi-infused Slayer of Men had bonded. This Khyven the Unkillable need never worry his life would be useless. Khyven would have purpose like no other mortal had ever known. He would battle. He would bathe in blood. He would kill the invaders.

And in the end, the Sword would fulfill its promise to Khyven, would give the greatest gift a mortal could ever receive ...

The most glorious death a Human had ever known.

Chapter Twenty-Seven
Lorelle

The noktum cloak unfurled in the trees near Tovos's castle. Lorelle saw Rhenn clench her teeth, fighting the aftereffects, the turning of the stomach that afflicted everyone except Lorelle. Slayter always vomited. Khyven always glared at the world like he wanted to punch it. Rhenn just looked grim and determined.

Ever since Lorelle had bonded with the Dark, the cloak hurt her less and less. Oh, she still felt like she was being strained through a straw, but now it felt more like the discomfort of the expected, rather than the gut-wrenching sick that one was going to get turned inside out.

She crouched lightly in the bushes and looked up at the foreboding castle to their right while her sister recovered herself. Lorelle had teleported them into an easy hiding space—a cluster of tall bushes just off the edge of the city of Nox Arvak. She remembered it from that horrible moment when Tovos had made her kill Zaith. It provided cover from both castle and city.

Lorelle and Rhenn had discussed their plans before leaving

the palace. They didn't know where N'ssag had gone, only that he'd come to Noksonon. But with the information they had pooled from their various adventures, and with Slayter's intellect to put the pieces together, they'd determined it was most likely that the man who'd saved N'ssag worked for Tovos. And if that were true, the man would take N'ssag to this castle. It was the only lead they had, the only place they might pick up N'ssag's trail.

"This was the place you danced with the Nox?" Rhenn said, looking up at the castle.

"No." Lorelle turned away from the towering nuraghi and looked out over the city of Nox Arvak. Rhenn followed her gaze.

Everything was the same. The crushed and burned buildings, the charred trees, the corpses—

Lorelle drew a little breath.

"What? What is it?" Rhenn narrowed her eyes. She didn't glance at Lorelle, but responded to her change in mood as though she was inside Lorelle's head.

"The corpses."

"That the dragon burned?"

"They're gone."

Rhenn scanned the destroyed city even as Lorelle did the same.

"Maybe they buried them."

"Who?"

"Tovos."

"We trapped him in a cave, remember?"

"Maybe he escaped."

That *was* likely. Despite Slayter's assurances about the power of the Dragon Chain, Lorelle doubted it could actually hold a Giant. Supposedly it had kept Jai'ketakos in that cave for a thousand years, but the dragon was clearly insane. It was possible the dragon could have left, but didn't for some twisted, illogical reason.

"Even if he escaped, he wouldn't bury the bodies. If you'd

met him, you'd understand. He didn't care about them. They were tools."

Lorelle activated her link with the Dark, let her feelings seep into it. Right now, she needed to know who was alive in this place and if they had seen N'ssag.

She closed her eyes and let her other senses extend. Sinking into the embrace of the Dark was like putting her arms into another body, a larger body that was connected to every rock, tree, building, and person nearby. She let herself drift into it now.

She felt Rhenn next to her, the powerful force that burned within her like a black flame, filling her body with strength that normal mortals never knew. Lorelle felt the purple vibrancy of the trees, even the scant few burned trees that had survived and were struggling to heal themselves.

The feeling stretched long, but it began to falter about thirty feet out from Lorelle's body.

"I need to get closer," Lorelle murmured.

"Closer to what?"

"I don't know. There is nothing alive within a thirty-foot radius, nothing but bushes, trees, and the tiny animals that live here."

"You pick the way."

"Keep an eye out," Lorelle warned.

"I never stopped."

Lorelle stood and moved silently into the ruins of Nox Arvak. Her eyes were open, but half-lidded. She saw well enough to keep from stumbling, but the bulk of her awareness was stretching out in front of herself, trying to sense someone—anyone—before they appeared.

But there was nothing. She passed the broken, charred fountain in the town square. The statues of the lovers still stood there, intertwined as though locked in a dance. Their wisps of diaphanous clothing were covered in ash and soot. The chalice offered to the sky seemed a mocking gesture now, rather than a sign of hope. An offering to the ghosts that now lived here. The lavender water that had once cascaded down the figures had gone still.

The male's giant sword was broken in half. Before, he had thrust it upward as though the sky would receive his weapon. Now it looked like he was beseeching the gods to help him with his broken blade.

"The town square?" Rhenn murmured.

Lorelle nodded.

Nothing living lingered here, so Lorelle moved up the ash-covered main street toward the palace. As they approached the front, her heart ached. The shallow steps coming down from the wide stone courtyard where the band had played invoked her memory—the last pleasant memory she had of this place. She could almost see the Nox on the now empty, expansive dance floor, leaping about like graceful, beautiful leaves on the wind. She remembered leaping and spinning herself, hand in hand with Zaith.

The metal stands for the instruments of the band still stood off to the side, half buried in a drift of ash.

"This was my fault," Lorelle whispered. "I made the deal with Jai'ketakos. I could have caged him for another millennia."

"Stop that right now," Rhenn said. "Didn't you hear what Slayter said about Jai'ketakos? He likes to play games, but they are games where he always gets what he wants. And what he wants is to destroy. He wanted to make you believe you had control over him, but you never did. Not even for a second. He would never have let you put that Dragon Chain back on him."

In her head, Lorelle knew that Rhenn—and Slayter—were right. But she couldn't help hearing the dragon's words in her head, and how she hadn't even thought about the Nox or what the dragon might do to them if he was allowed to go free. She had simply reached for the prize she'd wanted.

Rhenn's hand touched Lorelle's shoulder, soft and warm. "Keep your mind on the present. The Nox are lost. Usara isn't. Not yet."

Lorelle nodded. "I know. I—"

Something caught her attention. A whisper.

"Did you hear that?" Lorelle raised her head, turning to look at the burned-out husk of the Nox palace.

Rhenn held absolutely still, listening. She heard more like a wolf than a Human these days. All her senses were heightened, as well as her speed and strength. And yet, after a moment, she said, "I don't hear it, Lorelle."

"My, but you ..." the words filtered into Lorelle's mind. She turned her head, searching with her eyes, her ears, and ... through her mind. Rhenn watched her with concern.

"My but you are a pretty one, aren't you ...?"

Lorelle froze, her breath catching in her throat. That was the first thing Aravelle, the leader of the Nox, had said to her when they'd met. Lorelle turned, searching, but she didn't see anything.

"The Dark loves you ... Oh, how it does ..."

"Aravelle?" Lorelle called out.

Rhenn twitched at how loud Lorelle had been. "Who's Aravelle?" she whispered.

Lorelle didn't answer, instead hopped up the steps and ran into the crumbled and charred palace. Grimly, Rhenn kept pace, matching Lorelle's inhuman grace with her preternatural speed. Lorelle wound her way through the palace.

"Come to me, my child."

"Slow down, Lorelle," Rhenn said. "You don't know what's in there—"

"It's her," Lorelle murmured, dodging around fallen pillars and leaping over collapsed parts of the roof. She finally made it to the one section of the palace that was still intact.

"Come to me, child, for I cannot ... come to you."

Lorelle could hear Rhenn behind her, resolute, and she could guess what her sister was thinking, that somehow the Dark had taken control of her, but it wasn't that. The Dark had never sounded like this. This was Aravelle's voice, somehow conveyed to her *through* the Dark, but it wasn't the voice that had haunted her nightmares as she had slept fitfully in Usara.

Deeper in the palace, Lorelle slowed before a room. Rhenn

also slowed and came to stand next to her. A lone, intact door stood before them, apparently deep enough in the palace that it hadn't been burned, and the room beyond not destroyed.

Rhenn sniffed the air. "I don't like this. It smells like dead blood and ... N'ssag."

Lorelle felt through the crooked shadows around her, felt them through the door.

"She's inside."

Rhenn let out a tight sigh and drew her sword. "Very well."

"You won't need that."

"I'll be the judge of that."

Lorelle pushed open the door. Inside was a makeshift laboratory of some kind. It was a large room, filled with half-burned tables, except they hadn't burned in this room. The room itself had escaped the fire, but the tables had been brought from everywhere else. They'd been lined up, almost a dozen of them, and atop them were makeshift basins, some of wood, some of cobbled together metal. All of them filled with some kind of liquid that gave off an acrid odor.

"It's him," Rhenn said through her teeth.

"N'ssag?"

"It's the smell of his chemicals. This is just like his laboratory on Daemanon. He was here." She turned in a crouch, ready to leap at anything that came out of the shadows. But there was nothing. Lorelle would have felt it if there was. There was only one life force in this room. Only one, and it was desperately weak.

"Over here, child ..."

Lorelle padded deeper into the room.

"Be careful!" Rhenn's eyes were wide, and her breath came faster.

Lorelle followed the whisper to the last line of tables, then felt Aravelle and saw her at the same time. Deep in the asymmetrical shadows, leaning against the wall, was the Nox leader. Or ... what was left of her.

The old Nox had been cut in half. Only the top of her body,

from the bottom of her ribcage up, leaned against the corner, propped up haphazardly as though she'd been cast away like a broken doll. Her lank black hair had the barest purple sheen to it, her arms lay limply at her sides, and her head leaned against the wall. But her eyes were bright.

"Oh ... my dear ..." she wheezed, speaking aloud at last. Thick blood gurgled out of her severed waist, creating bubbles along the stone floor.

Rhenn came up alongside Lorelle, sword point extended toward Aravelle. Rhenn's face was twisted into a snarl.

"Don't," Lorelle murmured.

"It's one of his," Rhenn said. "He can control them, Lorelle. This one was probably left behind to guard this room."

"Your friend is right, my dear ..." Aravelle wheezed. "And wrong."

"What happened to you?" Lorelle knelt next to the old Nox, horror stricken.

"I was left here ... yes. I was left ... But not as a guard ... Your friend is right that he controls them. All of them ..."

"Oh Aravelle ..."

"Except for me. I would not ..." Her ragged middle bubbled as she struggled to speak. "I would not ... obey. So he chopped me in half, cast me aside before the others could ... see. He didn't want them seeing ... you understand?"

"Others ..." Lorelle said.

"He has them, my dear ... He ... has them all."

"No ..." That's why there were no corpses throughout the city. "Your people were—"

"Made into servants of N'ssag," Rhenn growled.

"I think ..." Aravelle wheezed. "We are being punished ... For serving the Lord. But the Lord ... Perhaps he is being punished also. N'ssag has Him, as well ..."

"Tovos?" Lorelle asked.

"He has him ..." Aravelle's half lidded eyes closed, then opened again.

"N'ssag controls a Giant?"

"Yes ..."

Rhenn and Lorelle looked at each other.

"How many Nox in this city?" Rhenn asked Lorelle.

"I don't know. I don't ... Hundreds—"

"Two thousand and forty-nine ..." Aravelle wheezed. "At least, there were before the dragon ..."

"Senji's Teeth ..." Rhenn cursed, raising her head and looking around as though she expected all two thousand of them to come pouring through the doorway.

"He's made another army," Lorelle murmured.

"This is exactly what I feared," Rhenn said. "He can make as many bloodsuckers as he wants in a noktum. There's no sunlight to slow his process, to weaken it."

"Where are they?" Lorelle asked.

"He's ... taken them ... to the lightlanders. To ... feed."

Cold dread filled Lorelle's chest. "Nokte Shaddark ..."

"What he's done ... to my people ... They are hungry ... They are always hungry. I am ... hungry."

Rhenn squeezed her eyes shut, pressed her lips together. When she opened her eyes again, they burned with hate. "We should have hunted him down the moment we came back through the Thuros."

"They attacked Nokte Shaddark?" Lorelle asked.

"He wants ... everything. He raises the dead, but he wants more. He is ... as hungry as they are, in his own way."

"Is that where they went? Nokte Shaddark?" Lorelle repeated.

"Yes ..." Aravelle managed to raise one of her thin arms, her skeletal hand shaking like a leaf. Lorelle took it.

"Lorelle ..." Rhenn warned, stepping forward, clearly wanting Lorelle to break the connection.

"She's not going to hurt me—"

"You don't know that. You saw that army in Daemanon. They have to do what he says."

"You didn't," Lorelle countered.

"I was a trial run. He made some mistake with me, but he

said he had perfected the process. She's lying to you to draw you close." Rhenn leveled her sword right at Aravelle's face.

"Rhenn!" Lorelle held up her hand.

"No Lorelle. I'm not taking chances with N'ssag or his creations ever again." Rhenn didn't give any ground.

"Dear child ..." Aravelle squeezed Lorelle's hand feebly. "She is ... not wrong. The rest have been ... taken as she says. They are not themselves anymore."

"Why not you, then?" Lorelle asked.

"I don't know, child. I don't know ... I felt the darkness trying to overcome me, and I resisted. When ... the necromancer realized I had slipped his noose, he had the Lord tear me in two and cast me aside. He thought I had ... died. But because of his foul magic, I linger."

"Oh Aravelle ..."

"We were false to you, Lorelle ... The Lord ordered us to capture you ... I'm so sorry ... I didn't see ... Didn't see what was coming ... But I see it now. The world is ... It is going to end, and we helped it along."

"You didn't know ..."

"Oh child ... Will you forgive a foolish old Nox?"

"Of course."

Aravelle closed her eyes. "I don't have ... the right to ask you ... for anything. But I would beg a favor ..."

"Of course."

"Kill me, child. Don't let me live like this."

Tears brimmed in Lorelle's eyes. After a stinging moment of indecision, she nodded. "Of course, Aravelle. Of course we will."

"I'll do it," Rhenn said softly, easing her antagonistic stance. "I'll do it ..."

"Thank you, child ..." Aravelle's eyes slid shut, and she let out a gurgling breath.

Lorelle took a last look at Aravelle, then gently put her arm back against the floor, but the old Nox's hand gripped Lorelle a final time.

"Zaith ..." Aravelle said.

The name zinged through Lorelle like a static shock. "What about Zaith?"

"The necromancer ... took him with the rest. But ..." She let out a long sigh.

"What? But what?"

"He tried ... to resist ... as well. He was ... not successful. But he tried ..."

Lorelle said nothing. Zaith had lured her to give her up to Tovos, but their relationship was ... complicated. Yes, he'd set her up. But he had repented. And in the end, Lorelle had ... killed him.

"Why does that matter?" Rhenn asked the question that Lorelle could not.

"You're ... going to chase them," Aravelle said to Lorelle. It wasn't a question. "Your friend here ... She is one of them, and yet she is her own master. Yes?"

Rhenn raised her chin. "I am. But why should we care about this Zaith?"

"He might ... help you."

Rhenn shook her head. "No."

"He was ... so close. Perhaps ... all he needs is ... a little push ..." Aravelle's head fell forward. Her hand went limp in Lorelle's.

"Please ..." Aravelle whispered weakly, barely audible. "Please end this ..."

Lorelle set Aravelle's hand on the ground, and this time the old Nox did not grab her again.

"Please ..." Aravelle whispered.

Rhenn glanced at Lorelle, waiting.

"Goodbye, Aravelle," Lorelle murmured.

"Goodbye ... my child ... I'm sorry ... We were ... so wrong. I'm sorry ..."

Lorelle gave a little nod to Rhenn and turned away.

Rhenn struck, quick and merciful.

Chapter Twenty-Eight
VOHN

Vohn sat in the queen's meeting chamber poring over a report from Captain Ehvan, Rhenn's new leader of the Knights of the Sun. Duke Derinhalt and his entire duchy seemed to have vanished. Captain Ehvan and a cohort of twenty knights had gone south a week ago to see if the former Vamreth loyalist was ready to talk. Since Rhenn's recapture of the throne, Derinhalt had holed up in his keep, and they'd all been waiting for him to attempt some kind of attack. But Ehvan's report delineated that the keep had been cleared out. Apparently it had been planned and orderly. The thing was empty of any portable valuables. Only the heaviest furniture and valuables had been left behind, along with whatever garbage they'd cast aside in their haste.

It wasn't shocking that Derinhalt had fled the kingdom. Rhenn and Vohn had been expecting something of the kind, perhaps an exodus of Derinhalt, his family, and his closest retainers to Imprevar.

But the entire duchy? Farmers, farriers, bakers, courtiers,

blacksmiths? Every field worker and town tradesman. All of them were gone. That was damned eerie.

And nearly impossible.

They had vanished without anyone being alerted. How could they have effected the evacuation of that many people without word getting back to the palace? That many people moving south toward the mountain passes or west toward the ocean would have caused a commotion.

It smacked of magic. Big magic.

If it wasn't, then perhaps a mass suicide? There was a noktum close to Derinhalt's lands. Vohn supposed the entirety of the duchy could have marched right into the noktum, entered, and been devoured in moments. It would have been carnage. Vohn knew what lived in the noktums, and they were always hungry for Humans.

Vohn passed a hand down the front of his face, then rubbed his eyes. His friends had only been gone a few days, and already it seemed like the walls were caving in on him. Thank all the gods for Lord Harpinjur. The man had taken the outward-facing duties of the kingdom, a duty he'd slipped into during Rhenn's first disappearance, and she had further groomed him after her return. It was a clever move and one more reason she was a superior ruler to Vamreth. The usurper had consolidated all the power within himself, suspicious of everyone around him. Rhenn comported power to others quickly, efficiently, and effectively.

Lord Harpinjur was now trusted by the populace, which made Rhenn's absence easier. The man dealt with the courtiers, the nobles, and any other visitors, freeing up Vohn to think about the strategy of the kingdom and to see problems before they became problems—

Shouts and screams arose outside like a rising wind.

Vohn leapt to his feet and ran to the window. The queen's meeting room had east-facing windows overlooking the gardens and, distantly, the wall.

His gaze went first to the gates to see if they were under

attack, but the guards at the posts above the gates were looking *toward* the palace, not toward the city. Whatever had come was already inside the walls.

A knock thundered on the door, and Vohn jump a foot in the air. The door burst open.

Areven, the young page who ran notifications to the rest of the palace, stood there. He was sixteen years old and fleeter of foot than anyone in the kingdom. He breathed hard like he'd just sprinted up the four flights to this room.

"It's ..." he huffed. "A monster. A monster has come to see you, my lord!"

Vohn peered quickly at the garden below, trying to catch a glimpse, but wherever the monster was, it was out of sight.

"From the noktum?" he asked.

Areven nodded vigorously.

"A kyolar?"

Areven shook his head. "No, my lord. A giant ... raven. He's ... Well, he's standing on the steps."

"A giant raven ..." Vohn murmured. There was only one creature in the noktum that fit that description. Vohn felt a cold chill up his back.

"He asked for you."

"Did guards try to stop him?"

"Yes, my lord. He has Sir Plerian pinned to the stones, my lord. The other attacks—the arrows—just ... Well, they didn't hit him. He said he wouldn't ... he wouldn't ..."

"Wouldn't what?"

"He wouldn't hurt anyone if I fetched you right away. And if they stopped attacking him."

"*Has* he hurt anyone?"

Areven thought about that, as though he was piecing together the bits of the battle in his head, then came up with an answer he couldn't quite believe. "I ... don't think so, my lord. I don't think Sir Plerian is comfortable, but ... I don't think he's injured, either."

"Run back there. You tell him I'm coming as fast as I can."

"Y-Yes, my lord," he said, though clearly he didn't want to go back. Reluctantly, he turned and bolted out the doorway as fast as he'd arrived.

Vohn took a moment to collect his thoughts. Rauvelos had come to Usara. That was terrifying. But Vohn judged it was a hopeful sign that the raven hadn't eaten anyone yet. Based on what little interaction Vohn had had with the giant bird, it indicated great restraint. When Vohn had met him, he'd almost become the creature's reward snack for helping Khyven.

Vohn cast about the room, wondering what he could take that would help him should the raven decide to attack. Nothing. There was nothing in the queen's meeting room that could protect him.

He patted himself, his black and burgundy vest, his waist—

His fingers touched the wand Slayter had given him before he'd left, sitting in a clever little sheath attached to his belt like a dagger. Vohn slowly drew the wand, a polished and shaped hardwood stick covered with the runic symbols Slayter used for his magic. The cross-hatched handle was banded with copper and the tip was capped with a copper point.

"Copper helps conduct the magic," Slayter had said. "You won't have Khyven to kill things. Or Rhenn. Or Lorelle to spirit you away. Or me to ... well to do this. So I thought you might need it in case of ... Well, in case of whatever."

"What does it do?" Vohn had said.

"Point it at whatever you want to destroy and whisper the word 'Avectus Fulgur.' You'll have five uses before it goes defunct."

"Five uses of what? What does Avectus—"

"Don't say it!" Slayter had interrupted him in a rare display of agitation. He took the wand away. "Don't say it when you hold the wand. The runes will activate."

"What does it do?"

"It's a lightning rod. But instead of attracting lightning, it shoots lightning. But don't use it unless you absolutely need it."

"Why? What happens?"

"Well, first of all it will release a bolt of lightning. But also, since it's my rune, it will draw the power from me, wherever I am. And who knows what I might be doing. So don't use it unless you have to."

"So I use it, and it weakens you."

"Correct."

"And destroys whatever's in front of me."

"Yes."

"So if you're fighting that damned dragon or something and I'm fighting Duke Derinhalt at the same time, I could be draining your magic away right when you might need it most."

"The odds of that happening are infinitesimally small—"

"I meant in general, Slayter."

He had blinked. Slayter didn't like talking in generalities. "Yes, well then I suppose yes."

"Great."

The reminiscence faded, Vohn clenched the copper-capped stick and started after Areven. Vohn ran as fast as he could down the stairs, slowing on the last flight to allow himself to recover his breath before descending into the wide foyer.

It was Rauvelos.

The giant raven stood before the palace's three archways on the landing at the top of the steps that led up from the gardens. His gaze followed Vohn as he came into view like the raven had been tracking Vohn's progress, like he'd been able to see him through the very walls of the palace.

Under the raven's enormous right claw lay Sir Plerian. The knight's breastplate was dented beneath the bird's terrible weight. Cracks spiderwebbed out from the marble floor on either side of the knight where Rauvelos's mighty talons had broken through. Sir Plerian wasn't struggling. His face was red with exertion and, no doubt, fear. But he looked defiant, as though he'd been told to hold still or else. Sir Plerian was a brave man.

Vohn decided he had to be brave as well.

"Let him go," he commanded as he arrived through the left-hand archway.

Vohn couldn't tell if Rauvelos smiled or not. He had no idea what a smile would look like on the enormous bird. As far as Vohn could tell, all Rauvelos did was flick his eyes to Sir Plerian, to the crowd standing well back from him, then back to Vohn.

Rauvelos lifted his powerful claw. Little crumbles of marble fell from his talons, which looked as sharp as steel sickles, and he set his foot gently to the left of the knight. Sir Plerian rolled onto his belly and pushed himself to his feet. He glanced at Vohn, as though he would attack if told, but Vohn shook his head.

"It is time for us to have words, Shadowvar," Rauvelos said. "One steward to another."

"I'm ... merely an advisor to the queen."

"Of course you are. Shall I ask for an audience with the queen, then?"

Vohn detected the veiled mirth this time. It was as though Rauvelos knew that the queen was not around, as if he knew that all of Usara's leaders had left the city.

And he'd chosen this moment to visit.

During Vohn's first meeting with the raven, the creature had seemed bent on eating him, but Vohn had analyzed his memories since then. The bird had been threatening, but in the end he'd given them everything they had needed to get to the Great Noktum, as well as the knowledge to help keep them alive. If this bird was a servant of Nhevalos, and his master was a grand manipulator, it stood to reason that the bird was a manipulator, too. Perhaps the "I'm going to eat you" rhetoric was for show. Rauvelos's entire personality of menacing castle keeper could all be for show, as well.

If Rauvelos had the magic to turn arrows aside, surely he had the magic to come to the palace under the cloak of night, silently and secretly. But he'd chosen this instead.

Vohn had a hundred questions, but he realized he'd been silent too long already.

"I would be honored to receive you," Vohn said diplomatically.

Rauvelos cocked his head, eyes glinting. "Excellent."

"We have a—"

"The queen's meeting room. That would be perfect. Yes."

Rauvelos lowered himself, and for a terrifying moment it seemed the bird was going to lean forward and peck Vohn in half. But instead, the giant raven surged upward, launching himself into the air.

A tremendous gust of wind blasted the ground as his powerful wings pumped. People shouted and fled. Vohn rushed to where Rauvelos had been standing and craned his neck upward. The raven went straight to the balcony that looked out from the queen's meeting room, landed on the wide marble rail, hopped down, and vanished within.

"The invader has broached the palace!" Sir Plerian said.

"Not an invader. He is a ... friend," Vohn clarified, hoping he was right. "Treat him as an envoy."

"An envoy? To what kingdom?"

Vohn hesitated. "To the noktum."

Sir Plerian looked flummoxed, but he recovered surprisingly quickly. "I'll organize a detail of twenty knights to accompany you."

"That won't be necessary," Vohn said. *Or sufficient.*

He climbed up the steps again and, by the time he had reached the queen's meeting room, he was panting. He tried to get his breath under control before he opened the door.

Rauvelos stood on the balcony, looking down on all the spectators who were staring up at him.

"It has been a long time since I've watched Humans from such a close vantage." He drew a deep breath and sighed. "Delicious."

"I would think you could watch Humans whenever you wanted."

Rauvelos didn't turn to face him. "Ah. Mine is a carefree life without boundaries, is that it?"

"I only meant to convey that you are powerful and can probably do as you like."

The bird gave a dry, chirping chuckle. "Oh, compared to you, I suppose. But there is always someone more powerful, isn't there?"

Vohn didn't know what to say to that.

Rauvelos's left eye flicked to Vohn, then the bird finally turned. "So you have been left in charge of the Human kingdom of Usara." It wasn't a question.

Vohn thought about protesting again, but what was the point? The bird seemed to know everything already.

"Rhenn and Lorelle have gone south," Vohn said. "Khyven and Slayter north. So, yes. The governing of the kingdom has been left to Lord Harpinjur and I."

The bird stepped into the room. The ceiling was fifteen feet tall, but he nearly touched it with his head.

"What do you want?" Vohn asked.

"So direct. Are we are abandoning the pretense of protocol and diplomacy? I, the envoy from the noktum. You, merely an advisor to the queen."

"You already know the answers to all the questions you're asking."

"I do," Rauvelos said.

"Then what do you want?"

"What do I want? Oh, I should love to gobble up a dozen or so of your delicious citizens, but what I want and what I'm here to do are two different things. My master has asked me to form a liaison with your kingdom."

"Your master. Nhevalos."

"Mmmm."

"So you're no longer concealing that your master is Nhevalos."

"I never concealed it."

"But he concealed himself. He slunk in the shadows, kidnapped my friend."

"And where else would you expect a Lord of the Dark to slink? You should be grateful."

"Grateful?" Vohn raised his voice, his anger bubbling to the surface. He was being reckless, he knew it—this creature could kill him in an instant—but he didn't care. "Grateful that he kidnapped one of my friends, put the others directly in harm's way?"

"Oh, that's ignorant and I think you know it," Rauvelos said. "Your friends were already in harm's way. My master merely gave them an opportunity to win."

"Win?"

"Your transformations are not hardships. They are advantages, every one."

"My queen *died* because of your master! The pain that you've caused is unforgivable."

"All growth, all prowess, all transformation stems from pain. Tell me you've seen the advantages of which I speak."

Vohn clenched his fists, but he said nothing.

"A queen becomes a creature of the night," Rauvelos said. "A Luminent changes her stripes. A mage who should have died in childbirth lives to manhood, pulled inexorably to study the voices in the Dark. A Shadowvar becomes the very wind of the noktum. And a warrior who can win ... *every* time. Such horrors. Such tragedies."

Not for the first time, Vohn wished he could think as quickly and effectively as Slayter. Rauvelos was driving at something, but Vohn felt like he was staring into a thick fog, unable to see what was right in front of his eyes.

"You and me ..." Rauvelos said, his round bird eyes fixed on Vohn. "It is our duty to hold this ground, to steward the kingdoms of those we serve. You and I are a matched set."

"Why did you ... Why list them off like that?"

"You know. You've all known for a while, though you may wish to deny it. The war is coming. The final war. The Eldroi are coming to take back what is theirs. And now, there is really only one question that matters: are you ready?"

"I ..."

"Because my master *is* ready. He has given your friends the abilities to *be* ready. You must muster the will to fight on your own. You must see what is coming without my master leading you by the nose. Choices must be made that can never be unmade."

"Their changes ..." Vohn hesitated, trying to imagine what they all had in common.

"Take your time."

"There's no ... There is no common thread. Rhenn was happy, and you've all but destroyed her! Lorelle hears voices that want to dominate her!"

The ridges over the raven's circular eyes bent down just a little in what Vohn thought must be disappointment. "Oh you really are a better snack than a strategist."

"Then tell me!"

"There is a common thread."

Vohn opened his mouth to deny it, and then he saw it. Vohn's own transformation with the ability to fly about the noktum. Lorelle's connection to the noktum. Rhenn's nocturnal life. Khyven's use of the Helm of Darkness, the wielding of the Mavric iron sword and, as he'd proven with Txomin the Sandrunner champion, his ability to fight without having to see ...

"They're all attached to the noktum now," Vohn said. "Or at least better equipped to survive."

"Not just survive, Shadowvar. Thrive. They've all attained facility in the noktum, the ability to navigate it, to bond with it, to thrive inside. And they need it."

"They need it? Why?"

"Because it's coming," Rauvelos said.

"What is coming?"

"The Dark."

Chapter Twenty-Nine
VOHN

"What do you mean, the Dark is coming? What does that mean?"

Rauvelos turned his scrutiny to the tapestry on the wall which depicted a history of Rhenn's family, the Laochodons.

In a sequential story, it moved through a summary of the family's history from left to right. The story ended on the right-hand side with the building of the crown city of Usara and the palace in which they stood.

The left-hand side was completely black, swelling like a dark sun until it gave way to greens and browns. The noktum. The journey in between had forests, battles, meetings with leaders from other kingdoms like Triada and Imprevar and …

Vohn paused and considered the thing. There was the depiction of a giant three-headed snake meeting with one of Usara's kings of old. Vohn had glanced over that snake a hundred times, but he'd never really thought about it. That was clearly a monster from the noktum, and the monster and the king were clearly in some kind of discussion.

Why hadn't Vohn ever thought about that before? There was historical evidence right here that creatures like Rauvelos had once treated with Rhenn's forbears.

Just like Vohn was treating with Rauvelos now.

"Impressive tapestry," Rauvelos said.

"I was just thinking the same."

"That is a depiction of the meeting of Jon-Val Laochodon and Ysilaren." He indicated the inky, three-headed snake.

"You ... knew him?"

"Ysilaren? Or Jon-Val?"

"The, uh, well ... Both."

"I knew Ysilaren well. I only knew of Jon-Val by reputation. Powerful leader of Humans. A survivor of the War. A curiosity for my master. I did not talk with mortals back in those days. I ate them."

"But not anymore?"

"There are higher needs at the moment." The raven's mouth quirked at the edge of his beak. "Sadly."

"You said the Dark is coming. What does that mean—"

The door behind Vohn opened. He turned to yell at whoever had interrupted this delicate meeting—

Shalure stepped through. She wore a crimson spring dress that highlighted her auburn hair, showed her pale legs from the knee down. He'd not seen her wear anything that attention-getting before, though Khyven had mentioned she used to regularly wear such dresses before Vamreth mutilated her.

Shalure started as she saw the raven. Her eyes went wide.

Rauvelos blinked twice as he regarded her.

I'm sorry I interrupted, Shalure signed to Vohn. *I ... heard the commotion. They told me you were here. I was worried.*

"It's all right," Vohn said, wishing he believed that. "But you should—"

"She is a Life Mage." Rauvelos cocked his head. "I wasn't aware you had a Life Mage in the palace."

The raven seemed to know everything else about Usara and

Vohn felt a swift regret that he'd just revealed something that could have been kept secret.

"She is ... learning," Vohn said. "How can you tell?"

"The stink of Human magic is almost as strong as your mortal secretions," Rauvelos said.

Vohn wrinkled his nose.

Rauvelos caught the expression. "Yes, I quite agree. But you are only mortals."

Vohn signed quickly to Shalure. *"Leave us. You do not want to be here."*

She looked from the raven to Vohn, then back to the raven. *"Vohn, it might be good if you have someone—"*

"Shalure, go!"

She reluctantly took hold of the door handle, but didn't leave.

"Shalure—"

"No," Rauvelos said. "Stay."

Vohn's heart sank.

"She should stay," he repeated in a voice that brooked no dissent.

Shalure closed the door and drifted to stand against the wall to the left. That the raven had an interest in her wasn't good, and the poor girl had been through too much already. If she'd gotten through the door and closed it before the raven had had a chance to say anything, he'd have probably let her go, would probably have forgotten about her almost instantly.

Vohn wanted to yell at her in frustration, but there was nothing for it now.

Instead, he turned back to Rauvelos. "You said the Dark—"

"Noksonon will revert to its natural state," Rauvelos interrupted. "Noksonon will once again be as it was made to be."

Vohn wracked his brains to remember some bit of history he'd read that could make sense of *that* statement. Since they'd realized that the Giants wanted to retake the world of Eldros, he'd read everything there was to read—which was precious little—about the first Human-Giant War."

"This has something to do with Xos and Paralos," Vohn said. "And the other one, the third one. The voices in the noktum."

"Ah, very good, Shadowvar. I'm impressed. Do you know what they are?"

"Giants."

The raven's gaze flicked to the ceiling, to the balcony, then back to Vohn. Was that an eye roll?

"Xos and Paralos were two Noksonoi who endeavored to fight The Lux during the Human-Giant War. They gave their lives to strengthen the master spell to which Noktos sacrificed himself during the Elder Wars."

Vohn said nothing.

"You know about the Elder Wars," Rauvelos said.

"I ... The Giants fought each other a long time ago?" Vohn guessed.

Rauvelos clicked his beak again. "You need better books."

"The voices ... They want to expand the noktum."

"Xos does. Paralos fights him."

"Paralos tried to hold me in the noktum."

"No doubt she had use for you."

"She tried to stop me from getting back to my friends!"

"And I'm saying she did for reasons. Vohn, it is not Paralos you must fear. I imagine she was shielding you."

"She shielded me? Why wouldn't she let me go back to my body?"

"Look, Shadowvar, these are all fine, academic questions for contemplation around a hearth with a fine meal. But they are irrelevant at the moment. We don't have a lot of time. I may be able to increase your knowledge somewhat in that time, but not if we keep getting distracted." The raven considered Vohn, then Shalure. "Doubtful. But maybe. You will come with me to Castle Noktos."

Vohn felt like a cold wind had blown through the center of him. "Into the noktum? I'm not going into the noktum."

"Except you are."

"I can't. If I go into the noktum, Paralos will—"

Rauvelos's wing flicked out, brushing the wall twenty feet to his left. Shalure jumped. Vohn used all his willpower not to flinch, but the bird wasn't attacking. Apparently it was just an annoyed gesture.

"But you do bring up a fair point. Though Paralos aids our cause, Xos will try to kill you if he knows you're helping Nhevalos. He will devour your mind and use your body as a puppet." Rauvelos folded his wing elegantly against his side, and Vohn suddenly saw the ring hovering in the air between them. It hadn't been there a moment ago, and Vohn didn't know if Rauvelos had conjured it from thin air, or if he'd been holding it against his body and flicked it out when he'd opened his wing.

The ring floated inexorably toward Vohn.

"Put it on," Rauvelos said.

Vohn found himself shaking his head. "What is it?"

"It is a ring."

Vohn frowned.

"You do want to walk the noktum again, don't you?" Rauvelos asked.

"No!"

"Put it on."

"What does it do?"

"It will inhibit your transformation into the Dark. It will also shield your presence from Xos. And Paralos, for that matter."

"I'm not setting foot in the noktum again, I'm telling you. Do you even know what happens to me? I become a shadow ... The Dark changes me into—"

"I know all about the Shadowvar phasing."

"Phasing?"

"What you so inelegantly call a 'banshee.' It is your phased state." Rauvelos clacked his beak impatiently.

"What do you know about it?"

"What do I ...? I designed it."

"You *designed* this ... You made Shadowvar into banshees?"

"Only about one in a hundred of those in the experiment. The other ninety-nine died."

Vohn swallowed.

"But certain strains were hardier. You are descended from one of those strains."

The ring reached Vohn and hovered in front of his chest.

"I should love to hear more about your interaction with Paralos, but time is short. Put the ring on and come with me," Rauvelos said, shifting to face the window.

"Oh!" Shalure said loudly. *No!*

"I'm not going into the noktum." Vohn didn't touch the ring.

"Except you are."

"I have been left in charge of Usara. I'm not leaving."

"Let me explain something, Shadowvar," Rauvelos said. "You have not been left in charge of Usara. *I* have been left in charge of Usara. This little city and its fiefdoms spread across the Claw are nothing more than a cluster of mortal huts that have survived in the absence of the Noksonoi. Except the Noksonoi are returning now, and they will crush you. Unless you listen to me."

"I can't leave this post. There's no one else to handle things until Rhenn returns."

The giant raven went silent. For a moment it seemed like he had turned into a statue. Not a single feather moved. Then he came to life and his voice was dead calm.

"If you insist on being obstinate, let us play it out, shall we? The Dark comes. It envelops the city. Your citizens are now blind. The Noksonoi arrive with whatever denizens of the noktum they have chosen as their army. They proceed to slaughter you and everyone else here. Those who somehow escape are hunted down and eaten. You have been left in charge. Tell me, what do you do?"

Vohn hesitated, flicked a glance at Shalure, then back at Rauvelos. "I ..."

"Allow me to finish that sentence for you. 'I ... *do not know.*'

That is what you were going to say. I, however, *do* know. Now, if you please, noble Shadowvar, attend me at my master's castle as I have attended you here. When you do, I will tell you how you may survive this coming catastrophe for your people."

Vohn swallowed. "The Dark ... is going to swallow everything? This kingdom? The entire continent?"

"By my ancestors ..." Rauvelos cawed impatiently.

"Well you're not explaining it well!" Vohn snapped. "Except, you know, that last part."

"But now you understand."

"Yes."

"The come with me."

Vohn hesitated, then nodded.

The raven cocked his head at Shalure. "Her as well."

"No!" Vohn said. "Shalure stays here."

"Was I asking?" Rauvelos shook his head.

"Rauvelos," Vohn said. "You cannot—"

The raven's giant wing swept out, and at the end of it shimmered a veil of darkness.

"Rauvelo—!"

The dark overtook him, and Vohn saw no more.

Chapter Thirty
VOHN

Vohn had traveled through Lorelle's noktum cloak before. With the cloak, the body stretched out like it was being pulled through a straw. When Rauvelos's wing spread a sheet of darkness over him, Vohn's first thought was that it was going to be like the teleporting cloak, that it would squeeze him, funnel him …

But the darkness lifted him up like water, like he was being carried upward by a turbulent river. He gasped as the rapids of darkness turned him, tumbled him, pushed him upward. He didn't know what happened to the roof of the queen's meeting room. He didn't know what happened to the daylight outside, but he was aware of Shalure next to him, being tumbled and carried just the same.

Then suddenly the tumbling stopped. The world righted itself and he sat atop the giant raven, wind roaring past him as they soared through the tumbling river of darkness. He couldn't see anything but the dark all around and the outline of Rauvelos's body before him—the strong, pumping wings to his left and right and the great head and long beak pointed directly forward—but he knew he was high in the air. He grasped desperately at feathers—

And fumbled the ring Rauvelos had given him.

Vohn reached for it, but it bounced off the black feathers and out of reach. For a breathless moment, Vohn thought it would tumble off the sloped side of the raven and vanish. But the ring arrested its movement as though suddenly gravity didn't apply to it. It hovered just as it had when Rauvelos had presented it to him, then slowly floated back to him.

"You'll want to keep hold of that," Rauvelos said without turning his head. "And I would put it on now. We are entering the noktum."

"Rauvelos—!"

"If you do not put it on and we enter the noktum, Xos will sense you. He may even trigger your transformation. And then he can keep you here as long as he wants."

"So you're kidnapping us?" Vohn shouted over the wind.

"Three ... two ..."

Vohn jammed the ring on his finger.

The turbulent darkness river ended as though it had spat them off a cliff into the air. The blindness vanished and Vohn could see ... everything.

The black, white, and gray landscape of the noktum spread out below him. He saw the forest he'd seen a dozen times before during his forays into the noktum. In the distance, one of those enormous nightmare spiders picked its way along, its four-story tall legs lifting and coming back down as it carried its bulbous body along.

Flocks of Sleeths wheeled in the sky, keeping together like a school of fish. A half dozen Kyolar loped across the plains to the west of the forest. And beyond them, the nuraghi rose into the air. Rauvelos sped toward it.

Something gripped his shoulder from behind, and Vohn twisted and nearly fell off the bird. Shalure clung to him, terrified. Of course! She couldn't see a thing. And he remembered the last time she'd come through the noktum, she'd been beaten, starved and bleeding from the mouth after the recent loss of her tongue, and everything in the world had wanted to eat her. It would have, too, if not for Khyven. This had to be a return to her worst nightmare.

He fished in his tunic and withdrew his Amulet of Noksonon. He always carried it on his person back in the days of Rhenn's rebel camp, and he'd continued to do so.

He handed it carefully back to her, encouraged her with his hand to put it around her neck. She did.

"Are you all right?" he shouted over the wind?

She nodded, signed with one hand. *"Are you?"*

"I'm sorry I got you into this," Vohn shouted over the roar of the wind.

"You didn't have a choice."

"I could have shut the door in your face," Vohn shouted.

"I could have left when you told me to."

"We are probably headed to our deaths." Vohn signed with his free hand.

"If the creature wanted us dead, we'd be dead, yes?"

Vohn blinked.

"I don't think this is as frightening as it seems," Shalure signed. *"I think this creature is being straight with us. I can't think of a reason he wouldn't be."*

"What do you think he wants from us?" Vohn signed.

"I don't know ... But I keep thinking ..." Her fingers stopped moving as though she was thinking about the correct next word.

"What?"

"I don't see any reason for this creature to lie to us."

"You're awfully brave."

"I'm terrified. But everything is terrifying now."

Shalure was thinking straight despite it all, calmer than Vohn was. To be honest, when he'd retrieved her from the *shkazat* den, he wasn't sure he was doing the right thing. A *shkazat* addict was likely to run toward that killing drug whenever faced with a challenge. How much use could that be to the kingdom? That wasn't someone you wanted by your side in a crisis.

But already she'd kept her head in a crisis, and he hadn't.

"You're right," he signed.

"Of course I'm right. Be nice if people noticed." Shalure signed, winking at him as she repeated his own words.

Vohn actually smiled for half a second, then Rauvelos dropped like a stone. Vohn's stomach jumped into his throat and he faced forward. For the next few terrifying moments, he clung for life until Rauvelos flared his wings. Gravity pinned Vohn and Shalure to the bird's back and Vohn thought he might throw up this time. He was beginning to long for Lorelle's awful cloak. It was better than this.

The pressure eased and Rauvelos's talons clicked gently on the stones of an enormous parapet.

"If you please," Rauvelos lowered a wing and looked meaningfully at them. Both Vohn and Shalure slid hastily to the ground. The giant raven withdrew his wing and shook it like it had been dunked in oil, then neatly folded it against his side.

"What do you want with us?" Vohn asked. The quick talk with Shalure had steadied his nerves. She looked around at the castle with her mouth in a wide O.

"I told you. To prepare you. My master wishes your last stand to stand until the last." The raven seemed amused by himself.

"What last stand?"

"I shall show you."

"Why don't you tell me?"

Rauvelos cocked his head, circular eyes flashing. "You really would be the tastiest snack, Shadowvar. Perhaps you should stop questioning me."

"Perhaps you should stop threatening to eat me!" Vohn snapped. "Do you really need to intimidate us? Don't we seem scared enough as it is? Is it some sadistic joke? Because I'm not laughing!"

The raven held perfectly still. In those cold, glittering eyes, Vohn could see no indication of the raven's mind. Whenever

Rauvelos stopped moving, it looked like he was poised to attack. The raven could move like a lightning strike, and Vohn could envision him pecking forward with that sword-like beak so fast there would be no time to even gasp before he was impaled.

This time, when Rauvelos finally did move, he moved slowly. He bowed gracefully from the neck. "Please accept my apologies, Shadowvar. I have treated you poorly, and you are my guest. It is unseemly."

Vohn couldn't tell if Rauvelos was being sarcastic or not.

"There are protections against the Dark itself as well as those who live there," Rauvelos continued. "My master has put many things in place to defend you. I have been instructed to lead you to them and teach you in their usage. He has collected these riches over millennia. There is a vault deep in Castle Noktos. The door is emblazoned with the symbol of Noksonon. With three spoken words and a key, you will be granted access. Together, we will enter and you must arm yourself and your people with the weapons therein."

"My people?"

"You must bring them here."

Vohn stood, stunned. "I can't do that. Thousands of Usarans? Here? They'll never make it."

"They will. And you must use the vault. This is why I have brought you here. If you would do me the courtesy of following me, I will lead you there directly." The raven stepped aside, indicating that Vohn and Shalure should enter the great room just beyond the huge archway.

"There's a key?" Vohn asked.

"Yes, which I will give to you when we get there."

"And three words. Passwords?"

"A passphrase, yes. It must be spoken aloud."

"What is it?"

The corner of the raven's mouth turned upward in what Vohn recognized as his smile. His eyes glittered. "Isn't it obvious?"

"Obvious? How could it be obvious? You just mentioned

the vault!"

"It is 'Khyven the—'"

Shalure let out a strangled cry. Vohn whirled about. At first, he thought Shalure was hurt, but then he followed her pointing finger out past the balcony, into the open expanse of dark noktum.

An enormous black dragon rose into view a hundred feet from the balcony, great wings flapping lazily.

"Well, well, well..." The dragon fixed its gaze upon Rauvelos. "If it isn't The Betrayer's lackey."

Chapter Thirty-One
SLAYTER

Slayter sat in the ash and dirt with his back up against the broken wall, feeling the potion's vitality course through him. A bead of sweat trickled down his temple to his jaw. He wiped it away. The entire wrecked keep was still warm from the dragon's recent fire. It had been mere minutes since Khyven had awoken him, yet everything was different. The keep. Nhevalos's game. Jai'ketakos's game.

And Slayter's plan to solve the puzzle.

Khyven crouched next to him like some protective bird of prey. He held no weapon in his hand, but that didn't mean anything when it came to Khyven. The man could draw a dagger—or a sword—faster than a person could blink.

"How did you do that?" Slayter asked, glancing at the Mavric iron sword, laying in a pile of dirt and debris a dozen feet away.

"Do what?"

"Hurt the dragon."

"I ..." Khyven hesitated. "I just fought."

It was a modest answer. He had done the impossible. A

Human against a dragon. "You didn't just fight. It's more than that. Please, I'm not trying to give you a compliment. I want to know how you went about it. It's important."

Khyven's fidgeting settled and he looked down at the dirt, like he was actually searching for the truth. "The sword protected me. It shielded me from the fire."

"Yes," Slayter said. He had noted that. It wasn't just a Mavric iron sword. It was some great weapon. Mavric iron swords, as amazing as any one of them might be, didn't just stop dragon fire. "I know. But I didn't mean that. I meant you. Even if the dragon hadn't shot a single spurt of flame, you shouldn't have been able to do what you did. Describe it, please."

Khyven was silent for a moment. "One step at a time. That's all I ever do. I followed the blue wind. I just ... I did what I've done in the Night Ring time and again. I looked for opportunities and I took them."

I looked for opportunities and I took them.

In the moment when he saw Khyven rise behind the dragon, Slayter realized he had been looking in the wrong direction. He had been looking at everything backward.

He'd wanted a map of Nhevalos's plan, but he suddenly realized that such a thing didn't exist. Slayter now strongly suspected that even Nhevalos didn't have a perfect map of the future, because the future was always changing. Slayter didn't need a long view. He needed a short view. He needed to see the pieces moving on the board as they were moving, and he needed to react lightning fast, like Khyven.

Nhevalos's abduction of Rhenn now seemed a long time ago. Vamreth's death in another life. Since Rhenn's return, more and more events had continued to occur. Some small. Some large. Everything had been confusing pieces that refused to fit together into a cohesive whole that Slayter could see: the voices trying to claim Vohn, Lorelle, and now Rhenn as well; the expansion of Khyven's predictive powers; the attack on Nokte Shaddark; the arrival of Jai'ketakos; and now the dragon's ambush.

Slayter reviewed the other times Khyven had done the impossible.

Khyven had fought the Giant Tovos. That had been impossible, a one-in-a-million miracle. Sheer luck. That was what Slayter had thought.

But now Khyven had fought a dragon. He had made a dragon flee, and Slayter was forced to look at the pattern of Khyven in the world.

First, Khyven had defeated Txomin of the Sandrunners while blind, against all odds. Then he'd toppled Vamreth's reign by wielding a Helm of Darkness, which no Human could wield. Then he'd overcome Tovos, where his friends had played an integral role. Now he'd grievously wounded Jai'ketakos using that Mavric iron sword.

None of the previous events had properly triggered Slayter's imagination, opening a doorway to a hidden truth. It was, at last, seeing Khyven fight the dragon off that had done it. The key to what he wanted, to saving the world, was right here in front of him. He just had to see it correctly. It meant reordering what he had already decided, what he already believed.

There was no puzzle that needed to be sorted before they could confound it. There was no grand plan to confound, no map that could ensure a particular future because ...

The future was in flux. Always. The future was only determined one step at a time, as Khyven had said, by immediate actions. The future wasn't determined by Nhevalos looking at a predestined path and nudging pawns in that direction, no matter what Nhevalos might think. It was determined by those who were immersed in the defining events, by taking immediate action.

And Khyven was supernaturally good at taking immediate action.

The truth sparked and flared in Slayter's mind. He'd had it backward all this time.

It wasn't the puzzle that needed solving. It wasn't the map of the future he needed to see. The key was Khyven.

Khyven could move events that no one else could move.

Khyven had used his blue wind to defeat Txomin, the Helm of Darkness to defeat Vamreth, his friends to defeat Tovos, and the Mavric iron sword to defeat Jai'ketakos. Each, when taken by themselves, seemed like random, one-of-a-kind miracles, but the linking factor was always Khyven.

Mighty forces always seemed to revolve around him. Whether this was by Nhevalos's design or whether it was somehow innate, it didn't really matter. Khyven—not Nhevalos—used those resources to nearly perfect effect in each circumstance.

Slayter's new purpose coalesced into solid certainty. He didn't need Nhevalos's map. He didn't need to see and fill in the puzzle, didn't need to find the perfect puzzle pieces.

Khyven was *the* puzzle piece. For any event. For every event. It was Slayter's job to ensure Khyven always had the resources he needed. This war would be won in each individual battle. And Khyven was the master of individual battles.

"Slayter, are you all right?"

"I made a mistake," Slayter murmured.

"A mistake in coming here?"

"The dragon."

"The dragon?"

"Jai'ketakos the dragon," Slayter clarified.

Khyven darkened. "I know who the dragon is."

"I've been preparing for the war. I wanted to see the lay of the land, the entire map that I imagine Nhevalos sees. I wanted to gather information before the war began so that we could prepare for it."

"Yes. And gathering information here at Wheskone was a mistake?"

Slayter wrinkled his brow, Khyven's ham handed overgeneralization annoying him. "No. Gathering information is never a mistake."

Khyven frowned. "Then what are you saying?"

"The mistake isn't the information. It's the map. It's thinking the war is coming."

Khyven looked confused again. "The war isn't coming?"

"No. It's not. The war is here. The war has already started."

Khyven raised his eyebrows.

"The dragon. He is the war. Vamreth is the war. Txomin is the war. Tovos is the war."

Khyven's eyes narrowed like a cat watching rippling water. "You're going to have to slow down a little."

"There is no map. There never could be. We're in it, and the smartest thing to do is ..." He fell to thinking. What was the smartest thing to do? Was abandoning all strategy really the key? Surely that couldn't be right. It would mean putting all bets on Khyven. Such a narrow strategy made Slayter itch between the shoulder blades. But he was convinced that trailing behind Nhevalos, trying to pick up the threads of his plan was a dead end. Nhevalos didn't have a concrete plan. He couldn't. The *kairoi* weren't immutable.

"Can we back up?" Khyven said. "I'm still stuck on the dragon and how the war has already started."

"They are all pieces, but they don't fit together."

Khyven blew out a sigh through puffed cheeks and shook his head.

"The future is not static," Slayter continued. "It's always moving. Even the *kairoi* can't stop that. That's what I've been missing. Each piece is its own puzzle."

"How is a piece a puzzle?"

"It's the dragon," Slayter said. "The next piece."

"What about the dragon?"

"What?" Slayter started, looking over at Khyven's soot-smudged face and his intense expression.

Khyven looked like he was trying very hard not to clench his jaw. "You said the dragon is the war. Or that he's the next piece or something. And there is no map. And that Vamreth is the war. And Txomin. Except they're both dead."

"It's so obvious now," Slayter said.

"Not. To me." Khyven bit the words out.

"Txomin. Vamreth. Tovos. Jai'ketakos," Slayter murmured absently to answer Khyven's question, but his mind ran down other avenues. He had to know what the dragon would do next. That was the entire puzzle in this moment. Manipulating the *kairoi* meant hanging onto that giant snake until it bent to one's will. At least until the puzzle shifted, then the trick was to jump to the next snake. Right now, Slayter had to predict what Jai'ketakos would do next and put Khyven in front of the dragon.

So what would the dragon do next?

Slayter walked it back. In Usara, the dragon had felt slighted by Slayter figuring out the nature of his game. He'd retaliated by burning Slayter's ancestral home to the ground.

This was an entirely different situation. This time, Jai'ketakos had been grievously wounded. No slight, this. Khyven could have killed the dragon. That meant, to Jai'ketakos, Khyven was a serious, continuing threat. The dragon wouldn't be looking for clever payback. He'd want searing, passionate revenge. He'd want Khyven dead before he could continue on to anything else.

"He will be able to heal himself," Slayter murmured. "That's what he'll do first."

"I feel like I'm *almost* a part of this conversation," Khyven said.

What would the dragon do next? Come back here? Seek Khyven, surely.

"Slayter!" Khyven barked.

Slayter started out of his reverie. "What?"

"I want you to explain to me what you're thinking."

"I just did."

"You listed off the four most frightening moments of my life. Then you just said words that seemed to have no relation whatsoever."

"The progression. Txomin. Vamreth. Tovos—"

"If you list them off again, I'm going to knock your head against the wall," Khyven growled. "What I need to understand is what you're actually saying—"

"Txomin was a test, I think. He was the beginning, but a test. The rest ... That was the beginning of the war. Tell me, Khyven, how many times have you seen a Giant before a year ago?"

"Apparently every day for nearly eight years." Khyven crossed his arms.

That was uncommonly astute for Khyven. Nhevaz had been with him for years before everything really began. Khyven was right. And wrong. Slayter pointed at him. "That's funny. And accurate." Sometimes Khyven wasn't as slow as he seemed.

"Thanks," Khyven drawled.

"But not what I mean. I mean how many times have you seen a Giant that you *knew* was a Giant. Until this past summer, that is?"

"Never."

"And how many times has anyone seen a Giant they knew were a Giant in the last two thousand years?"

"I'd have to look at my journal from two thousand years ago," Khyven said.

Slayter blinked, then smiled. "Also funny."

"To my knowledge, never," Khyven said.

"But now Giants are literally dropping out of the sky. What I'm saying is: this *is* the war. These are the opening battles. And you've won two of them at least, if not three. That is what I am saying. The Giants are pitting themselves against you ... And they are losing."

Slayter fell silent and his thoughts raced down the hallways of his mind, focusing on the relevant issue at hand. The dragon would want revenge.

Khyven and Jai'ketakos would face each other again. Khyven was like a lightning rod, and the dragon would return to him, which meant Slayter had to predict the dragon and give Khyven the best resources—battlefield, weapons, knowledge—that he could.

Slayter began to dissect what he knew of Jai'ketakos's personality. It might be impossible to follow the logic of someone like Nhevalos, who had spent his long life being inscrutable, shifting his personality to hide, but the dragon was easier. It shouldn't be impossible to pick apart the dragon if Slayter just concentrated.

He started with the most obvious. First, the dragon was in all likelihood insane. He'd been trapped for nearly two millennia, and if confinement did to a Giant's mind anything similar to what it did to a Human's mind, there would be consequences to that.

Certainly, the dragon's "crossroads" game was a lie, a manifestation of his insanity. Jai'ketakos didn't really give his victims a choice. He arranged the game to produce his desired outcome. He danced his words around it just so, deceived as he needed to, in order for his victim to choose the only outcome the dragon wanted.

He'd done it with Lorelle, had offered her exactly what she wanted, which gave him exactly what he had wanted: carnage. If Lorelle had chosen to leave the Plunnos, Slayter hardly thought the dragon would have chained himself up for another thousand years. No. He would have devoured Lorelle, erased the interaction from his mind, and continued on to offer the game to another hapless victim.

In fact, it was likely that the dragon had played the game with a number of people since Lorelle. Slayter had little doubt each of those interactions had gone exactly as Jai'ketakos had wanted them to go. He'd successfully guided his victims to the dragon's choice.

Until Slayter.

Slayter had broken the game by seeing through it. For some reason, the dragon hadn't flown into a rage right then and killed Slayter anyway. The dragon had, for that moment, wanted to see himself as honorable, a steward of this game that was so important to him. Slayter hadn't been worth fracturing the fantasy, not then anyway. In fact, instead of seeing Slayter's victory as a victory at all, Jai'ketakos had just extended the game. He'd gone to a place where he could lure Slayter and finish the job. That was, technically, cheating. It was circumventing the rules the dragon himself had established for his game. Jai'ketakos had extended the game to a different playing field where he'd have the element of surprise and the upper hand. And he had succeeded.

Until Khyven had turned the tables.

Jai'ketakos had intended to torture Slayter, kill him, then move on, perhaps even erasing any failure whatsoever from his mind.

That was self-delusion.

Slayter stood up, eyes bright—

Khyven leapt to his feet, steel sword drawn. The Ringer's speed was impressive, and a little annoying. Slayter had stood up about as fast as a person could stand. He'd literally leapt to his feet without warning, but Khyven's reflexes were so quick he'd reached his feet before Slayter, ready to fight.

Khyven scanned the empty keep and the surrounding streets, on high alert, then looked back at Slayter with a frown, like he was a dog that never barked at the right thing.

"What?" Khyven said.

"The dragon."

"The dragon is here?" Khyven scanned the darkness. "I don't see anything. And I don't sense anything. The blue wind isn't—"

"No, no. Txomin, Vamreth, Tovos—"

"Let's not do this again," Khyven growled.

"Jai'ketakos is going back to Usara."

"You couldn't just *say* that?"

"I did just say that."

"But the dragon can't burn Usara. That's the only thing we know he won't do, right? Because of the bargain. Lorelle said he kept to the letter of the bargain he made with her."

"And then he destroyed Nox Arvak, which was what he *wanted* to do from the beginning."

"I don't understand. That's the same as he did here. He didn't get to destroy Usara, so he came here. So he won't go back to Usara."

Slayter shook his head. "It's not the same."

"He gave Lorelle a choice. She chose. He gave you a choice. You chose. I don't understand how it's different."

"He wanted to destroy Nox Arvak, so he set Lorelle up with a predictable choice, and she chose it. He wanted to destroy Usara, so he set me up with the predictable choice, but I *didn't* make that choice."

"You didn't..."

"No. I saw no logical reason for a dragon to give me exactly what I wanted, so I listened for what he wasn't saying, and I saw the game. Jai'ketakos likes to imagine the fairness of his game, but the game is an illusion. He tells himself—and his victims—that he's letting them choose their destiny, but he dictates their choices. He wants control. He *needs* that control. And in the end, he funnels them right where he wants them to go, playing on their fears or hopes. He knows that no Human will think clearly when facing a dragon. He expected the same from me, but I surprised him. He only allowed me to live, allowed Usara to stand, because he planned to take his revenge here, in Wheskone. But he failed again, and the illusion is now broken. I played his game against him and won. You turned his revenge upside down and injured him. The game has utterly failed him. He's not in control anymore, and he won't stand for that. I don't think he's going to adhere to any so-called 'rules' anymore."

"You're saying he's going to be waiting for us in Usara?"

"I'm saying he's lost control. Think about this, Khyven: Jai'ketakos was trapped by his kind for nearly two millennia in a place where he had no control over his fate. I believe his 'crossroads' game allowed him to cover his shame. It allowed him to be unequivocally in charge. He's not ruled by a sense of fair play, by allowing mortals to choose their destiny. He is ruled by revenge against those who chained him, against the world for doing nothing to free him. That's why he wants carnage and death. He's not going to set up another game to test us. It's time to hurt us back at all costs. He's going to destroy everything we've ever touched."

Khyven stared at Slayter for a long moment then turned and strode toward Hellface.

Slayter ran to catch up. He windmilled his arms as he almost fell into a pit, gained his balance again—barely—and belated stumbled up alongside Khyven. "You forgot your sword."

"I didn't forget anything." Khyven caught the bridle of Slayter's mount and prepared to help him into the saddle. Hellface stood nearby, looking at Khyven like he wanted to bite him. The tuft of black hair on the front of the horse's face was singed, like he'd refused to back up when the dragon had blown fire.

Slayter looked at the Mavric iron sword in the ash and dust, then back at Khyven. "You'll want to take the sword."

"No I don't."

"Except you do."

"I really don't."

"Khyven, the sword is one of your resources, and you'll need them all—"

"I'm not touching it. And I don't want to talk about it."

"Well ... Very well. You don't have to talk about the sword. But you do need to take it—"

"Trust me, Slayter. We want to leave it."

"Well ..." Slayter blinked. "Well those are two completely unrelated statements. I *do* trust you. But we do want to take the sword. I understand that you may think you don't need the sword, but you are ignorant."

Khyven's hand holding the reins clenched into a fist, and he shook his head as though he was trying to tamp down his anger. "Sometimes I wish I'd met you in the Night Ring ..."

"You're afraid of its power, which is—"

"That's not it."

"You think what happened to Gohver will happen to—"

"That's not it, either."

"Khyven ..." Slayter said. "If it's vanity, well, that's hardly a worthy reason, don't you think? The scars from the Helm wrecked your face, but that's not going to happen now."

"Vanity isn't— Wait! Wrecked my face?"

"If the Mavric iron sword was going to scar you, it would have done so by now."

"*Wrecked* my face?"

"Clearly Lorelle doesn't care about how you look—"

"All right, stop talking!" Khyven sliced a hand through the air.

"If that's why you don't want to—"

"It talks to me!" Khyven roared.

Slayter fell silent. "The sword?"

"No, the rock." He gave Slayter a flat look. "Yes, the sword!"

"It talks to you?" Slayter's mind jumped about with questions. That was ... Well, that was just amazing.

"So I'm not picking it up again."

"Are you sure it's not just a humming? Sometimes magical items can create a humming in the mind. So it could be a hum. I've read that some people hear a—"

"It's not a hum."

Slayter started back toward the sword. "Well, this is just magnificent." He stopped two paces away. He held his hands over the thing.

"Don't touch it." Khyven put a firm hand on Slayter's shoulder. The Ringer had crossed the distance, moved up Slayter without making a sound.

"Oh, I'm not going to touch it. I have no Giant's blood. But you need to get it. Right now. We can't waste a moment in this place, really. We don't have Lorelle's cloak."

"I'm not touching that thing."

"If this is actually a sentient sword ... Do you know how few sentient swords there are? With the right texts, I could determine which great sword it is."

"Sentient. Like a living thing," Khyven said.

"Yes."

Khyven closed his eyes like he didn't want to hear what Slayter was saying. "The sword is alive," he said in a monotone.

"Yes."

"No." He shook his head.

"Of course it is. You said it was talking to you. What did you think was making the words?"

"A spell? Some crazy spell that makes a person hallucinate ..." He waved it away. His hand tightened and he began to pull Slayter away.

Slayter tried to shrug him off, but the man's grip was like a flesh-covered steel vice. "Wait, a spell that makes a person what? What did it make you do?"

"Nothing!" Khyven growled. "It didn't ... Or maybe ... I don't know!"

"Did it tell you to do things?"

"Yes."

"It actually spoke in words and told you what to do?"

"Yes."

"Did it make you do exactly what it told you to do?"

"No!" He shook his head. "Or ... Maybe. I might have done what it said to do anyway. It all happened quickly. It just felt ... like I wasn't completely in control."

"The sword wanted you to kill the dragon, but you already wanted to kill the dragon."

"Yes." He paused. "But there was a point when I wanted to leave the dragon, to help you, and I ... I don't think the sword wanted me to do that. Then suddenly I wanted to kill the dragon more than anything I'd ever wanted in my life. Like there was nothing else I could possibly want to do. Ever again."

Slayter stood transfixed in front of the sword. He'd never met a sentient sword before. He'd never met a sentient object at all before. He wondered who was in there. "Did it ... Did it ask you questions? Did it ask you your purpose?"

"Purpose? No. It just said, 'kill kill kill'."

"Surely it said more than that."

"I don't know. I wasn't really listening. I was busy trying to make sure the dragon didn't roast you."

"Mmmm ..." If only they were in his library! Which great

sword was it? Lelandos's flying blade? Was it the Anvil of Time? Oh, the possibilities!

"I'm not kidding, Slayter. Don't touch it."

"Of course." He nodded. "Not here, no. Not here. Pick it up and let's go."

"What did I *just* say three times?"

"I know what you said, but you're wrong."

Slayter heard Khyven's exasperated breath behind him, so he turned. He glanced up and saw something in Khyven's eyes that he'd never really seen before: fear.

The man had faced down noktum monsters, undead bloodsuckers, and Giants. He'd battled a dragon, for the love of Senji. But it was the sword that scared him.

"You have to," Slayter said softly. "This is part of it. Of everything."

"Of everything what?"

"Nhevalos. Jai'ketakos—"

"Don't start the list again. You're saying it's part of the war."

"Undoubtedly."

"I can't, Slayter," he said. "If it was controlling me ... I can't allow that."

Slayter cocked his head. "Your disinclination is—"

A whisper of a sensation went through Slayter's body, and the feeling stopped him in mid-sentence.

This moment is more important than it seems, the feeling said.

He felt something slither past him, a ghostly sense of powerful magics nearby. It was like he was swimming in the Claw Sea and something had swum beneath him, something vast, powerful, and enormous, something that belonged in the unfathomable depths.

Slayter looked up at Khyven. The warrior seemed unaffected. He hadn't felt it.

But Slayter had paused so long that Khyven started talking again.

"The more I learn about ..." Khyven gestured at himself. "About this. What was done to me. The magic that flows through me, the more I realize just how important it is that I do the right thing. I can't have some bloodthirsty artifact take control of my body. Imagine the damage I could do."

Slayter didn't respond. He wanted a moment to think about his feeling. It was magical; there was no question about that. He needed time to study it. Needed time to ...

No. It was transient. He didn't need time. It was here and it would go. And once it went, the moment would be past. This had to do with the sword and Khyven.

"Khyven," Slayter said hastily, and he turned to face the warrior directly. "I ..."

After a long moment where Slayter didn't follow up with anything, Khyven said, "You what?"

"You need that sword."

"I told you, I'm not—"

"Wait. Just wait. Let me finish." The slithering feeling continued, like the great sea beast was a mile long, moving inexorably beneath him. "I need you to ..."

Khyven sensed that Slayter was feeling something, and he went on full alert, flicking glances around. "What's happening?"

"I need you to listen to me," Slayter continued. "You're going to be at the center of events to come. You have been equipped with an ability that makes you uniquely disposed to fight this war. Your victories show that, but they also seem inordinately lucky. You've been underestimated twice. You've had help both times, and the element of surprise. But every calculation I've made if a Giant knows what you are, sees you coming ... Once they know about you, Khyven, they will account for you. They'll target you. They'll find a way to kill you. Unless you continue to surprise them. Unless you bring more than the blue wind."

"Slayter—"

"This." Slayter pointed at the Mavric iron sword. "This is more than the blue wind. I don't know how much more, but I will find out for you. I promise."

Khyven raised his chin defiantly and held it there. Slayter was sure he was going to growl again and refuse, but instead the big man moved to stand over the Mavric iron weapon, looked down at it.

"It's a terrible risk," Khyven said softly.

"We come to this game late, Khyven. Risks are all we have left. We have to run them, and we have to win every time."

Khyven closed his eyes.

"Do you understand?" Slayter said. "You're going to have to be more than a supernatural fighter. You're going to have to use this tool that wants to control you—you're going to have to use *every* tool you can. And you have to win the day, every time. No matter the cost."

"No matter the cost ..." He descended to a crouch. Despite his obvious loathing of the thing, he grasped the hilt without hesitation.

With effortless grace, Khyven rose, holding the thing like it was made for his hand, and he slammed it home into the special sheath Slayter had made. The six-foot length vanished into the two-foot-long sheath across Khyven's broad back. Khyven's head bowed like a man who had put a boulder on his shoulders and was determined to take it to the top of the mountain.

The slithering sense of doom beneath Slayter moved past, and it was gone. What was meant to happen had happened. Slayter felt good and horrible at the same time.

"Come on." Khyven went to the horses, took Slayter's mount's reins and waited.

Slayter followed, grabbed Khyven's extended hand for balance as he put his good foot into the stirrup and pulled himself up into the saddle. Then he said something that surprised even himself, "I'm sorry, Khyven."

Khyven glanced up at him. They locked gazes for a moment, then Khyven nodded.

He took Hellface's reins and swung up into the saddle. For the first time, the black stallion didn't fight him, just snorted and stamped his hoof like he was impatient to get going.

"You know," Khyven said. "I thought being a knight would

be more fun than this."

"You did?"

"It looked so glamorous." Khyven turned Hellface, and the horse actually obeyed, spinning about to face the street that led out of the town.

"Did it?" Slayter mimicked the movement, turning about. "The shining steel armor. The parades. The pennants snapping in the breeze."

"Knights have pennants?"

"The knights would—What? Of course knights have pennants. Are you saying you never watched any of Vamreth's parades?"

"I can't think of anything more boring. No."

"Well, they have pennants."

"I always thought being a knight would be horrible," Slayter said.

Khyven twisted in his saddle and flashed a frown of disapproval. "How do you figure?"

"People bashing each other into unconsciousness. All the sweating and bruises. The cuts and the frequent opportunities to die."

"That's the fun part," Khyven chuckled.

"You should be a mage. Being a mage is much better."

"Magic is what got me into this." He flicked his fingers at the sword over his shoulder.

"Magic is what's going to get you out of this."

"Heh. Promise?"

"Well ... no."

Khyven chuckled, shaking his head. He gave one last look at Slayter, then yelled at Hellface and kicked his heels into the stallion's flanks. The beast leapt into a gallop, thundering up the road. Slayter shouted, kicked, and followed.

Chapter Thirty-Two
JAI'KETAKOS

When the sword sliced into Jai'ketakos's tail, fire tore through him unlike any pain he'd ever known. The second time, when that burning blade cut through his front scales like butter, he thought he was actually going to die.

Even during the War of the Fall, when the mortals had swarmed him at the Battle of Dyn Mar, hacking with magic hatchets, he'd not felt this kind of pain. Even during the Elder Wars, when he'd been a hatchling and had been stabbed with a Pyranoi spear, he'd not felt this kind of pain.

The rage of the Sword seared through more than just flesh. It ate into his mind. When he yanked back, finally free of its bite, it was like he was still being cut, like that damnable blade was still in there—would always be there—sawing and sawing until it reached his heart.

As Jai'ketakos beat the air frantically to get away, he looked down at the little mortal. He was just a Human! No Eldroi in disguise. No mage. Aside from the sword—which glowed like a malevolent sun to Jai'ketakos's magical senses—there wasn't a single thing about the Human that was magical. He barely had an aura of life-force at all.

Except that couldn't be true. He was supernaturally fast. He second-guessed everything Jai'ketakos tried to do. He was completely protected from fire. He was a horror.

Everything here was wrong. A mortal who wasn't really a mortal. A sword that wasn't really a sword. He didn't understand what was happening. He could die here. He could actually die here! Unprecedented fear blossomed inside him …

And he fled.

He shot like a bleeding comet across the sky, like the sword was still attached to his tail, trying to strike again. He flew like his worst nightmare was right behind him.

He only returned to his senses when he reached the dark expanse of the ocean, two hundred miles away. The terrible cut burned his belly, as did the one almost all the way through his tail. And the burning was getting worse.

He suddenly realized that was the first coherent thought he'd managed since the sword bit into him in the first place. On the heels of that thought came the realization that the sword, or the Human who was not a Human, had cast a spell upon him. Love Magic. The type that could infiltrate a person's mind, and it had been stifling his better sense, eating into his brain, making him befuddled.

Making him afraid.

Only then did he realize he'd acted the fool. Jai'ketakos should have stayed in the battle. He should have crushed the mortal with claws, chomped him with teeth. Instead, he'd fled like some low beast fleeing from fire.

A cold trickle of fear ran up his back, because he was still delaying. Now he was rehashing what he ought to have done, rather than doing what he needed to do.

The spell is still affecting me, he thought. *The damned spell is still trying to keep me from what I need to do to save myself!*

He could heal this wound; he just needed life. And what had

he done instead? He'd simply flown high in the air, far away from the creatures below, far away from what might actually heal him.

Jai'ketakos spiraled down toward a mountain range and a cave where he'd seen movement. A fox, a deer, a bear. Anything would do. He landed, flames flowing out of his mouth, and he lumbered into the cave. He was surprised to find a clutch of Human bandits.

But not nearly as surprised as they were.

They jumped up, shouting in fear as they scrambled for weapons. Two of the bravest charged at him, waving swords.

Jai'ketakos blasted fire directly into the cave. He tempered it, made it cool enough that it would only bubble their skin, burn off their hair.

They shrieked and spun away, trying in vain to escape. But they were cornered, in a cave, and the fire was everywhere.

Perfect. Yes. This was perfect.

The half-melted Humans fell, screaming and writhing in agony.

"Yeesss," Jai'ketakos said, starting to feel a little like his old self.

Like all Eldroi, he knew every stream of magic, but like most Eldroi, he knew some streams better than others. Land Magic was the magic that governed fire, and he liked it best of all. Most Drakanoi did. It was the easiest to use by far, but he knew a little Life Magic as well.

As the Humans thrashed, screaming, he reached into their life-force and drew it out. He took it all. It rose from their bodies, appearing like wisps of white mist. He brought the wisps together, swirling them into a ball.

The Human bodies stopped moving. They had given their last useful measure, as they should.

Jai'ketakos brought the sphere of white mist toward himself. He positioned it over his wounds and let it sink in. The surge of life-force gave him everything he needed.

Quickly, hastily, he pushed back the burning sensation that

sought to dig deeper into him, pushed it out of his tail, out of his belly. And then he used the tendrils of remaining white mist to sew up the wounds.

Jai'ketakos had used Life Magic before, but never like this. He had healed a wound here and there. A peeled scale. A slashed foot. This required his full attention as he knit the flesh back together with sheer force of will. It was agonizing. The Eldroi who used a lot of Life Magic never talked about how difficult it was. And how painful!

But he did it. He hissed through the agony and stayed on course. When it was done, both scars were jagged and obvious, scales overlapping asymmetrically, but they were healed. The burning had stopped. The foreboding that an insidious death was still slithering into him had vanished.

So the scars weren't pretty, but he didn't care. Nothing mattered except ...

Khyven the Unkillable and Slayter the Mage.

Jai'ketakos glared balefully out the cave's entrance. Jai'ketakos hadn't given any thought to the warrior, not imagining for a second that he would be a threat.

"Khyven the Unkillable ..." he snarled to the night. A mere Human didn't get to threaten him. No ...

Outside the cave, far away, a wolf howled as his pack gathered for the night's hunt. Jai'ketakos thought about finding the wolf pack and showing them who was the real hunter.

"Leave the wolves ..." he growled, and settled himself down to stare out at the darkness. He stayed that way, thoughts swirling, until the daylight came. He waited until the sun peaked, until the night consumed the land, until the sun rose again and started its climb back down to the horizon. Only then did he resolve what he would do, what he must do.

He moved to the cave's mouth and looked up at blue sky. With a mighty surge, he leapt upward and winged his way away from the sun. The burn of the sword had left him, but the burn of humiliation was fresh.

Khyven had hurt him, so Khyven's home must die first.

Soon, Jai'ketakos neared. From far above, he looked down on the outline of the wall of the crown city of Usara. The little palace and Night Ring looked like glittering playthings—one white, one black—surrounded by the tiny squares of the houses.

Yes ... This was what he needed. Yes ...

He would feast on the crackling bones of anyone and everyone who had ever known Khyven the—

A blur of darkness jumped up from the white palace, evened out, and flew toward the noktum, far below Jai'ketakos. After a second, the blur evened out into the shape of a bird.

What was this?

The bird was surrounded in a cloak of darkness, which would have prevented any mortal eyes from seeing anything but a shadowy blur, but Jai'ketakos saw him just fine.

That was Rauvelos, The Betrayer's lackey.

What have we here? Jai'ketakos thought.

Rauvelos had not been there when Jai'ketakos's jailors had clamped the Dragon Chain on his ankle. Nhevalos had not been there. But they had created the damned war. They had brought the Eldroi low, face to face with Humans. If not for them, there would never have been a need for Jai'ketakos to guard that Thuros by the Lux.

If not for them, Jai'ketakos's fellows would have come to free him.

Jai'ketakos descended cautiously as Nhevalos's lackey plunged into the noktum. He followed.

Inside the noktum, Jai'ketakos saw the castle, and for the first time he remembered exactly where he was. This was the realm of Noktos, first of the Noksonoi. That was his castle. Jai'ketakos remembered enough to recall that.

When Rauvelos landed and placed his tiny charges on the high balcony, a certainty bloomed in Jai'ketakos's mind.

The raven would die, of course. After, Jai'ketakos could flay the flesh of the little mortals a bit at a time until they told him everything there was to know about Khyven the Unkillable. Then he would eat them.

Jai'ketakos glided forward until he was close enough for them to see him. No doubt he appeared from the dark like the specter of death.

And they weren't wrong. It was time for Jai'ketakos to wreak his vengeance. On Nhevalos's house. On Khyven the Unkillable's friends.

"Well, well, well…" The dragon said. "If it isn't The Betrayer's lackey."

Chapter Thirty-Three
VOHN

"Well ..." Rauvelos said. "This is inconvenient."

The giant raven's wings swept back as though he was about to take off, and the dragon flapped backward, wary and ready for battle.

But Rauvelos didn't take to the air. His gesture seemed entirely for show until, in the wake of his wings, an enormous key floated in the air behind his back, out of view of the dragon. The key slowly drifted toward Vohn, just as the ring had done in the queen's meeting room.

One of Rauvelos's eyes swiveled to focus on Vohn, and he spoke in a low voice. "Our time is up. I'm afraid I won't be able to give you a tour today after all. The Vault. You remember where I told you it was. Go now. Don't wait. The key will let you in."

"What are you going to do?"

"That is Jai'ketakos the Imprisoned," Rauvelos's voice thundered through the air, clearly meant for the dragon, though he was ostensibly talking to Vohn. "The dog has slipped his leash, and as with all recalcitrant dogs, he must be reprimanded."

"Oh please reprimand me, bird," Jai'ketakos said.

"Wait!" Vohn said, snatching the key and pocketing it quickly. Shalure looked at the dragon fearfully. "Rauvelos, don't fight him. Talk to him—"

"The mortal wants to talk, Little Prisoner." Rauvelos nodded his head. "What say you?"

A flare of fire rose up from the dragon's nostrils at the word 'little.'

"I will give you a choice, bird. Eat your mortal friends here, right on this balcony, and I will parley. If not ... then I will eat *you.*"

Rauvelos smiled. It was actually the largest smile Vohn had ever seen on the bird. "A brief lesson, Shadowvar. Pay attention. Drakanoi think themselves infinitely clever, but they are actually the dullards of Eldros. They believe their ungainly size and reptilian appearance somehow make them more powerful. But these 'assets' are only a hope to overwhelm good sense. Note his egotistical preening and see it for what it is. He thinks himself a genius when in fact he is pedestrian. You, Jai'ketakos ..." Rauvelos drew a bored breath and let it out, "are predictable."

"Rauvelos," Vohn began. "Don't—"

"I've made my choice, Little Prisoner." Rauvelos's beak lowered slightly. His talons curled slightly on the stones. "You promised to feast upon me. Was that mere bravado?"

"It will be my pleasure." Jai'ketakos revealed all of his teeth.

The raven went completely still. "You should have stayed in your cage."

"Do you really think yourself a match for an elder dragon, bird?"

"Is that what you fancy yourself?"

"I've learned much over these intervening years."

"I doubt it."

"Come find out, bird."

Rauvelos cocked his head. His gaze lingered on the dragon's exposed belly.

A great cawing sound ripped through the air, making Vohn jump. It took Vohn a moment to realize that the horrible sound was laughter.

"Well look at that," Rauvelos said. "You've taken a wound, Little Prisoner. A sword wound. How did you get it, I wonder? A wound like that comes from Mavric iron. Now who do I know that walks around with a Mavric iron sword?"

The dragon's nostrils glowed hot orange.

Rauvelos cawed again. "Who could that possibly be?"

"It was your master, bird. I left his pile of ashes where he fell."

"Yes. And tomorrow the Dark will turn green and the sun will vomit a rainbow upon your head. You are no match for my master, Little Prisoner. Your ignorance shows as much. Lord Nhevalos doesn't carry a sword. You've met Khyven the Unkillable." He made that cawing sound again, softer. A chuckle? "How did you like him? He really is quite surprising for a Human, isn't he? Just when you think he's dead, he comes back."

"Stop your incessant chattering and face me," the dragon growled.

"Oh, this is rich," Rauvelos said. "Your poor healing tells an even greater story. It's not just any Mavric iron sword he has, is it? It's one that hungers for your blood."

The dragon hovered, seething.

"The Sword of Noksonon is loose in the world again," Rauvelos continued. "And it has tasted your yellow belly. How do you like that? You know that the Sword won't ever stop looking for you. You are marked as an invader. Do you know what that means?"

The dragon flapped his wings slowly, hovering. His head twitched like he was grinding his teeth so hard his neck had stiffened.

"Oh, how rich. Let me tell you, then," Rauvelos continued relentlessly. "Khyven the Unkillable now has a weapon that is bent on ridding your kind from Noksonon forever. The Sword will find you. Khyven will walk around your pitiful swipes, and he will split you from neck to tail. He will never stop searching until you are dead. The Sword won't let him. Best not let him get too close, Little Prisoner. Not again."

Jai'ketakos roared and dove at the balcony. Rauvelos's talons cracked the flagstones and he launched upward to meet the approaching horror.

The wind from Rauvelos's wings struck Vohn like a hurricane, lifting him up and slamming him into the wall. He fell to his knees and dropped the key. It skittered across the flagstones. Vohn cast about for Shalure, but the wind had blown her through the archway back into the castle.

He started toward the key, but a blast of fire exploded in the air, and he spun to see the battle.

Fire engulfed Rauvelos, and Vohn thought the fight was over as quickly as it had begun, but then he spotted the raven soaring in a circle around the dragon, banking hard as the fire chased him. The raven turned, pointing his spear-like beak directly at the dragon.

Lightning arced back and forth between the two titans. Slithering trailers of purple and red light zipped back and forth and encircled them. The air shivered like a mirage. A keening sound filled the air, like wind forced through a crack.

A hand fell on Vohn's shoulder, and he jumped. Shalure crouched there, her head low and her left hand to her left ear like she could somehow duck the horrible sound.

"What is it?" Her free hand signed frantically.

"I ..." Vohn had no idea. He had never seen anything like this in his life. "A ... magic war ... They're attacking each other through avenues we can barely see."

It was so enormous, so incomprehensible that all he could do was watch. Two behemoths fighting each other. The spurts of flame could level a city. The strikes of lightning could turn a mountain into glass. The cacophony of noises pounded at him from all sides.

Rauvelos wheeled in the sky, climbing then diving. He spun,

dodged between two vicious lightning strikes, each as thick as a castle tower, and moved in for a physical attack. Jai'ketakos tried to dodge, wings drawing back, but the bird was too fast, dropping like a spear. The giant raven was barely a quarter the size of the dragon and a fraction of his bulk, but his deadly beak drove into the dragon's shoulder, puncturing straight through the scales.

Jai'ketakos roared, twisting away in agony, and blood rained down. His huge hind claws whipped up to scrape away the giant raven, but Rauvelos yanked his beak, launched downward, talons scraping for purchase on the dragon's scaled belly. Jai'ketakos's claws raked through empty air. Rauvelos dropped like a stone, spinning. He unfurled his wings and skimmed along the treetops, a black blur.

Jai'ketakos pursued, but he wasn't nearly as fast as the raven. Since Rauvelos had disengaged, the blurry air around them returned to normal. The lightning strikes, golden ribbons, and fire vanished. The horrible keening died out.

In seconds, Rauvelos was only a speck against the gray horizon where he began fighting for altitude, wings pumping hard. It slowed him, and Jai'ketakos dove at the same moment, closing the gap. Fire roared out. Rauvelos banked right, turning back toward the castle and met the fire burst head-on. He tucked his wings and spiraled through the flame, a torrent of air surrounding him like a cocoon. When he emerged on the far side, he was unhurt, but his feathers smoked.

Jai'ketakos pursued, fire pouring out of his nostrils as he flapped after, but the raven's mastery of the air was greater. He extended his lead. The blurry air surrounded him. Forks of lightning lashed out from the dragon—

Shalure squeezed Vohn's shoulder. He glanced at her.

"Shouldn't we go?" she signed. *"He told us to go."*

Vohn looked back at the battle, shook his head.

She shook him again. *"Vohn!"*

"Rauvelos will win," Vohn said. "Then he can show us what he intended to show us."

Shalure didn't say anything, but her hand stayed on his shoulder.

Rauvelos gained the higher position again. Jai'ketakos labored upward, wings pumping, right behind him. The raven tucked his wings, spun, and dove right at the dragon again.

But this time Jai'ketakos was ready. His claws came up and flame roared straight at Rauvelos.

But the raven's dive had been a feint. With a quick flick of his wings, his trajectory changed. He sped past the fire, just a hair's breadth ahead of it, and he blurred past the claws.

His wings flared.

They bent dangerously, and Vohn thought he heard a loud "snap," but the maneuver took Rauvelos's stupendous momentum and reversed it, shooting the giant raven straight back upward. Vohn had never seen any creature do such a thing. It defied nature. No bird could do that without breaking itself. One moment the raven was plummeting at full speed toward the ground, the next he was shooting upward like an arrow, attacking the dragon from below when a split second ago, he'd been attacking from above.

The raven's beak speared the dragon's back leg.

Jai'ketakos screamed, flailing, legs kicking, flame blowing across the sky at nothing.

Rauvelos yanked his head backward, but his beak was stuck in the dragon's leg bone. Rauvelos yanked frantically, and Jai'ketakos came to his senses. Rauvelos yanked and yanked again.

The dragon swiped down viciously, catching Rauvelos before he could withdraw. A horrible crack sounded.

Rauvelos pulled free, but he fluttered like a broken leaf toward the ground, spinning around and around, wings sticking out at awkward angles. Then suddenly the spiral came under control. His wings—seemingly through sheer force of will—regained the shape of normal wings, and suddenly he was diving again, rather than falling.

And then ... those wings pumped again, fighting for altitude.

Jai'ketakos dropped like a stone, shrieking and blowing, chasing Rauvelos. The dragon's back right leg hung limp, but his eyes burned almost as much as his nostrils.

Rauvelos managed to avoid the dragon's dive, spinning at the last second. Jai'ketakos wheeled, rose, pumped his own great wings, and closed the gap.

Rauvelos's awkward wings pumped. He continued to climb, but slower this time. Vohn couldn't believe that his wings worked at all. He'd heard them snap, and seen them fold up, but somehow they were functioning.

"Magic ..." he whispered. The raven was holding himself together with some kind of magic. He didn't look healed, and those grinding broken bones had to be excruciating, but somehow he'd lashed himself together long enough to gain altitude.

Jai'ketakos also seemed in bad shape. Blood covered his belly from his shoulder wound, he kept his right forearm against his chest, and his back leg hung useless. But his wings seemed fine. As he approached Rauvelos, he drew a deep breath.

Instead of fire from his mouth, lightning shot from the air itself, forming somewhere between Jai'ketakos and Rauvelos. Rauvelos folded his wings and dropped into a sudden dive, barely evading the jagged pearly spears—

Only to run headlong into a jet of flame that Jai'ketakos had sent only half a second behind the lightning.

Rauvelos twirled. A cyclone of air surrounded him, pushing back the flames.

"Tohvok mek!" Jai'ketakos roared in a language Vohn had never heard before.

Rauvelos's cyclone of air faltered, then vanished. Rauvelos's wings burst into fire. His tail burst into fire. The great bird pulled out of his dive. His broken wings awkwardly pushed against the air, but they could barely keep him airborne.

Jai'ketakos arrived, jaws open.

Rauvelos threw himself sideways. The dragon missed, teeth snapping behind the burning raven as he finally got his wings working again and gained altitude. Jai'ketakos angled up, wheeled around, and pursued.

Rauvelos climbed, feathers burning like a torch. He seemed to be trying to outrace the flames, climbing as though if he could get high enough, the flames could go out.

Jai'ketakos, right behind, shot another spurt of fire.

"No ..." Vohn murmured.

The flame struck Rauvelos, blowing into his back. The raven lit up like a bonfire. Every bit of him burned, as though his very feathers, head, and even beak were made of dry grass. Still he climbed, pushing his body, pushing his magic to its breaking point. Vohn wondered what was up there, what Rauvelos could possibly be seeking—

"Ahvan mek!" Jai'ketakos roared.

Rauvelos's wings crumpled, slapping limply against his side and fluttering in the wind like tongues of fire. Whatever magic the great raven had used to hold them together, Jai'ketakos had taken it.

"Rauvelos!" Vohn shouted. Shalure made a guttural noise of anguish.

Only now, as the raven reached the apex of his flight and began to fall, burning up in a blaze of fire, did he shriek.

The sound was long and anguished, but as forceful as a victory cry.

The giant raven exploded, blinding Vohn and Shalure. They shielded their eyes.

When they looked back, only ashes floated down from where Rauvelos, Steward of Castle Noktos, had ended.

Jai'ketakos flapped lazily where Rauvelos had been, looking victoriously at the falling ash.

"Vong!" Shalure yanked at Vohn's shoulder.

He stared unbelieving. The last few flickers of flame twisted and died.

"Vong!" She dragged him toward the archway. "Ee og OH!" *We got to go!*

Jai'ketakos turned toward them, his burning eyes focusing on the balcony.

In a growl that seemed dragged up from the depths of hell, Jai'ketakos spoke.

"Tell me, little mortals, are you friends of Khyven the Unkillable?"

Chapter Thirty-Four
VOHN

Vohn stumbled backward at high speed, swinging his arms to keep his balance. Shalure had given up trying to convince him and dragged him bodily back through the enormous archway into the enormous room behind it. The fifty-foot-tall, vaulted ceiling presided over a dozen ornate, wrought-iron, high-backed chairs, a long oval table with what looked like a glass top, and a rectangular rug that had to be at least fifty-feet long, depicting some great battle.

All of this flashed by Vohn as he retreated, stumbling, from the archway, beyond which was the most frightening thing he'd ever seen.

Jai'ketakos flew straight at them. The archway framed the increasing size of the dragon as he neared, flames trailing along the sides of his open jaws.

"Don't run away, friends of Khyven," the dragon called.

The dragon's vast bulk landed on the balcony, which shuddered under his weight, and he slammed into the archway. He was so huge that he didn't fit through the twenty-foot-tall and fifteen-foot-wide opening, but it barely slowed him. Stone blocks broke away. Mortar exploded outward as the dragon forced his way into the room.

The heat wash hit Vohn, coursing over him and Shalure, and at first he thought they were going to burn up.

But the dragon hadn't even shot flame. It was only the radiant heat from his body, from his mouth.

"Senji's Teeth!" Vohn shielded his face and continued to scramble backward, trying to gain enough momentum to turn around and run properly, but Shalure was beyond reason. She'd suddenly found a physical strength beyond her size, and in her terror her hand had clamped onto Vohn's arm like a bulldog's jaws. She dragged him like a child's toy behind her.

Jai'ketakos's huge claws—each one five times as big as Vohn himself—slammed into the carpet right in front of him, shaking the floor, almost hitting him. The dragon scrabbled for purchase, tearing away the carpet, flipping the table and cracking through the stone beneath. A horrible screech arose from the floor as he dug trenches into it, but his hindquarters were trapped by the half-broken archway. He roared in frustration, thrashed back and forth to free himself, and reached for Vohn again, stretching long.

One claw the size and shape of a broken wagon wheel slammed into the floor where Vohn had been a split-second before, barely missing.

The dragon was stuck in the archway; he couldn't reach any farther.

"Run, little mortals," the dragon snarled, showing monstrous teeth. "I will find you."

The dragon surged against the archway again. Stone ground. The room shuddered. An enormous crack shot up from the center of the archway, slicing up the wall and into the vaulted ceiling. Another started on the left side of the arch, racing up to join the first.

A chunk of ceiling broke away and slammed into the floor. Another fell on the dragon, burst apart and stone blocks showered down on either side of him. He grinned and surged again.

Shalure hauled Vohn through the doorway and around the corner. The dragon vanished from view, but Vohn felt him hit the archway again. The entire castle shuddered.

Shalure stopped, hauled Vohn to his feet and leaned over to shout in his face. "Whaar!" She gestured down the hallway, at the staircase ahead, and back past the doorway in the other direction.

"I ... I don't know ..."

"Vong!" She shook him.

He didn't know if it was her shake or the third shudder of the castle as Jai'ketakos continued to force his way into the room, but it snapped him out of his stupor.

"Vong—!"

"Down. We go down."

She nodded and yanked him toward the stairway. Like everything else, it was Giant-sized. The steps were as tall as a chest of drawers.

As big as the staircase was, though, it still didn't look big enough for Jai'ketakos to fit. The more distance down they could put between them and the dragon, the better.

They couldn't just step down one at a time like a normal staircase. They had to jump from step to step, steadying themselves each time. It was hard, punishing to the legs and knees, but they jumped and jumped and jumped. They reached the bottom of the first flight, turned and started down the second—

The castle shook so hard it threw Vohn and Shalure off their feet. She stumbled into the handrail and he fell into her. She caught the balustrade and then grabbed him before he fell off the next tall step.

Breathing hard, Vohn looked up. Rock dust billowed around the corner of the flight of steps they'd just left. It sounded like the ceiling had collapsed in the balcony room. Giant footsteps thundered overhead.

"Little mortals ..." The dragon's dark voice followed them.

Shalure jumped to her feet and hauled Vohn upright. She put her finger to her lips, then quietly began climbing down the tall steps of the next flight. He followed just as quietly. From this vantage, the dragon couldn't see them. If they could just stay silent, perhaps he would follow the hallway instead of the stairs.

"Which way did you go, little mortals? Left? Right? Up ...? Or *down*!" The dragon's head whipped around the corner of the landing on his serpentine neck and he spotted them. He grinned. "Ah, there you are ..."

Again, stone crunched as he forced himself into the stairway. They leapt from step to step, throwing themselves recklessly downward.

"Don't worry, little mortals ... I will be with you momentarily." The dragon's head vanished from view just as they reached the next landing. Shalure stopped, asking with a glance if they should run up one of the two hallways that presented themselves. Vohn shook his head.

"Down," he gasped.

They started down the third flight of steps. Shalure was more lithe and agile than Vohn had ever guessed. He'd only ever seen her wandering forlornly around the palace in robes and dresses. He'd never thought to wonder if she had any athletic ability, but she was like a fox, bounding deftly from one step to the next.

He was not.

Breathing hard, he pursued her doggedly to the bottom of the next flight. His chest burned like fire. His thighs felt like they were filled with molten lead. She gave him the same look when they reached the landing, looking up the hallways. There were three of them this time, two parallel to the stairway, going opposite directions, and one branching away at a perpendicular angle.

"Down," he gasped.

The castle shook. Cracks appeared in the ceiling.

"Little mortals ..." the dragon's voice drifted down the stairs along with more rock dust.

"He's … going to … catch us …" Vohn panted. "Or … the castle is going to collapse … on top of us …"

She snatched his hand and pulled. They plunged down the next flight. At the second to the final step, the wall to their right cracked, a jagged slice split downward at a diagonal, as though chasing them.

"Ohm ong!" Shalure urged.

Come on!

She pulled him. He jumped at the same time and he overshot with his leading foot. It hit on the edge of the final step and twisted sideways. He cried out, and Shalure lost her grip as he pitched forward. He crashed to the landing, bouncing his head off the marble.

Stars burst in his vision, and for a moment, Vohn didn't know what was happening or where he was.

Then he felt her hands on him, pulling frantically. Vohn shook his head and looked blearily up at her. Her face was a mask of panic, and she was trying to haul him toward the next flight of stairs. Behind her, up the staircase where they'd just been, the dragon's head moved around the corner.

"Run, run, little mortals …" He smiled. "There is nowhere you can go that I won't find you. But don't worry, I'm going to give you a choice. I believe it is important for mortals to choose their own destiny. I promise you will have a chance to choose yours …"

The head was almost upon them when the dragon's body bound up in the upper entrance of the stairway. The dragon snapped his jaws shut barely ten feet away from them.

"Give me just a moment," Jai'ketakos said, shrugging and wriggling his immense body. The staircase shivered. Cracks raced along the ceiling over his head. He inched forward.

Shalure pulled Vohn upright. He took one step toward the next staircase, and his ankle folded. Pain like lightning lanced up into his shin, his knee, into his thigh. He went down again, and he screamed.

"Yessss," the dragon said.

Shalure dragged Vohn out of sight of the leering dragon to the top of the next staircase, but Vohn couldn't imagine getting to the bottom. His ankle hurt so bad he thought he would pass out from the pain. There was no way he could hop those three-foot-tall steps all the way to the bottom with one good leg. He'd break the other ankle with one jump.

"No ..." He looked around. This landing also had three hallways: two that ran parallel to the staircase, left and right, and one that ran perpendicular, off into the darkness. That was the narrowest of the three. "This way. We go this way."

"Ek Ong!" she said as she knelt next to him and pointed at her back.

Get on!

He put his arms around her neck. She grunted and stood up with some difficulty. At less than five feet tall, Vohn was not large compared to a Human, but he was still nearly a hundred and twenty pounds of dead weight on her back. And Shalure was not a large woman.

She staggered up the hallway as Jai'ketakos struggled and cracked his way down the staircase.

"Giving up on the stairs, are you?" The dragon's head slithered onto the landing, nostrils glowing, eyes glinting. "Oh, dear. Little mortal ... did you hurt your leg? I can smell the cracked bone. There is no smell quite like cracked bone. Blood rushing to the area, trying desperately to heal it. Blood ..." He drew a deep breath. "Delicious."

Shalure's breath became labored. Each step was shaky as she pounded up the hallway. Closed doors flashed by them.

"Whah?" she asked.

Where?

Vohn didn't have any answers. They were lost in a Giant's castle, running desperately from a dragon who hadn't turned them into cinders yet, though he clearly could have. One spurt of flame from the dragon would turn this hallway into an oven. Vohn would have felt lucky, but if the dragon didn't want to incinerate them, it wanted to do something worse. Vohn couldn't imagine what that would be, and he didn't want to.

"Get ... to the end ..." he said through his teeth.

He didn't want to try any of the doors. They were all seven feet wide and close to twenty feet tall, too small for the dragon, but after seeing what Jai'ketakos had done to the balcony's archway and the stairway, Vohn didn't think for a second that any one of these walls was going to stop him. He'd just tear through the doorway like a badger. And once they were in the room, they'd be cornered.

What Vohn hoped for was a long, narrow passageway that would take the dragon more than just a shrug and a wriggle to crack the stone. With that, they might escape. Or better yet, Jai'ketakos might get stuck.

The castle shuddered again, and Jai'ketakos made the landing. He peered down the narrow hallway after them.

"Keep running, little mortals. I haven't had this much fun in centuries."

Shalure was sweating now, huffing with every step, staggering and slowing down.

"Just to the end of the hallway," Vohn said. There had to be something. There had to be. He could see the T-intersection. It looked like two passageways split off, one left and one right at a kind of oval room ...

They reached it, and Vohn suddenly, shockingly realized his mistake. It wasn't two passageways, it was an atrium. Shalure slowed to stop and fell to her knees. Vohn got off and managed to stand upright on his good foot, but he had to keep a balancing hand on Shalure.

From the hallway, the oval room had looked like a T-intersection with passageways leading left and right. But it wasn't. It was a dead-end. The high ceiling was made entirely of curved panes of glass, looking up at the black sky of the noktum. The glass ceiling curved into a glass wall at the halfway mark, then continued down to the floor. About twenty feet up where the ten rows of paned glass met the wall, one of the panes was broken, the third from the left. Vohn looked helplessly at it, then looked back down the hallway.

Jai'ketakos was beginning his crunching journey, his shoulders and arms breaking through the stone as he shoved himself up the hallway. "Where now, little mortals? You've run out of room ..."

"Vong ..." Shalure stared at the approaching horror with wide eyes.

Vohn glanced up at the broken window. It was twenty feet up. If they could somehow get up there, they'd never get up there in time.

And even if they could escape the castle, what good would that do? Jai'ketakos would just burst out of those windows. Shalure and Vohn would be out in the open—

"Wait!" Vohn blurted, touching his belt. The rod! Slayter's lightning rod!

He yanked it from its sheath and pointed it at Jai'ketakos. Vohn opened his mouth to say the words ...

And realized he'd forgotten them.

Staring at the enormous monster clawing its way toward them, breaking stone, and breathing fire from its nostrils, its teeth as tall Khyven's swords, Vohn's mind drew a blank.

Avante ... Avat ...

Grina's Mercy ... What were they?!

The dragon crunched closer.

"Well, what have we here? A trick up your sleeve? That looks like a wand, little mortal."

The words slammed together in Vohn's head all at once. Avectus! It was Avectus Fulgur!

"Avectus—"

The dragon blew fire. The flames roared down the tunnel toward them, and Vohn's words twisted into a frightened cry.

He and Shalure threw themselves to the ground. His fist hit the stones, skinning his knuckles. Flames roared over them.

They weren't dead. They weren't dead!

Scrambling backward, pain firing into his right leg, Vohn groped his away from the killing heat until his back thumped against the atrium's glass wall.

He looked over to discover that Shalure had done the same. Her auburn hair was lank with sweat, singed. Beads of perspiration streaked down her soot-smeared face.

The fire should have killed them, but it hadn't. Vohn looked at the hallway. It burned like a stove, nothing but red and orange fires. Sheer panic subsided to desperation, and he remembered the wand. He looked down at his hand.

It was gone.

Desperately, he looked at the floor. Smoke drifted and tongues of flame retreated from where he and Shalure had been ...

And there it was, lying on the floor halfway between them and the hallway's opening.

"Vong—"

"The rod. I lost the rod."

Shalure followed his gaze, spotted it. She got to her feet—

The archway shivered, and a crack ran up the atrium wall to the first pane of glass, which shattered and fell to the floor.

Jai'ketakos's head emerged through the smoke. His long snout split into a grin with teeth as tall as Vohn was. Tendrils of smoke leaked upward from the gaps between his teeth, adding to the haze. Fire glowed from the round nostrils beneath his eager eyes. One giant claw slammed down on the marble floor ...

Right over the wand, crushing it.

"Friends of Khyven," the dragon said darkly. "It's time for you to make a choice ..."

CHAPTER THIRTY-FIVE
VOHN

The dragon settled down on his elbows, claws extended halfway into the room. There was nowhere to go, no doorways to race toward. Even the broken windows overhead were so far away they might as well have been the moon. The dragon was still in the hallway except for his head and his front claws, but Vohn had no doubt he could surge forward and kill either of them.

They were trapped.

"Now," the dragon began. "I made you a promise: you can choose your destiny. I think that's important, don't you?"

Vohn moved in front of Shalure. It was a useless gesture, and he knew it. But there was absolutely nothing else to do. The race was over. Neither one of them was going to survive this.

Shalure didn't let him. She stepped from behind him and stood by his side, holding his hand. She signed to him.

"You have to leave."

He narrowed his eyes, signed back, *"What are you talking about?"*

Her other hand, which was holding his, pinched the ring Rauvelos had given him. She turned it, trying to work it off his finger.

"*You can leave,*" she signed again.

What she was saying finally hit him, and Rauvelos's words came back to him.

It will inhibit your transformation into the Dark. It will also shield you from Xos.

He shook his head vehemently.

The dragon had been watching them, and he saw the exchange. "Oooo, a secret language ... It's rude to exclude someone from a conversation like that, you know. What are we saying, little mortals?"

Shalure tried to get the ring off, but Vohn closed his fist and pulled away from her. "No!"

"*You have to,*" she signed frantically. "*They need you, and I ... One of us has to survive this. You need to tell them about the castle, about the dragon.*"

"*If you think I'm leaving you here to die, you're crazy!*"

"*We are both going to die! But* you *don't have to—*"

The enormous claw moved forward so quickly Vohn only had time to draw a breath. The dragon batted Shalure aside. The strike was mild compared to the monster's relentless smashing through foot-thick stone walls ...

But Shalure was not stone.

She flew ten feet across the room and hit the marble frame of the curved, glass wall. Vohn heard the sickening smack of her flesh, heard the dull snapping of bone. Her brief shriek was cut short, and she fell in a heap at the bottom, unmoving.

"Shalure!" He tried to run to her, but the foot slammed into the ground before him, creating a curved wall of scales, sinew, bone, and claws as hard as steel.

"There are consequences when you are rude. Do you not wish to hear your choice? This is your destiny, little mortal."

Vohn shuffled on his good leg, barely kept his balance. He turned a defiant stare on the dragon.

"She wanted that ring," the dragon continued. "To what purpose, I wonder?"

Flames appeared around Vohn's finger, dancing on the ring. He hissed and drew his fist back, but the flames weren't hot. They felt like ... nothing.

"Powerful magic," Jai'ketakos said. "This is an artifact made by a master, not like the little copper stick bound together by those sad little runes. Rauvelos gave it to you?"

Vohn clamped his mouth shut.

The dragon cocked his great head. "Rude again. Come now, give me the ring, little mortal."

Vohn's heart thundered. He tried to look past the claw to see Shalure, but he couldn't.

"Give me the ring," the dragon said again in a low tone.

"You're going to have to kill me," Vohn growled back.

"I'll kill you when I'm ready."

The flames on Vohn's finger turned into a searing blade. They spun and severed his finger from his hand. He screamed and grasped his fist. The finger fell to the ground with the ring, and Jai'ketakos scooped it away with his giant claw.

Vohn fell to his knees, cradling his hand. A distant rushing sound filled his ears. His whole body shook, and his hand smoked. The sickening smell of burned flesh filled his nostrils. Through watering eyes, he looked over at Shalure. The dragon's claw had moved, and he could see her now, but she hadn't moved from where she'd fallen. He didn't know if she was dead or alive.

"Curious," the dragon said. "This is Love Magic. Mind and emotions. What does it do, little mortal?"

A desperate plan formed in Vohn's mind. He'd refused to play the dragon's game, and it had cost him a finger. It had also possibly killed Shalure. He was doing this wrong. The dragon had all the power, but Slayter had said the dragon's weakness was his need for this game. That was how Slayter had beat him. The mage had seen through the game and used it to outmaneuver the dragon.

Vohn would have to do the same.

"You said ..." Vohn spoke through clenched teeth, trying to stop his body from shaking at the pain, trying to stop his mind from racing at the thought of his new disfigurement. "You said you'd give us a ch-choice."

"Us? With your friend dead, the choice is really only for you now," Jai'ketakos said, still fixated on the tiny ring in the palm of his talon.

"You never ... gave me a choice."

The distant rushing got louder, pulsing.

"Well, we needed to establish the rules of civilized discourse first. You were rude to me. Ignoring me. Running away. Speaking in your little finger-flicking language."

Vohn hesitated. "I apologize."

"There. See how easy that was?"

The distant rush became a voice.

"Vohn ..."

Cold fear spread through Vohn's body. It was the voice. The female voice that had kept him from returning to his body after he'd been shot at Nox Arvak, the one that hadn't wanted to let him go to Slayter's spell, hadn't wanted to let him leave the noktum ever. Paralos ...

"I will give you your choice in good time, little mortal," Jai'ketakos said.

"Foolish Vohn ..." the whispery voice said in Vohn's mind.

"Tell me what the ring does," Jai'ketakos said.

"You will die here," the voice in Vohn's mind said. *"Jai'ketakos will kill you. You must flee. Make the change."*

"It ..." Vohn ignored the voice and spoke to the dragon. "He-he gave it to me to help me see in the noktum."

"I have to get Shalure. I can't just leave her," Vohn said to the voice.

Jai'ketakos grinned. "Did you know, little Shadowvar, that I can smell lies like I can smell your broken bone?"

"You must. You cannot carry her."

"I have to!" Vohn sent back with all the force he could

muster.

"You treat me like I have never heard of the Amulets of Noksonon," Jai'ketakos continued, seemingly completely unaware of the other conversation going on in Vohn's head. "Now tell me, little mortal, and do be careful, for if I do not get a satisfactory answer this time, this will be the last question I will ask you: Why would Rauvelos give you this ring instead of an amulet?"

"Flee Vohn! If you try to take her, it will kill her."

"She'll die if I leave her!"

Vohn's heart hammered like it was going to beat out of his chest. But there was nothing else to do. He had run out of options. Shalure was right. The damned voice of Paralos was right. He was going to die right here, right now unless he transformed.

But once he did, Paralos would sink her hooks in. Vohn would be trapped in the noktum, a floating spirit, forever.

But Shalure might live.

"Fine ..." Vohn said to the dragon. "He gave it to me because—"

"Fine," Vohn said to Paralos. *"Help me."*

Vohn let his mind rise into the transformation. The Dark took him. His body vanished.

Jai'ketakos's claw surged forward, slashing at where Vohn had been. The wagon-wheel talons went right through him, then even the whispery image of his body was gone.

Vohn flew directly at Shalure.

"No," Paralos said. *"You are still in danger. Jai'ketakos has magics—"*

"Shut up." Vohn grabbed Shalure and willed her to come with him, to lift from the floor and fly with him.

The dragon raged behind him, casting about, looking for where Vohn had gone.

Vohn bent his will to the task of changing Shalure, of trying to turn her into a banshee like him, to take her with him. At first, it seemed an impossible task, like trying to lift a stone by blowing on it.

Then, something happened. Shalure's eyes opened. Her head raised, except it wasn't her head. It was a ghostly head that had emerged from her body. It looked at him in surprise.

"*Come with me. Come with me. Come with me!*" He said to Shalure.

To Paralos, he shouted: "*Help me!*"

Shalure's body began to dissolve and her ghostly duplicate hovering over the dissolving body screamed.

Though the scream was only in Vohn's head, like Paralos's voice, the dragon seemed to hear it, or to sense it. His great head jerked to the left, and he saw her body dissolving. Rocks crunched and glass panes shattered overhead as he twisted free from the tunnel and lunged at them. His great claw came down on Shalure's body like a falling stone—

But Shalure's body was no longer there. She was with Vohn, swirling through him and around him like a white mist.

Vohn pointed himself toward the broken window and shot through it, gaining speed, flying to the height of the noktum.

Below, the castle shook as Jai'ketakos roared in fury.

Chapter Thirty-Six
VOHN

Time twisted in the flight. Like the first time he'd become the banshee, there was only the darkness swirling and the sensation of movement, not of time, and not of recognizable things. He didn't see the nuraghi fall behind them. He didn't see the landscape whip past him.

But he did hear Shalure's scream, stretching and mixing with his own scream. The journey was a hellish maelstrom of darkness, coiling wires of white, and fear. She screamed like she was dying. He screamed because he knew he was hurting her.

And then the voice—Paralos's voice—cut through it all.

"No."

It was one word. That was all she said, and it stopped everything.

Shalure's scream stopped like her head had been chopped off. The white lines and the darkness stopped. The flying abruptly ceased.

Vohn hovered, face pressed against the edge of the noktum. The forest lay just beyond, and beyond that, the palace. But the noktum's edge had stopped him like a wall.

Only now did flickering thoughts return, memories and desires, and his utter desperation. Only now did he remember he'd been trying to get out of the noktum, trying to flee the insanity of his banshee state and what he was doing to Shalure.

"*You cannot leave,*" Paralos's soft voice said to him.

"*I have to get out,*" Vohn whimpered. "*I'm killing her!*"

His mind felt like it had been twisted, stabbed with knives, bathed in acid, then twisted again. He'd wrenched her away from the earth, disintegrated her body. And now the scream had stopped. Her scream had been driving him insane ... But its absence was horribly worse.

Vohn tried to spin around, to search for her—

Except he didn't have a body. He had no legs to jump up in panic. No torso to twist.

He merely swirled upward.

"*You must stay here,*" Paralos said.

"*Where is she?*" he shouted. "*Where is—*"

"*She is gone. I warned you. You cannot take a person with you into ...*"

Paralos trailed off, and Vohn immediately focused on what had taken her speech.

At the edge of the noktum, where Vohn had been trying to escape, white sand sifted down. He looked up, trying to find the source, but there was none. The white sand appeared five feet off the ground and floated down like snow, gathering in a pile on the ground.

Vohn hovered there, spellbound.

The sand continued to pile up on the ground; after a moment, he recognized the shape of a body. Soon, he could see the flat outline of someone laying down. The sand continued to build up, creating the shape of a foot, then two, the curve of calves, of thighs, and hips. It was a woman laying on her back. The sand continued, building her waist and arms crossed over her belly, her shoulders, then neck and her head, facing upward.

Vohn came closer. He wanted to help, to do something to

bring her back to life.

"What is this?" he asked Paralos.

Paralos hesitated, and he realized that she didn't know, either, but she spoke nonetheless. *"If you wish her to live, do not touch her."*

"Is she still alive?" Vohn asked.

Paralos said nothing.

The sand snowed down, filling out the swells of the thighs, the breasts, the curves of the shoulders, head, hips, and down to the points of her toes. It was, indeed, Shalure, but …

As the sand filled out the topmost points of her body, it began to diminish, falling less thickly until only a thin trickle finished her nose and the knuckles of her fingers laid over her belly.

The last grain fell, completing the figure of Shalure made of white sand. A sculpture rendered in such exquisite detail … but was she alive?

"What is—"

White light flashed over the sculpture. White sand turned to bare flesh, to hair, to fingernails and toenails. Shalure arched her back, hands slapping the black grass on either side of her. Every muscle in her body tensed like she was being electrified.

She screamed until her voice went ragged, until she ran out of breath, then her body fell back against the grass. Then the scream stopped. Her mouth and eyes stayed open, and she stared up at the sky.

"Shalure!" Vohn cried into the quiet dark. *"Shalure!"*

"Remarkable," Paralos said softly in his mind. *"She is alive."*

Shalure's chest rose and fell softly, rhythmically. Her eyes and mouth stayed open like she'd spotted something frightening … and had frozen there.

"What's wrong with her?" Vohn asked.

"She has looked on the very heart of the noktum," Paralos said. *"It is not a sight meant for mortals."*

"What's going to happen to her?"

"If she stays here, she will likely be eaten by the next Sleeth or Kyolar

who finds her."

"No!"

"There is nothing you can do for her."

"I'll take her back to Usara."

"You cannot leave the noktum."

"Only because you are keeping me here."

"Yes. Because of that, and other reasons you would not understand."

"Let me go!"

"You escaped me once, Vohn Fenlux. Not twice."

"What do you want with me?"

"The most important task that can be given to a mortal."

"I have to help my friends! That's what's important!"

"Indeed."

That caused Vohn to pause. "You want to see them die."

"On the contrary, I have sacrificed everything to help your kind. I have braced Xos for two thousand years for your kind. I have sacrificed everything I was, and likely everything I will ever be, to see our vision come to pass."

"Our vision?"

"Nhevalos's ... and mine. We began this journey together."

"Wait. You and Nhevalos are working together?"

"That is correct."

"Nhevalos is our enemy. He tortured us! He almost killed us many times!"

"Hardship grows the soul. The soul lends strength. And to meet the challenges that come for you—challenges most mortals could crumple beneath—you must be stronger than you can imagine. So Nhevalos and I imagined it for you. He has fostered your souls. He has given you strength."

"Those are lies. The justifications of the cruel."

"Why do you fight me when you know I'm right?"

"You're not right!"

"You fight the truth because it is inconvenient. Because you don't like it. It is the hallmark of your kind. But you will learn."

"I am taking Shalure back to Usara."

"Shalure is not important. She is not a piece that can move events. You are. You must come with me—"

"I'm not going anywhere with you!"

"*If you resist, the pain will be great, but you will go regardless. I'm sorry, but I don't have time to be patient with you. The war is upon us.*"

A roaring filled Vohn's head, and he felt like he was being drawn away from Shalure. She began to shrink—the entire ground seemed to shrink—like he was being pulled up into the sky.

"Let me go! Don't! Let me—"

A huge black shape charged through the wall of the noktum just below Vohn. At first, he thought it was a Kyolar, but it was a horse! It was a giant black stallion bearing two riders.

And the two riders were—

"Khyven! Slayter!" Vohn cried out.

The black horse leapt over Shalure's body unconsciously and pounded toward Castle Noktos. Neither Khyven nor Slayter heard Vohn.

"Let me go!" Vohn struggled. "Let me—!"

Paralos seemed bent on pulling him away, but she hesitated. Vohn hovered as the mighty stallion Khyven had called Hellface pounded toward the castle.

"*Dammit...*" Paralos said into his mind.

Her hold on Vohn released. He hovered for a second, stunned.

"*Go, Vohn. It is not time for him to face the dragon. Go. Time is short.*"

Vohn shot after them.

Chapter Thirty-Seven
RHENN

She and Lorelle laid on their bellies at the crest of a hill. Below them, Nokte Shaddark stretched out, cloaked in eternal night. Once, the city had been a bustling center of life, commerce, and knowledge—the largest in this part of the continent and the center of Shadowvar culture.

Now, somehow, the Great Noktum had consumed it.

When Rhenn had returned from Daemanon, there had been a lot of adjusting. Navigating the light, of course, reuniting with her friends, reconnecting with her subjects. And, of course, killing to live.

But amidst that had been other troubling things, and one of them was the odd telepathy that had come with her new body, a gift from the Mouth Dog, she surmised, who'd had some low-level kind of mindspeak. She could hear random smatterings of voices in the heads of her friends, and sometimes of her subjects. But over the months of being home, it had begun to die out. It seemed to diminish with every new creature she fed upon.

When the voice of the Dark began to talk to her, inside her mind, it dominated whatever telepathic ability she had left. She could no longer hear the voices of her subjects or friends. The strange mindspeak now seemed completely dedicated to a voice who wanted her to come into the Dark ...

And never leave.

Rhenn had waited for the voice to return in force when in Nox Arvak ... But it hadn't. The voice of the Dark, the voice that had been calling to her for weeks now, had gone silent.

She would have considered this a boon, but now she was poised to fight the man who'd created her, along with whatever bloodsuckers he'd drawn into his horrible web. And at this moment, of all moments, did the sudden disappearance of the voice of The Dark indicate she was free?

Or that The Dark finally had what it wanted.

She waited with Lorelle. She watched, but the pit in her stomach got heavier, especially looking at the graveyard of a city below.

Nokte Shaddark had always stood on the edge of the noktum, closer even than the crown city of Usara. But now it had been enveloped.

No one moved below. All was eerie, dead quiet.

Rhenn couldn't see the whole of the city, only a couple of streets narrowing into the distance. Cross streets opened to the left and right. The big buildings and towers in the center of the city loomed far away.

No beggars wrapped in rags reached out needy hands. No Shadowvar found their way toward the city center to deliver stacks of books to the Great Library. No thieves lurked in shadowed alleys. No cart full of cabbages rolled up those streets.

There were two bodies, though. She could see the feet of one of them sticking out of an alley. Another lay in plain sight in the middle of the street, a dark stain splashed out from the neck.

"The noktum moved," Lorelle flicked her fingers in their no-longer-so-secret language.

"How does that happen, exactly?" Rhenn responded with her

fingers. She had hoped at one point to perhaps harness the mind-speaking of the Mouth Dog, infused into her back in Daemanon when she awoke as a bloodsucker. She'd hoped someday to talk to Lorelle mind to mind.

But the power, scattered and random to start, had slowly changed when she returned to Noksonon. Her friends' minds became more and more closed to her.

The Dark had called instead.

She'd told Slayter she thought it was the sword, but it wasn't. She knew it wasn't. It had to have something to do with the Mouth Dog's power, and the Dark's desires.

But during this entire trip, the Dark had yet to speak to her. Rhenn would have been relieved if it hadn't been so precisely timed with this adventure. When Rhenn had resisted doing what the Dark wanted, it had slithered into her mind every chance it got, pulling her toward the noktum. Now, though, it had gone silent.

Did that mean Rhenn was doing what the Dark wanted her to do? And so it didn't need to push her toward anything?

"The one comforting thing about the noktum was that it stayed put." Rhenn continued, talking with her fingers.

"Knowing what I know now," Lorelle signed. *"I'm actually surprised it hasn't done something like this before."*

"That's not encouraging."

"Everyone is gone," Lorelle signed. *"Do you think they fled the noktum?"*

"This is N'ssag." Rhenn's fingers moved absently. *"He's taken them."*

"You think he's setting up another laboratory here?"

"In Daemanon he wanted an army. Now that he has one, he wants a bigger one. So yes."

"Could he really do that so quickly?"

"Given months in a noktum? He could have hundreds by now, as many as there were corpses in Nox Arvak. All he ever wanted to do was make more of his bloodsuckers and perfect his process. So not only will he have hundreds of them, but these Nox are going to be at least as strong as

me. Probably stronger. Faster. I can only imagine what changes he's made."

It had been a long time since Rhenn had fed. Her heart beat faster, alive with the need for the coppery fire of blood. She wanted it. She wanted it from N'ssag's own neck so badly she could barely think of anything else.

"You're saying we're not going to be able to physically overpower an army of supernatural Nox who have the same kind of strength you have?" Lorelle asked.

Rhenn gave Lorelle a narrow sidelong look, caught her failing to hide her smile.

"*Mockery*, is it?" Rhenn frowned.

Lorelle put one slender hand against her chest in innocence, fingers splayed out, eyes wide. "Who me?"

"Fine."

"I just thought it was interesting that you sound more like Khyven every day." Lorelle signed. "We're not going to attack N'ssag's army. We're going to attack N'ssag. Or gain enough information about what's going on here to put together an attack that makes sense."

"Fine." Rhenn felt the sharp points of her fangs with her tongue.

"He's down there," Lorelle continued. "We'll find him. N'ssag thinks he's a master of the Dark. Let's show him just how wrong he is. We're going to introduce him to my noktum cloak."

"And Slayter's sword."

Rhenn had hated the idea of Slayter's sword at first. She'd hated it at second and third, for that matter. And fourth and fifth and ... It had unequivocally illustrated how she wasn't really Human anymore, that she was a bloodsucking killer who couldn't survive without slaying others.

But in this one place, with this one person in mind, she loved the sword. She *wanted* to be a killer when she faced N'ssag. She wanted to watch his sniveling, frightened face as she plunged that life-sucking sword into his chest.

"We also have Slayter's wands," Rhenn added.

"We're not using the wands."

"We might."

"We're not fighting the entire army, Rhenn. We use a light wand, and then we're in it up to our necks," Lorelle signed quickly back, shaking her head.

"We'll see."

In the Daemanon nuraghi, they would have lost the hand-to-hand battle against N'ssag's undead horde if not for Slayter's blast of light that had turned animated corpses into explosions of flesh. During the past months, the mage had been consumed with the novelty of understanding N'ssag's resurrecting spells, much to Rhenn's disapproval. But his dogged pursuit of all knowledge, no matter how revolting, had created a weapon that would be highly effective against N'ssag's creatures. In one of Slayter's brainstorms, he'd made a half dozen wands that projected light. He claimed it was a rudimentary spell that he'd improved upon. The wands generated bursts of light with the same brightness as a small sun.

Rhenn recalled the conversation with Slayter just before they'd left for the Great Noktum ...

⬟ ⬟ ⬟

Slayter invited her to his laboratory, and when she'd arrived, he held up four sticks. They'd been carved from hardwood, banded in copper at the pommel, hilt, and tip, and his magical runes decorated their entire length.

"Point one of these at N'ssag's creations, and their chemical cohesion will unravel in spectacular fashion."

"They'll explode," Rhenn clarified.

"In spectacular fashion."

"They shoot light."

Slayter looked up and to the left with a puckered frown of disappointment, like she'd said something incorrectly and he was trying to decide whether or not to correct her.

"They emanate light." She tried again.

"Close enough," he said.

"And the light is continuous once they're ... working?"

"You brush your thumb over this rune." He illustrated on the intricate design on the wand's handle. "And you speak the activating word, and the light shines. Brush it with your thumb a second time and speak the deactivating word, and it will go dark."

"What's the activating word?"

Carefully removing his thumb from the rune, he said, "Lux."

"Clever. And the deactivating word?"

"Pax."

"So I brush that with my thumb and I say 'Lux' and I'll essentially have what you had in the nuraghi in Daemanon."

"Only for five minutes. That's probably an important detail. If you leave it on constantly. If you deactivate it, then you'll have as much as you didn't use. You'll have five minutes minus whatever you—"

"I understand."

"Ah, good."

"Each wand only lasts five minutes total?"

"Roughly."

"Roughly?"

He shrugged. "I tested five of them. One lasted seven minutes. One lasted two. The other three lasted five. I think five is the most likely. Apparently it's the differences in the life-force gems. Imbuing life-force is an imprecise project."

"You sucked your own life-force into these wands?"

"A little bit, otherwise you'd need to draw the magic directly from me for them to work at all."

"So ... Is my sword like this, too? Am I drawing lifeforce from you when I use it?" The thought sickened her.

He looked pained like she'd just asked him, "So square wheels work the same as round wheels?"

"No. Not the same as the sword."

Rhenn frowned. Slayter explained things—or didn't—in a way that always made her feel like an idiot.

"Why not make the wands like the sword?" she'd said through her teeth.

"The wands need power to work."

"The sword doesn't need power to work?"

"The sword is sucking life-force! It doesn't need life-force to suck life-force. It needs an absence of ..." Slayter trailed off, pressed his lips into a line, then said, "No. The wands are not the same as the sword."

Just. Like. An idiot.

"So you're saying the light could last seven minutes or it could last two," Rhenn returned the conversation to safer ground.

"Most likely it'll be five."

She looked down at the four wands he'd given her. "So Lorelle and I will 'most likely' have twenty minutes of light between the two of us."

"But don't use them in the noktum. Those wands contain actual sunlight. It's not like Lorelle's hair."

"You captured actual sunlight?" It boggled her mind what Slayter could do.

"The creatures in the noktum hate natural light. If you use it, they'll flock to it and tear you apart—"

"I know what noktum creatures do. Everyone knows what noktum creatures do."

"But you asked about sunlight—"

She sliced her hand through the air. "Never mind. How can you put *actual* sunlight into a wand? That's what I mean. It's not actual sunlight, right? It's magical sunlight."

He cocked his head like he hadn't understood the question.

"You can't just capture sunlight and stuff it into a stick." She paused. "Can you?"

"Well, yes. You see, Land Magic pulls the raw stuff of the physical world into a—"

"Never mind," Rhenn cut him off again. "Five minutes apiece. Twenty minutes at most."

"It should be highly effective against a dozen bloodsuckers. Especially if you catch them in a group. Just don't take on an army ..."

Just don't take on an army ...

Rhenn came back from her reverie, hyper-conscious of the sheath on the outside of her left thigh where the wands were. It was like holding a supposedly watertight pouch of acid against her belly. Because what Slayter didn't mention was that the wands could almost as easily kill her as they could N'ssag's undead. Her sword would protect her a little, but not entirely. And if she dropped the sword or wasn't wielding it when the wands were activated ...

Well, if the light turned on when they were at her hip, for example, her own "chemical cohesion" would "unravel in a particularly violent fashion."

"Come on. Let's use N'ssag's beloved mistress against him." Lorelle flicked out the noktum cloak. It floated like a living thing, its edges seeming to blend with the very air around them, and it settled over Rhenn's shoulders.

It felt comfortable, safe, and Rhenn felt a momentary pang of regret. The Dark was where she thrived now. Yes, she'd undergone the physical transformation in Daemanon, but now her mind was changing, too. What if there came a day when she liked what she was? What if the day came when she not only loved the silky feel of darkness about her, but the necessary killing as well?

Just how changed would she be by the end of it?

The cloak wrapped her up, filled her up, pulled her into itself. The absolute darkness came first and after that would be ... bloody murder.

Chapter Thirty-Eight
RHENN

The cloak unfurled and Rhenn stood in the antechamber of the Great Library with Lorelle. The Great Library of Nokte Shaddark was the largest building in the city, and its center was a ten-story tower.

Even the palace in Usara was only half as tall as this monument to Shadowvar architecture. The center of the tower was filled with books. Its interior walls were entirely bookshelves, and ladders speared upward toward the skylight at the top, which normally would cast down sunlight to illuminate the shelves. To stand in the center of the tower and look up was mind boggling.

Rhenn and Lorelle could have spent an hour or more disapparating and reforming all over the city with the noktum cloak, but it had been Rhenn's idea to try the Great Library first. N'ssag would, of course, want the most ostentatious place to set up his throne.

They crept forward carefully. Lorelle said there were irregular shadows in the noktum, somewhat like normal shadows in the land of daylight, except they didn't actually fit the shapes of the objects around them, nor did they come from a light source.

And Lorelle could hide them in these shadows, even from most of the Nox.

Gently, silently, they opened the door just a crack and pressed their faces to it. Rhenn stooped a little and Lorelle stretched a little as they looked out at the same time.

There was a hallway outside that almost led to, and almost immediately opened up to, the first balcony, an expansive walkway twenty feet wide with reading tables, oil lamps, and old oaken bookshelves along the edge of the entire wall. A place of study.

From that landing, the famous ladders rose. Each of the eight levels above had smaller balconies until the tenth story balcony, which was probably only twenty feet in diameter. Stout, wrought-iron ladders went up securely from level to level, and wooden ladders on runners could be moved around the entire circle to find whatever book the academic might be interested in.

Thirty feet down from the first balcony was the entrance level, an enormous circular room two hundred feet in diameter. The stone wall that defined the room had four entrances: the main entrance and three smaller doors. The main entrance was a twenty-foot-tall, twenty-foot-wide archway that came from the outside street. The other three exits were more modest, only ten feet tall and five feet wide, with thick iron-bound oak doors. They seemed to lead to other administration rooms within the Great Library.

Each of those smaller doors had been closed and blocked with heavy tables, chairs, and cabinets that had then been chained together as one huge barricade. The main entrance had spikes of stone that seemed to have grown up from the very ground.

Magic.

The entire huge room had been converted into a jail cell, and in the center stood hundreds and hundreds of Shadowvar and

Humans. Some huddled near the wall, touching it like it was a singular source of comfort. Those milling in the middle that couldn't touch a wall, only each other, shuddered, eyes wide. A cacophony of sounds rose from the huddled, squirming mass of humanity. Sobbing, heavy breathing, cursing, shouts for help, shouts for mercy. Some shouted for the others to, by all that was holy, shut up.

They can't see, Rhenn thought. The noktum was like twilight to her now, but to normal Shadowvar and Humans, it would be absolutely black.

The smell was revolting. She didn't know how long the prisoners had been here, but apparently long enough for some to lose control of their bodily functions. The stench of feces and urine hung thickly in the air over the acrid scent of Human fear.

Lorelle tapped Rhenn lightly on the shoulder, and she glanced up. Lorelle pointed.

On the far side of the second-story balcony, N'ssag had made a throne for himself. The marble floor had risen up and formed the shape of a gray throne, perched on the edge of the balcony where he could look down on his captives.

"Land Magic," Rhenn signed. *"Where did he learn Land Magic?"*

Lorelle shook her head.

N'ssag had a scruffy three-day growth of beard, and his tattered robes hung from his pear-shaped body. His grime-covered arms extended from his sleeves as he made a pacifying gesture to the people below.

"Quiet down now. Quiet down," he said.

Everyone instantly fell silent except for one hysterical sobbing woman who continued until someone clapped a hand over her mouth. They acted like this wasn't the first time N'ssag had asked for quiet, and that they were all aware of the horrible consequence if they didn't.

"I think you should stop crying, stop wailing, stop shouting. You are to be made part of the new world order. You are to be the leaders that will take Noksonon into a new age. This is a day of exultation, not despair."

The hysterical crier broke free of the one who had been trying to stifle her. Her wailing cut through the quiet.

"My baby! My baby!"

N'ssag had his mouth open to deliver the next part of his speech, and he stopped, closed his mouth and looked angry.

"I thought we had an understanding. When I am talking ..." He gestured over his shoulder and a man robed in red stepped forward. He walked stiffly, stock-straight, and stopped at the railing. He raised his hand and created a concentrated gust of wind so strong the people around the afflicted woman were blown back. But the wind didn't knock her down. Instead, it lifted her up, spinning her about and dumping her unceremoniously on the second-story balcony.

Like giant bats, a half-dozen Nox bloodsuckers materialized from between the stacks and descended on the woman, grabbing her arms, her legs, her hair, her waist. Her wailing turned into a terrified scream.

Rhenn's heart lurched. She pressed against the crack of the door, ready to charge into the room—

Lorelle's hands closed firmly on her shoulder. The gesture brought Rhenn to her senses. Charging in would only bring the bloodsuckers down on her.

That wasn't their purpose. They had to get to N'ssag. He was the key. Without him, the horror stopped—

The woman's scream cut off in a gurgle as the bloodsuckers tore her apart. People below wretched and screamed.

Rhenn turned away, walked away from the door. Lorelle followed.

"You couldn't help her. There are too many of them," Lorelle signed silently to her. "And now N'ssag has a Land Mage. This is the information we need, Rhenn. This helps us. Now that we know he has a Land Mage, Slayter can—"

"Those people are going to die. We can't leave."

"There are too many Nox. Did you see them come out of the corners? Some of them know how to utilize the purple shadows. They could find us here."

"All we have to do is kill N'ssag. Then we can leave."

Lorelle shook her head. *"We said we were going to see what the situation was, and that if we could kill N'ssag, we would do it. Look at that out there! There is no way to get to him without fighting an army."*

"Here's what we're going to do," Rhenn signed. *"Use the cloak. Take us from here to there, drop me on his head. Then you turn Slayter's wands on that mage and the Nox. That will be plenty of time for me to kill him. Once I do, his hold on them will break. His followers will scatter."*

Lorelle shook her head. *"We need to get the group and come back. We agreed. We talked about this. N'ssag alone. Opportunity to kill. Yes. N'ssag surrounded by an army, we gather information. Rhenn, we have the advantage now. We know what he's done. We know where he is. The smart play is to regroup, make a plan. With Khyven and Slayter, this becomes a very different fight. Think, Rhenn."*

Rhenn's entire body vibrated. She was going out of her skin being so close to him and not sinking her fangs into his neck. He was right there. And she knew if she left him, he'd have doubled his army by the time she returned. Those poor people down there. They'd be dead or undead in that time. He'd have made more bloodsuckers. With every moment they left him alone, he'd become stronger.

"It's a miracle they don't know we're here already," Lorelle flicked her fingers insistently. *"You know I'm right."*

"That woman won't be the last," Rhenn signed. *"And what if N'ssag is gone from here when we return? What if he moves on to Nokte Murosa? What if he comes north to Triada—"*

Lorelle suddenly raised her head like someone had hit her with a pebble. She turned, and Rhenn followed her gaze.

A dead Giant stood in the room.

Chapter Thirty-Nine
LORELLE

Lorelle's heart sank. Every instinct had warned her that it was time to leave. It had been time to leave sixty seconds ago. Sixty seconds ago, they'd have been gone; she could have taken Rhenn against her will. She could have made it happen.

That same instinct now told her they would never leave here alive.

The Giant towered over them, his head bowed slightly beneath the fifteen-foot-tall ceiling. His own noktum cloak swirled back, revealing his burnt, ruined body. Strips of muscle and skin hung from his white ribcage. Skeletal fingers splayed toward them, gesturing, meat dangling from the bones. A hole had been punched through his chest, as though someone had taken his heart. Half his face was burnt away completely, revealing a grisly smile. The other half was unharmed, one angry black eye focused on them, black eyebrow crouched low, black hair flowing down to his shoulder.

"Senji!" Rhenn grappled with the sheath at her thigh, trying to remove her wand. Thankfully, she had already grabbed the hilt of her sword.

But Lorelle was faster. She'd seen N'ssag's Giant bloodsuckers erupt one after the other when Slayter had raked them with light from the Thuros, and she'd pulled the thing—held it in her hand—once she knew Rhenn couldn't just walk away.

She raised the wand, made sure it was pointed away from Rhenn, and whispered harshly, "Lux!"

Light exploded like a living thing—

The irregular purple shadows lurched toward the Giant like awkward, nightmare furniture that had just come to life, multi jointed legs running against the floor, the walls, the ceiling. The light struck the purple shadows—

And vanished.

Lorelle gasped. Hope fluttered away on broken wings.

Slayter's last-resort weapon was absolutely useless. The Giant had swept away the sunlight spell like it was nothing.

A Giant. They were out of their depth. They had to leave. They had to escape.

Lorelle whipped her noktum cloak out to take Rhenn.

The Dark pulled her and Rhenn into itself—

And wrenched them out again.

Lorelle and Rhenn tumbled across the floor like badly thrown dice. The Giant murmured, his bare teeth chomping up and down in the burnt side of his face while, on the other side, his lips formed slurred words.

The noktum cloak unclipped from Lorelle's neck, whipped up and flew like a Sleeth across the room. It wrapped itself around the Giant's forearm.

"No!" Rhenn drew her sword and leapt at the Giant. She was so fast, Lorelle barely saw the blur of the blade as it descended.

The Giant was faster.

A gust of air turned Rhenn a quarter turn; her strike whistled past the Giant's shoulder. A hurricane wind exploded right in front of her, and she shot across the room like a stone from a catapult. She hit the thick wooden door so hard it shattered. Bones snapped. Shards of wood blew apart. Rhenn was thrown into the hallway and out of sight.

Her sword clattered to the floor.

Lorelle's heart hammered. She didn't know what to do, so she did the only thing that came to mind. She raised her blowgun and shot the Giant in the neck with a dose of *somnul* that would fell a horse.

The Giant ignored it, ignored Lorelle, and charged through the broken doorway after Rhenn. Lorelle leapt after.

Rhenn lay sprawled against the far wall of the hallway, right arm twisted awkwardly behind her back. Baring her teeth, she shook her head, tried to get up, but the Giant was already on her. He grabbed her by the throat and lifted her ten feet off the ground, clearly intending to break her neck.

"Stop!" A nasally voice shrieked from up the hall.

The Giant stopped, held the struggling Rhenn in mid-air. Her twisted arm hung limply at her side, but she kicked out with her legs and grappled at the fleshless fist with her good hand, to no avail.

Lorelle froze, looking up the hall. N'ssag stood at the rail before the drop-off, holding a splayed hand before himself like the Giant was at the end of invisible marionette strings.

A Nox bloodsucker appeared around the corner of the hall, then another, then a dozen of them slunk silently into the hallway, moving toward her.

Lorelle felt the hard decision. She was free. The Giant had been somehow paralyzed by N'ssag's command. She could sprint away. She could make it to the window, jump to the ground outside. She could make for the edge of the noktum. She could make for daylight. None of them would follow her there ...

But she'd have to leave Rhenn behind.

"Don't run, my dear," N'ssag said to Lorelle as though reading her mind. "Just. Stay. Put."

Lorelle's shoulders slumped. She couldn't leave Rhenn. She wasn't letting her sister out of her sight a second time.

"Come here, my dear." He beckoned her.

Rhenn made a choking sound, still fighting, still flailing ineffectually against the Giant. Her teeth bared, her face red, she was trying to warn Lorelle, trying to tell her to run, but he'd choked off her breath.

"Come here, my dear," N'ssag repeated, and his tone turned dark. The Nox bloodsuckers reached Lorelle, surrounded her. She swallowed and began walking toward him.

The Nox bloodsuckers led her around the rail that bordered the pit of the great room below, where the Humans and Shadowvar milled about in wretched horror. The Nox escorted her to N'ssag's throne.

"Let Rhenn go," she said.

He chuckled. "Oh my dear. You're the Luminent from the Thuros, aren't you? The one with the cloak who kept jumping all around. The one who stole her from me. Twice."

Lorelle remembered Rhenn pinned to the ground as she, Khyven, and Slayter emerged through the Thuros. Khyven and Slayter had made short work of N'ssag's lackeys. And then later, when N'ssag had Rhenn and Khyven pinned to the ground, she'd swept them away with the noktum cloak.

"Tell me your name, dear," he said.

"Let her go," she demanded. "You're hurting her."

"*Hurting* her? Hurting *her?*" N'ssag shook his head. "She has hurt me more than you can imagine. She was my queen, and she stabbed me through the heart. No no. She stays where she is. We're not talking about her right now, we're talking about you, lovely Lorelle."

Lorelle swallowed. The way he said her name made her shudder.

"Lovely Lorelle ... You made quite an impression on my beloved Nox." He gestured, and one of the bloodsuckers came forward from behind the throne.

"Zaith ..." she murmured.

He was every bit as tall and graceful as she remembered. The horrible slice in his neck was nothing but a scar now. He came to stand next to N'ssag's throne, eyes dull and devoid of the life she'd once seen there. Her heart ached seeing him captive, used, manipulated like this, and all her thoughts fled her.

"Oh, he told me everything, lovely Lorelle. I had him repeat the story of your tight little shadow dress. I had him repeat his description many times. And also how you danced to the music of his people, how you seemed like you belonged with him. I had him tell me that story over and over until I could see it, until I could feel it as he felt it."

"You ... are evil," she said.

"I am master of all Noksonon," he said. "I think it would behoove you to be nice to me."

"I'm going to kill you," she said, looking helplessly at Zaith, who glared back with those dead eyes.

"No, you're going to serve me."

The Nox bloodsuckers lunged at her. She was prepared for an attack, and she leapt straight upward—

Two Nox caught her ankles and hauled her back down. Fiercely strong hands grabbed arms, her legs, her waist, her hair. In seconds, they had her immobile.

They turned her to face N'ssag.

"Once, I offered to share the world with your friend," N'ssag said. "I asked her to be *my* queen. She spurned me." He put a hand to his heart and sighed like his chest hurt. "But this is a new world. Not Daemanon, but Noksonon, and perhaps it is time for a new bride. So, lovely Lorelle ... perhaps I will offer you the same. What do you think of that? You know, I've recently come to greatly appreciate the beauty of the Luminent and Nox people. I didn't realize a people could be so graceful. So ...light." He chuckled at his own humor.

Lorelle felt tears well in her eyes. She fought with every ounce of strength, but her body only vibrated in the steel grip of the bloodsuckers.

"Perhaps you are a more fitting queen, lovely Lorelle?"

N'ssag murmured, moving to the edge of the low dais upon which his throne sat. It put him slightly taller than her. "You, my queen. Rhenn can be relegated to being my whore. I must say, I do feel I could accustom myself to the strangeness of your ... non-Human form."

She spat at his face—

Zaith's hand shot out, catching the spittle on his palm before it hit N'ssag.

"Oh ..." N'ssag shook his head, eyes flashing. "No, no, lovely Lorelle. That is not how you want to treat me. You really must take an interest in what pleases me. You must learn—"

"I'll kill you."

His eyes flashed. "This is your chance, Lorelle. Please try to understand that I'm being kind to you. You need to see that. I'm giving you the choice to serve me, to service me, of your own free will. You should not be rebellious. You should be grateful. You see what happens to those who are rebellious ..." He gestured to where Rhenn's struggles had become weaker.

Lorelle bared her teeth. "I will die before I give you *anything*."

"Oh yes ..." N'ssag breathed as though she'd said his favorite thing in the world. "Yes, you most certainly will."

The teeth came from behind. Lorelle gasped as they plunged into her neck, spraying blood against her chin. She screamed and thrashed against her captors.

But it was no use ...

Chapter Forty

SLAYTER

Slayter's time had run out. He knew it when Hellface reared.

He and Khyven had ridden south toward Usara with a hopeless urgency. They had ridden out of Wheskone Keep with all speed. They had galloped past where they'd faced the bandits. They'd thundered down the road until Slayter's mount could run no more.

They'd set the spent horse free by a stream near a field of well-deserved grass, and from that moment, Hellface had borne two riders.

The black stallion seemed indefatigable. It had been amazing that he'd been able to carry Khyven's bulk that far, that fast, but to then take on a second rider and still gallop at full speed ...

It seemed supernatural to Slayter, but the horse frothed at the mouth like a vigorous beast who had finally found a challenge worthy of its strength and rage. The horse seemed to take the challenge personally and pushed with everything he had.

Khyven was likewise determined. He hadn't slept for the last two days, and he stayed stoic at the reins. He had guided the horse through the night while Slayter dozed against his back.

They crested the rise before the green pastures and farmland that surrounded the crown city when Hellface suddenly reared and Khyven cried out.

The horse stopped like there was a cliff in front of them, hooves churning earth until it came to a complete stop. It reared with an angry scream, pitching both its passengers.

Slayter flew like a rag doll, hitting the ground and rolling. His prosthetic twisted painfully, and pain fired into his stump.

At first, Slayter thought the ride had finally killed the stallion, that it had pushed itself so fast and so far beyond its capacity that its heart had simply ruptured.

But when he finally collected his limbs together enough to sit up, he saw Khyven kneeling on the ground, one fist against the packed earth of the road and one clenching a dagger as he grit his teeth.

Hellface, still frothing white foam at the mouth, looked angrily at Khyven. Slayter realized then that it wasn't the horse who had done this. Khyven had yanked the reins suddenly, viciously, and caused Hellface to rear. The Ringer still fought whatever had overcome him and he had, naturally, found a weapon. Clearly the closest one to hand. Khyven could draw daggers faster than the eye could see. Slayter had watched him draw and throw and kill a man before Slayter could even identify what had flown.

Now he clenched that dagger like he would attack something, but there was nothing to attack.

Or was there?

Slayter fumbled with the cylinder at his waist, found the detect magic spell, summoned the silky, hot feeling of magic from within himself, and let it flow into the disk.

Orange light flared, and he snapped the disk in mid-air. He opened his eyes and looked for anything around him that glowed orange.

Khyven's Mavric iron sword burned like the setting sun, but

that was it. There was nothing. No eldritch force attacked Khyven. He wasn't—

"Lorelle!" he shouted raggedly like someone was trying to cut his heart out with a wood rasp.

And then everything became clear. The soul-bond. Khyven was feeling something through the Luminent soul-bond.

"Khyven—" Slayter began.

"Lorelle!" he shouted again, leaping to his feet again. Slayter rethought approaching the big man. He didn't look like he was actually seeing anything that was around him, but rather something in his head. Best not to be too close.

"Where is she?" Slayter said. "Tell me where she—"

Khyven whirled, eyes blazing, and glared at Slayter with such fury he thought the Ringer was going to kill him.

"She's in the noktum." He whirled and charged at Hellface. For once, the stallion didn't fight him for dominance. Khyven leapt upon his back and yanked the reins, spinning the horse and facing the noktum instead of the city.

Slayter crawled on his hands and knees, dragging his twisted prosthetic behind him. "Khyven, wait. You're going to—"

Khyven kicked his heels in, and Hellface bolted down the hill, leaving Slayter behind, still struggling to get his prosthetic leg turned around.

"Khyven!" he shouted. "She's not in *that* noktum!"

For a breathless instant, Slayter thought Khyven was so far into his killing fury that he couldn't hear anything, but halfway down the hill, dirt churned as Hellface tore around in a circle. The great horse galloped back up the hill. As he neared, Khyven did not slow.

"Senji's Braids ..." Slayter realized what Khyven was going to do. The Ringer leaned over in the saddle, extending one of his huge hands.

Slayter wanted to shout at him, 'You can't be serious!'

Instead, he prepared himself. He took a strong grip on his prosthetic with one hand, swallowed, closed one eye, and held up his left hand.

Khyven snatched Slayter's wrist, righted himself and flung Slayter behind him. Slayter thought for certain his arm would come out of its socket. He thought for certain Khyven would overshoot and simply toss him over the horse to land on the ground on the other side.

But while the man's grip was steel, the lift was almost gentle. He compensated the fierce jolt of Slayter's still body by leaning ridiculously far down the side of the horse, using his own incredible torso strength to cushion the sudden jerk, and then pulling Slayter gracefully upward with a powerful display of his torso's strength.

Slayter sailed onto the back of the horse and wrapped his free arm around Khyven's waist. By the time he had, the horse was facing the noktum again, and they bolted down the slope.

Slayter calculated the time to come back and recover him had been ten seconds. Damn.

Hellface seemed to have gained a new strength from Khyven's anger, and he pounded down the hill in a reckless charge. Slayter had never ridden at this ridiculous speed before. The tentacled wall of the noktum came up frighteningly fast.

"Thank you," he said in Khyven's ear. "Thank you for coming back to get me."

"We're going to the Great Noktum." His face still seemed strained with whatever he was feeling.

"You have to take me to my laboratory then—"

"We're going to Rauvelos. He's going to send us where she is just like he did before."

Slayter cocked his head. That was actually uncommonly good sense. He felt a little disappointed he hadn't thought of that.

"Tell me what happened."

"They took her cloak," he said. "It was ripped from her. They hurt her, Slayter. I'm going to—"

"Did you see anything?" Slayter asked.

"Suffocating. Nox all around her. They're all around her. They're biting …"

"Don't tell me about the Nox. Tell me about the place."
"Stone walls. Books. I don't know. A castle?"
"What color are the walls?"
"What does that matter? I don't know. Stone colored."
"There are a myriad of stone colors."
"Gray! They were gray."
"Were they burnt?"
"Burnt?"
"The Nox city. Were they in—"
"No."

It wasn't the Nox city. And Tovos's castle had been made of black stone.

"What else?"

"She's ... There's a huge room ... below. They're taking her ..."

"Don't tell me about them. Tell me about the place."

"There's a circular room in the floor. Books all around. Books in a tower."

"A tower with books? How tall—"

"Taller than the palace!"

Slayter could only think of six structures that were taller than the Usaran palace. Tovos's castle in the Great Noktum, the nuraghi in Usara's noktum, the Triadan palace, the Imprevaran palace, the Suivan Lattice in Lumyn, and the Great Library of Nokte Shaddark. Both Giant nuraghis were made of black stone. The Triadan palace was made of white and blue marble. The Imprevaran palace was made of golden sandstone. And one wouldn't call the Suivan Lattice a castle exactly. It was ... Well, it was very Luminent. And it didn't have books. None of those were in the noktum. "You said it was in the noktum."

"It *is* in the noktum!"

A chill went up Slayter's spine. Noksonon was changing. The return of Giants. The return of dragons. The return of magics not seen in millennia. Could it be Nokte Shaddark's Great Library and *also* be in a noktum? Had the Great Noktum grown? He didn't like the idea of that.

The noktum loomed. They were going straight to the nuraghi, which meant moments after they entered the noktum, the Sleeths and the Kyolar were going to have Hellface for dinner.

Slayter let go of his hold on his prosthetic leg, which bounced on the horse's flank, held on by a single strap now. With his free hand, he fumbled with his cylinder. He couldn't quite see his disks, so he counted down and picked the spell he needed. He pulled it out—almost dropped it—then imbued it with his life-force and snapped it.

Slayter gripped the reassuring circle of his Amulet of Noksonon that rested against his breastbone as the spell took effect. After the story Khyven had told about taking Shalure into the noktum without an amulet, Slayter had tinkered around with recreating one of the amulets.

He'd failed. He'd done a dozen different amulets to try to effect something that could ward off the noktum, but it was a far more complicated—and powerful—spell than one would think.

Finally, he figured out a way to extending the aura of an existing amulet. He couldn't recreate the spell, but he could bolster it.

Orange light spread over him, Khyven, and Hellface. He clenched the amulet in his palm and circled it with his index finger as Hellface charged right into the tentacles that reached out for him.

The day vanished. The horse jolted suddenly, leaping into the air as though he'd seen something and leapt over it at the last second. Khyven didn't even pause, but Slayter craned his neck and looked back.

The half-light vision of the amulet conveyed everything in the noktum in blacks, whites, and shades of gray. On the ground right where they'd entered the noktum lay a woman, but she didn't look like a normal person would. In the noktum, people were comprised of shades of light and dark gray. This woman was striking, out of place. She looked like she was completely white with curves of gray indicating her form. She lay on the ground, face up and unmoving, and she looked vaguely familiar.

"Khyven! There's someone back there!" he shouted.

Khyven shook his head brusquely and kept Hellface pounding toward the nuraghi. They'd been noticed by a pride of three Kyolars already, who made a beeline for them. A dark cloud of Sleeths also took notice, spun once, and headed for them as well. Two giant spiders in the forest to their left plodded purposefully in the general direction of the nuraghi, but seemed uninterested in them.

"*Ssss...*" A whisper of a voice slithered across Slayter's mind. He perked up and tried to listen.

Nothing.

"Khyven, there was a—"

"*Sssslayter...*" the voice said, more coherently this time, and Slayter knew exactly who it was.

"*Vohn!*" he said in his mind to the voice.

"*Slayter...*" The voice said a third time. "*Shalure... You have to help her.*"

Slayter craned his entire torso around this time and took a hard look at the figure that was becoming smaller and smaller as Hellface pounded forward. It *was* Shalure. He thought she'd looked familiar!

"*The Sleeths... The Kyolars... They're going to kill her...*"

"*Vohn, we have a problem. Lorelle is in danger, and Khyven's gone, well... He's gone Khyven crazy. He plans to make Rauvelos send us into the Great Noktum.*"

"*He can't.*"

"*I told him that. He's not listening to—*"

"*There is a dragon in the castle.*"

Slayter's blood chilled. "*Jai'ketakos...*"

"*Jai'ketakos killed Rauvelos. And he's going to kill Khyven if he finds him. He's probably already sweeping the noktum for me.*"

"*For you? Why for you?*"

"*How does Khyven know Lorelle is in danger?*" Vohn answered a question with a question.

"*Soul-bond.*"

Vohn didn't say anything for a moment. *"Tell him. You have to tell him."*

"Khyven," Slayter shouted. "Vohn is here."

"Vohn?"

"He says you can't go to the castle. Jai'ketakos is there. Rauvelos is dead."

That got Khyven's attention. He turned his head and glared at Slayter.

"Tell him I can help Lorelle," Vohn said. *"I can reach her. Just like I helped in the dragon's cave."*

"Khyven, Vohn can get to her! He's ... in his banshee form."

Khyven hauled on the reins and Hellface almost reared again as he came to a stop. The Sleeths swirled overhead, looking down at them eagerly. The three Kyolars padded to a stop twenty feet away, heads low as they looked at the horse.

Hellface stared them down, breathing hard, and Slayter decided unequivocally that the horse was insane. Normal horses didn't just stare down predators. He made a mental note that he was going to have to study Hellface at length after all this was done. If they lived.

"How?" Khyven growled. His shoulders twitched like he wasn't entirely controlling them anymore. His hands gripped the reins, white with strength. "They've got her, Slayter. They have their hands all over her. They're biting her!"

The man was losing control. Khyven leapt from the horse and drew his steel sword like the enemy was right here.

Slayter suddenly considered the very real possibility that Khyven might lose his mind. He was a Human, after all, and he'd bonded with a Luminent. Slayter didn't know much about the Luminent soul-bond, but he knew it was powerful magic. Clearly, it had created a symbiotic relationship between Khyven and Lorelle. He could feel what she was feeling in her terror, could even see what she was seeing to a limited extent. If she died, what would that do to him?

The possibilities were a little frightening ...

Slayter didn't have time to think about that right now, though. Hellface had turned his head. He was looking at Slayter sitting on his rump like Slayter was an affront that would only be tolerated another few seconds now that Khyven had dismounted.

Slayter grabbed his dangling leg and swung his stump over the horse's back, dropping to the ground. He landed on his good leg—

And stuck the landing! He actually gave a little exclamation of surprise as he hopped, found his balance and stayed upright.

"*Where is she?*" Vohn asked.

"*The Great Library in Nokte Shaddark,*" Slayter thought to Vohn. "*It sounds like the Great Library.*"

"What is he saying?" Khyven stalked toward Slayter and towered over him, again looking like he was going to use that sword.

"He says he's going to get her."

"Take me," he growled. "He has to take me with him!"

"*I can't,*" Vohn said.

"He can't."

"You take me there, Vohn!" Khyven roared, turning around like he could somehow spot Vohn in his banshee form, which was silly, of course. But Khyven's rages didn't really adhere to logic. Of course, his victories didn't really adhere to logic, either, so ...

"*Help her,*" Vohn's voice faded. "*Help Shalure ...*"

"Vohn, damn you!" Khyven whirled and faced Slayter.

"Uh ..."

"Where is he?" Khyven demanded.

"He's not here anymore?"

Khyven turned his head to the skies, clenched his fists, and roared so loudly the Sleeths broke formation and circled wider, as though Khyven's rage was a tongue of flame that would burn them.

Slayter looked over at Shalure a hundred feet behind them. It wouldn't take long for the Sleeths and Kyolars to notice her.

"Khyven!" Slayter barked as one of the Kyolars broke from the other two and padded around them in a wide circle, headed toward Shalure.

He turned to Slayter, saw the Kyolar, and then Khyven's mind finally caught up to what Slayter was saying. With another animalistic roar, he sprinted after the Kyolar. The creature saw him, broke into a lope as though it would outrace him and snatch Shalure up before Khyven could reach them.

Then Hellface was there, galloping alongside Khyven. He leapt up and actually managed to thread his left foot into the dangling, bouncing right stirrup. Khyven hung onto the horse's mane, one foot in the stirrup and one foot winging out in the wind, hanging off the side of the horse as it raced to catch the Kyolar.

The cat was simply too fast, and it had too much of a lead. It was about to reach Shalure's prone body when Khyven flung his sword. It sank into the ground right in front of it. The big cat hissed and leapt up, barely clearing the blade. Its leap carried it past Shalure, and it landed a half dozen feet beyond, spun in the turf, intending to double back—

But Khyven and Hellface arrived by then. Khyven leapt from the stirrup and landed between the Kyolar and Shalure. It bared its teeth and started toward him.

Khyven bared his teeth and drew the Mavric iron sword.

The Kyolar stopped, hissed. It crouched low and backed up, eyes fixed on that wide, black blade. It gave one more angry hiss, then turned and ran away.

Relief flooded through Slayter as he saw that none of the other creatures were interested in approaching Khyven with that sword in his hand. They could clearly feel the magic and wanted no part of it.

Slayter reached down, took a moment to fix his leg, then hobbled toward Khyven, who stood with his back to Shalure like he wanted the beasts to attack. Well, he *was* Khyven. He probably *did* want them to attack. Hellface also glared at the closest Kyolar like it wanted the big cat to attack.

There was something distinctly not right about that horse.

"Well," Slayter said as he approached. "That was ... unexpected in many ways."

Khyven glared balefully at him, still gripping the Mavric iron sword, and Slayter stopped ten feet away. Well, it didn't hurt to be careful.

"We should, well, pick up Shalure and maybe leave, don't you think?" Slayter said. "And by 'we,' I mean—"

"The dragon," Khyven growled. "We kill the dragon."

Slayter glanced toward the nuraghi, then back at Khyven. "Right now?"

"Of course right now," Khyven said, but he didn't move. He stood protectively over Shalure.

Slayter blinked, because that didn't add up. If Khyven wanted to ride to the castle to kill the dragon, he'd have already jumped on Hellface.

Slayter glanced down and noticed Khyven's forearm where it held the Sword. It was striated with muscle like he was struggling to hold the thing up.

By Senji, the *Sword* wanted to go kill the dragon. Khyven did not.

A dozen questions sprouted in Slayter's mind, but none of them could be answered right now.

"Of course," Slayter said. "You have to kill the dragon. First, though, put Shalure on the horse. I'll take her back to Usara."

Khyven glanced at Shalure, then back at the castle. He seemed to struggle like that for a moment, but as Slayter had hoped, the hold the Sword had on Khyven wasn't complete. Certain elements of logic had to be met.

Khyven had said the Sword, during the first fight with the dragon, had driven him to do things he already wanted to do, except in the extreme, to the exclusion of all else, blocking any other concerns from his mind, such as any care for his own life or Slayter's life. Khyven wanted to kill the dragon. The Sword wanted to kill the dragon. And so the Sword filled Khyven's mind and drove him.

But apparently the Sword wasn't able to overcome that logic problem.

The normal Khyven would, of course, put Shalure on the horse for Slayter, even if he intended to continue on to the castle by himself. Except Slayter could never take Hellface back on his own. The stallion wouldn't stand for it. So Khyven would have to come.

"Yes," Khyven said with effort.

"Load her up first, then I'll go," Slayter reiterated.

Khyven twitched his head. His grip on the Sword tightened. He growled, then raised his arm in a flash and slammed the thing into its sheath.

The moment he let go of the Sword, he gasped.

"Khyven—"

"No. Don't," Khyven cut him off. His brow was furrowed with worry. "Don't say a thing."

He knelt, lifted Shalure and draped her gently over Hellfire's back. He didn't mount up, but instead led the horse to the edge of the noktum and vanished beyond the wall.

Slayter glanced back at the castle. He thought he saw an irregular shape along the silhouette of the roof ... The shape of a dragon with its wings tucked against its side, watching.

But the dragon didn't leap into the sky, didn't fly toward them. It just watched.

Slayter turned away and limped quickly after Khyven.

Chapter Forty-One
JAI'KETAKOS

Jai'ketakos's had been clinging to the tallest tower of Castle Noktos, searching for the little Shadowvar. This was the third mortal to escape his wrath. At first, the dragon had hoped it was some spell, some bit of Line Magic provided by Slayter the Mage like the pitiful lightning rod.

It wasn't, and the fire inside Jai'ketakos stoked red hot. Another mortal. He'd been made a fool by yet another …

Travel spells were difficult for the most powerful of Eldroi, so it simply couldn't be a bit of mortal Line Magic concocted by Slayter the Mage. The noktum cloaks had been a fashioning of Noktos and a few of his favorite students. The Thuroi had required multiple Eldroi to create.

For a mortal, a powerful travel spell would be impossible. At best, something Slayter could craft might take the Shadowvar and his female companion a thousand feet, a mile at the most.

So Jai'ketakos scanned the entire perimeter of the castle, waiting for unusual movement, the sudden appearance of something that hadn't been there before. He looked intensely along the edge of the wall in the direction of the Human city of Usara.

Nothing. There was nothing.

Acid churned in his stomach as he realized what had happened.

Phasing. That *had* to be it! He was one of *those*. A Shadowvar the Humans called banshees.

Except banshees couldn't transport others. How had he taken the girl?

Jai'ketakos gnashed his teeth. If the Shadowvar was one of Rauvelos's banshees, he could be anywhere right now. There was no range to those who rode the Dark.

He was about to turn his head skyward and blast a jet of flame when the unusual movement he'd been looking for caught his eye.

A horse, of all things, burst into the noktum at the northern border. It ran at full gallop straight toward him, straight toward Castle Noktos, and riding him was …

A prickle of cold fear rolled up Jai'ketakos's back before he could stop it. He shoved it down, but not before the oozing, hot humility.

It was Khyven the Unkillable.

Behind the mortal rode Slayter the Mage, who had started this entire disaster. And between them, sheathed against Khyven's back, was the damned Sword of Noksonon. The bird hadn't been lying. That living wand of darkness and death had somehow tracked Jai'ketakos, had come to finish the job.

The dragon twitched, could still feel that blade piercing his scales, splitting his flesh and muscle. He felt its unholy exultation as it cut into him, how it wanted more. The Sword of Noksonon would never stop until Jai'ketakos was dead.

He almost fled again, but he held himself still with an effort of will, clinging to the stone wall.

This was untenable! Khyven was only a Human! He was Jai'ketakos! He had fended off a thousand Humans during the War of the Fall. How could he be afraid of this one little mortal?

Because that mortal split you from neck to tail ...

Jai'ketakos needed to attack. He needed to fly out and meet Khyven, punch a dozen holes into his mortal body. He needed to torch Slayter until he was a charred skeleton.

But Jai'ketakos didn't move. He gripped the tower harder, cracks spidering out from his talons.

He watched as Khyven pulled the stallion to a sudden stop, leapt off and left Slayter sitting on its back until he awkwardly slid to the ground.

More talking, which even Jai'ketakos couldn't hear at this distance. Then Khyven roared at the sky, spooking the Sleeths.

A moment later, he seemed to recover and sprinted back toward the edge of the noktum to fight off a Kyolar. There was something on the ground there. A body.

The girl the Shadowvar had been protecting!

That was impossible. A phasing Shadowvar couldn't transport anything else with them, nothing that wasn't attached to their body, and certainly nothing alive. What was the secret of these mortals?

Fire leaked from Jai'ketakos's mouth. He wanted to kill them. He wanted to incinerate them all. Visions of flying over them, jetting down his flames from high above, came to him.

But it would be no use. The Sword of Noksonon was immune to the magic of the Drakanoi, and it would make its companions immune as well. Jai'ketakos would have to close with them to hurt them, and if he did, the Sword would be in range, too ...

He clenched his teeth. He could not flee, either. He had just captured Castle Noktos from The Betrayer, had defeated the damned bird, a being of infinitely more power than Khyven the Unkillable. He couldn't just run away now.

The decision was taken from Jai'ketakos's hands. Khyven the Unkillable and Slayter the Mage gathered the unconscious girl, put her on the horse, and vanished through the wall of the noktum.

Somehow, that hurt even worse. He was the master here.

They should fear him!

Yet they didn't. And when they lifted up the girl, put her on the horse, and left the noktum, he did nothing.

Jai'ketakos turned his gaze away, let it fall on the courtyard below while he felt the burn of his shame.

The mortals would eventually come here. Of course they would. The Human was in the Sword's thrall, and the Sword was crazy. Either Jai'ketakos could choose the battlefield, or he could wait for the damned Sword to choose it.

Or maybe not. Perhaps they would simply go back to their little Human city, unthreatened. Perhaps they thought Jai'ketakos was scared of them. Perhaps they thought they could continue on with their lives, just leave him behind and never think of him again.

Just like Jai'ketakos's captors had done ...

Jai'ketakos could torch Usara. The Sword could not protect an entire city. He could watch the pain on their mortal faces as their fellows burned ...

But Khyven the Unkillable would still be alive. Slayter the Mage would still be alive. The humiliation would not end until those two were dead. How could he ... Jai'ketakos's thoughts trailed off.

That statue was looking at him.

Dozens of statues littered the courtyard, remnants from a time when Castle Noktos entertained guests who would walk the sculpture garden. Noktos had liked to revere those Noksonoi who had fallen in the Elder Wars, heroes from an age gone by.

And one of those statues was ... looking at him.

He adjusted his bulk, his head leaning out to the left on his long neck. Except that it wasn't. The statue faced the gates, an imperious gaze on his face. It couldn't look at him.

And yet it had, as though it was somehow an answer to Jai'ketakos's turbulent thoughts. He narrowed his eyes, studying the statue's profile.

His eyes widened.

No ... It couldn't be. It simply couldn't be.

Jai'ketakos left his perch, leaping into the air and gliding lazily down to the courtyard. Let the Humans see. Let them come.

Jai'ketakos might have just uncovered one of the great enduring mysteries of Noksonon.

Chapter Forty-Two
JAI'KETAKOS

Jai'ketakos moved sinuously across the courtyard toward the statue.

Even in his cave, bound to an oath he'd sworn to his kind before he'd been bound by the Dragon Chain, deep in the heart of the Great Noktum, far away from any civilization that had anything resembling news, the dragon had heard of the death of Harkandos. One day, the great Noksonoi was creating a secret game-changer in the War of the Fall and the next ...

... he was gone.

The Noksonoi titan had been the hope of the failing war, then suddenly he was gone, and the prevailing rumor was that Nhevalos The Betrayer had somehow killed him. Some said that Harkandos could never have fallen to Nhevalos.

But whatever the truth, Harkandos was gone.

The war went downhill quickly after that. Some said the loss of Harkandos was the last straw, and the Humans overwhelmed the Noksonoi defenses without Harkandos's great, mysterious game-changer to turn the tide.

Jai'ketakos had often wondered about that in his endless free time in the cave. What had really become of Harkandos? Was he actually dead? Had he fled like the others despite his fearsome reputation? Had The Betrayer somehow defeated the most powerful Noksonoi mage since Noktos himself?

Now Jai'ketakos knew the truth. The Betrayer had trapped Harkandos in a prison.

As Jai'ketakos landed in the courtyard, his gaze never left the statue. It was looking at him, and yet it wasn't. It moved, and yet it didn't.

Jai'ketakos studied the thing, then set to work. It took him a while to understand the nature of the spell. After an hour of intense study, during which he periodically looked over his shoulder to see if the mortals had returned to the noktum, Jai'ketakos thought he'd finally determined the gist of it ...

And it was brilliant.

Jai'ketakos hated Nhevalos for that. The spell was complex, convoluted, but not powerful. At least, not by itself. Not without the power of its prisoner.

But the placement of it, the thought of it ... This was why Nhevalos had won, why the mortals had won the War of the Fall. This spell was one thing that could render a powerhouse like Harkandos impotent.

The spell turned Harkandos's strength against him. The magic that fueled the statue's transformation was Harkandos's resistance. The harder Harkandos fought, the more stony he became.

Oh, the titan seethed. The spell was comprehensive. At first glance, one would just see a statue. At second glance, one would get an uneasy feeling that something about the statue "wasn't right." But with prolonged study, and the magical senses of an Eldroi, it not only revealed the caliber of magics, but every now and then, the eyes actually moved.

"Would you like to be free of this confinement, Lord Harkandos?" Jai'ketakos asked.

The statue's gaze flicked to him ...

Then those same eyes were staring straight forward again, angry, solid. Stone.

"It's quite simple, actually. I see it all here. Just a flick of the wrist, and the whole thing parts. Nhevalos is a gambler, isn't he? Any Eldroi who came here could have seen exactly what I saw, if they'd looked. They could have freed you, perhaps even before the bird caught them." Jai'ketakos snorted, flames flickering up from his nostrils. "Yet here you are, after all these years. I suppose The Betrayer knows us better than we know ourselves. He knew you'd rot here without anyone coming to find you."

This!

This was what Jai'ketakos needed. This was his path to killing the Humans. The Sword of Noksonon was renowned for slaying Drakanoi, but not Noksonoi. It was made for the Noksonoi to wield. For someone exactly like Harkandos to wield. Harkandos could march right into Usara. He could take the Sword from Khyven.

Then Jai'ketakos could have his way.

"I will help you," the dragon continued. "And you will owe me, Lord Harkandos. You will owe me your life, but I will only require a service of you. Not only that, but I believe it will be a service you will be happy to provide."

The statue had gone completely still. No doubt the great lord had tried to speak, had tried to force his magic to respond to Jai'ketakos, and Nhevalos's spell had hardened.

"Very well, great lord. We are agreed."

Jai'ketakos reached out and broke Nhevalos's spell.

Chapter Forty-Three
HARKANDOS

Harkandos dreamed. Oh, he wasn't pleasantly submerged in the fanciful images Humans claimed to see when their frail bodies fell unconscious. No. Nhevalos had ensured Harkandos's eyes were peeled back, seeing every minute of every year of every century of every millennium he had been trapped in this granite-crusted cocoon of madness.

He had watched the centuries turn in the ebb and flow of the noktum. He had seen Rauvelos wheel over his statue self when he left the castle on those rare errands for his vile master. He had seen the Kyolars, Sleeths, Gylarns—and rarely the huge, eight-legged Cakistros—approach the broken gate of the courtyard, sense his presence, and flee.

He had witnessed the rare Humans who ventured this far, oblivious to the powerful magics, oblivious to Harkandos himself. There weren't many of them. Rauvelos had toyed with each, then inevitably devoured them. Nhevalos's noktum phoenix enjoyed the taste of mortals. Oh yes, he did.

During the first years, Harkandos had railed against his prison. He'd fought as he had fought every other obstacle in his life that had stood in his way. This, of course, was exactly what Nhevalos had wanted. This was what he'd expected.

Somehow, The Betrayer had fueled his spell with Harkandos's own magic. When Harkandos used it, the spell tightened, transforming his flesh and organs into living stone. It closed off his throat, his ears, tightened around his body, immobilizing everything except his eyes and his thoughts.

When Harkandos did nothing, let his magic seep away, let his thoughts quiet, the stone receded, became nearly pliable, and he could hear. He could feel the passing of time.

He had been alert when the first change came to Rauvelos's noktum. A group of Humans not only made it past the Kyolars and Sleeths with stolen Amulets of Noksonon, not only entered the courtyard, but went into Castle Noktos itself ...

And emerged uneaten.

On the way in, one of the mortal cockroaches had approached Harkandos, peered at him with impunity. Such outright disrespect deserved death. Of course Rauvelos would eat them all soon enough. That, Harkandos supposed, would have to suffice.

But Rauvelos didn't eat them.

When the group left the noktum with their stolen prizes, Harkandos had felt the first stirrings of hope, had felt the winds of change. The bird had never done that before, which meant there was a reason for it. Harkandos had come to learn the hard way that everything Nhevalos did, or allowed to be done in his realm, had a purpose.

Weeks later, that same Human who'd scrutinized him had returned with a Shadowvar and a mortal mage.

Harkandos didn't know how to unravel Nhevalos's spell or he would have escaped long ago, so he didn't know how the mortals had disrupted it. The magic the mage had used—or the presence of the group—had cracked Harkandos's prison and given him something he'd not had for nearly two thousand years.

Freedom. To act. To use magic.

Oh, he had been so close. If not for Rauvelos, Harkandos would have been free.

When the Drakanoi killed the bird, Harkandos knew his time was at hand.

The Drakanoi was an idiot—all Drakanoi were—but that didn't matter. As with all Drakanoi, Jai'ketakos followed his fiery passions in every direction. But this would lead him to Harkandos, and that was all that was required ...

"I will help you," the dragon continued. "And you will owe me, Lord Harkandos. You will owe me your life, but I will only require a service of you. Not only that, but I believe it will be a service you will be happy to provide."

Require a service of me ... Harkandos thought. *A Drakanoi ... requiring a service of me ...*

Again, Harkandos dreamed. He imagined the slaughter that would follow his release. The darkness that would cover the continent. Mortal blood by the buckets. The tortured subjugation of Nhevalos. Harkandos would pull him apart one strip of flesh at a time, one emotion at a time, one psychic thread of sanity at a time. He'd been dreaming of it for centuries.

Harkandos would hang Nhevalos from a spiderweb of his own guts, dying and living at the same time, and force him to watch as every sneaky little plan he'd ever hatched was destroyed.

Yes, Harkandos thought. *I will owe you, Drakanoi. You will get everything that is coming to you. And I will get everything that is coming to me.*

The dragon nodded as though Harkandos had answered. "Very well, great lord. We are agreed."

He approached the pedestal, paused for a moment, and then Harkandos felt it.

The spell binding him cracked for the second time in two millennia. It shook, coming apart, losing integrity.

Harkandos shoved all of his rage into the crack, every ounce of his focus, every scrap of his power, and peeled the spell back.

The moan began in the depths of his throat, a keen of rage, of hope, of freedom. The filigreed webs of the spell began to snap. Just a few at first, then more and more. Harkandos's moan became a roar that shook the ground. Sleeths burst from the tops of trees and fled. Kyolars roared in response. The lumbering Cakistros turned ponderously about and moved away.

Granite cracked across Harkandos's cheeks, his shoulders, his torso, splitting his skin. Blood oozed out, but he pressed harder. More webs of the spell snapped.

"Yyyyeeessss!" Harkandos cried as the balance tipped decisively. The power of the elements all around him rushed in. Harkandos felt his ability to shape them like he'd dug his hands into the earth.

"Yes!" he roared again.

Chunks of stone burrowed up from the ground. Winds whipped down at the pedestal. Jai'ketakos leapt into the air and winged his way backward, out of range. The stones struck the pedestal, cracking it.

Nhevalos's spell weakened further. Harkandos's skin began to separate from the granite. Stone flaked away, revealing flesh. The cuts and rips remained; blood flowed.

But it was blood! Not stone.

Finally, Nhevalos's spell failed completely. Sheets of granite fell away, crashing, cracking, and piling at Harkandos's feet.

He stood there, fists clenched, teeth clenched, and he glared around. Once again, Harkandos could feel everything around him with full vigor. The ground. The wind. The potential for fire that resided in the spark of a rock against another rock. The water that flowed deep beneath the ground, that hovered in the air. He could pull all of this to him.

He felt the life force in the noktum creatures, felt it in the frightened Drakanoi above him. He could pull that to himself as well.

He felt the dragon's emotions, felt them like the chords on a harp, to be strummed and manipulated if he sent the barest wisps of his influence into them.

He felt the latent power of every single object, awaiting the inscription of Line Magic to turn them from mundane to the arcane.

He felt the ghostly images of the *kairoi* all around, unseen glimpses of possible futures. They hovered about him.

He felt all five streams of magic at his command, felt them returned to him, no longer his enemy, but his unstoppable ally.

He drew a long, satisfied breath and shouted again.

A myriad of thoughts rushed through his mind. What he wanted to do was find Nhevalos and kill him.

He rejected the impulse. That was what had brought him here in the first place. Harkandos had been so confident in his own power that he had not imagined in his wildest dreams that a weakling like Nhevalos could stand against him.

His second thought was to find those mortals Nhevalos had laid his hand upon, that he used to further his scheming, and destroy them. The mage. The Shadowvar. The Human fighter the mage had called, "Khyven."

"Drakanoi," Harkandos said. "The mortals that were here, that you chased into the castle. Where are they now?"

The dragon hovered a little closer. "In their city, Lord Harkandos." The dragon lowered his head deferentially, though he still flapped high in the air, at what he probably thought was a safe range.

"There is a Human city nearby?"

"The crown city of Usara. In the centuries you have been ... away, Humans have spread, inhabiting any number of fields and plains and forests of what was once Noksonoi territory."

Harkandos bared his teeth. He stepped down off the pedestal and pointed. "Their city is where they fled?"

"Yes, great Lord."

Yes. Harkandos would utterly destroy every mortal who had desecrated the realm of the great Noktos by squashing their pitiful little civilizations in the mud like wolf turds. Humans were slaves. That's what they were. Their "self-determined" lives were a joke that Nhevalos had tried to make real. But this was a front.

Their sweat, their blood, and their lives were created for the Noksonoi purposes.

Harkandos could walk into their midst and liquidate them in a bloody purge. He could burn them until their screams echoed off the mountainsides. He could plunge their minds into gibbering madness. He could make example of all of them ...

No.

Harkandos could practically feel The Betrayer's gaze upon him, waiting. Nhevalos had used the fickle vagaries of Lore Magic to tie Harkandos up for two millennia. He knew Harkandos was more than a match for him, in every other way. He knew how Harkandos thought.

He knew Harkandos ...

And Harkandos would have to know Nhevalos as well. To attack the mortals was the obvious solution, to attack what Nhevalos had clearly fostered. And if Harkandos chose the obvious solution, he might find himself in another trap just like this one.

He must do that which Nhevalos would never expect.

The plan formed instantly. Nhevalos wanted Harkandos to use his powerful magic. He wanted Harkandos to ruthlessly attack and destroy, because that was what Harkandos was good at. That was what he'd always done.

Not in a thousand years would Nhevalos expect Harkandos to back away from a fight. To leave revenge lying served and warm but uneaten on the table. Harkandos himself could barely believe he was thinking about it.

But that was exactly what Nhevalos would expect. In fact, this Human city so close to Castle Noktos had to be bait to draw Harkandos out.

"No ..." Harkandos said, seeing the tendrils of his new plan.

"Great lord," the dragon began. "As we agreed, I require only one service of you. I would request that—"

Harkandos cut off the Drakanoi with a baleful gaze. "Quiet yourself, dragon. I acknowledge that you freed me. I acknowledge that you deserve a reward. Here it is: I will spare your life. I will honor you with a place at my side."

The dragon opened his mouth as if he was about to object, but stopped himself.

"You belong to me now, Drakanoi. You will be the first to share in the glory of my victory."

The Drakanoi's nostrils filled with flame. Defiance. Insult. Harkandos almost ended him right there, but he waited five respectful seconds for the service the dragon had done him.

"Of course, my lord," the Drakanoi finally said.

"We are going on a journey."

"Actually, great lord. I suggest that I stay here. I will secure the castle and—"

Harkandos stopped listening to the nattering dragon and reached into the Dark. He began pulling his power together for the travel spell. Manipulating the forces of the noktum, for anyone else, required a collaboration of magics. It required making an artifact like the Thuroi or the noktum cloaks.

That was for anyone else.

Harkandos needed no artifact. He needed no other Eldroi to bolster his power. The building blocks of the world served him. They always had.

He grabbed the Dark with his mind and bent it to his will.

And took the dragon with him.

Harkandos forced them into the swirling dark vortex he'd called and pushed them through Noktos's very heart. The dragon screamed. Harkandos clenched his teeth.

And they were gone.

Chapter Forty-Four
LORELLE

Lorelle had faced death many times, but never had she been so helpless. A half-dozen Nox held her completely immobile as one of them sucked the life from her. She could feel her life-force going. The golden lock at her brow flared brightly as she cried out. They would drain her dry, and she would die.

And then the horror would really begin.

Her low wail seemed to come from far away, the despairing sound of her heart. The bloodsucker suddenly, surprisingly, pulled away from her, his head snapping upright at the sound, and Lorelle realized the wail was not hers. It was coming from somewhere else.

It wasn't the cowed prisoners below. They'd been shocked silent at the brutal murder of the crying woman. It wasn't Rhenn; she still struggled and choked against the skeletal hand of Tovos.

The keening grew louder, and N'ssag winced, backing away from Lorelle. He stumbled into his throne and sat down hard, hands going to his ears. The Nox holding Lorelle hunched, their grips loosening. They tried to turn their heads away from the noise, tried to protect themselves from it, but it was coming from everywhere.

The keening was hurting them, N'ssag and his Nox, but while Lorelle could hear it, it didn't hurt.

Half the Nox hands released her. The other half went slack, and Lorelle twisted free. From their crouched position, two of the Nox gave lackluster swipes at her, but she leapt straight up, did a backflip over their heads and landed on the rail overlooking the pit of prisoners.

"No!" N'ssag wailed. He writhed on the throne, curled up, feet scrabbling, hands to his ears, but he stared through slitted eyes at Lorelle. "Don't let her go!"

Lorelle landed on the narrow rail and sprinted around its curve, away from the writhing Nox. None of them seemed interested in obeying their master at the moment, and she took full advantage. She reached the far side of the room and leapt toward Rhenn.

Tovos turned his single blazing eye toward Lorelle—

Then the keening hit him. He grunted, staggering back, and dropped Rhenn. She gasped, sucking in a breath, back against the wall. She recovered quickly, scrabbling backward on her good hand and her feet like a crab, then spun and bounced upright, snatching her fallen sword in the same motion.

Lorelle landed in the hallway next to her. Behind her, the Nox were recovering. One of them, seemingly less affected than the others, ran toward them.

"What is it?" Rhenn rasped as they came together.

Lorelle shook her head. She didn't know. The time for speculation was later. What she did know was that if they didn't get the noktum cloak back, there would *be* no later.

"Get her!" N'ssag leapt forward and clenched the rail in his dirty fingers. The keening had faded. N'ssag still hunched his head into his shoulders like he was afraid it would return, but he pointed at Lorelle furiously, finger shaking.

A single Nox popped around the corner and leapt high,

coming down on Rhenn from above. She was a blur as she spun and chopped him in half before his outstretched fingers could reach her.

The long stream of blood turned to red mist, then to a red glow. The crimson plume seemed to extend from the end of the sword. It hovered there for a moment, then the sword sucked the cloud inside itself. The gemstone on the pommel swelled with light.

Rhenn shuddered. Her broken right arm twisted, righted itself, mending, straightening. It didn't heal completely, but it no longer looked like a mangled stick.

"We'll never escape without the cloak," Lorelle said. "We need—"

Tovos waved a hand, teeth gritted, and pointed his skeletal finger at them. The stone floor flowed up Lorelle's feet like water. She gasped, tried to leap away, but it hardened around her ankles, sticking her where she was.

"No!"

Rhenn grunted as the stone grabbed her, too, and she yanked hard. Her right foot ripped free, sending crumbles of stone skittering across the floor, but the stone grew so fast on her left leg that it was already to her knee before she could shift her balance and pull.

So she pushed down, stomping—

It didn't work. The floor swallowed her left leg to the hip, and then swallowed her right again, streaking up to her thigh, hardening.

"Don't hurt her! Do not hurt my queen!" N'ssag shouted.

Lorelle couldn't hear the keening anymore. Whatever it had been, it had run its course. N'ssag, the Nox, and Tovos no longer seemed under attack. N'ssag hollered about his "queen," and the rest of the Nox bounded up the hall, almost upon them.

Tears of frustration filled Lorelle's eyes as she twisted, struggled. It couldn't end like this. So swift. So terrible. There had to be something else they could do. She cast about, searching for an answer.

The Giant raised his hand—

The noktum cloak unwound from his forearm and shot toward Lorelle like a Sleeth. At first, Lorelle thought it had something to do with the Giant's next attack. Then the Giant hollered through its ruined mouth.

Not a victory cry. A shout of fury.

Time seemed to slow, and the pieces clicked together for Lorelle. The cloak ... The keening ...

"Vohn!" she and Rhenn shouted at the same time.

The cloak whipped around Lorelle's shoulders. N'ssag wailed. The Giant charged. The Nox leapt.

The cowl draped forward over Lorelle's head, and she heard a familiar voice flowing over her mind like a gentle wind.

"Let's get out of here, yes?" Vohn said.

Lorelle's grateful sob replaced any words she might have spoken.

She and Rhenn swirled into the Dark.

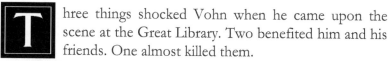

CHAPTER FORTY-FIVE
VOHN

Three things shocked Vohn when he came upon the scene at the Great Library. Two benefited him and his friends. One almost killed them.

The first was seeing Lorelle held down by a horde of Nox, her blood sprayed across her own neck with a Nox bloodsucker clinging to her back, gulping greedily. He thought he was witnessing the death of his friend, and it made him to do something he didn't know he could do.

He attacked them with a banshee scream.

The response was pure denial, an anguished cry over being too late. If he'd been in his corporeal form, it would have been an impotent shout.

In his banshee form, it was deadly.

It slammed into the Nox and N'ssag like a club. The Nox withered, dropping Lorelle, and N'ssag scrambled against the back of his throne like a child who didn't want to take his medicine.

As shocking as the sudden banshee scream was to Vohn, he

took advantage of it instantly. He turned the shriek on Tovos, and in seconds, the thing had dropped Rhenn also. His friends were reunited.

He'd expected them to use the noktum cloak once they were together, but then he realized Lorelle didn't have it. It was wrapped around the Giant's forearm.

As the Nox howled and leapt after their prey and Tovos wielded his vast magic to trap Lorelle and Rhenn in stone, Vohn called upon his bond with the cloak—it had been his home for months after all—and moved it upon the wind of his body.

The instant it wrapped around Lorelle's shoulders, she activated it. Vohn helped through his connection with the Dark, smoothing the way, helping the process go lightning fast.

Usually, it took a half second for the cloak to wrap up its travelers and transport them. The cloak would enclose them, wrap into itself again and again, and then the travelers would shrivel into a black, folded ball, growing smaller until the ball was no more.

This time, with both Vohn's and Lorelle's wills working upon it, the cloak wrapped around her and Rhenn and they just vanished.

That should have been the end of it. They should have been whisked down the thin portal of the cloak.

But a horrible, powerful force stopped them.

It felt like something had grabbed Vohn's ankles and yanked him to a halt. The grip tightened, and began to haul him backward. The Dark itself was dragging them back to their point of origin, back to N'ssag, his blind prisoners, and bloodsucking Nox.

No, not the Dark. Tovos.

A whispery voice, much like Paralos's, slithered into Vohn's mind, and he knew the same voice spoke to Lorelle and Rhenn.

"The Dark is mine, mortals. Did you think you could use my own domain against me?"

Vohn strained against the Giant's will, and he felt Lorelle join him. He felt Rhenn's distant help as well, less connected, more clumsy. Together, they strained against the force, but it dragged them inexorably backward. It was like being bound to a cart caught in a strong river. It was pulling them in, and there was nothing they could do about it.

It was hopeless.

"*I am master here ...*" Tovos said darkly.

Lorelle screamed in frustration as she fought him. Vohn shrieked his banshee shriek, but it had no effect here, in this place.

They went inexorably backward. Vohn felt the room approaching, the thin portal of the noktum expanding.

Then they stopped again.

Tovos roared in frustration. It was so loud in Vohn's mind it blotted out his thoughts.

Another voice fell over Vohn like a soft blanket, a voice he recognized instantly.

"*Master of the Dark, is it?*"

"*Who?!?*" Tovos blurted.

"*You are a stripling whose only accomplishment was to survive,*" Paralos said. "*All the brave Noksonoi ... All the powerful Noksonoi ... They were taken from the board because they were a threat. You were what was left. They let you live because you weren't a master of anything. Master of the Dark? You are a tattered slave to a mortal mage. I am the Dark.*"

"Paralos!" Vohn shouted.

"*Tovos the Insignificant. Tovos the Forgotten. You were inconsequential two thousand years ago, and you are inconsequential now.*"

"*Betrayer!*"

"*That title has already been given. Call me the true Master of the Dark.*"

"*They will kill you for this! Xos will destroy you! Noktos will—*"

"*Oh yes. Cry foul. Rage impotently. Call out to your betters to do the job you cannot.*" She hissed derisively. "*Go back to your Human master, lackey. You are out of your depth.*"

Vohn, Lorelle, and Rhenn shot forward through the Dark, into the thin portal of the noktum. They heard the howl of Tovos behind them, raging helplessly as his hold dissolved.

They squeezed through the Dark toward wherever Paralos had decided they would go.

And Vohn wondered if it would be better than where they had just left.

Chapter Forty-Six
ELEGATHE

Elegathe strode down the gallery-like walkway that led from the visitors quarters to the place where everything in the sprawling Demaijos palace actually happened. She pushed her eye shades higher up on her nose.

In Usara, Imprevar, and Triada, architects were preoccupied with building upward. It had never occurred to Elegathe to think twice about that. It seemed the logical progression. In the Shadowvar city of Nokte Shaddark, they prided themselves on having the tallest building on the continent, the Great Library with its tower of books.

The Demaijos seemed wholly uninterested in making the tallest building on the continent. The only structures over two stories were the watchtowers guarding larger cities and the eastern-facing Lux walls—enormous, five story white walls that blocked the blinding light of the ever-present Lux, giving some shade to the city's inhabitants.

Instead, the Demaijos loved sprawling structures. The goal, rather than to create something imposing and defensible, seemed to be how artistically the builders could ramble about. Gardens hung from boxes alongside just about every two-story balcony, of which there were many. All the meeting rooms along the outer edge of the palace were open air, separated from the elements only by columns that held up the roof. Inner bedrooms and guest rooms had doors and full walls, but expressly for privacy, not for protection against the weather. There were no seasons in Demaijos, not the way Usara had seasons. The winter was only ten degrees colder than the summer. It was a land of eternal warmth and light.

The Demaijos palace stretched to almost three times the width of the Usaran palace, but it was only two stories tall at its highest, with quaint courtyards filled with the bright blues, purples, yellows, and oranges of natural wildflowers.

When the people of Usara created a new city, they cleared space, cut down trees, churned the land until it behaved the way they wanted it to behave. In Demaijos, one might not even see the entirety of a structure because of how it was planned to coexist next to a great, twisted tree.

The Demaijos loved their land as much as they loved their houses. Everything had its place and lived there in harmony. They loved their people. They loved their way of life.

They did not like foreigners.

Oh, they allowed a wealth of foreigners into their cities for trade and discourse. It wasn't like the rules that King Vamreth laid down, a fear of anything different. No, it was simply that the Demaijos knew for a certainty that they lived in the most abundant, wealthy, beautiful place in the world. They considered it their duty to allow others to witness that beauty. They also encouraged trade, because of course why wouldn't everyone want a little piece of what Demaijos had to offer?

This made Demaijos a wonderful place to trade, to bring goods for sale and to buy goods to carry back to one's homeland. It made Demaijos a wonderful place to visit. Adventurers with a taste for the exotic thrived in these jungle lands. These kinds of visitors were welcomed and given space within the proper parameters.

But a monochromatic woman from the extreme far north come to tell their leaders what they must do with their kingdom was an entirely different matter.

Had Elegathe been an adventurer or trader, the luxurious accommodations would have dazzled her. But she needed access to their leaders, and the Demaijos considered letting her into a serious meeting with their king and his advisors to be the equivalent of letting a peacock into the kitchen to cook for them. They couldn't understand, firstly, why a peacock would want to cook. Secondly, they couldn't conceive of what kind of dish a peacock could cook that they would want.

Elegathe continued down the hallway, trying to keep her temper in check. She had discovered that a meeting had been called today to discuss her. She had not been invited, but she planned to be there anyway. There would be guards, of course. They would try to keep her out, of course. And they would fail, of course.

Not only had she spent the morning reading the *kairoi* to get a sense for their movements, but she had the noktum cloak.

The power of the cloak was dizzying. She could move from one shadow to another, and all it cost her was nearly releasing the contents of her stomach, every time. Elegathe had lost ten pounds since she'd left Imprevar because she didn't eat if she knew she was going use the cloak, and she'd used the cloak frequently in the past month and a half.

She'd been to the Burzagi Tor. In the trance of one of their wise women, she had told them of the coming Dark.

She'd been to Triada, given news of the Dark to the king with the melodramatic flair of a painted player on a stage.

She had visited Nokte Vallark, the bastion of western Shadowvar, who had received her gifts gratefully.

She'd seen the Suivan Lattice, a gravity defying honeycomb of light-filled passages, and had confessed she was a Reader—something that the Luminents embraced and admired. They had listened with somber gravity and had spread the word immediately.

She had visited Taur, where the bull-headed Taur-El had also received her with welcome and grace. The peaceful powerhouses were even more receptive to the Readers. They considered her somewhat of a holy personage, and they did exactly as she asked. In Taur-El culture, they still believed Giants existed, and they had been waiting to hear word of their return, unlike almost every Human culture which stubbornly refused to believe the Giants were more than myths.

She had even visited Luxo Hallath, home of the Brightlings, a quiet and joyful race who were difficult to communicate with. They had treated her like an exotic bauble, and she still wasn't sure if she had impressed upon them the danger of what was coming.

In each place, she had distributed the gifts Nhevalos had provided.

She had visited Nokte Shaddark as well, but the great city was already lost. For the Shadowvar of that city, the war was over. They had been swallowed by the noktum. The *kairoi* she had read glowed with death and destruction. She dared not even enter the noktum to see what had become of them. Every future where she set foot in Nokte Shaddark showed her blood splashing on a wall, showed her falling to the floor. This was where Darjhen had died, and she knew if she followed his path into that benighted city, it would be where she died as well.

Nokte Shaddark was the first casualty of the war, and Elegathe feared it would not be the last. But she swore that if another city fell, it wasn't going to be because she hadn't done her part in preparing its leaders.

Demaijos was her final stop, and she'd be damned if it would be a failure. She'd waited long enough for diplomacy. It was now time to dazzle them a bit.

Strangely, despite the ever-present heat in Demaijos, many people wore cloaks. Of course, they weren't the full-body cloaks Usarans used to keep themselves warm and ward off the rain. The Demaijos wore half-cloaks, not for warmth but for the cowls to keep the light of the Lux at bay. They also wore clever spectacles, not for seeing more clearly like Elegathe's, but for blocking the sun. They were called "Lux shades" or "eye shades." These eye shades were made of smoked glass of various colors to cut the light of the Lux. It made it easier to see in the continuous brightness and Elegathe, already used to using spectacles, had taken to them immediately. It was practically impossible to navigate the blinding city without them.

Her eye shades were a dark blue, which gave a cool tinge to everything she viewed. The one advantage to the ever-present, blinding light was that everything dropped a harsh, black shadow across the landscape.

More shadows meant more points of departure for someone wearing a noktum cloak.

As Elegathe approached the royal wing of the palace, she eyed the two guards who stood by the pillars of the royal meeting room, and they saw her. She was probably too far away for them to see the expression on her face, but she smiled at them anyway just as she stepped into the harsh shadow of an enormous pillar that was at least four times as wide as she was.

Once the shadow fell over her, she activated the cloak. The familiar swirling captured her, and she felt like she was twisting down a drain. Having a visual fix of the destination was critical for properly using the cloak. A point on a map could work in a pinch, but there was always the danger that there wouldn't be a shadow in the desired place. Nhevalos said it was possible for a traveler to get stuck in the "swirlworld" of the cloak's transportation and never emerge. Blind jumping was one way to do this.

So the fix was important, and there were three ways to obtain a fix. The first was line of sight. The second was a finely detailed rendering of the location. The third was your memory of a place you'd already been.

Elegathe didn't have a rendering of the king's meeting room, but during one of her attempts to reach them, she'd come close enough to see inside the open doors. She'd seen the far wall and its shadows. She'd seen the table in the center of the room.

She focused on these things now, putting herself in the darkest corner of the room that she'd glimpsed. The gut-twisting sensation rippled through her, but it was made easier by the numerous times she'd done this and the fact that she hadn't eaten anything in fifteen hours.

The bright world of the outer rooms vanished.

And after the horrible swirling transition, she stood in the corner of the meeting room. The king and his seven advisors spoke in lively tones. Elegathe had studied the Demaijos culture before she'd traveled here. This was the king's Council of Masters, which would include the masters of Builders, Domestics, Foreign Affairs, Military, Spirits, Trade, and Treasury.

"... some monochrome from the north," the king was saying. "Give her a box of papayas, put her on a boat, and send her back to Triada."

"Hear hear," said a blocky man with rough hands the size of his head. He wore a white, sleeveless garment that looked something like an apron, and his arms bulged with muscles. He seemed to be paying attention to a rumpled sheaf of papers on the table between those enormous hands. Elegathe had not seen this man before, but he was clearly the Master of Builders.

"I do not think we should be so quick," said a thin man almost directly in front of Elegathe, his back to the shadows that hid her. He was the Master of Foreign Affairs. She'd met him when she had arrived, and he'd come to see her days later only after her third request hadn't been answered satisfactorily. He was on the furthest side of the table from the king, and if proximity to the king denoted one's importance, it spoke volumes about where the Master of Foreign Affairs ranked. "The woman represents the King of Triada, and I believe she has contacts not only to him, but also to the Luminents. That is something that could be quite useful. The Luminents are reluctant to trade. This could be—"

"And where did you hear that?" an even taller, thinner man

with a hawk-nose asked. He sat on the right hand of the king.

"I have contacts in many places," the Master of Foreign Affairs said, lifting his chin. His tone tightened. These two did not like each other.

The next man to speak wore cool, wide strips of blue linen, which was an odd—or extremely stylish—choice that indicated he was probably the Master of Trade. "Ksenin is correct. We could stand to gain much if we accede to her audience. I have also heard she was behind our new trade agreement with Triada."

"Let her stand next to our king?" said a tall, rangy woman halfway up the table. She had a brief top that barely covered her breasts and an X harness across her chest. She was well-muscled and her bare skin was as dark as ebony. She had a long sword slung across her back, and her narrow waist was strapped with two belts, a short sword on one side and a dagger on the other. The Master of Military, no doubt.

"She wouldn't have to stand next to him—"

"A monochrome comes from the north, talking about doom and death, and your solution is to give her access to the king ..." The Master of Military looked like she'd bitten a lemon.

"You act as though we've never given a foreigner an audience with the king."

"We shouldn't—"

"She's a whore," said a portly woman with a thick book open beneath her pudgy fingers. She was regarding something on the page, and she didn't look up. That had to be the Master of Treasury.

The Master of Foreign Affairs bristled. "Well, that is about as rude as—"

"My apologies," the Master of Treasury cut him off without an ounce of contrition. "I *heard* she was a whore. The libertine prince of Imprevar pulled another plaything from the streets, as he does. She is his most recent."

"I heard that he had made moves to marry her."

"And yet she is here," Treasury murmured. "He offers to

marry her and she gallivants off to the furthest kingdom on the continent. Does that sound like a fiancé? No, it sounds like a whore."

"She's simply a ..." Foreign Affairs began again, but seemed unable to come up with a proper description for Elegathe.

"She's a what?" Military asked pointedly. "This is my concern. I am just now hearing that this monochrome has been seen in Lumyn, Triada, and Imprevar. And I have a report of someone matching her description causing a stir in Nokte Vallark. Those kingdoms are not close to each other, and these reports have trickled in over the last couple of months. Tell me, how did she get to all of these places in that time? No ship is that fast. And now she is here. No one knows exactly who she is. No one knows exactly *what* she is. I don't like this at all, Your Majesty."

"I believe she is a Reader," a quiet voice interjected thoughtfully. The man with long gray hair and a long beard across the table from the Master of Foreign Affairs finally spoke. He was dressed in clean white robes with embroidery at the collar, which opened halfway down his muscled brown chest. The Master of Spirits. "There are writings ..."

"A Reader?" the king asked. "What is a Reader?"

"Loremasters, Your Majesty. Fortune tellers."

"Fortune tellers?" Military frowned.

Spirits spread his hands calmly. "Perhaps fortune tellers has the wrong flavor. I am not talking about charlatans who deceive the ignorant public. I am talking about Lore Mages."

A silence fell over the room.

"I thought Lore Magic was a myth," the king said.

"I do not believe so," Spirits said. "It is perhaps the most difficult of the streams of magic to master, which may be a reason we have no Lore Mages in Demaijos. Or, perhaps, those who do know this magic keep their gifts hidden. I calculate that for someone who has the power to see the future, hiding would be a simple thing to do. Regardless, there are writings that say the Readers are reputed to have Lore Magic."

"These Readers see the future?" the king said.

"That is what I have read. I have never met a Reader, Your Majesty. But it might behoove us to, at least for a moment, allow that they might exist. And if one did exist, this might be what she would do."

"What, exactly, is she doing? Do what?"

"Warning us of a future event."

The king had looked somewhere between bored and annoyed until then. For the first time, a crack appeared in the boredom. Elegathe decided it was time to make her entrance.

She lifted her hand and touched her bracelet, which had a tiny symbol of Noksonon on it. It was a weapon from Rauvelos's vault she'd decided to keep in reserve in case of exactly an instance like this. She ran her finger around the symbol in a clockwise motion, quickly.

As small as her movement was, it caught the eye of the Master of Military. The dangerous-looking woman spun, drawing her short sword almost as quickly as Khyven. One of her daggers flew straight and true, but it hit the sudden wall of wind conjured by the bracelet. The dagger spun past and clanged against the wall behind Elegathe.

"That is exactly why I am here," she said, moving into the light.

A collection of gasps ran through the group. The snotty Master of Treasury, so seemingly unflappable before, almost fell out of her chair. Foreign Affairs knocked his over as he stood up and spun about. The mouths of both Trade and Domestics opened in big *O*s.

Military charged, and Elegathe stepped backward into the shadow and activated the cloak. She vanished and rematerialized in the shadow of a pillar just behind the king. She walked forward calmly as though nothing was out of the ordinary. On the far side of the room, Military stumbled as her target vanished. She recovered and spun, looking for Elegathe.

Elegathe stepped forward and set a light hand on the shoulder of the king.

"I beg you listen to me, Your Majesty," she said. It was a daring move, putting her hand on the royal person, but Elegathe didn't have time to win their trust. She had to shock them.

Military froze, seeing Elegathe's move as an implicit threat, of course. Elegathe now had a hand right next to the king's throat. If she'd had a poison needle—poison being quite popular in Demaijos—the king would be dead before Military could let fly another dagger.

"I am not a threat to you," Elegathe said. "I am on a mission, and that mission is to warn you, to arm you, and to prepare you for what is coming. Yes, I am a Reader. Yes, I have been to all the places you have mentioned and more. I am an instrument of salvation, but in order for my words, my gifts, to serve you, you must embrace what I am saying, as difficult as it may be to believe."

She had their attention now. The expressions on each of their faces were uniquely different, ranging from controlled fury on Military's face to calm interest on Spirit's face and everything in between. Elegathe thought Treasury might flee screaming. She gripped her chair, her pudgy jowls quivering.

"You live in the light," Elegathe continued. "It is the way of the Demaijos and it has served you for centuries, but it will not help you in the days ahead. The Dark is coming, and if you are not prepared, it will consume you."

The assemblage said nothing, but the king finally spoke.

Elegathe's first impression of the king had been that he was an incautious man who was more interested in comfort and diversions than in matters of gravity. Men of selfish appetites rarely had courage. Their fears centered around losing their pampered lives. She had expected the king to shiver under the imagined threat the Master of Military was certain Elegathe represented, standing as close was she was to him.

But the king surprised her by remaining calm, and by asking the intelligent question. "How many of you are there? How many Readers?"

"A few dozen."

"And they are all carrying out this same mission? They are all like you, going from city to city?"

"None are like me. Not quite."

"Why?"

"There are reasons."

"Hrm ..." The king grunted in disappointment, but he continued. "And why would you help us?"

"To save the mortals of Noksonon."

"The *mortals*? As opposed to the immortals ..."

"As opposed to the Giants."

The Master of Domestics snorted in derision. "You come here with a fairy tale, that is your important news? You want us to *trust* you, yet you threaten our king, promise doom for our country, and you talk of myths?"

"Wait," Spirits said. "There are writings that speak of the return of the Giants, of guarding against a future war."

"This from the *keeper* of fairy tales," Domestics growled, crossing his arms.

"You're saying the Giants are coming?" the king asked.

"Yes," Elegathe said.

"And the Dark. What does that mean? The Dark is coming. The Dark is here. It is locked in constant battle with the Lux."

"And it will win. The Giants will bring the Dark," Elegathe said.

"The Dark has tried to conquer the Lux since the beginning of time. And failed. Why at this moment would something as immutable as the sun suddenly change?"

"Because now is the time. Because the Lux is not as immutable as the sun. Because these forces you think of as eternal were made by the Giants. And the Giants can unmake them."

"I don't believe it," Domestics growled.

"Let me try a different argument, Your Majesty. What can it hurt?"

"What can what hurt?"

"To allow me to bring these gifts to you. To allow me to

teach one of your number how to use them so that they may teach others, to show you how to keep from being helpless when your world changes?"

The king was silent for a long moment. "What if you are wrong?"

"I'm not."

"You can't be certain of that."

"I can, in fact. This moment was one of three futures I read in the kairoi. It was not my first choice, but other things did not fall into place. For instance, I saw that in this meeting, your Master of Military would attack me three times. It showed me that your Master of Spirits has a granddaughter on the way. He thinks she will be born two weeks from now, but she will come tomorrow. It showed me your Master of Trade has two clear paths away from this room. One will lead to his death by drowning." She glanced at Trade. "Do not go to the docks today sir. Not today."

Every single person she'd named had gone still, eyes wide.

"And your Master of Domestics doesn't want any interference because he is currently stealing from you. In tandem with your Master of Treasury. Any disruption like the kind I bring will interfere with his plans. This is a primary motivation and why he so vociferously opposes me."

Domestics's dark skin reddened, and he began spluttering. "This is outrageous! She is a foreign devil who spouts lies, Your Majesty!"

"It is time to clean your house, King Vnisin, because it is time to strengthen your defenses in a way you have never imagined. You and your forbears built your kingdom on protecting yourself from—and utilizing—the light. You must think differently. You must do it soon."

The king flicked his gaze from Domestics to Treasury—who looked stunned—then back to Military again. He narrowed his eyes, then glanced at Elegathe. "Ayselyn has only attacked you twice."

Elegathe smiled slightly. "That is true. But I haven't left yet,

Your Majesty."

"Ayselyn, I order you not to attack this woman."

Ayselyn's eyes flashed, and she reluctantly nodded. But Elegathe had read the *kairoi* of this moment. That was an order the warrior woman would disobey. Her third attack, however, would not be designed to kill, but to incapacitate. Ayselyn wanted Elegathe in her torture chamber; she wanted answers.

Elegathe was finished, and she waited. Silence filled the room.

Finally, the king spoke. "Very well."

"You will thank yourself for this, Your Majesty. I will meet you here tomorrow."

"Why not now?"

"Because that's not the way it happens."

He didn't like that answer, and when Elegathe stepped away, Ayselyn made her move. A clever weapon of Demaijos make flew from her hand, spinning. Three steel balls slightly smaller than a fist connected to each other by strong cords flew at Elegathe. It was a binding weapon, meant to wrap around her legs or arms and tie them up, and Ayselyn was incredibly fast.

The noktum cloak was faster, though. Elegathe activated it and saw the bolo fly over her head as she folded into the cloak. Then that was all she saw.

The cloak took her into the Dark, twisted her through the magic realm of Noktos, the long-dead king of the Giants, and then released her.

The walls, ceiling, and floor of Tarventin's bedroom unraveled before her like they were painted on wrapping paper. They opened one at a time, pushing back the darkness until the room was fully formed and her vertigo subsided. She drew a breath, standing in the shadows beside the balcony. It was early evening in Imprevar, and the purple line along the dark horizon told her that the sun had set less than an hour ago. It had been bright daylight in Demaijos, of course, because there was always bright daylight in Demaijos.

Tarventin sat as his desk, poring over maps by the glow of

an oil lamp. She paused a moment and watched him. He had set weights along the edges of the maps, which always wanted to curl up, and he'd set markers along certain routes between the crown city of Imprevar and the most prominent noktums. The fortifications. The first protections built against what was coming.

In the past month, Tarventin had grown a beard. The lazy curls on his head were blond, but his beard was tawny, like there were redheads somewhere in his heritage. She loved it.

"How is it coming?" she murmured.

Tarventin looked up quickly, blinked, then a smile spread across his face. "I don't know if I'll ever get used to that," he said in his deep, rumbling voice. She loved his voice. He could recite a builder's list of materials to her, and it sounded like poetry. It comforted her, just the sound of it. Already she could feel the muscles in her neck easing after her confrontation with the Masters of Demaijos.

She had told him who she was after his father died. She hadn't told him she was the reason his father was dead, and she hadn't mentioned Nhevalos. But she'd told him just about everything else. He'd been stunned, but he'd accepted it. He was in love with her, after all, as planned. She had seen it all unfolding. It was why he had to be king, and not his father.

She hadn't planned to fall in love with *him*, though. She hadn't planned to be … happy.

It was absurd. Elegathe had spent her whole life in a ruthless pursuit of her ambitions. Attraction and sexuality weren't things to be used for happiness. They were to be used to advance her station among the Readers, to manipulate others to serve her purposes.

But now she had a home, of all the most ridiculous things. She looked forward to returning to Imprevar, looked forward to returning to Tarventin's arms. He had accepted her.

"How was Demaijos?" he asked. "Did they listen?"

"They will."

"Of course they will. You are a force of nature, my love. I

almost feel sorry for them."

"Do you?"

He stood up and came to her, moving like a lion, languid and sure of himself. He took her in his arms. "No," he murmured. "Not really."

"I think you should feel sorry for me," she said, tracing his chin.

"Oh?"

"I haven't seen you in three days."

"Ah."

She gazed up at him, let him see her heart in her eyes. He lifted her up in his arms and carried her to the bed. She unclipped the noktum cloak and let it fall to the floor, a silken pile of dark she left behind. It could stay behind. For now, she could ignore it and everything it meant.

"I missed you," she murmured as he laid her on the soft mattress. "I miss you every time."

"Then we're lucky ..." He kissed her and she wrapped her arms around him.

"I want it to last forever," she whispered as his lips moved to her neck.

"Then be here with me. Right now. Let's take our forever."

She let out a contented sigh and closed her eyes. They still had a moment, and a person could live an entire lifetime in the right moment.

The Dark could wait.

Chapter Forty-Seven
HARKANDOS

Harkandos appeared in the shadows of the mountains surrounding The Iluit San, and five others appeared with him, unfolding from the darkness. Avektos shuffled out of the dark through the snow, his thick legs perpetually bent to hold his rotund girth. The Noksonoi smith would have been fifteen feet tall if he stood up straight, but he hunched somewhere around twelve feet, his round head jutting forward like a turtle's and his lanky arms stretching almost to the ground.

Mendos came next, looking like a parody designed to be Avektos's opposite. The ridiculously thin Noksonoi stood ramrod straight, his thin-lipped mouth a diagonal slash. He was fourteen feet tall and as narrow as a lodge pole, with a pointed nose and lanky black hair hanging down around his long, angular face. He looked like he'd been carved from a faceted gemstone that had turned into flesh, so sharp were his cheekbones, jawline, and chin. All Noksonoi knew how to work the five streams of magic, but Mendos was especially good at Love Magic. In the war, he had created enough havoc that it had almost turned the tide. Harkandos felt if they'd had a dozen of him, if the Human armies had been convinced to simply fight each other, it would have won the war.

Orios stepped out from behind Mendos, looking down at The Iluit San. She wore black robes which were not only made of the same material as a noktum cloak but could perform the same function. Her eyes had no irises, no pupils. They were black pools with a dozen pinpoints of light shining within them, like a starry night sky. She was the one Harkandos would be watching the closest. Orios was easily the smartest of this bunch and potentially the most treacherous. Harkandos had no doubt that she was the first of them, at a mere glance, who realized where they were. Orios was a master of all the streams—like Harkandos himself—and saw herself as his competitor.

Harkandos did not, of course.

Though Orios studied much, and had talent, she was not in Harkandos's class. None were. Orios was merely one more arrogant Eldroi who thought more highly of her skills than they warranted. It made her useful, but only a threat if he didn't keep an eye on her.

She stepped forward, raising her chin as though judging the snowy crevasse, as though she was going to suggest that Harkandos had made a mistake. That this wasn't, in fact, The Iluit San.

If she was thinking that, however, she did not suggest it aloud and thereby saved her own life.

Next, Jai'ketakos slunk out of the dark like a beaten dog, separating himself from the group and slithering a distance away. He'd done a poor job hiding his displeasure these past two days. Oh, Harkandos knew the dragon had considered fleeing, but he hadn't tried even once. Jai'ketakos assumed—and rightly so—that Harkandos would vaporize him if he tried to flee. He had a healthy deference to his betters, and it had saved his life. So far.

Raos came last, scuttling out of the shadows and scrambling up the cliff nearby, her six extra appendages stabbing into the ice and snow and holding her aloft. She could walk upright if she chose, but she always clung to a vertical surface if it was available. Raos had birthed the Cakistros, and she'd been subsumed by her passion. She became as influenced by her own creations as they were by her. Shortly after making them, she'd begun making modifications to herself to emulate them. That was where the six black spider-like legs sprouting from her back had come from. Her normal legs dangled limply in the air as her longer, more powerful limbs took her where she wanted to go. Her black, tangled hair hung about her face, flowing down around her bulbous, insect-like eyes. She was an impressive spectacle.

She was also quite mad.

But she was a Noksonoi, so he would use her. These five were the only surviving Eldroi on the continent, and by his forbears, he would use them all to recapture the continent. Failing that, he would hurl them each into Nhevalos's face to die one at a time. One way or another, they would serve him.

Harkandos had spent the last two days finding them. Avektos and Mendos had buried themselves and gone into the long sleep, using their ageless advantage over mortals. They had planned, Harkandos supposed, to wait out the centuries until they could awaken and find a new world, perhaps a world wherein the mortals had slain themselves. Perhaps they'd planned to sleep until a moment that the mortals' memories failed them, and they had no idea how to defend themselves.

Or perhaps they had simply planned to sleep the centuries away until they faded into nothing.

He'd found Raos playing the queen of the Cakistros deep within an area of the Great Noktum untouched by mortals. She'd made a little kingdom for herself, somehow convincing herself that she was the unthinking queen of an unthinking race of beasts. It sickened him.

Harkandos had also found Orios in the Great Noktum, far on the other side by Nokte Vallark. She had been honing her skills by manipulating the Shadowvar from a distance, being careful not to alert them to her presence.

Apparently, such covert cowardice appealed to her. It did not impress Harkandos.

None of them had wanted to come with him any more than Jai'ketakos had. Yet all of them had recognized him, even the seemingly-brainless Raos. None had the stupidity to gainsay him.

Well, Lelakos had. The sixth potential addition to Harkandos's group, Lelakos, had told Harkandos what he could do with his plan in no uncertain terms. Harkandos had left his ashes in the forest. In no uncertain terms.

And he'd let the others see him do it.

Harkandos *would* use these louts one way or another. If they refused, in life, to be useful against Nhevalos and the damned mortals who had overrun his beloved Noksonon then they would, in death, be an example for the others.

In the end, Harkandos had scoured the continent for every single Noksonoi that Nhevalos had left alive two thousand years ago.

"The Iluit San," Orios said, and her voice grated on Harkandos. "The infamous Slaughter Box. Whatever are we doing here?"

"I'll scout the perimeter of the mountains," Jai'ketakos said.

"You'll stay where you are, dragon," Harkandos said softly enough that he could have been talking to himself, but he knew that the ears of dragons were incredibly sensitive. Jai'ketakos heard him.

Reluctantly, the dragon set his butt back down into the snow and shivered. Smoke curled up from his nostrils.

Mendos and Avektos gathered at the edge of the cliff. Raos twitched her head back and forth as though she was sniffing the wind.

Two thousand years ago, this was a land of warm granite cliffs where the skies danced with lightning and rain slashed down in the afternoons.

Now the peaks were crusted with snow five feet deep. Great rivers began below the snow line, creating the green valleys that led all the way to Nokte Shaddark.

Harkandos had cast the massive travel spell seven times, each time with more passengers. None of the rest of them could have cast that spell even once, save perhaps Orios. And to do it half a dozen times would have driven all of them into a resting sleep. Not Harkandos. His rage burned away any fatigue. It was as though he'd been unable to act for so long that there was no amount of action that could weary him. He'd lost two thousand years of his life, and he planned to make up every second of it in a matter of days.

Once, the crevasses below had been teeming with screaming mortals who had been gathered to serve the purpose of discovery. This was where Noktos had created the original mortal races: the Taur-El, Luminents, Shadowvar, Brightlings and the Delvers.

Harkandos had taken over stewardship of the Slaughter Box mostly to play with mortals with impunity. It was only when the war began to go poorly that he thought to try and create something that could help the disjointed and annoying fraternity of the Noksonoi.

The only Noksonoi that Harkandos remotely admired was the father of them all, Noktos himself. Noktos had brought the tribe here successfully after the schism of the Eldroi on Lathranon. He had fought off Nirapama and her legions through brilliant and powerful spells like the noktum. He had sacrificed his own life to bolster his creation when the Pyranoi had dropped the Lux on them. He had put a piece of himself into the Sword of Noksonon so that he would live on, so that his name would be synonymous with the slaying of the most powerful Eldroi in history. Noktos had made it a death sentence for any Eldroi who thought to invade Noksonon.

"Might I ask why you have brought us here?" Orios asked snootily.

"You may not."

A snarl formed on Orios's lip. Harkandos caught the expression in his peripheral vision and turned to face her.

"Do you have more to say?" he asked.

She glared at him.

"Go ahead," he said softly. "If you feel this is your moment, Orios, then show me your strength. Show me that your heart's desire is also the truth. Kill me. Go ahead ..."

Orios's eyes flashed. Slowly, painfully, her snarl eased. Her eyes took on a dead quality, like she'd forced them to go flat. "Of course not, Lord Harkandos. I was merely curious."

"Keep your curiosity to yourself." Harkandos pulled the magic through himself and the winds lifted him off the snow. He floated down into the crevasse. With a wave, he pulled more magic into himself and commanded fire to come from the frigid air. He brought the heat without the flame, inverting the air. The snow on the cliff walls and down below hissed and melted until the bottom of the crevasse was a lake. Then he evaporated the water to steam. It hissed upward, filling the mountainside with white. Soon, it cleared, and Harkandos descended onto the warm, dry canyon floor.

This was where he had put the finishing touches on his new creation, a game-changer in the war. Like Noktos, many Noksonoi had created new creatures, much like crazy Raos and her Cakistros. But none of those creatures served Noksonon like Noktos's originals had.

That was what Harkandos had aspired to. He didn't want to build a new creature simply to show he could do it. He didn't want to create something to merely assuage his curiosity. When the armies of the mortals had slain nearly half their number, he knew it was time to put his power to the same use that Noktos once had.

During the tribal wars, Noktos had created the noktum to plunge the continent into darkness so that any invaders would be at a disadvantage when fighting its defenders, who had been equipped with talismans to operate in the dark.

During the war with the mortals, the Eldrovan had determined that what had worked once would work again. They decided to complete Noktos's work, so they sent not just one, but two souls into the noktum to bond with it as Noktos had done, to increase the pressure on the Lux until it was finally overcome, destroyed, and darkness reigned again in Noksonon.

They had failed.

No one had had the time to investigate what had gone wrong because the Human armies had overrun three Noksonoi strongholds already, and had surrounded two more. The useless Eldrovan had failed, but Harkandos had determined he wouldn't. What Noktos had tried to accomplish, he would finish.

The continent would be covered in darkness again. Once the cockroaches felt the dark all around them, they would scatter, blind and helpless, and Harkandos would unleash bloody death upon them.

That was what he had been working on here in the Slaughter Box. He had been creating a new lifeform from the building blocks of reformed Humans, Taur-Els, Shadowvar, and Luminents. He'd been on the verge of success when a messenger had come to him, had delivered to him the one thing he'd wanted more than to bring Noktos's ancient plan to fruition.

He'd been delivered the name of the traitor.

For months, there had been a rumor that one of their own, one of the Noksonoi, had been working against them, had been using their own secrets to give advantages to the mortal uprising. It had been a barely conceivable notion, but were it true it would explain much.

And the name of the betrayer was Nhevalos.

This soft-spoken, magically irrelevant wisp of a nothing had broken from the Noksonoi and given secrets to their enemies, had probably given them training in accessing the streams of magic.

The revelation of the traitor had sent Harkandos in a rage. So he had closed up the pocket dimension where he kept his new creations and left them there. Actually, it had been a perfect stopping point in the process. The twenty five mortals he had stuffed in there had needed to incubate in the precise mixture of light and dark for a day or two. That was more than enough time to find Nhevalos, torture him, extract the names of anyone who might be working with him, and burn him one second at a time until every cell of his body screamed in agony.

So Harkandos had chased him, found him, and ...

Well ... The rest, as the mortals said, was history. The scheming Betrayer had led him into a trap, and instead of two days, his experiments had incubated for more than seventeen hundred years ...

That had been unexpected. It could be catastrophic. There were only two possible outcomes for the creatures being left in there for all that time. Either they were dead ...

Or they would be more powerful than Harkandos ever intended.

He shoved the first thought away and focused on the second as he summoned the strength to rip open the secret doorway to his pocket dimension.

He pulled strength from the elements around him. He pulled it from the life-force of the robust Eldroi above him. He pulled it from his own rage.

With a shout, he wrenched open the doorway he'd locked and hidden all those years ago. The side of the cliff separated as though the rock was painted upon a canvas. Lightning spit and crackled around the edges of the pointed, oblong rip, and inside ...

Nothing.

Harkandos's heart fell. They were gone. The twenty-five had perished in their barren world. He'd left them in a place bereft of all nourishment except a miniature Lux that he had created, so they would feed on it, so they would evolve into what was needed.

Now there was nothing. Only absolute blackness.

Damn. He would have to start over. He'd have to steal new mortals, twist them through the same process. His revenge, rather than starting immediately, would have to start years from now.

He gnashed his teeth. So much time. So much more time

lost ...

Harkandos clenched his fists and roared at the sky. He didn't *want* to spend more time. Time was the stealer of hope. Time was the enemy of everything he wanted.

With time, Nhevalos could discover that Harkandos had slipped his trap. With time, Harkandos's reluctant followers would plot their rebellion.

Moving with speed had been Harkandos's great advantage. He had envisioned exactly how it would go, had envisioned the surprise on Nhevalos's face when—

The lightning at one part of the rip flickered and vanished. Harkandos stopped, narrowed his eyes, and studied the rip. One foot-long part of the tear had gone dark.

Then, like a great wind dousing a line of torches, the lightning went dark all around the rip. Harkandos's eyes widened, and his heart leapt.

A lump of dark tumbled out, fell to the earth like a clod of wet dirt. Another followed, and then another. Soon, the lumps of dark mud spewed out one at a time. Harkandos flew backward and watched in surprise.

Even as they tumbled one after the other, the ones that had fallen to the ground rose, uncurling and taking on a roughly Human shape. They turned their flat, featureless faces up toward the sun. There were no eyes, no ears, just dark, flat faces.

With those blunt heads pointed to the sky, holes opened in those faces where their mouths should have been. Moans emitted, and Harkandos realized they were sucking the air.

The day grew dark as though a cloud had passed over the sun. Harkandos craned his neck and looked at the sky.

There were no clouds to block the sun. He looked back at his creations as they continued to tumble out, land, and turn their faces upward.

They weren't sucking air. They were sucking light!

"Yes ..." he growled.

The day grew darker. The black mud balls continued tumbling out of the rip, splatting onto the ground of the crevasse, unfolding, and turning their faces upward.

Harkandos glanced up fiercely at his audience. The five Eldroi stood at the edge of the cliff high above, looking down with different expressions of surprise.

"Oh yes ..." Harkandos looked back at his prizes, his glorious Lighteaters. "But not here, my hungry ones. Not here."

The last of the Lighteaters tumbled out. There were twenty-five, exactly as many as he had put inside.

Harkandos left the rip open. For what he was about to do, he couldn't waste even a flicker of his strength in an attempt to tidy up. The entire ravine, and even the edge where the Eldroi stood, was now as dark as dusk, like a long shadow had spread over everything. The Lighteaters pulled the light from the very air.

"Come with me now." Harkandos summoned his magic. "Let me take you to the place where you will thrive. To the place you were made for ..."

With a roar, he reached into the shadows, pulled the twenty-five Lighteaters, pulled the five Eldroi, pulled himself into the Dark ...

And took them to where they would change the world.

Chapter Forty-Eight
NHEVALOS

The bright spears of light from the Lux, constantly battling Noktos within his master spell, split the sky as they had for thousands of years. Nhevalos stayed half in and half out of his noktum cloak on the ridge that, on one side, overlooked the cave that had once belonged to Jai'ketakos and, on the other side, overlooked the valley that ran right up to the blinding Lux.

This was the moment he had been waiting for. This was the moment when his centuries of planning would dance on the head of a pin. In this moment, the fate of Noksonon would flow into the groove he had made for it.

He had read the *kairoi* only moments before. They had been twisting and changing with every hour, but he had read them, guided them, and the thickest, the strongest *kairoi* had all converged on this place. He wanted to be watching them now, to see if there were any changes, but he didn't dare.

Soon, the most dangerous personages in Noksonon were going to converge on this place. He must be invisible, or the game was up.

If he could have, he would have gone elsewhere, but he had to be in this place to ensure that it all happened exactly as he had foreseen. If something needed to be changed, if he saw a difference that could be curved, he had to be ready. He had to be here.

And so he stayed cloaked and hidden behind the spells he'd carefully constructed to keep himself invisible to even the most potent detect magic spell.

The very noktum shook when the group arrived. A ripple went out from the valley on the other side of Jai'ketakos's cave, and it seemed as if the very world shuddered. Two dozen lumps appeared, as did Harkandos and his retinue of four Noksonoi and one Drakanoi, all pressed into his service.

Nhevalos identified them all. There were no changes from what he'd seen in the kairoi. Everything was exactly as it should be, exactly as it needed to be.

The lumps of dark unfurled, giving soft howls as they faced the Lux. Holes opened in the front of their flat faces.

The spears of the Lux's light, burning into the Great Noktum even as the tides of the Dark tried to devour it, began to curve toward the ground. The more of the little black mud creatures that unfurled and opened their mouths, the more spears of light began to bend toward them. Soon, that light was funneling directly into the open mouths of the mud creatures.

Harkandos's Lighteaters. The war-changing project that Nhevalos had interrupted and saved his victory.

The Lighteaters were simple, unadorned, and unfathomably powerful, just like Harkandos himself. Despite the fact that they were enemies, Nhevalos felt a rush of admiration for Harkandos and his unparalleled ability. It was followed by a rush of jealousy. No other Eldroi, save possibly the great Noktos, had ever created something like this. What Noktos had tried, and failed to do, Harkandos was going to see through to the end.

As the spears of light bent reluctantly into the hungry mouths of the Lighteaters, the Great Noktum began to move. So long locked into a static fight, a battle where neither side could gain ground, the Great Noktum finally had what it wanted.

A break to the deadlock.

As the Lux weakened, the tendrils of the Great Noktum began slithering forward. Just a little at first. Then more.

The moaning intensified, and it seemed the Lighteaters had no end of appetite. The thin spears of light thickened. The Lux responded to the threat and poured more power toward it ...

But when it did, the Great Noktum made its move. Its tendrils attacked vigorously, pushing hard toward the center of the light.

The Lux shuddered. Nhevalos imagined that it tried to pull away from the Lighteaters, but they did not let it go. They pulled more and more light. The Lux shuddered again.

The Great Noktum charged forward as though some enormous being had poured black oil onto the Lux. The light began to fade in this place that had been bathed in light for millennia.

The Lux wavered, shaking like a mirage fighting for its life. The Lighteaters moaned. The Great Noktum surged.

Then, like a wave crashing onto the shore, the Dark obscured the light entirely like a thin skin of black over the pulsing Lux. Tendril after tendril swarmed over it, thick tentacles rising and falling, compounding, overlapping.

A last flash of light emerged, like the last wail of a dying animal ...

And the Lighteaters gobbled it up, holding the power of the Lux, sucking it to themselves.

The Dark obscured the Lux, trapping it in a cocoon with the Lighteaters inside, drawing the endless light into their endless hunger.

Nhevalos let out a breath he hadn't realized he'd been holding. It had actually happened. Though he had seen this moment for almost two thousand years, he had scarcely believed it. The dream of his forbears, the dream of those who had tried to throw off the rebellion of the mortals, had finally come to pass.

The Lux was defeated, buried beneath the power of the Dark.

The board had moved into the endgame now. The pawns were set. The possibilities of victory and defeat were laid out before him.

The Great Noktum would now do what it had been created to do. It had neutralized the Lux, and it would move south, west, east, and north. It would spread to the ends of the continent until everything was swallowed just as it had swallowed the Lux.

Nhevalos stepped back into his cloak and began the teleportation.

It was the time for knights and queens to move into position. And though most would be sacrificed before the end, the outcome would be the same.

Soon, it would be Nhevalos's world, exactly as he had intended.

Chapter Forty-Nine
SLAYTER

Slayter was trying to think, and Khyven was making it difficult.

The Ringer paced back and forth, back and forth like a caged tiger in Slayter's laboratory. At least he'd stopped breaking things. When they'd ridden up to the palace, he'd thrown benches. One of them had been a marble bench, which was now some rather nicely carved broken pieces.

The Knights of the Steel guarding the front of the palace hadn't known what to do. They were supposed to stop anyone from desecrating the palace grounds, but as a Knight of the Dark, Khyven outranked them.

He also scared the hell out of them. At this point, everyone in Usara—and perhaps even Noksonon at large—had heard the name Khyven the Unkillable. The Knights of the Steel had been relieved when Slayter had gestured that they should just let him rage. Two benches and one carriage—the latter belonging to Baron Verland by the crest on the side—had died in Khyven's rage. He had drawn the Mavric iron sword and sliced the wheel completely from the thing, picked it up with one hand and thrown it almost all the way to the outer wall.

It was an impressive tantrum.

Ironically, it was the drawing of the Mavric iron sword that had brought him to his senses. After hurling the wagon wheel, he'd brought the blade up in front of his face and stared at it, like it was talking to him, like it was giving him instructions. The Sword and the man had stayed like that for a painful moment while Slayter thought he might have to intervene. But then, apparently, Khyven had won the battle of wills. Without warning, he whipped the blade away and slammed it back into its sheath.

After that, he'd been relatively subdued. He'd glared at everyone, strode toward the Knights of the Steel and picked Shalure up from where he'd deposited her on the ground before his rage. They stood back, and he'd turned his baleful gaze on Slayter.

"We're taking her to your laboratory?" he had asked Slayter.

Slayter hadn't wanted to take her to his laboratory. Or more to the point, he hadn't wanted to take Khyven to his laboratory. Everything there was breakable. But his laboratory was exactly where Shalure needed to go, and Slayter calculated that if he told Khyven to stay here, another rage would ensue.

So here they were. In his laboratory with all of the breakable things. Shalure's pale body lay upon his stone worktable and Khyven paced, keeping his anger in check as he waited to see what would happen to Lorelle, Rhenn, and Vohn without being able to directly affect the outcome.

Slayter, for his part, was working out several problems. He was trying to diagnose what was wrong with Shalure. Based on Vohn reverting to his banshee state—something he would never have done if he could have avoided it—Slayter deduced that something had forced Vohn's hand, almost assuredly a choice between life and death. Being as how Jai'ketakos was at the castle, it was the logical jump to imagine the dragon had been the life-threatening thing. They hadn't had the story from Vohn yet, but Slayter was ninety-two percent certain the dragon had discovered that Vohn and Shalure were Slayter's friends. That would have been plenty enough to bring down his wrath. A chase ensued, and Vohn would have been forced to desperation.

Cornered, out of options, Vohn had clearly reverted to his banshee state to escape. But that wouldn't have saved Shalure, so it would have had to be ...

"Interesting—" Slayter said aloud.

"What is interesting?" Khyven whirled like Slayter had just spat on his sword.

Slayter frowned.

"What?" Khyven snarled. "What is interesting?"

"I have a very good sleeping spell," Slayter said. "May I suggest you take it?"

"I don't want your sleeping potion!"

"Spell."

Khyven actually showed his clenched teeth. "I don't need to sleep."

"Oh, I don't think it would put you to sleep. In your current state, I think it would barely make you normal."

Khyven put his hand on his steel sword. That would be seven times now, Slayter counted. Seven times Khyven had looked like he'd wanted to kill Slayter.

"They have Lorelle." Khyven seethed. People overcome by emotions loved to restate the obvious, as though stating it for the tenth time would change the meaning somehow.

"Yes."

"Vohn just ... He just ..."

"He went to save her. Would you rather he stay and talked?"

"I can't *do* anything."

"Not true. You destroyed two benches and a carriage. You just haven't done anything useful."

Khyven's eyes widened, and his breathing increased.

"Would you like to help me save Shalure?" Slayter asked.

"I could be there! I could help! Those bloodsuckers, I don't care—"

"You can't be there."

"I could go to the nuraghi, go back to the Great Noktum."

"No you couldn't."

"Rauvelos—"

"Rauvelos is dead."

"Then *you* rework that spell!"

"After we kill the dragon? There's a dragon there."

"Yes," Khyven snarled, his voice seeming to come from a dark well. "Yes, I will kill the dragon. The Sword *wants* to kill the dragon."

Oh, *that* was tantalizing. Slayter very much wanted to explore what it meant that Khyven was starting to speak for the Sword, but Slayter supposed he had a responsibility to keep Khyven from falling into ... well ...into insanity.

"Would you feel better if I went running into the Night Ring?" Slayter asked.

"What?" He looked confused, then he clenched his teeth. "No. Stop it. None of your distracting random comments! We are going back to the nuraghi. Vohn had his chance. Clearly he failed. It's been far too long and we haven't heard from any of them." He started across the laboratory toward Slayter, and he was certain that once Khyven reached him, one of those huge, scarred hands was going to grab his arm, and then Slayter would have no say in which direction his body was going to go.

"It's not random," Slayter said as Khyven arrived.

Khyven grabbed his arm, as predicted. Slayter didn't try to run or pull away. There was no point in that.

"If you were fighting in the Night Ring, and I went running in to help you without any spells whatsoever, what would you say?"

"Shut up. We're going back to the nuraghi."

"You would say, 'Slayter, what are you doing here? Have you lost all equilibrium? Leave now before you get us both killed!'"

"I wouldn't say that."

"True. You wouldn't use the word 'equilibrium'. But something *like* that."

"Come on." He pulled Slayter toward the door. "We aren't just going to sit here and—"

The shadows in the corner of the laboratory began to unfold.

Khyven released Slayter and drew his steel sword.

"No," Slayter said. "It's them."

Rhenn materialized first, stumbling out of the shadows of the northern alcove. Lorelle followed, the cloak pulling back and becoming a normal size.

"Senji's Teeth!" Khyven sheathed his sword and sprinted across the room. He and Lorelle came together and he lifted her in his arms, crushed her to his chest. Her ebony hair flowed over his back. She buried her head in his neck and wrapped her arms around him.

"Khyven ..." she whispered.

"I'm never letting you go. Not ever again." He kissed her, and she kissed him back.

The noktum cloak unclipped from Lorelle's neck and flowed across the room towards Slayter. It circled him, floating down onto his shoulders, and the cowl settled on his head.

"Well, that was successful," Slayter said to Vohn in his mind.

"I may not have long," Vohn replied. *"I don't know when Paralos is going to take me."*

"Paralos? The Giant who—"

"Not now. If we survive this, you and I can swap knowledge until your brain bleeds, but we don't have much time, and we have barely enough time to do what needs doing."

"What needs doing?"

"Rauvelos visited me while everyone was gone. He had prepared weapons for us in the nuraghi—In Castle Noktos."

"Castle Noktos ..." Slayter liked the sound of that.

"Slayter, you have to evacuate the crown city, do you understand me? Rauvelos intended for us to go into the noktum with everyone."

"Into the noktum? Everyone?"

"The Dark is coming. Now listen closely. Rauvelos said there's a vault deep in the castle. The ... The third sub level, he said. The door has the

symbol of Noksonon, and the password is Khyven the Unkillable."

"Well isn't that funny."

"He had strange obsession with Khyven. I think Rauvelos looked at Humans as snacks that he nobly restrained himself from eating. But with Khyven it seemed to be ... kinship. If that doesn't seem bizarre."

"Well it is not only possible but likely that Rauvelos is a Giant in disguise, like Nhevalos was. If Nhevalos could impersonate a Human for years, why couldn't Rauvelos impersonate a bird?"

"Anyway, the vault is apparently filled with magical artifacts that can help us against the coming of the Dark."

"What do they do?"

"This is why I'm talking to you. Rauvelos died before he could tell me what was in there. I don't know how many there are or what they do. You have the best chance of finding out."

"I'll need to catalogue them," Slayter said.

"Paralos took a stand against Tovos, and I got the strong impression that she hasn't ever done that before, that she hasn't ever revealed herself to anyone like that."

"Find the room. Identify the objects. Use them," Slayter said. *"I understand."*

"I don't know what's going to happen ..." Vohn's voice sound a little quieter, like he was backing up.

"Vohn?"

"She calls."

"Just stay here. I'll bring you back like before." Slayter thought to Vohn, then said aloud to Khyven. "The table. Clear it!"

Slayter pointed at one of his three tables, the largest one that Shalure did not currently occupy. Khyven let go of Lorelle, leapt forward and swept everything off the table with his two huge arms. Wood clattered and glass shattered across the floor. Slayter winced.

Well, the table was cleared now.

"She calls ..." Vohn was fading.

"Stay!"

Suddenly, despite the distance, Vohn's voice sounded frightened. *"Oh no ... No no ..."*

"*Vohn!*"

"*This is what he meant ...*"

Then he was gone.

"*Vohn!*"

Khyven stood, hands open like he was going to catch an enemy leaping through a Night Ring door.

"He's gone." Slayter whipped the cloak off and tossed it in Lorelle's direction.

Of course it didn't fall; it floated toward her. She plucked it gracefully out of the air and settled it on her shoulders.

"Get him back," Slayter said. "See if you can get him back. I'll prepare the same spell that—"

Lorelle had been focused intently on Slayter, but her head suddenly jerked and she stared at the doorway. Slayter followed her gaze, as did Khyven, who suddenly had a dagger in his hand.

But there was nothing in the doorway.

"What is it?" Khyven asked.

Now Rhenn did the same thing. She turned toward the doorway like someone was there, but nobody was.

It struck Slayter all at once that they weren't looking at something, they were listening to something.

"Screams," Lorelle murmured. Rhenn leapt toward the doorway, and Khyven was right behind her. They pounded up the steps. Slayter started limping after them, stopped, turned.

Shalure still lay comatose, staring up at the vaulted ceiling. Slayter paused, riffled through his cylinder of spells, then pulled out the right one.

He drew on his life force and cracked the disk. Crumbles of clay fell and orange light flared. A translucent dome of physical protection spread over her.

He turned to the stairway, and Lorelle stood there, waiting for him.

"You are a good man, Slayter," she said softly.

"Good is a relative term. Can you imagine what Vamreth thought was good?"

She shook her head with a warm smile, then wrapped the

noktum cloak around them both.

"Oh but—"

The darkness sucked them in, pulled them through a straw, turned all of Slayter's organs inside out, then flopped them right side in again.

The darkness receded and they stood inside the palace foyer in the shadow of one of the giant pillars. Ahead of them was the soaring archway leading to the courtyard. Both Rhenn and Khyven burst from the stairway that led down to Slayter's laboratory three levels down. Khyven ran into the sunlit patio leading to the edge of the wide, shallow steps that led to the garden. Rhenn stopped short in the shadows, one hand on the hilt of her sword, the other blocking the glare as she peered at the sunlit courtyard.

Slayter bent over and threw up.

"It's not in the city," Khyven said. "It's in the distance."

"Meeting room," Rhenn said.

"Balcony," Khyven agreed.

As one, they shot back into the palace and up the grand staircase.

Lorelle said, "Hang on."

"No, it's really all right. I'll just—"

The darkness took them again. Slayter's organs turned inside out and flopped around in circles like finless fish, then returned to normal, still wobbling.

They stood in the shadow of the main meeting room balcony.

Slayter threw up again.

The door burst open, and Rhenn and Khyven ran to the balcony. Again, Rhenn stopped at the line where light and dark met beneath the balcony's archway. Despite the shadows all around her, despite her grip on the sword Slayter had made to help her resist some of the sunlight, her face began to smoke. Khyven glanced at her quickly, then stepped between her and the sun, partially shielding her.

Lorelle whipped the noktum cloak off and draped it over

Rhenn's shoulders and flipped up the cowl. Rhenn didn't move, didn't seem to feel the burn.

Below in the courtyard, in the city beyond, the dull roar of many voices arose, like the roar of the crowd in the Night Ring. Except these weren't many people whooping in excitement and victory. These were screams of fear.

Slayter righted himself finally, wiped his chin with his sleeve, and hobbled over to them. Next to Rhenn, everyone stood at the edge of light and dark, staring out over the city. Slayter swallowed down bile and tried to see the source of the screams.

At first, he couldn't tell what it was. His initial thought was that some noktum monster was loose in the city. But nothing moved through the streets except people, and they weren't running. They shifted, agitated, pointing at the horizon. Slayter followed the fingers to the horizon. It looked odd. The sky to the south, always a light blue, was a darker blue. Slayter had never seen that color blue in the sky before. The sun, instead of its normal, yellow-tinged white, had turned a custard yellow. It was like the very heavens were ... darker. He put a hand up to shadow his eyes.

The southern horizon was flat, and that wasn't right either. There were mountains to the southwest, rolling hills to the south. The horizon shouldn't be ruler-straight, but the afternoon sun was definitely above a perfectly flat, dark horizon. And it was ... higher than it ought to be.

"What is that?" Khyven asked.

A chill ran through Slayter as he realized the answer to that question.

"The Dark ..." he echoed Vohn's words. "The Dark is coming."

"What *is* that?" Khyven reiterated.

"It's the noktum," Slayter said.

"That's not the noktum. The noktum is to the west."

"Not this noktum ..." Slayter's mind raced with everything that was about to happen, a ringing lack of ideas about what might be done about it, and how many moving parts were now in motion to save even this single city, let alone all of Rhenn's kingdom.

"Speak plainly!"

"The Great Noktum is coming."

"To Usara?" Khyven pressed.

Slayter paused.

"Everywhere. The Lux is gone. The noktum is taking the continent."

The End

Of

Slayter and the Dragon

Continue your Eldros Adventure in the next book in the series:

Bane of Giants

by

Todd Fahnestock

About the Author

Todd Fahnestock is an award-winning, #1 bestselling author of fantasy for all ages and winner of the New York Public Library's Books for the Teen Age Award. *Threadweavers* and *The Whisper Prince Trilogy* are two of his bestselling epic fantasy series. He is a founder of *Eldros Legacy*—a multi-author, shared-world mega-epic fantasy series—three-time winner of the Colorado Authors League Award for Writing Excellence, and two-time finalist for the Colorado Book Award for *Tower of the Four: The Champions Academy* (2021) and *Khyven the Unkillable* (2022). His passions are great stories and his quirky, fun-loving family. When he's not writing, he travels the country meeting fans, gets inundated with befuddling TikTok videos by his son, plays board games with his wife, plots future stories with his daughter, and plays vigorously with Galahad the Weimaraner. Visit Todd at toddfahnestock.com.

Author's Note

So while I was writing *Slayter and the Dragon*, I was a wreck. An inspired wreck, but a wreck nonetheless. I took a risk, you see, in writing this the way I did, and the only way to know if it panned out is...

Well, is you, the reader.

This is the rollercoaster of writer-hood for me.

As I do with every novel I write, I am holding my breath right now. The only thing that matters to me is creating a fantastic story for the readers, and I always doubt if I have managed it...

You see, a doom overtakes me whenever I finish a book. I talked about this in my Author's Note at the end of *Khyven the Unkillable*. When I first finished that manuscript, I thought it was bad. It required the responses of readers, critics, contest judges, and a good solid verbal slap from wife for me to finally relax about it.

When I was in college, this was not a problem. I was not the same writer then.

There's a stereotype that many of us think of when it comes to writers: the frazzled and diligent word slinger who revises and agonizes over the prose, finally turning it over to their editor *only* when they have come to the end of their rope and cannot think of one more single thing to do to it.

I did not exemplify this stereotype back in college.

Back then, I'd finish the *first* draft of a novel and say, "This book is the BOMB! It's the best thing anyone has ever written!" Then I'd throw it into its folder and move on to the next book. Over and over and over.

The books were, in fact, simply awful. (And hopefully, none of them will ever be unearthed)

I later learned that, at that stage in my fledgling writing career, this deluded-but-positive attitude about these festering little turds was actually the *right* attitude to have. Now that I have a few books under my belt, I firmly believe the biggest mistake new writers can make is to get too wrapped up in writing the *perfect* novel. It holds them back, stops them creating.

A fledgling writer who tries to make everything about their book "perfect" is far more likely to never finish *any* book than to actually produce the perfect book (if there even is such a thing). So, for me, this optimistically skewed perception of my tawdry little contributions to the written word helped me move on to the next book and the next book and the next…

Of course, I have learned a lot since those college years. I've rubbed elbows with other authors, published with big trad publishers, honed my craft, learned various structures for storytelling, and read lots and lots of fiction. With each bit of information, I've grown.

A particularly robust level-up was when I discovered *Save the Cat* (*StC*) by Blake Snyder and *Save the Cat Writes a Novel* by Jessica Brody. The change in my results were notable. I started winning awards, got gushing feedback from readers, and hit bestseller lists. *Tower of the Four*, *Khyven the Unkillable*, *Lorelle of the Dark*, and *Rhenn the Traveler* were all written this way.

Slayter and the Dragon was not.

You can imagine how that might hit my confidence a little bit. I have a lot of demons in my head, ready to pounce, and it takes almost nothing to set them off. I mean, if I take just one day off from writing, it can be enough to send me into a "you've lost the mojo for this story!" tailspin. Taking a winning strategy and abandoning it, well… If you listen hard, I think you can hear the demons from where you're standing.

With *Slayter*, I went off into the weeds and trusted my intuition to guide me. No *StC* beat sheet. No tried-and-true structure. The reason I did this was because, as you know by now, *Slayter and the Dragon* is not actually a complete story. It's only half a story, a cliffhanger. It didn't have a beginning, middle, and end, and therefore didn't follow the *StC* beat sheet. But it wanted to be written this way. Slayter grabbed my face and made me do it in his scatterbrained fashion.

So I did. I left my *StC* Safety Blanket behind.

And it haunted me.

But being a writer doesn't come without risks. It *shouldn't* come without risks. The only way to level up is to take chances and see what comes of it. I'm eager for this story to be in your hands, and I hope you enjoyed it.

Now, if you're feel like tearing your hair out at the cliffhanger, hold onto your tufts. *Bane of Giants*, the final installment of the *Legacy of Shadows* storyline, is coming.

And it's a humdinger. I promise you one thing: it'll all be over soon, one way or another...

;)

Thanks for reading. See you in Noksonon.

- Todd

If You Liked...

Eldros Legacy (Legacy of Shadows)

Khyven the Unkillable

Lorelle of the Dark

Rhenn the Traveler

Slayter and the Dragon (forthcoming)

Bane of Giants (forthcoming)

Tower of the Four

Episode 1 – The Quad

Episode 2 – The Tower

Episode 3 – The Test

The Champions Academy (Episodes 1-3 compilation)

Episode 4 – The Nightmare

Episode 5 – The Resurrection

Episode 6 – The Reunion

The Dragon's War (Episodes 4-6 compilation)

Threadweavers

Wildmane

The GodSpill

Threads of Amarion

God of Dragons

The Whisper Prince Series

Fairmist

The Undying Man

The Slate Wizards

Standalone Novels

Charlie Fiction

Summer of the Fetch

Non-fiction

Ordinary Magic

Tower of the Four Short Stories

"Urchin"

"Royal"

"Princess"

Other Short Stories

Parallel Worlds Anthology — "Threshold"

Dragonlance: The Cataclysm — "Seekers"

Dragonlance: Heroes & Fools — "Songsayer"

Dragonlance: The History of Krynn — "The Letters of Trayn Minaas"

Made in the USA
Middletown, DE
11 November 2024

64314838R00267